Outtakes

Selecte

First published by Route in 2021
Pontefract, UK
info@route-online.com
www.route-online.com

ISBN: 978-1901927-86-3

First Edition

Cover Design:
John Sellards

Typeset in Bembo by Route

Printed & bound in Great Britain by TJ Books

For all those who've sailed with me

CONTENTS

Preface

This book collects writing of mine about Bob Dylan's work, dating from 1967 to now: writing that wasn't part of either the *Song & Dance Man* trilogy or *The Bob Dylan Encyclopedia* – and of which only the odd trace can be found in those books.

It brings together in one place, for the first time, accurate versions of articles originally published in disparate places. These include pieces in some of the mainstream media (*The Guardian, Times, Observer, Independent* and *Telegraph*); in papers from the Underground (*OZ*, and the short-lived UK edition of *Rolling Stone*); in Dylan fanzines (*ISIS* and *Homer, the slut*); in other journals from *Canadian Folklore canadien* and *Sight & Sound* to the English-language *Japan Times*; in music magazines (*Let It Rock* and *Melody Maker*); in contributions to books from *Conclusions on the Wall* (UK, 1980) and *Professing Dylan* (Memphis, 2016) to *New Approaches to Bob Dylan* (Denmark, 2019); and newly written, unpublished work (2021).

It amounts to work of varying degrees of depth and success, written over a period of almost 55 years, and arranged almost always chronologically.

There is one exception to the chronology: a piece written in the second half of the 1990s comes first because it looks back to how the world was in 1966 – at least as seen from Britain – and makes for a personal introduction; but then comes the earliest piece, reproduced here (though in black and white) as it looked in the pages of *OZ* magazine in October 1967.

By then I was feeling I needed to write about Dylan's canon at length, whether I was up to it or not. Naturally, no-one had a clue, back in the tumult of the mid-1960s, what a small proportion of his work that first burst of his albums would form. I certainly didn't think about either Bob or me still being alive in the 2020s.

I'd graduated in May '67, from the University of York, and was staying for part of that summer in London, in a cheap flat in Chapel Market, Islington (now posh but then emphatically not), which was shared by ex-student friends Nigel Fountain and David Phillips, and mutual friend David Widgery, a freelance radical political writer and trainee doctor who became, in the end, an East London GP. He died in 1992.

Through these three I was given a connection to *OZ*. The first thing I wrote for them, co-written with David Phillips, was about pirate radio stations, centred on an interview we did with John Peel as he was agonising about whether to join the new BBC Radio 1. Our piece was published in the supposedly fused one-off publication of *OZ/ Other Scenes* (the latter an issue of John Wilcock's US underground paper), but it was really *OZ* No.6.

I don't remember when I first met Richard Neville, the *OZ* editor, but the day before my 21st birthday that August, he commissioned me to write a Dylan article. He said, 'Do an F.R. Leavis on Bob Dylan's songs.' ('Marvellous – right up my street', I wrote in my diary...)

That suggested stance surprised me, given how very Old School F.R. Leavis was and how underground *OZ* was, but the way they made it less Leavisite – more groovy for their Alternative Readership – was with graphics splodged all over the text. Which I didn't mind, having not been especially satisfied with this first concerted attempt at Dylan Lit Crit. In early October I received a published copy... and realised the piece had been drastically cut. Happily, I no longer have a record of the uncut version, so it appears here exactly as then.

I was never paid for it, which seemed wrong, underground press or not, since I was trying to be a freelance writer and needed money to survive (especially in London). On 28th December 1967, I went to an *OZ* dinner. They held at least one a month, asking chosen contributors to a meal instead of paying them. So I went to this intimate, hushed Chelsea restaurant, Muffins in Ifield Road, where about twelve of us, including film critic Raymond Durgnat, sat round one big table and had beautiful wine and food.

Richard Neville and Felix Dennis were the hosts. It struck me that these hippies were rich, and treated themselves very agreeably on a mix of the proceeds of *OZ* and their own inherited wealth.

I was given something valuable that night too. A waitress whispered in my ear that if I was the person interested in Dylan, they'd just acquired an unreleased tape of some new tracks of his, and would I like to hear them... Thus I first encountered the 14 originally circulated 1967 Basement Tapes tracks sent out to get the songs covered by people like Manfred Mann. It was my exciting initiation into the world of bootlegs, to use a term very new to us all at the time.

Martin Sharp, the graphic artist who designed so much for *OZ*, was at the dinner too – an extremely likeable man. Whether his iconic 'Blowin' in the Mind' poster was designed first for the magazine cover, I don't know, and I haven't been able to find out. All I can say is that, at the time, I was given the impression that my article prompted the design, and that the beautiful poster version in rich red, black and gold came after. It's nice for me to think this, but it may not be true.

In the end, I wrote *Song & Dance Man: The Art of Bob Dylan* and it was first published in the UK in late 1972, in early 1973 in the US, and that August, on my 27th birthday, in Japan. I continued to write for small magazines, and brought out an updated 2nd edition, reversedly titled *The Art of Bob Dylan: Song & Dance Man*, in 1981 in the UK and '82 in the States. I wrote an under-funded and therefore under-researched biography of Frank Zappa first published in the mid-1980s, which achieved Italian and German translations; I edited, with John Bauldie, the first anthology of pieces from his great fanzine *The Telegraph*, namely *All Across The Telegraph: A Bob Dylan Handbook*, in 1987; I co-wrote *The Elvis Atlas: A Journey Through Elvis Presley's America* with Roger Osborne in 1996; and after spending most of that decade writing *Song & Dance Man III: The Art of Bob Dylan* in North Yorkshire, it was published in the UK a fortnight before the end of the 20th century, and early in 2000 in the USA. My last book on Dylan was *The Bob Dylan Encyclopedia*, 2006, with a revised and updated paperback in 2008.

Meanwhile I'd also been researching a biography of Blind

Willie McTell, *Hand Me My Travelin' Shoes*, which came out in 2007 in the UK and 2009 in America.

It's a great pleasure, six decades after it all began, to still be listening to Bob Dylan's music, the old and the new, and to see it recognised far more widely as of substance and importance. I look forward to being able to research it further in the immensely rich archive in Tulsa, Oklahoma.

As for this book, you'll find it isn't of the depth or loftiness of my two huge Dylan tomes. I've always been a freelance journalist, working without salary and outside the newspapers I've written for and (with one term's exception as a Visiting Fellow Commoner at Girton College Cambridge in 2005) outside the academy. That said, the key point about *this* book, for me, is the opportunity it gives to make readily accessible some of the other material I've written about Bob and his music across the decades.

Crucially, it restores cuts made the first time around for space reasons and on editors' whims, and recovers material trashed by sub-editors. It allows me to offer it in accurate, convenient form; to include some previously unpublished pieces; to conclude with a piece of new critical work; and to see it out here in the world in the year Bob Dylan turns 80.

Bob Dylan, 1966 & Me
(1997)

This was written thirty years after the moment it describes. First published in an earlier form in the US fanzine On The Tracks *in March 1997 and then in* ISIS *No.73 in June that year.*

Bob Dylan, of course, began 1966 at the soaring peak of his inestimable genius, leaping from crag to lofty crag at giddying, undreamt of heights of incandescent inspiration, shaking his curls above the clouds, hearing that wild mercury sound in a rarified wind. He was to become 25 that year – which seemed, at the time, rather old for anyone to keep on being the hippest person in the universe.

His newest album was *Highway 61 Revisited*, and his revolutionary hit single 'Like A Rolling Stone', the longest thing you'd ever heard on the radio, had been released in the summer of 1965. In Britain, Bob had charted for the first time in March 1965, with 'The Times They Are A-Changin'', which was still climbing when 'Subterranean Homesick Blues' entered the charts a month later; both reached the Top 10 while an immaculately cool, Carnaby Street Bob toured England with his giant light bulb, dark glasses, Chelsea boots and acoustic guitar. Two months after that, 'Maggie's Farm' arrived in the lower reaches of the chart, and on 19th August 'Like A Rolling Stone', soon giving Dylan his first Top 5 hit record in the UK. (It would be his only one, excepting 'Lay, Lady, Lay'.) At the end of October, the lilting yet scathing 'Positively 4th Street' charted, soon becoming another Top 10 hit. Within four weeks of New Year's Day, 1966, Bob's next single, 'Can You Please Crawl Out Your Window?', would join the hit parade too.

It was all go for Bob, the folk singer who'd 'gone pop'. Except that it was obvious he hadn't. He was on his way somewhere else. Pop was all the others. The Beatles in 1965 were still moptops;

their hit singles in Britain that year were 'I Feel Fine', 'Ticket To Ride', 'Help!' and 'Day Tripper' c/w 'We Can Work It Out': all No.1 smash hits and only just beginning to hint at something less vacuous than 'she loves you yeah yeah yeah' and 'I Want To Hold Your Hand'.

Where Bob Dylan was going, nobody knew. Where the 1960s were going, nobody knew. It's as the original generation of rock'n'rollers always said decades later: it wasn't experienced as history-in-the-making at the time; at the time it was just how-things-are. But the feel of the period was upbeat: however fitfully or apparently randomly, we were escaping from 1950s drabness, its caution, predominant snobberies, poverty and grime.

A boom economy meant that to be young then was to be allowed to be young: you no longer had to go down the mine, or work in that factory, or go to college solely to launch a sensible career along traditional lines. You could be fussy about which job you chose. You could go to university to postpone going to work. You could feel there was all the time in the world – unless they dropped The Bomb – before you condescended to write that great novel, or direct those films. The corollary was a freeing-up of the whole culture.

I was to become 20 in 1966 – which seemed a pity, since 19 felt the ideal age: old enough to have escaped school and the family home, young enough to feel immortal and unbrushed by decay. I was in the middle of being a student. One of the tracks on Bob Dylan's newest album was 'Tombstone Blues', which referred to 'the old folks' home and the college'. I thought he was disparaging the deadness of college more directly than by juxtaposition: I always thought he sang 'the old folks home in the college'. Either way, it sounded a fine put-down but a false analysis to me. In Britain there had been Oxford and Cambridge, or else the so-called Redbrick Universities, mostly mediocre institutions scattered across large and inhospitable cities. Now, suddenly, there were also the New Universities, lavishly funded, human in scale, on purpose-built campuses, and standing for flair and an abrasive modernity yet also claiming the academic excellence of Oxford and Cambridge without its snobbish decrepitude.

The University of York was one of these, and I was thrilled to be there. I had escaped not just from the 1950s into the 1960s, but from a particularly Old School school into a particularly libertarian New University. For me, this was all a fantastic, invigorating transformation and as it turned out, all so well timed: the best time to be young since the 1920s.

Yet things work on multi-layered time-delays. You don't experience a particular period in isolation; not only is the new shaped by what it strives to replace, but parallel input from many other periods still crowds around you, like the furniture and objects in your house. If I was excited by Bob Dylan, and by the sexual liberation of the times, by the input of working-class informality into everything from the way we talked to the way we dressed, and by reading *On the Road* for the first time, I was also excited by the 19th-century novels of George Eliot, and much exercised by what now seem the rather obscure moral niceties that had exercised the Victorians.

Unwilling to forsake my loyalty to Elvis and Little Richard, I resisted the slapdash blandishments of Merseybeat. I was as entranced by the British waspishness of Evelyn Waugh's traditionally structured comic novels as by the brand-new American anarchy of Joseph Heller's *Catch-22*. The Surrealists and the Pre-Raphaelites, Art Deco and the Impressionists all lived alongside us; Magritte and Aubrey Beardsley coexisted with Raymond Chandler and Keats.

York itself, a medieval city enclosed by medieval walls, was damp and poor in the 1960s, in spirit hardly free of the Great Depression of the 1930s. York Station, with distinctive curved platforms and sweeping ironwork roof, is a triumph of Victorian industrial architecture. In 1966 we still had steam trains. A chocolate factory and the railways were the main employers; both had an interest in preventing a car factory moving in and putting up the below-average wages. Arty-farty students with their silly scarves, Black Sobranie cigarettes and increasingly long hair were an unwelcome novelty to the bowed-down, malnourished townsfolk with their cloth caps and Woodbines, their sticky beehive haircuts and white high-heeled shoes.

Bob Dylan squirrelled into this time-space jumble. It had taken me a while to get used to his voice, but once I could hear that within it lay such riches of expressive thought and feeling, such resources of intelligence, such clear-sighted, uncompromising purpose, I was hooked. He was crucial, the authentic contemporary heavyweight, an agent of the radical future, not as now a guardian of the past. He had cultural clout, not mere celebrity.

He was also popular. You could play his albums without apology. On the other hand he wasn't that popular: most of his records were still the pre-electric ones, you couldn't dance to him, and he was thought too doomy and intellectual for parties.

On campus, it was hard to avoid two equally gruesome developments: sanctimonious, tone-deaf sociology students with acoustic guitars playing 'Masters Of War' interminably in the common rooms, and over-lit parties in soulless seminar rooms hostessed by nicely-spoken, brittle girls who avoided Bob Dylan records in favour of The Beatles' 'Eight Days A Week'. Gerry Rafferty told me, many years later, that for him at the time the girls who liked The Beatles could be 'pulled', and the ones who liked Bob Dylan couldn't. This was not my own experience.

Either way, Dylan was becoming, for me as for so many others, an ever-present, formative influence. From late 1965 onwards, my diaries and letters begin to alight more and more on moments and incidents for which a Dylan aphorism comes as the natural bon mot – and they were all the more bon for their freshness. It was sparky then to throw off a line from 'Desolation Row' or 'To Ramona'. These records were but a couple of years old. The York student newspaper too began to feature Dylanisms, sewn among its headlines and sub-heads. This was not unconnected with the fact that at one point I edited it, and over a much longer period wrote two columns for it, one reviewing formal student debates, the other 'pop records'.

Dylan's influence could also be detected briefly in some surreal gibberish I wrote, imagining it to be Dylanesque poetry, as in a 'letter' in rhyming couplets to a bemused ex-school-friend, starting 'The man outside your door who tries so hard to wash your lawn / Is waiting, while his kettle boils, to see if he's been born', and carrying on in like vein for four closely-written sides of foolscap. I soon snapped out of this.

Mostly I just played the records. In the university vacations I went home to Merseyside (I'd grown up just across the river from Liverpool) and played Bob Dylan records to my sister and the ex-schoolfriends; in term-time in York I played them with clusters of people in college rooms and city lodgings. Mark Knopfler talks somewhere about listening to *Blonde On Blonde* over a million cups of coffee. That was us.

But there were no Bob Dylan networks then, nor any such concept, and things came through slowly. There was often a gap between when a record was released in America and in Britain, and often another gap between when it might be available in London and in the small provincial record shops of the North. In most towns, you could only buy records at antiquated, infuriating hardware/electrical-goods shops with a small record section somewhere behind the vacuum cleaners, fridges and lampshades: and the manager would be a tweed-jacketed, middle-aged man barely familiar with the name Elvis Presley, let alone Bob Dylan. The upshot was, for years, that if a record was in the Top 10 they'd sold out of it and if it wasn't, they'd never heard of it.

Under these conditions, and with news a matter of leisurely-paced rumour rather than fanzined, hotlined, internetted instant dispersal, I'm pretty sure I was unaware of the release in Britain of a couple of singles taken from *Blonde On Blonde*, one ahead of and the other to coincide with, Dylan's visit (with hindsight his historic visit) of May 1966. 'One Of Us Must Know (Sooner Or Later)' came out in March/April, and because it didn't do much, 'Rainy Day Women #12 & 35' was issued in May, hitting the charts on the 12th, by which time Dylan had already played dates in Stockholm, Copenhagen, Dublin, Belfast, Bristol and Cardiff and that night played Birmingham Odeon.

Two nights later, he played the Odeon in Liverpool, and with my only moderately interested girlfriend Gillian, I went to see him – my first Dylan concert. So under-publicised was the tour, as far as I could tell, that I almost couldn't get tickets by the time I found out that he was coming. We sat in the stalls, a long way from the stage.

I don't remember it in the degree of clear detail I'd like to. Mainly I remember how admirably un-showbiz he was, and how astonishing the new acoustic songs, especially 'Visions Of Johanna'. There was no support act and no MC. Dylan just wandered on, unannounced, at some indeterminate point, and stood around on a bare stage, wearing what looked like this shapeless but thin brown suit. Then he started interminably tuning his guitar (which nobody ever did in those days, though it would become highly fashionable later: almost an indicator of the 1970 singer-songwriter's sensitivity of soul). Then he coughed and muttered and paused – a gamut of anti-showbiz gestures – and started singing these extraordinary, quiet, long songs, into the rapt silence of two thousand people. Songs like 'Just Like A Woman' were undreamt of till that magical night because *Blonde On Blonde* wasn't yet released at the time of this astonishing 1966 tour of Europe. In America, the album was issued two days after that Liverpool concert. In Britain, it didn't come out until July.

Not only had we never heard these songs before: no-one had heard songs like this before. 'Visions Of Johanna' with its amazingly long, complex verse-shape, its piled-up lines and rhymes: there was no precedent for this, and, sung solo, it came soaring through the auditorium, delivered with mesmerising, unhurried mastery, as if Bob Dylan were dreaming it all into existence right in front of us. It was heart-stopping.

After an interval, the band came on and Bob strapped on his electric guitar, and the noise they made was unbelievably loud, and so badly amplified that it was largely indecipherable. I don't remember much booing: it was more like tolerant puzzlement under fire, though later another York student told me he'd been to the Sheffield concert two nights later and at the end, as people were filing out, he'd heard someone say, 'Well, Bob Dylan died tonight.'

Why didn't I go to all the concerts? Because nobody did. Back then, nobody conceived of that level of fandom. You went to the one concert nearest your home town, and you greeted this superlative genius, this pinnacle of 20th-century art-in-action, with restrained applause from your seat. And all the better for the artist, too, it seems to me, than the habit which has long since superceded it, of greeting even his most tired, sulky, blurred performances by going apeshit, baying and whooping and crowding forward like a mob at a public execution.

In July, my sister and I flew to New York – first trip to America! – and there, in the heatwave – it was 106 degrees Fahrenheit on Fifth Avenue – I suddenly saw that unmistakable, muzzy double-album cover in Sam Goody's window. I still sometimes get a flash of how it felt on those first few playings in a funky borrowed apartment on West End Avenue, #915. In that room the heat just coughed. The insinuating purr of Dylan's voice, the gurgling of the organ and the piercing dancing reveries of harmonica: all these are intermingled for me with the shine of wooden floors, smells of polish and cockroach-powder, the strange thinness of the American vinyl and the redness of the Columbia label, the taste of graham crackers, the exotic noises of the cosmopolitan hot night. I could wish I had not been foolishly uneasy at first with what seemed Dylan's excessive concessions to pop: the easy R&B and the meaningless words on songs like 'Obviously 5 Believers'. I couldn't fully relax into the album's radical sumptuousness. That took time. But New York City was a great first place to hear it.

My first evening there, we walked up into Harlem and found the Apollo Theater, but was dissuaded from going in. 'Joe Tex is on next week, with the Shirelles and the Exciters,' I wrote wistfully in my diary. Next day, Greenwich Village. It wasn't specifically a Dylan pilgrimage, though it was discovering America; but in Boston I took a bus to Cambridge to walk the green pastures of Harvard University, and another day I almost drowned in the cruel sea off Atlantic City (where eating on the beach was illegal yet the beach was full of ice-cream vendors).

Towards the end of my trip I took a Greyhound to Richmond, Virginia – first feel of The South – and there bought the Dylan single of 'I Want You' for the B-side, thrilled to find that it was 'Just Like Tom Thumb's Blues'… recorded live in Liverpool. That was me, somewhere on the fade-out handclaps.

What's So Good About Dylan?
(1967)

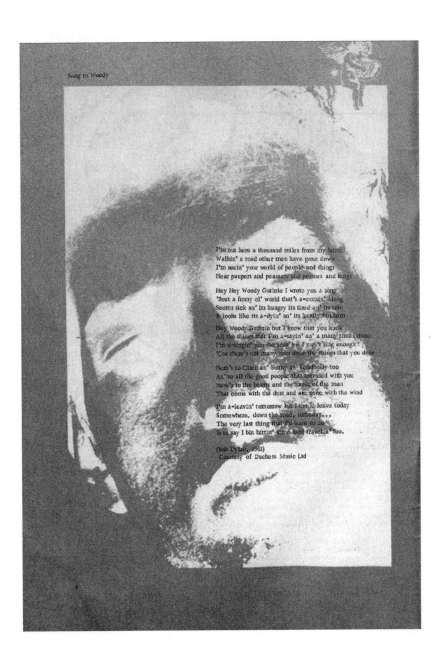

Song to Woody

I'm out here a thousand miles from my home
Walkin' a road other men have gone down
I'm seein' your world of people and things
Hear paupers and peasants and princes and kings

Hey Hey Woody Guthrie I wrote you a song
'Bout a funny ol' world that's a-comin' along
Seems sick an' its hungry its tired an' its torn
It looks like its a-dyin' an' its hardly bin born

Hey Woody Guthrie but I know that you know
All the things that I'm a-sayin' an' a many times more
I'm a-singin' you the song but I can't sing enough
'Cos there's not many men done the things that you done

Here's to Cisco an' Sonny an' Leadbelly too
An' to all the good people that travelled with you
Here's to the hearts and the hands of the men
That come with the dust and are gone with the wind

I'm a-leavin' tomorrow but I could leave today
Somewhere, down the road, someday...
The very last thing that I'd want to do
Is to say I bin hittin' some hard travellin' too.

(Bob Dylan, 1961)
Courtesy of Duchess Music Ltd

21

What's so good about Dylan?

Dylan's lyrics are not poems, they are parts of songs. This is not to assert that Dylan is not a poet but simply to remember that he is certainly a pop singer. The medium he has chosen involves more than language – and therefore a number of limits are placed on the selection and organisation of language within his works.

I don't think there are any other pop artists who experience the same difficulties the other writer-singers labour under strains of a different quality. They are inevitably less aware than Dylan of the tension between linguistic, musical and dramatic expression because – unlike Dylan – they lack the necessary sureness of touch, in one or more of those directions.

Jagger is usually worth watching and his records communicate the ethos of the sexual scene; but the words of a Jagger song are mere dilettante junkee-ism. Scratched inarticulate on its own prison wall, with methedrine as a deified scapegoat.

Paul Simon – record, stage or paper belongs to part of Americana which assumes that an indiscriminate eagerness plus Doe-Eyed sensitivity = creative intelligence. The latter has not yet revealed itself on his SON OF

'SEPTEMBER IN THE RAIN' LPs.

Lennon-McCartney compositions, the Beatles records, are at best, artistically disciplined, cameos: cave-paintings in the primeval pop-world. And like cave-paintings they do not need their authors to explain, accompany or complete them. This is a notable achievement – although the self-reliant is not always the valuable and The Beatles' writing seems to me to attain a standard that is fairly placed by being called Noel Cowardish. Nevertheless, Lennon-McCartney's compositions do not need blood-transfusions from Beatle performances in order to fend for themselves.

Dylan, on the other hand, is about 60% singer, musician and performer. This is one of the obstacles in the way of the attempt to isolate his lyrics. And though Dylan has often said "I am my words" this is more to invite further difficulty; for an analysis on these grounds tends to suffer also in assuming the form of a Great Message Hunt.

I am not against messages. A writer without message is without real interest – contrary to a public opinion which distrusts preaching and gives that label to anything

served up without clear bias. Literature is inseparable from the moral life of mankind cannot afford to give the public what it wants; the creative writer must offer as humbly as possible what he believes the public needs. And as the establishment knows, even as the Harold Robbinses prove by their passivity (for Mr. Robbins is one of humanity's drop-outs), giving the public what it wants is the easiest way to control what it wants.

Dylan is one of those who still continue to speak out against the humanising of society.

To Message Hunt through Dylan's lyrics is to pursue the precious notion of a cohesive whole or something cosier: a philosophy of life that is without contradiction. Dylan does not claim to offer this. He is still searching both for his essential beliefs and an appropriate form in which to express them. What I think he does offer is the artistic recreation of the experience of life within effort. The tough, and the virtue lies not in the immediacy but in the honesty. Dylan's work possesses that individual integrity which belongs to the artist who can be said to represent the age and this characteristic is essentially different from the ability to put

They're selling postcards of the hanging
They're painting the passports brown
The beauty-parlour is filled with sailors
The circus is in town
Here comes the blind commissioner
They've got him in a trance
One hand is tied to the tight-rope walker
The other is in his pants
And the riot squad they're restless
They need somewhere to go
As Lady 'n' I look out tonight
From Desolation Row

Cinderella she seems so easy
'It takes one to know one', she smiles,
And puts her hands in her back pockets
Bette Davis style.
And in comes Romeo he's moaning
You Belong To Me I believe
And someone says you're in the wrong place my friend
You better leave
And the only sound that's left
After the ambulances go
Is Cinderella sweeping up
On Desolation Row.

Now the moon is almost hidden
The stars are beginning to hide
The fortune-telling lady
Has even taken all her things inside
All except for Cain and Abel
And the hunch-back of Notre Dame
Everybody is making love
Or else expecting rain
And the Good Samaritan he's dressing
He's getting ready for the show
He's going to the carnival tonight
On Desolation Row.

Ophelia she's 'neath the window
For her I feel so afraid
On her twenty-second birthday
She already is an old maid
To her, death is quite romantic

She wears an iron vest
Her profession's her religion
Her sin is her lifelessness
And though her eyes are fixed upon
Noah's great rainbow
She spends her time peeking in
To Desolation Row

Einstein disguised as Robin Hood
With his memories in a trunk
Passed this way an hour ago
With his friend a jealous monk
Now he looked so immaculately frightful
As he bummed a cigarette
And he went off sniffing drainpipes
And reciting the alphabet.
You would not think to look at him
But he was famous long ago
For playing the electric violin
On Desolation Row

Dr. Filth he keeps his world
Inside of a leather cup
But all his sexless patients
They are trying to blow it up
Now his nurse, some local loser
She's in charge of the cyanide hole
And she also keeps the cards that read
Have Mercy On His Soul
They all play on the penny whistle
You can hear them blow
If you lean your head out far enough
From Desolation Row

Across the street they've nailed the curtains
They're getting ready for the feast -
The Phantom of the Opera
In a perfect image of a priest
They are spoonfeeding Casanova
To get him to feel more assured
Then they'll kill him with self-confidence
After poisoning him with words
And the Phantom's shouting to skinny girls
Get Outa Here If You Don't Know

Casanova is just being punished
For going to Desolation Row

At midnight all the agents
And the superhuman crew
Go out and round up everyone
That knows more than they do
Then they bring them to the factory
Where the heart-attack machine
Is strapped across their shoulders
And then the kerosene
Is brought down from the castles
By insurance men who go
Check to see that nobody is escaping
To Desolation Row

Praise be to ...
The Titanic sails at dawn
Everybody's shouting
Which Side Are You On?
And Ezra Pound and T.S. Eliot
Fighting in the captain's tower
While calypso singers laugh at them
And fishermen hold flowers
Between the windows of the sea
Where lovely mermaids flow
And nobody has to think too much
About Desolation Row

Yes I received your letter yesterday
(About the time the door-knob broke)
When you asked me how I was doing
Was that some kind of joke?
All these people that you mention
Yes I know them they're quite lame
I had to rearrange their faces
And give them all another name
Right now I can't read too good
Don't send me no more letters no
Not unless you mail them
From Desolation Row

(Bob Dylan, 1965)
© Warner Bros. Music / Levy's Music Ltd.

---

together a few common denominators as Amis did in the 1950s and as the Beatle-writers do today. Dylan' is a personal perception - the perception of an intelligent acquisitive mind. The focus is sensitive, the expression disciplined and therefore the product is art. At this point it is no longer useful to compare Bob Dylan with other pop stars; it may later be constructive instead to measure him against other poets. If Dylan is influenced by early Presley he is also influenced by Whitman; and though he is saying more than Simon-Garfunkel, Lennon or P.F. Sloan, he may be saying less than Yevtushenko, S.T. Coleridge or Stephen Wycherley.

So what is Dylan saying? •

SONG TO WOODY, the first of the two lyrics printed here, expresses the desire for an innocent drop-out, but also, as with Mr. Tambourine Man, the concern to find a new allegiance:

'Hey Mr. Tambourine Man play a song for me -
In the jingle-jangle morning I'll come following you."

- and the allegiance declared here is to the inner world. The intention is to come upon self-discovery (I doubt if one can 'come upon it' with quite that facility), to free the mind in the hope that its isolation will bring independent thought. I am not concerned to argue the pros and cons of whether this

works in general, or whether, if it does, the independent thinking is likely to be redirected towards "dropping back in" in any socially constructive way. It is enough to say that it has worked for Dylan. Drugs have not dulled the finer edges nor restricted his ability to perceive and remain articulate. "People should not know more than they can creatively digest," wrote Neitzche. That Dylan has the capacity for this creative assimilation - it is abundantly clear in his work - is what gives him his authority.

The allegiance sought in SONG TO WOODY is the "hard travellin'" ethos represented by Guthrie. In that sense it is, too, the world of the American West to which

6

Hemingway and his "Lost Generation" looked for fulfilment - and failed to discover. Hemingway could only find instead the masturbation-habit of attending Spanish bullfights. Guthrie, on the other hand, lived a life of Hard Travelin' and the intensity and compassion of Dylan's lyric is confirmed by a reading of the Guthrie autobiography 'Bound for Glory'. The lines:

Here's to the hearts and the hands of the men
That come with the dust and are gone with the wind

faithfully reflect Guthrie's ethnic sensibility but communicate also (they flow naturally from that undramatic statement of a personal admiration which makes the second line of this fourth stanza so effective) Dylan's pledge of involvement with Guthrie's America. That line in the opening verse acts, in retrospect, as confirmation:

I'm seein' your world of people and things

- confirmation that, as the rhythmic balance of the lyric insists, Dylan has an incisive grasp of that world and (as part of that reality) of its romantic implications. One notes too that the awareness of the latter is evidence also that Dylan can see the Guthrie World in the context of others. Guthrie's Hard Travelers shared a landscape of dust, wind and poverty, seen on foot and rattled through in over-crowded box-cars. And the wind and dust are evoked in the construction of the song. Lines and syllables take the form of a list: the suggestion is one of restless movement within a pre-ordained pattern of repetition. The felicity of Dylan's intimations of experience within and outside of the ethos described is focused by the combination of the general response personalised:

I'm leavin' tomorrow but I could leave today

Somewhere, down the road, someday . . . . .

and the personal response generalised:

Hey Hey Woody Guthrie I wrote you a song
Bout a funny ol' world that's a-comin' along
Seems sick an' its hungry its tired an' its torn
It looks like its a-dyin' an' its hardly bin born.

And there, most economically, is the rhythmic and onomatopoeic repetition. Also evoked, one notes, is the acquired fortitude of mild amusement which is the necessary survival-kit of the hard traveler. 'Hey Hey Woody Guthrie I wrote you a song' pinpoints this with a deceptive ease. That Dylan can render this with such felicitous poignancy is sufficient indication that neither the intention nor the effect is one of ill-considered sentimentalism. And although in 'God On Our Side' he lingers over the line:

The country I come from is called the Mid-West

and the romantic vision of dying on a freight train occurs in his version of 'Man of Constant Sorrow' and again in 'It Takes A Lot To Laugh It Takes A Train To Cry', the last two lines of 'Song to Woody' are of at least equal significance:

The very last thing that I'd want to do
Is to say I bin hittin' some hard travelin' too.

With those lines - deriving as they do a particular strength from the clipped reluctant flirtation of the cadence - we are given a greater understanding of the spirit of the lyric as it is stated in the title. To say he'd been hittin' some hard travelin' too is, emphatically, not the last thing he'd want to be able to do. 'Song to Woody'.

most pungently, includes in its pledge of involvement a plea for that involvement. And it expresses the same inner drive of desire which we find directed elsewhere in 'Mr. Tambourine Man' and again in, say, 'Pledging My Time'. In the one the desire is for the freedom to make a reality out of dancing:

beneath the diamond sky with one hand waving free
Silhouetted by the sea

and in the other the desire is to achieve an unknown fulfilment in a personal relationship. Strange that Dylan is so often dismissed as a professional protest-merchant.

When we ask what this rather crude label means, of course, there is no answer - except from those agents of the existing order who disapprove of people who sing for a living and who resent their having opinions. (The most offensive lapel-badge of all, in their eyes, is the one that reminds them in moderate type that BOB DYLAN IS A RATE-PAYER). The label Protest-Merchant, then, is hardly a critical term.

Dylan is, patently, a critic of society: I hope we all are. But Dylan's criticism, as it is presented in his writing, seems to me to be characterised by a personal insight unusually abrasive in quality. Some of his earlier criticism appeared then, and appears more so in retrospect, obvious and, to that extent, naive. 'Blowin In The Wind' and 'Masters of War' are not memorable pieces of writing. It is not simply the clichés that mar them but also the assumption that thier inclusion is necessary for the emphasised communication of his theme. The implication is that the listener needs to be spoonfed.

In his more recent work, however, Dylan has learnt to trust his public. The criticism of human values in society, though sometimes harsh and sometimes rendered as an ingenuous reproach, is always offered in a form dictated by his art, not by an anxiety based on lack of trust.

I should like to put a case for judging Dylan's 'Desolation Row' to be a distinguished and brilliantly sustained critique of modern American society.

Desolation Row is a Cannery Row, the logical consequence, in one way at least, of the society surrounding it. Dylan is writing from within Desolation Row and though part of his pessimism is the product of his living there

When you asked me how I was doing
Was that some kind of joke?

the intention is not to repeat the theme of, say, North Country Blues, which was basically a chronicle of a community's suffering in the face of encroaching poverty. Dylan's despondence in 'Desolation Row' is his reaction to what he sees around him. And what he sees is life regimented by false values, lived out with dishonesty; norms which produce a denial of humanity being acted upon by man. Dylan explores this unreal society, recognises it as pernicious in its denial of essential human truths and insists upon the urgency of the need to assert and re-establish these.

He communicates his conviction of society's perversity, in the first place, by a sustained reversal of norms within the logic of the poem: the beauty-parlour is filled with sailors and it is the riot squad that is restless. Casanova, the dominating lover, is being spoon-fed: Romeo is moaning. And the determined use of a

barrage of folk-heroes, in careful disarray, participants in and agents of this world of sick disorder, emphasises his theme. There is Bette Davis, Cain and Abel, the hunchback of Notre Dame, the Good Samaritan, Ophelia, Noah, Einstein, Robin Hood, the Phantom of the Opera, Casanova, Romeo, Nero, Neptune, Ezra Pound and T.S. Eliot - not to mention Dr. Filth. There is Cinderella too, but she is the exception. She is, with Dylan, on Desolation Row; she is victim, not agent, and therefore she is less of a victim. But though she can afford to be more honest - "to live outside the law you must be honest" is a line from a later song - the real "sweeping up" must be done outside: across the street, where they've nailed the curtains.

The other general characteristic of the poem is the recurring intimation of imminent disaster.

The commissioner, who is blind, is tied (by one hand) to the tight-rope walker; and:

All except for Cain and Abel
And the hunchback of Notre Dame
Everybody is making love
Or else expecting rain.

Now the moon is almost hidden
The stars are beginning to hide
The fortune-telling lady
Has even taken all her things inside . . . . .

But it is the single line:
'The Titanic sails at dawn'
which is most strikingly evocative of catastrophe. It summarises with the conciseness of the true artist the theme and colouring of the whole poem. It is the Titanic which epitomises present-day American society as Dylan interprets it: for the Titanic was the ship of the future, the proof of man's progress and civilisation, the unsinkable ship which, on her

maiden voyage, sank. And when she began to sink the majority of her passengers refused to believe it could happen; the palm court orchestra played on and the people in the ship's ballroom continued to dance.

he different kinds of denial - the various ways in which the "dancing" continues, as Dylan sees it - are presented with an incision which incorporates Dylan's essential sanity within an impressionistic evocation of escalating malaise. They're selling postcards of the hanging at the beginning of the song; but by the middle some local loser is in charge of the cyanide hole:

And she also keeps the cards that read
Have Mercy On His Soul.

The first two stanzas present a general picture, establishing the nature of the poem being offered and laying the foundations of its "Wasteland" connotations. The only specific criticism made is that contained in the observation that:

the riot squad they're restless
They need somewhere to go . . . . .

That the society has riot-quelling machinery out on the streets is a denial of its democratic basis; and that this arrangement is taken for granted - accepted as normal - is indicative of the malaise which a corrupted system of government inculcates in the process of rendering its citizens morally, as well as politically, impotent.

In the third stanza - again with a striking economy of language - Dylan questions the essential quality and effectiveness of modern humanitarian liberalism in the context of the society he sees

And the Good Samaritan he's dressin

He's getting ready for the show .....
When we meet the Good Samaritan
preparing for his carnival the
stars have already begun to hide,
The darkness is already closing in,
and it is not the sort of darkness
which should encourage dressing
for dinner. Like everybody's
making love it is an inappropriate
response. It exposes that lethal
unawareness against which Dylan
is concerned to speak out.

This is why, in the final stanza, Dylan
demands of his correspondent that
she submit herself to the experience
of being on Desolation Row – the one
place where it remains possible
to possess, or re-discover, an
honesty of response. There is,
after all, nothing Desolation Row
can offer in the way of compromising
or deluding alternative. Consequently
the letter received from outside
communicates nothing beyond what
Dylan knows already of that
outside society. His receiving it,
therefore, is of no importance to
him at all:

Yes I received your letter yesterday
(About the time the door-knob broke) ..

That pay-off line is beautiful, as
Dylan's put-downs usually are.

In this final stanza of 'Desolation Row',
The real emphasis is
on the hope that the girl from
outside will come to the Row, to be
redeemed, as it were:

Don't send me no more letters no –
Not unless you mail them from
Desolation Row.

This blindness which is under
attack (it is a society of
commissioners with which Dylan
is dealing) is examined in terms
of a kind of cause and effect
in stanzas eight and nine. Stanza
eight is an indictment of the
tightly-organised human betrayal
which the American educational
system represents. It is portrayed
as essentially a nightmarish
machinery for bringing the potential

enemies of the status quo – the
potential saviours, the independant
thinkers – into line:

At midnight all the agents
And the superhuman crew
Go out and round up everyone
That knows more than they do

Mockingly, Dylan shows that
the system's "education" consists
in the maintenance of ignorance.
Moreover, that "crew", in the
context, asserts in combination
with the opening phrase 'At
midnight...' the telling connotative
suggestion of collective vandalism,
political purges and press-gangs.
The over-riding element of
violence, then, is evoked in those
first two lines of the verse. We
are forewarned of the "heart-attack
machine", the kerosene and the
near-impossibility of escape.

The consequent powerlessness of
the individual, in the face of all
this, is a conclusion urged upon us
also by the link with Kafka's vision
of life contained in the remainder
of the stanza: the kerosene is

brought down from the castles
By insurance men who go
Check to see that nobody is
escaping
To Desolation Row.

Stanza nine deals with the result of
this examination of individuality
and returns us to the element of
urgency which Dylan finds
consonant with his analysis.

Everybody is shouting
Which Side Are You On?

Perhaps the palm-court orchestra
is playing it. And 'Which Side
Are You On?', one remembers, is
the song used by the Chorus in
Duberman's play 'In White America'

Now we have Dylan's
America, presented
with a power of
conviction for which
his artistry is
responsible. What
we have in
'Desolation Row' is far removed from
the blanket, grating assemblage of
accusation which pop-protesters
like Mr. Barry McGuire will always
assume to be adequate and worthy
of attention. Neither is it a
product of the easy occupation of
preaching to the converted: Dylan

does not preach – he offers his
comment, throws out the hint but
with the poet's virility. And even
for those who are, in a general
sense, "converted" to the view
that American society is nauseously
uncivilised, Dylan's analysis is
of a quality likely to make its
expression in the poem a means of
enhancing the reader's awareness.
That is its value.

Where I think Dylan is immature in
his judgement is in contending as he
does in that ninth stanza that Eliot
and Pound have sold out to the
non-human values. Eliot in

continued on page 27

particular must be acknowledged as a poet of greatness - far more so than say, Walt Whitman, whose influence can be detected in Dylan's early work. (It is, for example, prominent in the long, piled-up lines of 'A Hard Rain's A-Gonna Fall'.)

"Art," as Collingwood somewhat pompously suggests, "is

the community's medicine against the worst disease of mind, the corruption of consciousness." Eliot, unquestionably, has exercised his responsibility in this direction and is very far from fighting for the captaincy of the Titanic. Dylan's claim to validity as an artist must ultimately stand or fall by his

acceptance or rejection of this same responsibility. So too must the measure of his success as an artist be the quality of perception which he brings to bear in the struggle against this corruption of consciousness

It may be said that Dylan's claim is valid and his success appreciable.

That Million Dollar Serenade:
Isle Of Wight Festival
(1969)

This was commissioned by the short-lived UK edition of Rolling Stone, *back when that was still an underground paper, and published on 20th September 1969. I found out afterwards that while I'd been paid £20, the freelance photographer they sent had been paid £100. Jann Wenner didn't like my piece and didn't publish it in the US edition. I don't like it either: my shallow facetiousness has come back to bite me — but it's of its time and it gives some specific details I've not seen noted elsewhere.*

No-one not resident in the area claims to have heard of the 1st Isle of Wight Festival; everyone heard about the 2nd. The difference, of course, was Bob Dylan.

Yet in an important sense, he obscured the festival as an idea by the very fact of his presence. The festival was one thing, his appearance another; and the twain only fused in the reports of the national newsmen and for the small, cheery skinheads there for a weekend of adultless society, in which they could dart about among overworked shopkeepers, policemen and bus conductors, live and breathe deafening, nebulous music, show prowess at lighting tent-side fires and eat an impressive number of unpleasant hot dogs. For this minority faction of the participants, it was a Festival, of all things pop, in which the star turn was The Who.

But for a large majority, the festival didn't exist as an entity. It was all just a dream, a vacuumy scheme babe, for getting to watch Dylan live. They arrived, in the main, on the Friday, in order to make absolutely sure of a seat for Sunday evening — and most of the other acts were merely the reasonable purgatory to be endured before entering heaven. Only one day was of real importance — Sunday, 31st August: the 30th anniversary of Hitler's order to attack Poland; the first day of the International Book Fair in Leipzig; and the day Dylan played in England for the first time in over three years.

That the gates of Eden were so difficult to reach and yet were indeed reached by at least three times the number of people who made it to Trafalgar Square for the huge Vietnam demonstration in March last year, indicated graphically the change in supposed significance that Dylan's name has produced in those three years.

In the spring of 1966, he did a tour of major British cities after beginning in Ireland and finishing in London. The odd fanatic followed the tour nightly, as Pennebaker followed it in 1965 to get material for *Dont Look Back*; but most people didn't, in 1966, follow Dylan around. The average admirer went to one concert only and would have considered it extravagant – too much the teenybopper role – to have attended more.

In contrast, no-one in the enormous crowd at Woodside Bay gave even a hint of thinking it extravagant to have travelled from northern Scotland or the depths of Wales, along roads choked with holidaymakers bent on a few days splash and tickle, to have queued and pushed to catch a boat or hovercraft from the appalling town of Portsmouth and, at the other side, an overloaded bus to the Festival Site vicinity, to have sat through Gypsy, The Pretty Things, Gary Farr, Julie Felix (and her Going to the bloody Zoo song), Liverpool Scene, Fat Mattress, Free, Heaven, Blonde on Blonde and more besides, and to have paid two pounds ten shillings (£2.50) for a small square of squatting space – all to breathe the air around Bob Dylan for an hour. One hour. In 1966 the price of a good seat, warm and comfortable, was about 10/6d (52½p) and Dylan was on stage an hour and a half.

A few people, perhaps, went solely to hear Indo-Jazz Fusions, or even the Edgar Broughton Band, or maybe in the vain hope of seeing Marsha Hunt topless; but the vast, vast majority were there for Dylan, the one great artist of a generation.

This generation, Dylan and Dylan's public function – all these have changed so much since those British concerts of three years ago, when *Highway 61 Revisited* was the latest album.

Then, Dylan was giving a preview of what *Blonde On Blonde* was to offer with such impact – the sound and vision of chaos of which all the subsequent acid-rock albums of others were essentially imitative. Those concerts, though, were still largely a part of what Colonel Tom Parker and his boy Elvis had used in pop. Sequinned curtains, queues to the stage door, empty plushy orchestra-pits, elderly and uncomprehending men operating spotlight plans contrived for the likes of Bobby Vee, 12-year-olds wetting their pants. The only aspect remotely of sociological interest was that in response to all this, folk people wanted out in imbecile disillusion. At Liverpool what they walked out of was the Odeon Cinema – a large, central, flashy establishment which thrives on long runs of maudlin movies at extra-high prices. That day it boasted in puce plastic letters outside its foyer: 2PM THE SOUND OF MUSIC 7.45PM BOB DYLAN. It was easy to see without looking too far that not much was really sacred.

Dylan, in amongst all this, was staggeringly good and not at all phony – and he was clearly a contemporary. He was a great figurehead, an unpredictable superstar, but his greater vision and stronger integrity seemed to rest on similar experience, or at least on a similar perception of what was rotten in the United States of America. Dylan, in this sense, was one of us, defining our responses for us and living outside the law and being honest. He had put behind him a tainted and reductive humanitarianism (we shall overcome what?: the answer my friend is blowin' in the Greenwich Village wind). It seemed normal enough that Dylan was on the road again.

At Woodside Bay, he came no longer as a contemporary, the Wicked Messenger, but like Moses come down from the Mount. This was the essential relationship between him and his audience – and there was no hint that this was extravagant.

On the contrary, the more inconvenient it was to get there, the more essential it was to make the journey. And most people had a hard job concealing the radiant pride they felt in the achievement – the sense of having served the master well.

Their three-day penance was a mixture of abominable discomfort, localised outrages, illusions of collective grandeur, and caricatures of capitalism at work. A large majority of people found themselves caught in each other's company and accepted, with a committed curiosity, all the ludicrous drawbacks involved in such a sudden imposition of the beautiful people en masse on individual beautiful persons accustomed to public hostility. Life in the town of Ryde became a rehearsal for peaceful takeover. Everyone watched 200,000 mirror images acting out their chosen roles, spreading over the whole resort and changing, swiftly, the lifestyle of every street. It was so easy – just a matter of outnumbering the residents and day-trippers.

But this of course was an illusion of the kind most exciting to the apolitical hippie-cum-anarchists. Look, look, people said with middle-class mannerisms, they're being nice to us. Oh! thank you kind middle-class shopkeepers, thank you for taking our money warmly into your tills.

And it was this fundamental softness which made life on the site itself such an unprincipled theatre of bullying in the name of peace, incitement to pious violence in the name of things cool, and plain exploitation.

The walk down to the site on Friday afternoon, in a rare hour of sunshine, was an eerie re-creation of that sequence in the film of *The Grapes of Wrath* where the Joads are approaching the work-camp, still optimistic, and they are puzzled and then apprehensive because of the line of unhappy people coming away from the camp in the opposite direction. The hopes and fears of all the years.

The publicity about the festival beforehand was also reminiscent of the 1930s California scene. Just as the Okies etc. pinned their faith on orange bills boasting of non-existent jobs in the west, so the people shuttled out to the festival site from Ryde in Southern Vectis buses hoped that the Fiery Creations' People's Charter would all come true. People clutched at the *Melody Maker* full-page advert which assured them 'everybody will hear, everybody will see'.

The site looked like a sinister internment camp thinly disguised as an underground Butlin's. At the end of the dirt-track approach, the first view presented of the arena itself was the sight of twin towers, a closed gate, a high fence with wiring carrying 2,600 volts and long lines of submissive, uncomfortable people.

And when it became quite clear how badly these guys and gals were going to be treated, and that the response was to be all softness and tolerance, injustice was seen to be very successfully done. A fair estimate of the toilet facilities, for instance, would be one cubicle for every thirty thousand people. There were queues to filthy mobile bogs even at four o'clock in the morning. Similarly, if you were naive enough to try to get some breakfast between 7am and noon, then sure, there were hamburger stalls and pies were on sale and cups of milk and slices of melon, and all at reasonably normal prices too: but the time lags between conceiving of a desire for anything and coming into contact with it were enormous. Albert Grossman bet Ray of Fiery Creations that the food would run out by Saturday night. He was wrong. The underdeveloped masses could still buy a soup and roll on Sunday night, but they had to stand still hard to do so.

The sharp division between the manipulating few and the ordinary ticket-holders was perhaps most distastefully in evidence in the arena itself during the music. Up on stage, Rikki Farr, son of boxer Tommy Farr and brother of singer Gary Farr, spent three afternoons and evenings imposing his sanctimonious assumed personality onto 'you people who really count'. Clearly, he had been given a hipster's phrasebook and a series of hasty, anxious lessons in what to say and what not to say. (Listen, Rikki: don't say 'mate', say 'man'; don't say 'What-the-bleedin'-'ell-d'you-think-you're-bloody-doin'?', say 'that's uncool, people'.) Armed with this excruciating manual, Farr was able to manipulate his vast audience into frequent swings from pacificity to near fascism and back again. 'People – be cool.' 'If those bastards won't get down off the fence I'm going to ask you people to get them off.' 'People – people – with the fibres of your body, welcome, onto the stage, the incredible, beautiful, Moody Blues.' The people must have been glad of all the free speed, acid and hash that circulated. They certainly deserved some escape route.

On the other side of the barrier there was the press and the nasty pop aristocracy. Grossman, the only one with style, was there, detached and powerful, dismissing the rumours of a supergroup jam session after the Dylan performance. 'Of course

The Beatles would like to play with Dylan,' he said. 'I would like to go to the moon.' (This kind of point needed making, of course: the list of other artists reported ready and willing to join Dylan on stage was ludicrous. The Bee Gees were ready, Canned Heat was ready, let alone the Stones, Beatles, Blind Faith and all.)

So while the middle class, young and old, surprised each other with politeness, still waiting outside the arena, the music began inside. You can make it if you try.

The first night, Friday, there was a free concert, which ended with an excellent performance by The Nice. Each instrument, despite the tremendous volume of noise, was clear, and their programme, like that of The Who on Saturday, was very logical. Tchaikovsky really is their soulmate, the soupy classical equivalent of their brash, aggressive sentimentality.

Saturday included Marsha Hunt, Fat Mattress, The Pretty Things, Joe Cocker and Family.

Marsha Hunt wore black leather shorts and a black sleeveless vest cut away slightly at the bottom. Her whole message was sex. She had nothing else going for her but sex, plus a certain satirical glee. A big phallic microphone dangled between her legs, bumping against her crotch, and was occasionally brought caressingly up between expert-seeming fingertips, almost to the suck. Tremendous. Fantastic. Her excursions into satire consisted of sudden, smouldering looks fixed at random on a pressman and held till his eyes averted. She was having fun. She sang 'Wild Thing' even. But everything, really, including 'Walk On Gilded Splinters', sounded like another encore of the same striptease show. The pressmen slobbered at her brown, sexy feet.

Nobody slobbered at Fat Mattress' feet. It was their British debut performance. It was also a farce. Visually, they were nothing – no charisma, no focal point. The lead singer looked like an even more ridiculous parody of Christopher Logue than Christopher Logue did. None of the instruments escaped from the massive lump of formless, pointless noise that earned them a whisper of applause and no encore. Their regular attempts at frenzy were as ineffectual as their less frequent tries for delicacy.

The Pretty Things were as bad, and it seemed all too apposite that half of Fat Mattress joined them on stage at the end. They went together like dumplings and lumpy gravy.

The Who, having signed up months ago for £450, having phoned up the day before to say Kit Lambert had decided he wanted £5,000 for them instead, and having thereby ended up being paid £1,000, arrived by helicopter (which crash-landed), did an excellent, efficient show and flew away again. A sane, disdainful approach. They did 'I Can't Explain', 'Young Man Blues' and a selection from *Tommy*, which was interrupted by applause for 'Pinball Wizard'. At the end of this selection, there was a short standing ovation. Then 'Summertime Blues', then that other frustrated plea for ugly people to be allowed to make everything ugly, 'My Generation'. Then a couple more. Then another standing ovation. This was impressive till Rikki Farr came on to whip it up some. Result: a big sag, but enough response still for an encore. 'Shakin' All Over'. Perfunctory equipment-bashing. Further demands for more.

Joe Cocker was good if you like people pretending to be Ray Charles pretending to still have some musical integrity. Family was competent, pleasant and unremarkable. Saturday was over. People left the arena, went to sleep right outside the gate and were therefore in the queue for Sunday's show all through the night and all Sunday morning. 'Welcome to the camp / I guess you all know why we're here.'

The sun came out on Sunday afternoon and listening to the Third Ear Band and then to the more substantial Indo-Jazz Fusions was like the film *Jazz on a Summer's Day*. But by the time Tom Paxton came on, it had gone cold and windy again and people seemed none too happy.

Paxton began nervously and rather sadly. (On the Saturday he had appeared in the press area wearing a piece of paper saying 'Tom Paxton' on his lapel.) But after some old favourites – 'Where I'm Bound', 'Ramblin' Boy', 'Last Thing On My Mind' – he warmed up and got a very warm reception indeed. As an encore, he did a biting, brilliant 'Vietnam Pot-Luck Blues'. This caused a storm. Paxton had humanised the audience. He'd made them feel cared for. He treated them kindly and contrasted well with

Rikki Farr and all the nebulous Progressive shit that the audience had been exhorted to welcome with the essence of their beings. He had to do another encore. After this, there was a standing ovation that lasted longer than those accorded The Who. Back a third time? No, he really couldn't, because, it was explained (quite untruthfully), he had to fly back at once for a US concert commitment. (In fact he spent the rest of the afternoon drinking in the press bar and then came into the press arena to see Dylan's performance. But this was enough: he had been a bloody sight more sincere on stage than most people and anyway a third encore would have been a tactical error.)

Even after being told that he was emphatically not coming back on stage, the audience kept standing and fell into a chant of Paxton, Paxton, Paxton which lasted a full four minutes. It was, because so unexpected, an overwhelming and delirious incident. And when Paxton did, after all, come back, he came to the microphone and said 'Thank you. Thank you. You've made me happier than I've been my whole life.' Real tears came to people's eyes. It was fantastic. Following him, everybody got a bonus of applause. Pentangle benefited considerably from this. Theirs was an uninteresting and at times incompetent set, full of dreary sensitiveness signifying little. Julie Felix was worse, but better received. She asked what people would like to hear. She dithered. She smiled. She asked for a drink. She had a cold. Should she sing 'Masters Of War' or 'Chimes Of Freedom', she asked. Everyone shouted for the former, so she had to explain that she'd much rather sing the latter because it meant a lot to her. (A coy blush, a shy smile.) In the end she sang them both. An embarrassing half hour. Everyone was pretty fed up with being told how beautiful they were and that they were too much. And by the time Richie Havens came on to add his clichés to the weight of decadent philosophy already thrown down 2,000 watts at the crowd it was, well, too much.

'Groovy,' he said, several times. 'My guitar IS,' he said. 'My guitar has come a long way in the last twenty-four hours. It has probably touched every element known to man. It has been on the earth. It has been on the water...' One wished it had caught on fire.

No, his music was good. It began slightly off touch but by the time he reached the last number before his encore, 'Strawberry Fields Forever', he was exciting, assured, powerful, coherent: and his musicians, Paul Williams on guitar, Daniel Ben Zebulon on drums, were superb. He got two encores. The Grossman stable had justified its collective top billing.

After Havens there was over an hour's pause, during which the audience waited doggedly, a little cynically, and the 2,000 people in the press arena meant to hold 300 began pushing and shoving and taking more photographs of the famous (Françoise Hardy, Jane Fonda, even Cilla Black) and fighting for a better vantage point. There was precious little gentleness and love emanating from the press. The seating was arranged to allow 'Mr. Grossman's party', which numbered around seventy, to grab all the best places. Other people were asked to leave the arena and promised that they would then be re-admitted. Most people declined to take up this somewhat pointless offer; those that did found that for the second time, the necessary ticket had been swapped and that since they couldn't get through for these tickets there was no hope of their getting back in except by the adept use of force. The press still had a good deal. They could get a drink inside them within a quarter of an hour. The people in the crowd needed three hours to crap in.

Curtains came across before Dylan came on. Thick, proletarian microphones, one per instrument, were exchanged for elegant design-award microphones in large numbers, grouped tastefully around a cleaner, more ethereally lit stage.

The Band came on, technically perfect and as cold as ice, and played for 45 minutes. Another pause. The return of Rikki Farr to boss us around some more. A friend said the whole thing reminded her of being at boarding school.

'People! – Do you want the sound to be perfect?!' 'Yeah!' 'Then cool it, people. You've waited three days. Be cool and wait another five minutes and you'll have the sound 100% perfect! In fact you'll get it 200% perfect!'

And then, sure enough, on came Bob Dylan, the only performer who could afford not to wear flared, sexy trousers, dressed all in white with a yellow shirt, perfect. Like a worrying but ecstatic dream. He reinterpreted much earlier work in the light of *Nashville Skyline*. He serenaded, he smiled like Bugs Bunny, he broke some more rules by doing an encore, by pretending to be surprised to see so many people there to see him, and by repeating, in a shy voice, 'Great to be here, really great.'

There was nothing from the first two albums but something from all the others. More came from *Bringing It All Back Home* than any other. He did only two new (for him) songs: the traditional Scottish folk song 'Will Ye Go, Lassie' and a hammed-up encore song called 'Who's Gonna Throw That Minstrel Boy A Coin?' He did 'I Threw It All Away', 'To Ramona', 'One Too Many Mornings', 'I Dreamed I Saw St. Augustine', 'Lay, Lady, Lay', 'Mr. Tambourine Man', 'She Belongs To Me' and even 'Like A Rolling Stone'. Out of all these, he tried, by a fluttering, Orbison-like lyric eloquence, to take every nuance of cynicism and bitterness. In 'Like A Rolling Stone' he used the additional device of adding the word 'girl' judiciously: 'When you got nothing girl, you got nothing to lose'. Pretty gently, huh?

It was an exquisite con. It was brilliant. It was the best thing that's happened on a British stage since the 1966 concerts by the same untouchable, charismatic man. The crowd, knowing perfectly well that there was no practical point in doing so, stood and shouted for more for at least twenty solid minutes. Our Father, which art back in thy villa with thy £35,000 already, forgive thyself thy trespass against us.

Tarantula Jacket Blurb
(1971)

This was commissioned by Michael Dempsey, the editor I was working with on the manuscript of Song & Dance Man: The Art of Bob Dylan *(to be published the following November). I had to phone it through to him from a callbox down the track from where I was living in the oddly named hamlet of Lake, outside Barnstaple, North Devon. Then it had to be submitted to NYC for Dylan's approval, which he gave.*

'The very last thing that I'd want to do is to say I've been hittin' some hard travelin' too,' sang Bob Dylan in one of his first songs. But in less than ten years he has travelled farther than any artist of our time, and moved more mountains.

In the early sixties he took a snowballing folk music scene by the ears, destroying its cosy complacency and jolting it into a new mood of toughness and exploration. As a performer he stood out against all the hollowness of entertainer 'professionalism'; as a composer he broke the stranglehold of the Tin Pan Alley three-minute song.

And that was just the beginning. Dylan went on to set his poetry to electric music – at one stroke making rock'n'roll an art form and revolutionising its possibilities for a whole generation of listeners and other performers. Dylan alone made possible all the myriad creativity of what is now called 'progressive' music, shattering all the traditions of showbiz pop.

And while he has remained at the forefront of this creativity – pioneering with *Blonde On Blonde* what became known as acid rock – yet he has also pointed back to the roots of all this growth, and, perhaps especially, re-alerted us all to the strength of country music.

In 1965-66, the most crowded and energetic period of his career, the years that produced a vast array of his most vital songs, including 'Mr. Tambourine Man', 'Like A Rolling Stone',

'Desolation Row', 'She Belongs To Me', 'Love Minus Zero/No Limit', 'Visions Of Johanna' and 'Ballad Of A Thin Man' – in this period Dylan also wrote *Tarantula*, his first and only book.

It is an astonishing, exasperating book; a beautiful, flowing, stormy prose poem. *Tarantula* is surrealism on speed, a phantasmagoric trip through an America seen by an impatient, restless, brilliant man stabbing at life with a lethal humour and a strange narrative power.

Tarantula is crowded out with flashes and fragments of piercing, instantaneous portraiture: people and places and lifestyles snatched up and spotlit in a moment, as of America's chaos. Dylan pins down the pointlessness and the aimlessness and the lifelessness in a devastatingly eccentric way.

But he pins down hopes and dreams too, as *Tarantula* runs wild in a demanding, confusing, celebratory carnival of vitality and vision.

Notes On The Dylan Bootlegs:
To Live Outside The Law You Must Be Honest
(1972)

This was published in the November 1972 issue of the UK monthly Let It Rock, *under the pseudonym Tony White. (I can't recall why.) I hadn't read it since about 1974 (except for the chopped-up bits Robert Shelton chose to use, with permission, in his book* No Direction Home) *but in re-reading it in 2020 – to decide about including it in this book – I felt I should include it, and should correct only the typos from the original article, leaving alone all other errors – song mistitlings, for example, and guesses that proved wrong later – because the article and its Bootlegs Discography are now a real time-tunnel back to what was available at the dawn of Dylan bootlegs and Dylan collecting: recovering what we knew back then, what was available, how the technology was, and how things emerged into rumour and partial knowledge back in 1972 (existentially, still towards the end of the 1960s) – all such a very long time before the internet. I know, too, that anyone interested enough to be a collector of Dylan's work today will recognise and understand the errors in what follows. Many of these seem quaint now. (Besides, this* must *be of historical value, because Clinton Heylin has said it was reading this article that drew him to Bob Dylan in the first place...)*

When is a bootleg not a bootleg? That's not as simple a question as it seems, because if you've ever read the small print that runs in a circle round the edges of all your old singles' labels, you'll know that it's illegal to borrow a record from a friend and tape it for yourself on a tape recorder. You're a bootlegger. Now everyone knows that laws only work if they have the consent of a least some of the people some of the time, and if they can be enforced – if it's physically possible to enforce them. Precisely these difficulties have always meant that the copyright laws have *not* worked:

there must be at least a million bootleggers in Britain alone, not selling their illegal tapes like the big-boy pirate merchants, but managing to get their sounds without paying out for records. Your local library probably has a record library somewhere inside it (mine, a very small branch indeed, even has Dylan's *Self Portrait* in its Folk Section) and can offer you, therefore, a cheap and easy source of bootlegging material financed largely by your friendly neighbourhood rate-payers. And in innumerable schools, teachers with tape recorders – gracing themselves with the title Audio-Visual Aids Department – are busily bootlegging radio and even TV programmes all day long.

This situation of horrendous mass crime has, of course, been around for so long that it's part of the status quo, like drinking and driving or dropping your bus ticket (maximum fine for a first offence: £100). So nobody minds. And the only recent attempt to prevent everyone from cheating the gigantic record companies in this way came in the giddy days when Apple was pouring money into a diverse collection of doomed projects and hip ideas, one of the most ominous of which was for a device (and the press reports suggested it was already perfected and ready) which would be incorporated into every record marketed and would, somehow, jam and ruin any tapes anyone tried to make from records.

It never happened but the very fact that someone like John Lennon should have financed research on it shows up the peculiar double-think which 'revolutionary' rock artists can get trapped in.

The same applies to Dylan. Hunting down bootleggers who've been ripping off huge corporations like Columbia hardly ties in with all those celebrations of outlaws that recur in Dylan's work. The lines of morality get pretty blurred on the bootlegs issue, and all the sanctimonious crap from the record companies about violation of the artist's integrity don't help clear up the mess. What did the company care for the artist's integrity when their lawyers had the original *Freewheelin' Bob Dylan* album withdrawn because they were worried by the lyrics of 'Talkin' John Birch Society Blues'? Ironically, that withdrawal was the first major stroke in bringing bootlegs into existence. The album was first issued with four tracks – including 'John Birch' – different from those on the re-issued and now standard album. Copies that had already gone out were recalled, but a few, in California, got away. So right back then in 1963, there were people grooving around the West Coast clutching precious vinyl collectors' items. The later taping, re-taping and selling of those rare tracks was bound to come, as Dylan's following grew larger and more fanatical from '65 onwards.

The company provided that first invite to bootlegging; Dylan himself provided the second. In 1967, during the long wait between *Blonde On Blonde* (1966) and the next album *John Wesley Harding* (1968) brought on by the legendary motorcycle crash, Dylan recorded a big collection of songs with The Band behind him, and took the uncharacteristic step of sending it as a demo tape to his British music publishers. It was from this demo that Manfred Mann, for example, got 'The Mighty Quinn' and had a hit with it, thus creating a vast demand for Dylan's own unreleased version.

This is where another crashing irony comes in: for the British music publishers who now try to track down and prosecute the bootleg merchants, had that demo tape stolen from their own offices and turned into the first real bootleg. It's still the most famous bootleg – widely known simply as The Acetate – and a lot of stuff on it, from 'Tears Of Rage' to 'Million Dollar Bash', is really unsurpassable, top-quality Dylan. So again, the inevitable corollary of sending this tape out into the big wide world was that it got lifted and bootlegged.

You might even say that Dylan knew this would occur, and sent it deliberately. It fits in absolutely with his way of doing things. He's never got himself across by using the full battering-ram of the media, never takes up all the interview requests that most people are, in these truculent days, obliging about. He gets across largely by rumour, by setting up undercurrents.

It was certainly like that with his novel, *Tarantula*, which could have come out with a Madison Avenue bang from the publishers, American Macmillan, in 1966, but which, instead, was allowed to pass from hand to hand in bootlegged xerox form for five years before the 'official' version was issued in 1971.

Similarly, throughout his career – if that is the right word – he has made his concert audiences familiar with songs he's never released on albums, which provokes attempts at furtive acquisition. He continued to sing 'Talkin' John Birch Society Blues' long after its deletion from the album. In 1964, taking a 'special guest spot' on Joan Baez's concerts, he consistently featured the beautiful, unreleased 'Lay Down Your Weary Tune': sometimes, indeed, giving a forty-five minute version of the song. (Not all of Joan's fans, of course, appreciated this intrusion – the song got referred to as *War and Peace* – but for Dylan fans, what an incitement. If anyone happens to have a copy of this mammoth live performance, then I…)

The following year, Dylan did two half-hour shows for the BBC (easy enough to tape) and when he came to 'One Too Many Mornings' he used a distinctly different tune from the record version. Then in 1966, on that controversial British tour (the film version of which, edited by Dylan himself, came out in the States about six months ago – a long wait again – with the title *Eat the Document*) in which he appeared solo for the first half of each show and then had the loudest rock group that people had ever heard up on stage with him for each second half. He opened each rock section with a song that, unlike the others, did *not* emerge subsequently on the *Blonde On Blonde* album – a memorable, screaming, cynical song called (I would think) 'I Know And You Know' or maybe 'Tell Me Mama'. Those, at any rate, were the repeated chorus lines, and the verses included real gems in the Dylan Put-Down tradition already established by songs like 'Positively 4th Street'. An example: 'Everybody sees you on your window-ledge: / How long's it gonna take for you to / Get off the edge? / You're makin' everybody *jump* 'n' *roar*: / Now whaddya wanna go an' *do* that *for*?'

If you followed that concert around the country, you must have noticed that Columbia's video tapes were rolling all the time. So you knew, after, that all that incredible music, including the unreleased song and including a 9-minute version of 'Like A Rolling Stone', were somewhere in the Columbia vaults. The bootleg took a long time coming, but it's been available for about eighteen months now in this country, complete with all the dramatic (and now historic) audience participation of slow-handclapping the electric Dylan, and, just before the last number, the verbal clash where someone shouts out 'Judas!' and Dylan finally comes up to the microphone and speaks. 'I don't believe you!' he growls. The music begins again, quiet but ominous, and with perfect timing Dylan darts back and shouts 'You're a liar!' The instant he's said it, the band crashes into the apocalyptic opening of 'Like A Rolling Stone' and the song comes through harder than ever before, with Dylan literally hurling the words *at* his audience.

That bootleg is one of Dylan's most important records. It explains a lot and at the same time gives you Dylan at his best. Not many of the other bootleg albums manage that. To the question does the bootleg material reveal, as it were, new Bob Dylans, the answer is largely no. The Acetate is important, and that 1966 British concert tape is important, but the others are usually, in any case, disconnected collections of Dylan cuts, and so much lacking the unity of the two already mentioned that their importance lies only in the occasional particular track which might be said to give a 'new' Bob Dylan to the listener. And even then, the avid Dylan fan would hardly be surprised by any of these 'new' glimpses – he would have been able to guess their existence by understanding the Dylan already known. For instance, on the first of the various *Great White Wonder* bootlegs, there is a truly great track called 'Black Cross', an old Lord Buckley song about a black rural American hanged for being literate and irreligious. I'd say this track was essential to any proper Dylan collection: it differs from the released Dylan 'protest' stuff in being very funny as well as very serious, but it represents an extension of Dylan's range that anyone could have guessed at from listening to, say, 'Memphis Blues Again' or 'Motorpsycho Nitemare'.

Similarly, the bootleg commonly known as *VD Waltz* includes a complete Dylan version of 'Cocaine', which is nice for its rhyming of 'purple' with 'nipples' but which no-one familiar with Dylan's New York folk-club background could have failed to expect to find on tape somewhere.

The other isolated bootleg tracks which are important include two songs already mentioned, 'John Birch' (on two of the three bootleg double-albums which, confusingly enough, all bear the name *Great White Wonder Volume 2*) and 'Lay Down Your Weary Tune' (on the single bootleg album called *24*) which is long but nowhere near 45 minutes.

Apart from these, the most vital tracks are: the mock-pop song 'I'm Ready' – which confirms all the stories about the early Dylan wishing he was Gene Vincent / Little Richard / Elvis Presley, and the fantastically vitriolic 'She's Your Lover Now' (which makes 'Positively 4th Street' sound like 'I Got You Babe'), both of which appear on the *40 Red White & Blue Shoestrings* bootleg; the beautifully inconsequential 'Hava Nagila Blues', which crops up along with a *third* version of 'Corrina, Corrina' on a nicely packaged bootleg called *Talkin' Bear Mountain Picnic Massacre Blues*; plus, finally, a live version of 'Mr. Tambourine Man' (about the 12th available version), this one cut the night that 1966 'British' tour opened, which was in Dublin. It's an acoustic version from the solo half of the concert, but what is remarkable about it is the harmonica in the middle and at the end of the performance, an incredible, stoned, slurred, cascading tour de force not paralleled anywhere else in Dylan's work. The technical quality of this recording is atrocious but it's well worth having.

All these tracks, though, are the exceptions. The vast majority of bootlegged Dylan recordings are less than spectacular. Most of them come from the pre-1965, pre-electric period and are what you'd expect. All the songs were always in the Dylan songbooks but never on his albums – songs like 'Paths Of Victory', 'Eternal Circle', 'Seven Curses' and so on – plus slightly different versions of much of his album material: 'Gospel Plow' and 'Baby Let Me Follow You Down' etc. Then, predictably, Dylan's versions of a number of Woody Guthrie songs, and many live and studio versions of songs commonly featured in the pre-65 Dylan concerts: things like 'Who Killed Davey Moore?' and 'Walls Of Red Wing'.

Perhaps the most interesting side effect of the bootleg boom is the way this massive regurgitation of his early cuts has impinged on Dylan himself. It is almost certain that it was the huge interest in The Acetate which led Dylan to re-record three of the songs from that tape and have them issued on the official *More Bob Dylan Greatest Hits* album ('I Shall Be Released', 'You Ain't Goin' Nowhere' and 'Down In The Flood'). It's a nice touch, on Dylan's part, to include those bootleg songs under that collective title. And that (which is still Dylan's latest album) also includes a track cut live in 1964, the seductive 'Tomorrow Is A Long Time' (which happens to be the only song of Dylan's that has been recorded by Elvis Presley, though that's another story).

In fact, for Dylan in 1971 to release a track cut in 1964 is a big tribute to the boomeranging impact of Dylan bootlegs on Dylan, because previously one of his maxims had always been, in his own phrase, 'don't look back'. When Jann Wenner interviewed Dylan for *Rolling Stone* magazine in 1969 (and it's notable that Dylan has not done a single interview since then) Wenner kept referring to albums like *Highway 61 Revisited* and *Blonde On Blonde*, and Dylan kept saying 'Well, what was on that album? Which songs were those?' And while it may genuinely be the case that Dylan is less familiar with his own earlier records than every one of his followers, that response also indicates the habit Dylan had always (until recently) had of turning away from his past, never staying in one place. ('And here I sit so patiently / Waiting to find out what price / Ya have to pay to get out of / Going through all these things twice'.)

In contrast, since the great overflow of bootleg albums onto the market in 1970 and 1971 (before the latest round of new crack-down legislation), Dylan has indeed started to look back. He's returned to live in Greenwich Village, and he's certainly returned to a surprising extent to his older song material. Who could possibly have guessed that his performance at the 1971 Concert For Bangla Desh would have included 'Blowin' In The Wind' – a song he hadn't sung before that for almost seven years, a song he'd refused to sing way back in 1965 at the stormy Newport Folk Festival appearance that had marked his electric-guitar debut – a song he's spent years trying to escape from?

Dylan's Concert For Bangla Desh performance also included a similarly long-time-no-sing revisit to his 1963 song 'A Hard Rain's A-Gonna Fall'. I think there's no doubt that the release of so much bootleg Dylan has played a major part in re-kindling Dylan's interest in his own musical past.

Had Dylan's official album releases been as prolific as most of his contemporaries', he would never have got to the cult-adulation position whereby such a vast bootleg market could have developed. The first of his albums, *Bob Dylan*, could have been followed up sooner than it was, and by another album of similar material culled from the very substantial number of studio cuts made at the time. Likewise, after the largely 'protest' album *The Freewheelin' Bob Dylan*, it would easily have been possible to issue another twelve Dylan 'protest' songs of parallel focus (songs like 'The Ballad Of Omie Wise', 'The Death Of Emmett Till', 'The Ballad Of Donald White', 'Cuban Blockade' etc., as well as songs already cited like 'Walls Of Red Wing' and 'Who Killed Davey Moore?') before *The Times They Are A-Changin'*. And again, after Dylan's fourth album, *Another Side Of Bob Dylan*, enough tracks cut at around the same time and conveying the same distinctive sound and range of interests could have been put together and issued as a follow-up. (Tracks for this could reasonably have included 'Bob Dylan's New Orleans Rag', 'Sometimes I'm In The Mood', 'Tomorrow Is A Long Time', 'Eternal Circle', 'Lay Down Your Weary Tune', and those two great 1964 songs 'Mama, You Bin On My Mind' and 'I'll Keep It With Mine'.)

But if that had happened, if that much had come onto the market in the early 1960s, Dylan would not, I think, have been the seminal influence and outstanding force for good that he has been in rock music. People die very easily from over-exposure – and if they don't die, they certainly devalue their currency.

Dylan has always been keenly aware of this and has, over what is now a ten-year period, issued only eleven albums (plus the two *Greatest Hits* collections). In 1964 in New York City, one of Dylan's concerts was recorded by Columbia with a view to getting and issuing a live album. Columbia wanted a 'protest' album because they could see the Protest Boom coming up. Dylan had finished with 'protest', and certainly didn't want to get caught up in the imminent Boom (which came to a head in Britain the following year, 1965, with Barry McGuire's gold record of 'Eve

Of Destruction'). So that live album never came out. In 1967 Columbia released the first *Greatest Hits* album – with its dopey selection of tracks – against Dylan's wishes, to try to make up for the fact that no proper new Dylan album was there until, finally, *John Wesley Harding* emerged in 1968.

After that, it was heavily rumoured that Dylan would leave Columbia and probably sign with MGM instead. It's a safe bet that the reason Dylan did *not*, in the event, quit Columbia was that had he done so, Columbia would have poured around *seventy* unreleased Dylan tracks onto the market. If they'd issued it all, that would have been thirteen more albums. To call that over-exposure would be an understatement.

So Dylan re-signed with Columbia, making sure this time that he owned his own masters and that no-one expected more than one album a year from there on in. Since then, the only official releases have been: *Nashville Skyline*, 1969; *Self Portrait*, mid 1970; *New Morning*, late 1970; and the *More Greatest Hits* collection in late 1971.

Now, therefore, it is nearly two years since a completely new Dylan album and all that has appeared in the meantime has been the singles of 'Watching The River Flow' and 'George Jackson' – which was, in one sense, another astonishing throwback – plus a few scattered album tracks: five old songs on the *Concert For Bangla Desh* album, three Woody Guthrie songs recorded live with The Band back in 1968 and recently issued on the Columbia album *A Tribute To Woody Guthrie Part One*, and an instrumental duet between Earl Scruggs's banjo and Dylan's guitar doing 'Nashville Skyline Rag' on the LP *Earl Scruggs, His Family and Friends*.

It's hard to tell for sure, but again I'd say that this most recent gap in Dylan's output has to do with the Dylan bootlegs situation. I think Dylan must be feeling that the release of so much bootleg material, material which has got around so far and so fast, once again poses the over-exposure problem, and that the best way to counteract it is for him to hold back for a substantial period before issuing anything else at all.

With the latest anti-bootleg legislation, which imposes very heavy penalties indeed on shops that stock the stuff, the bootleg market is drying up. If you're Bob Dylan, this will please you, and will, after a suitable pause, leave you free to release a new record; if you're a fan who already has all the bootlegs, this will also please you, because then You're Alright Jack and there won't be so long left to wait for that *new* Dylan album. If, on the other hand, you haven't yet traced any kind of path through the maze of the Dylan bootlegs that are (just about) still around, then you'd better act quickly.

It's a maze in the sense that so many bootlegs duplicate tracks, so it's sometimes necessary to pay out for, say, ten tracks you've already got, in order to get one track you haven't got and can't get any other way.

The discography below has been compiled to try to minimise all this mixed-up confusion. It includes, along with the proper bootlegs, a round-up (I hope complete) of tracks officially released by various companies which in some way feature Dylan but which are not proper Dylan album / hit single cuts.

What follows is *not*, however, truly complete, because it isn't possible to know exactly how many unreleased tracks there are – or what they are – still in Columbia's vaults. And we'll never know that unless Dylan dies prematurely.

In *that* event, of course, the ultimate bootlegging will begin, and will be done by Dylan's own record company. We'll get those 70+ tracks together with every home-recorded track and every jam-session fragment that can be dug out, all, if it's deemed necessary, re-mixed, dubbed, electronically-reprocessed-for-quad-sound, and so on. The most prolific Buddy Holly Syndrome since Holly himself died will flush into action with indecent haste.

Here, then, is The Other Dylan Discography:

(a) Little-known Columbia (CBS) tracks:

1. 'Mixed-Up Confusion' c/w 'Corrina, Corrina': mono single issued & quickly withdrawn in US in 1963; re-issued in Holland in 1966 (CBS 2476); still available in various European countries. ('Corrina, Corrina' is not the same cut as on the *Freewheelin'* LP but was recorded at the LP sessions).

2. The *Freewheelin' Bob Dylan* Mk1. Issued in US, quickly withdrawn and most copies recalled. The tracks deleted were: 'Talkin' John Birch Society Blues'; 'Let Me Die In My Footsteps'; 'Rocks And Gravel', and 'Ramblin' Gamblin' Willy'. All four deleted tracks are now available on bootlegs (see Section c).

3. 'If You Gotta Go, Go Now' c/w 'To Ramona': mono single issued in the Benelux countries in 1967. Still available (CBS 2921). 'To Ramona' same as 4th LP cut. 'If You Gotta Go, Go Now' cut at the *Bringing It All Back Home* sessions 1965.

4. 'I Want You' c/w 'Just Like Tom Thumb's Blues': mono single. Issued everywhere 1966 – and a hit too! But those who only bought the LPs may have missed this out – a mistake, because the B-side is not the LP version. It's a live cut from Dylan's Liverpool concert of May 1966 (the only officially released cut from that concert tour).

5. *Carolyn Hester*: LP by Carolyn Hester (US no. Columbia CL 1796) cut before the release of Dylan's 1st LP, features Dylan on harmonica throughout.

6. *Earl Scruggs, His Family and Friends*: LP issued 1972. Has Dylan on one track, saying 'OK' & playing lead acoustic guitar in duet with Scruggs's banjo on 'Nashville Skyline Rag', cut at a private house in Carmel, NY (no date given).

7. *A Tribute To Woody Guthrie Part One*: LP cut live at Carnegie Hall 1968. Includes Dylan & The Band on 'Mrs. Roosevelt', 'I Ain't Got No Home In This World Anymore' and 'Grand Coolee Dam'. (This appearance was Dylan's first since 1966 and the subsequent motorbike crash). Issued 1972.

8. *Highway 61 Revisited*: in the US, this LP had, for a short time, a different take of 'From A Buick 6' on; then the usual version was reinstated. (1965).

NB. There are various other minor variations to note: the versions of 'One Of Us Must Know (Sooner Or Later)' on the UK *Blonde On Blonde* LP and on the first *Greatest Hits* LP are the same recordings as on the original US *Blonde On Blonde*, but are different mixes, so that a heavy piano riff disappears & a weak organ emerges instead. On the UK *Blonde On Blonde* also, 'Memphis Blues Again' was for a time given on the label as 'Stuck Inside Of Mobile With Thee'. On the US *Blonde On Blonde* the liner photos were rearranged shortly after the LP's release.

NB 2: the front cover of The Band's first album, 1968's *Music From Big Pink*, is a painting by Dylan.

(b) Officially Released Non-Columbia Tracks:

1. *Three Kings & The Queen*: LP cut 1961, issued 1964 in the US on the Spivey label (Spivey LP 1004). Victoria Spivey (the lady with Dylan on the back cover of the *New Morning* album: the photo presumably dates from this 1961 session), with Big Joe Williams, Lonnie Johnson & Roosevelt Sykes. Dylan plays harmonica on 'Wichita' and (plus back-up voice) on 'Sitting On Top Of The World'.

2. *Midnight Special*: LP by Harry Belafonte (US no. RCA LSP 2449) issued May 1962. Dylan plays harmonica on title track.

3. *Blues Project*: an Elektra LP (EKS 7264), various artists. Dylan plays piano on 'Downtown Blues' under the name Bob Landy.

4. *Evening Concerts at Newport, Volume 1*, 1963: Vanguard LP (VSD 79143), cut at the 1963 Newport Folk Festival. Dylan sings 'Blowin' In The Wind'.

5. *Newport Broadside*: Vanguard LP (VSD 79144), cut same time same place. Dylan & Pete Seeger duet on 'Ye Playboys & Playgirls'; and everyone joins for a version of 'Blowin' In The Wind' again. (NB. There is also an EP – I have no details to hand – from the same concerts, which includes a duet by Dylan and Joan Baez on 'With God On Our Side'.)

6. *We Shall Overcome*: Broadside LP (BR-592), various artists. Dylan singing 'Only A Pawn In Their Game' live at the 1963 Washington Civil Rights March.

7. *Broadside Ballads No. 1*: Broadside LP (BR–301) issued November 1963. Dylan features as Blind Boy Grunt on 'John Brown', 'Only A Hobo' and 'Talkin Devil'.

8. *Dick Fariña & Eric Von Schmidt*: Folklore Records LP (F-LEUT/7). Dylan, again as Blind Boy Grunt, plays harmonica on 'Glory Glory', 'You Can't Always Tell', 'Christmas Island' and 'Cocaine'.

9. *Concert For Bangla Desh*: Apple triple-album (STCX RE3385). Dylan live at Madison Square Gardens, August 1971, backed by Leon Russell, George Harrison & Ringo Starr, on 'A Hard Rain's A-Gonna Fall', 'It Takes A Lot To Laugh, It Takes A Train To Cry', 'Blowin' In The Wind', 'Mr. Tambourine Man' and 'Just Like A Woman'.

(c) Bootleg Albums:

1. The Acetate (more commonly circulated on tape than on record): Dylan & The Band, cut at Big Pink, New York State, 1967. The basic tape has 14 tracks but the full tape has a handful more. The 14 are: 'Down In The Flood', 'This Wheel's On Fire', 'I Shall Be Released', 'Nothing Was Delivered', 'Please, Mrs. Henry', 'Million Dollar Bash', 'Tears Of Rage', 'Too Much Of Nothing', 'Tiny Montgomery', 'Lo And Behold', 'The Mighty Quinn', 'Yea! Heavy And A Bottle Of Bread', 'You Ain't Goin' Nowhere' and 'Open The Door, Homer'. The full Acetate has, in addition, two alternative versions of 'Nothing Was Delivered' (one an Elvis parody), plus 'The Clothes Song', 'I'm Not There I'm Gone', 'Odds And Ends' and 'Get Your Eyes Off'.

2. *Motor Cycle*: LP of the 14 basic Acetate tracks.

3. *Great White Wonder Vol. 1*: double-LP, containing: 'Poor Lazarus', 'Baby Please Don't Go', 'See That My Grave Is Kept Clean', 'East Orange New Jersey', 'Man Of Constant Sorrow', 'Candy Man', 'Ramblin' Round', a conversation fragment, 'Black Cross', 'Ain't Got No Home In This World Anymore' – all recorded in a Minneapolis hotel room in December 1961. Plus:

'The Death Of Emmett Till', a snatch of interview with Dylan by Pete Seeger, and 'Fare Thee Well' – all from an unbroadcast radio show for WBAI-FM, recorded September 1961. Plus: 'The Mighty Quinn', 'This Wheel's On Fire', 'I Shall Be Released', 'Open The Door, Homer', 'Too Much Of Nothing', 'Nothing Was Delivered' & 'Tears Of Rage' – all from The Acetate. Plus: 'Bob Dylan's New Orleans Rag' (an incomplete studio version, 1963/4), 'If You Gotta Go, Go Now' (same as Section a, 3), 'Only A Hobo' (an outtake from the Broadside sessions, see Section b, 7), 'Barbed Wire Fence' (cut at the *Highway 61 Revisited* sessions, 1965, and more audible on the *Stealin'* bootleg – see below), 'Mixed-Up Confusion' (same as the single, see Section a, 1) and 'Living The Blues', cut live on the 1969 Johnny Cash TV show (Not same as the *Self Portrait* version). NB. In terms of technical quality, this is the worst bootleg. Try to get the tracks elsewhere.

4. *Great White Wonder Vol. 2* (Mk 1): double-LP containing: 'Can You Please Crawl Out Your Window?' (not same version as the single), 'It Takes A Lot To Laugh, It Takes A Train To Cry' (not same as LP version), 'Love Minus Zero/No Limit' (not LP version), 'She Belongs To Me' (not ditto), 'It's All Over Now, Baby Blue' (again, not ditto), 'That's All Right Mama', 'Hard Times In New York', 'Wade In The Water', 'Cocaine' (incomplete version) – all these obtainable with better quality on the *Stealin'* bootleg (see below). Plus: 'I'll Keep It With Mine', 'Talkin' John Birch Society Blues', 'Who Killed Davey Moore?' (one of several available versions, this one live), 'Eternal Circle', 'The Ballad Of Willie O'Conley / Willie The Gambler', 'Mixed-Up Confusion' (same as single and as on Vol. 1), 'I Was Young When I Left Home', 'Percy's Song / Turn Turn Turn', 'Corrina, Corrina' (not LP version, but same as B-side of single, see Section a, 1), 'In The Evening', 'Long John From Bowling Green', 'Your Best Form' – most of which are available in better quality elsewhere – plus the following The Acetate songs all over again: 'Million Dollar Bash', 'Yea! Heavy And A Bottle Of Bread', 'Lo And Behold', 'Please, Mrs. Henry', 'Tiny Montgomery' and 'You Ain't Goin' Nowhere'. Bad value for money though this is, with lots of

repetition of tracks better obtainable elsewhere, and in largely very poor quality, it is nonetheless vastly preferable to the double-LP listed immediately below, which purports to be the same as this one but which actually misses out several of the above and gives other tracks twice on the same double-album!

5. *Great White Wonder Vol.2* (Mk 2): double-LP to steer clear of, containing: 'Can You Please Crawl Out Your Window?', 'It Takes A Lot To Laugh, It Takes A Train To Cry', 'She Belongs To Me', 'It's All Over Now, Baby Blue', 'Love Minus Zero/No Limit', 'That's All Right Mama', 'Hard Times In New York' and 'Stealin'' (also, you've guessed, available – but not better quality – on the *Stealin'* bootleg). Plus: 'I Was Young When I Left Home', 'Percy's Song / Turn Turn Turn' twice, 'Corrina, Corrina' twice, 'In The Evening' twice, 'Long John From Bowling Green' twice, 'Bob Dylan's New Orleans Rag', 'The Cough Song' (also from the *Stealin'* bootleg), 'Wade In The Water', 'Cocaine', 'I'll Keep It With Mine', 'Talkin' John Birch Society Blues', 'Who Killed Davey Moore?', 'Eternal Circle', 'Willie The Gambler / The Ballad Of Willie O'Conley', and just one Acetate track, 'Down In The Flood'. All versions on this LP are on the *Great White Wonder Vol.2* (Mk 1), detailed above.

6. *Great White Wonder Vol.2* (Mk 3)(!) A totally different double-album, and the most difficult to obtain, containing: 'Somehow Somewhere', 'Great Times', 'Your Letter', 'In The Muddy Water', 'It Wasn't Easy Forever', 'I Love You', 'Never', 'I Can't Live Without You', 'You Are My Love', 'I'll Be Seeing You', 'That's It', 'Because You Care', 'Blue River', 'If Tomorrow You Are Still Here', 'No No And No', 'What Do You Say', 'You Can Do It', 'Don't', 'Oh Yeah', 'He Is Not For You', 'Three In A Basket', 'The Devil In You' and 'Like'. I've not heard this album and the titles are oddly pop. The only one I recognise is 'Oh Yeah', which is also available on the *VD Waltz* bootleg, and which sounds as if it – like the Dylan songs 'Sign On The Cross' and 'Don't Ya Tell Henry', which Coulson Dean McGuinness & Flint do on their *Lo & Behold* LP – is an extra part of the 1967 Acetate (though they don't appear on the usual 'full' Acetate tape). Possibly, therefore,

all this double-LP's other tracks are ones-that-got-away from the Acetate. Alternatively, they may well have been cut at the same time as the track 'I'm Ready' – mentioned above this discography – which is available on the *40 Red White & Blue Shoestrings* bootleg: see below. Anyone with information leading to the apprehension of this *GGW2*Mk3 bootleg please get in touch.

7. *Stealin'*: one of the best, containing 'Can You Please Crawl Out Your Window?' (different from the released single: at a guess, cut at the *Highway 61 Revisited* sessions, 1965), 'It Takes A Lot To Laugh, It Takes A Train To Cry' (ditto: a very heavy, fast rock version, new tune, many new words), 'Barbed Wire Fence/Killing Me Alive' (also from the *Highway 61* sessions), 'If You Gotta Go, Go Now' (same as single already mentioned); 'She Belongs To Me', 'Love Minus Zero/No Limit' and 'It's All Over Now, Baby Blue' – all three unused takes from the *Bringing It All Back Home* LP sessions, 'Blue' having a half-different tune. Plus: 'The Cough Song' (made at the 1963 *Broadside* session), 'Bob Dylan's New Orleans Rag' (same incomplete version already mentioned), 'That's All Right Mama' (probably done at the *Another Side Of Bob Dylan* sessions 1964), 'Hard Times In New York' (Minneapolis, 1961), 'Stealin'', 'Wade In The Water', 'Cocaine' and 'Lay Down Your Weary Tune' (again, probably from the *Another Side Of* sessions).

8. *Bob Dylan The Villager*: double-album, containing: 'Man On The Street', 'He Was A Friend Of Mine', 'Talkin' Bear Mountain Picnic Massacre Blues', 'Pretty Polly' and (with Dave Van Ronk) 'Car Car' – all cut live at the Gaslight Cafe, New York City, 1962. Plus 'Song To Woody', 'California', two talk interludes, 'Lay Down Your Weary Tune' (no details re those), 'I've Bin A Moonshiner' (probably done as a private demo tape for Witmarks – and Dylan calls it 'The Bottle Song'). Plus the following Guthrie songs taped at a house in East Orange, New Jersey in early 1962: 'Jesus Met The Woman At The Well', 'Gypsy Davy', 'Pastures Of Plenty', 'Jesse James' and 'Remember Me'.

9. *The Kindest Kut*: LP containing: 'Hard Times In New York', 'Stealin'', 'Wade In The Water' – all as on the *Stealin'* bootleg – plus: 'Baby Let Me Follow You Down', 'Sally Gal', 'Gospel Plow', 'Cocaine' (complete version), 'VD Blues', 'VD Waltz', 'VD City', 'VD Gunner's Blues', 'The Ballad of Omie Wise' – all these from the Minneapolis December 1961 taping – plus the Broadside cuts of 'John Brown', 'Only A Hobo' and 'Talkin' Devil'. Plus: 'There Was A Time When I Was Blind' (same tune as 'I Was Young When I Left Home' but different words – probably also Minneapolis 1961) and 'The Ballad Of Donald White', from the September '61 radio show for WBAI-FM (mentioned already).

10. *Blind Boy Grunt*: LP with same tracks as *The Kindest Kut*.

11. *John Birch Society Blues*: LP containing: 'Mixed-Up Confusion', 'I'll Keep It With Mine', 'Talkin' John Birch Society Blues', 'Who Killed Davey Moore?' (live version, I think), 'Eternal Circle', 'Willie The Gambler/The Ballad Of Willie O'Conley', 'Percy's Song/Turn Turn Turn', 'Corrina, Corrina', 'Long John From Bowling Green' and 'In The Evening' – all same versions as on *Great White Wonder Vol.2*, Mks 1 & 2 (see above). Plus: a piano solo (it isn't billed on *Stealin'* and *GWW2*Mks1&2, but it's there all the same), 'Ramblin' Round' (which is as on *GWW1*, from the Minneapolis 1961 tapes) and '900 Miles' (which is probably the same as 'Going To New Orleans' on the *Talkin' Bear Mountain Picnic Massacre Blues* bootleg below).

12. *Talkin' Bear Mountain Picnic Massacre Blues*: beautifully packaged colour-printed bootleg, containing: 'Quit Your Low-Down Ways', 'Worried Blues', 'Corrina, Corrina', 'Lonesome Whistle Blues', 'Rocks And Gravel', 'Talkin' Hava Nagila Blues', 'Adams Spring' (which is the same as 'The Ballad of Omie Wise' on the *Kindest Kut* bootleg), 'Wichita Blues', 'Talkin' Bear Mountain Picnic Massacre Blues', 'I'm In The Mood For You', 'The Death Of Emmett Till', 'Baby Please Don't Go', 'Going To New Orleans' and 'Milk Cow Blues'. NB. It might look from the tracks-list that most of these are duplicates, but in fact this album offers different versions of the most common ones so that eg: this

'Corrina, Corrina' is a third version. Likewise 'I'm In The Mood For You' and 'Baby Please Don't Go' are not the usual versions; nor is 'Rocks And Gravel'. And the technical quality of this LP is good.

13. *24*: single LP, despite any implications of the title; containing: 'I'm In The Mood For You', 'I Guess I'm Doin' Fine', 'Quit Your Low-Down Ways' (not the same as the *Picnic Massacre* version – see above), 'Gypsy Lou', 'Whatcha Gonna Do', 'Percy's Song/Turn Turn Turn' (not same as *GWW2*Mks1&2 version), 'Hero Blues' (studio version), 'Mama, You Bin On My Mind', 'Lay Down Your Weary Tune', 'I'll Keep It With Mine', 'Goin' Down South', 'I've Bin A Moonshiner', 'Only A Hobo' and, once again, 'Who Killed Davey Moore?'. It's hard to place most of the tracks on this and the *Picnic Massacre* bootleg but most are studio cuts from 1963 and 1964: mostly the latter, I'd say.

14. *VD Waltz*: a blue semi-transparent-vinyl single album, containing: 'VD Blues', 'VD Waltz', 'VD City', 'VD Gunner's Blues' – all as on the *Kindest Kut* bootleg – plus: 'Mama, You Bin On My Mind', 'Seven Curses', 'Paths Of Victory' – all studio cuts from '63/4. Plus: 'East Virginia' (a duet with Earl Scruggs, no date known); 'Will Ye Go, Lassie' (live from Dylan's Isle of Wight show, August 1969); and 'Mama But You're So Hard' (a fragment which sounds like the prototype for what became 'Temporary Like Achilles', but with the sound of the *Highway 61 Revisited* sessions). Plus these probably-from-the-Acetate tracks: 'The Clothes Song', 'I'm Not There I'm Gone', 'Oh Yeah', 'Odds And Ends' and 'Get Your Eyes Off'.

15. *Seems Like A Freeze-Out*: contains: 'Lay Down Your Weary Tune', 'Whatcha Gonna Do', 'California' (may be the same as 'Goin' Down South' on *24*), 'Dusty Old Fairgrounds', 'Who You Really Are', 'I'll Do It All Over You', 'Can You Please Crawl Out Your Window?' (as on *Stealin'*) and 'From A Buick 6' (the version briefly released officially on *Highway 61 Revisited* – see Section a, 8). Plus – all from the wonderful *40 Red White & Blue Shoestrings* bootleg (see below) – 'I Wanna Be Your Man', 'Visions

Of Johanna' and 'She's Your Lover Now'. This LP very hard to find. Again, I'd like to find it myself…

16. *40 Red White & Blue Shoestrings*: wonderful. Contains: 'I Wanna Be Your Man' (probably from the *Highway 61 Revisited* sessions, 1965), 'Number One' (an instrumental but sounds like a *Blonde On Blonde* backing-track), 'Visions Of Johanna' (sounds like a first try-out at the *Blonde On Blonde* sessions – some word changes), 'She's Your Lover Now' (search the world for this LP for this track alone: must be 1965?), 'One Too Many Mornings' (duet with Johnny Cash, from the film *Johnny Cash: The Man And His Music*), 'Let Me Die In My Footsteps' (studio cut, probably 1963), 'I'm Ready' (date unknown: maybe same session as *GWW2*Mk3), 'Rocks And Gravel' (not same as *Picnic Massacre* version) and 'Just Like Tom Thumb's Blues' (same as single: see Section a, 4).

17. *Black Nite Crash*: an all-live album, containing: 'Visions Of Johanna', '4th Time Around', 'Just Like A Woman' and 'Desolation Row' – all from Dylan's Dublin concert, May 1966. Plus: 'Ramblin' Down Thru The World', 'Bob Dylan's Dream', 'Bob Dylan's New Orleans Rag', 'Tomorrow Is A Long Time' (now issued officially on the *More Greatest Hits* LP), 'The Walls Of Redwing', 'Hero Blues' and 'Who Killed Davey Moore?' – all recorded live at, I think, Dylan's first solo concert at Carnegie Hall, 1964, or at his New York hallowe'en concert 1964.

18. *While The Establishment Burns*: LP with same tracks as *Black Nite Crash*. NB it has not got the song 'While The Establishment Burns' on it; perhaps the song doesn't exist and is just a myth. (Again, I'd appreciate being disabused of this suspicion.)

19. *Dylan With The Band Live 1966*: brilliant, seminal LP cut at the Albert Hall in May 1966. High quality sound (fallen off the back of a Columbia lorry, I would guess) and an aesthetically pleasing silver & black label with the witty trademark ZEROCKS. Containing: 'Tell Me Mama' (discussed in the article preceding this discography), 'I Don't Believe You', 'Baby Let Me Follow You Down', 'Just Like Tom Thumb's Blues', 'Leopard-Skin Pill-Box

Hat', 'One Too Many Mornings', 'Ballad Of A Thin Man', and 'Like A Rolling Stone'.

20. *Live*: appalling sound-quality double-LP containing: 'Tell Me Mama', 'Baby Let Me Follow You Down', 'One Too Many Mornings', 'Like A Rolling Stone' & 'I Don't Believe You' – all duplicating the *Dylan Live With The Band 1966* bootleg – plus 'She Belongs To Me', 'Maggie's Farm', 'Highway 61 Revisited', 'One Too Many Mornings', 'Like A Rolling Stone', 'The Mighty Quinn' and 'Rainy Day Women #12 & 35' – all badly taped from the 1969 Isle of Wight show, and all better obtainable on the Isle of Wight bootleg (see below). But, unfortunately, it is necessary to get this double-LP in order to get the only available version of 'If You Gotta Go, Go Now' cut live in Dublin in 1966, and of 'Mr. Tambourine Man' with unique harmonica solo.

21. *Dylan at the Isle of Wight*: disappointing sound-quality LP, containing: 'She Belongs To Me', 'The Mighty Quinn', 'Minstrel Boy' and 'Like A Rolling Stone' (which all appear on the *Self Portrait* LP but which, in a way, are better on the bootleg, because the *Self Portrait* re-mix cuts out one of the harmony voices, which is better left in); plus 'Highway 61 Revisited', 'One Too Many Mornings', 'I Pity The Poor Immigrant', 'I'll Be Your Baby Tonight', 'I Threw It All Away', 'Maggie's Farm', 'Will Ye Go, Lassie', 'It Ain't Me, Babe', 'To Ramona' (these last three are astonishing solo performances), 'Rainy Day Women #12 & 35' (this track not on all copies) and 'Lay, Lady, Lay'.

d) Other Recordings Known To Exist But Not Yet On Bootleg:

NB. If, of course, the bootlegs list above is not complete, then what follows will be, to that extent, affected. It is also easily possible that there are many other Dylan recordings which exist but which are not generally known and not on this list.

1. From the September 1961 WBAI-FM Radio Show: another version of 'Blowin' In The Wind'.

2. From the East Orange New Jersey early 1962 private-house tape: 'On The Trail Of The Buffalo' and 'San Francisco Bay Blues'.

3. From the 1963 Broadside Records session: 'Hey Hey I'd Hate To Be You On That Dreadful Day', 'Ye Playboys & Playgirls' (solo version), 'Train-a-Travelin', 'Cuban Blockade' and 'Walkin' Down The Line'.

4. From either the Witmark demo-tape or from the *Another Side Of Bob Dylan* sessions: 'Denise Denise', 'Walkin' Down The Line', 'The Walls Of Red Wing', 'Tomorrow Is A Long Time', 'Ain't Gonna Grieve', 'Farewell', and 'Born To Win Born To Lose'.

5. From the *Another Side Of Bob Dylan* session: 'East Laredo'.

6. From Dylan's first solo concert at Carnegie Hall, 1964: a Columbia acetate (Job No. 77110) containing: 'When The Ship Comes In', 'John Brown', 'Who Killed Davey Moore?' (though this one may be one of the bootlegged versions), 'Poem To Woody / Last Thoughts On Woody Guthrie', 'Lay Down Your Weary Tune', 'Dusty Old Fairgrounds', 'Percy's Song/Turn Turn Turn', 'Bob Dylan's New Orleans Rag' (i.e. third version), and 'Seven Curses'.

7. From Dylan's hallowe'en New York City concert, 1964: seventeen songs taped by Columbia (including 'If You Gotta Go, Go Now'), of which four were duets with Joan Baez, including 'Mama/Daddy, You Bin On My Mind'.

8. From Dylan's 1965 Newport Folk Festival performance: three tracks were taped for the film *Festival*: 'Maggie's Farm', 'Tombstone Blues' and 'Like A Rolling Stone'. Only the first was used in the film. (It was Dylan's first electric guitar appearance; he was backed by part of Paul Butterfield's Blues Band.)

9. From the 1965 BBC-TV Shows; many people privately taped these. Tracks are: 'Gates Of Eden', 'Mr. Tambourine Man', 'If You Gotta Go, Go Now', 'The Lonesome Death Of Hattie Carroll', 'It Ain't Me, Babe', 'Love Minus Zero/No Limit', 'One Too Many

Mornings', 'Boots Of Spanish Leather', 'It's Alright, Ma (I'm Only Bleeding)', 'She Belongs To Me' and 'It's All Over Now, Baby Blue'. (NB. Some private tapes exist of Dylan singing 'Swan In The River' in the BBC-TV play *Madhouse on Castle Street*, in which he appeared in '62.)

10. The soundtrack of the film of Dylan's 1965 British tour, *Dont Look Back*, contains incomplete live versions of: 'She Belongs To Me', 'All I Really Want To Do', 'Maggie's Farm', 'Only A Pawn In Their Game', 'To Ramona', 'The Times They Are A-Changin'', 'The Lonesome Death Of Hattie Carroll', 'Don't Think Twice, It's All Right', 'It's All Over Now, Baby Blue', 'The Times They Are A-Changin'' (again – different fragment), 'Talkin' World War III Blues', 'It's Alright, Ma (I'm Only Bleeding)', 'Gates Of Eden', and 'Love Minus Zero/No Limit'; plus non-performance fragments of 'London Bridge Is Falling Down', 'Lost Highway' and 'I'm So Lonesome I Could Cry'.

11. From the 1966 British tour: Columbia almost certainly taped the whole tour; the film of the tour, *Eat the Document*, includes fragments of many songs taken at various concerts.

12. From the 1967 Acetate: a second, and possibly third, version of 'Please, Mrs. Henry' was also put on tape at this time. Ditto with 'Tears Of Rage' and 'Open The Door, Homer'.

13. From the Columbia studios, Nashville, early 1969: duets between Dylan and Johnny Cash on 'I Walk The Line', 'Wanted Man', 'Big River', 'Understand Your Man', 'Careless Love' and possibly others.

14. From the *New Morning* sessions: at least thirteen unreleased cuts, including a reputedly staggering version of 'Jamaica Farewell'.

15. From other recent studio sessions: Dylan did a session with George Harrison in 1970 and another, in Hollywood sometime later, with Ringo Starr. Tracks not known.

16. From the Allen Ginsberg session: Ginsberg and Dylan cut enough material for an album, in New York in 1971/2, consisting

of William Blake songs set to music and/or set against musical backgrounds, with Ginsberg's voice and Dylan's guitar.

17. From The Band's New York concert, New Year's Eve, 1971/2: Dylan joined The Band on stage for their encore, and together they did 'Like A Rolling Stone', 'Please, Mrs. Henry' and another. They were recorded for a possible live LP.

18. Just a couple of months ago, Dylan did some informal recording with The Grateful Dead and they are reportedly considering doing an album together. Which makes for a tantalising note on which to end.

NOTE:

Perhaps two things do need retrospective explaining. First, the raved-about 1966 Dublin 'Mr. Tambourine Man' harmonica solos are unique *only because* of the early bootleg tape's terrible quality, which makes them sound like some magnificent organ played in a vast, surreal cathedral, transforming Dylan's playing thrillingly and completely from the very differently marvellous, beautifully filigreed, delicate harmonica-work we've long been able to hear on officially issued, clear recordings.

Second, the bootleg album *Great White Wonder Vol.2* (Mk 3) is not Bob Dylan. The track 'I'm Ready' was soon found to be by John Hammond Jr., and for all I know (or care) the rest of the tracks on this bootleg were also by him. They were not by Bob Dylan.

Robert Milkwood Thomas
(1973)

Dylan as session musician, published in Rock, NYC, April *1973 and in* Sounds, UK music paper, 3rd June 1973.

Session musicians become so from one of two main motives (if not some secret balance of both). Either they want to make a steady reputation and a steady living from the music they love to play, or they are on an apprenticeship, biding time and influencing people, until they get to be stars.

Witness Leon Russell, who's been on a ten-year spree from one extreme to not-quite-the-other – from the peak of anonymity as pianist on those old Phil Spector 45s (where even the artists up front were anonymous to the point of frequent interchangeability) to his more recent position as show-stealer for Mad Dogs & Englishmen and a star at the Concert For Bangla Desh.

So what it really amounts to is that the session-man story à la Leon is an updated boy-makes-good parable. But Dylan? Why is Bob Dylan electing at this time to take up the session-musician role? He doesn't (to go back to the first motive) need to make a reputation, after all: his immortality as an artist is already secured, and whether it's a halo or a millstone to him, it's unquestionably hanging there in the vicinity of his head and shoulders. And he needs a steady income like Grand Funk Railroad needs louder amps.[1]

---

[1] Of course, the Robert Milkwood Thomas side of Bob Dylan was not new, and his return to session work at that point was just one of the ways he had been breaking his dictum 'don't look back' around the start of the 1970s. Robert Milkwood Thomas was meeting Blind Boy Grunt, Little Joe and others.

From as early as February 1961 – the month after he arrived in NYC – Dylan started to be allowed to play harmonica at gigs by Village regulars like Fred Neil, Mark Spoelstra, Dave Van Ronk and Ramblin' Jack Elliott. His next step as a session musician was his first studio work: as the harmonica player, in 1961, on Carolyn Hester's eponymous album. Between then and the end of the sixties he also played back-up to one degree or another for Harry Belafonte (harmonica), bluesman Big Joe Williams (harmonica and back-up vocals), friend and folkie Happy Traum (Dylan playing second guitar under the name

As for the quest for stardom (second motive): the idea only makes any contact with Dylan's motivations if you stand it on its head. That is to say, Dylan may well be engaged in the impossible quest *from* stardom: a necessary road for an artist who wants to play music instead of God.

Perhaps for him, session work is a step towards sanity. It offers an opportunity to play a background role – and to avoid producing a new album after this burdensome gap of almost 2½ years. It may be simply a lot *easier* than doing a new album at this time (a time redolent with emptiness – with, despite the usual enormous output of albums, little of any consequence blowing in the wind). And in the third place, perhaps most importantly, Dylan can get from session work the pleasure of a kind of ordinary, earthly musical interaction with other creative people.

Those motivations explain not only the phenomenon of Dylan as Session Man; they also explain the kind of session work that has surfaced recently on the Doug Sahm and Steve Goodman albums.

Undistinguished. Especially by Godly standards, it is undistinguished.

As Robert Milkwood Thomas on the title track of Goodman's *Somebody Else's Troubles* album,[2] Dylan is almost inaudible. His piano work is far from being an irreplaceable part of the whole, and you'd need some kind of audio-microscope to detect any Magic Dylan element in the back-up vocals he contributes.

Dylan on the Doug Sahm album *Doug Sahm and Band* (appearing, oddly, under his own name, and with no statement

Blind Boy Grunt on his own song 'Let Me Die In My Footsteps' on a Broadside LP), then harmonica and vocal back-up, again as Blind Boy Grunt, on six tracks cut in London for the eponymous *Dick Fariña & Eric Von Schmidt* LP (1963), as Tedham Porterhouse on harmonica for one Jack Elliott 1963 album track, and on piano and harmonica for Geoff Muldaur for the embryo band that made the Elektra *Blues Project* album in 1965.

For more detailed information on these and Dylan's post-1973 session playing, see either the relevant years at www.bjorner.com/still.htm or the notes for the 1998 bootleg *Alias – The Complete Sideman Story* Box Set (the album set is very rare but the notes are online, starting at www.bobsboots.com/CDs/cd-a47.html), though oddly this omits the Happy Traum from its 1960s list.

[2] Dylan plays as Robert Milkwood Thomas on both the album's title track and on 'Election Year Rag', the latter issued on a single: *Somebody Else's Troubles*, recorded NYC, September 1972, released on Buddah BDS-5121, US, 1972; 'Election Year Rag' released on Buddah BDA-326, 1972. (It's said that Dylan was not just 'fitting in' by this point, at least not for Steve Goodman, who reportedly grew impatient with Dylan's turning up hours late.)

of thanks from Atlantic to Columbia, even though there is just such a statement to cover Dave Bromberg's appearance) illustrates the point even better.[3] You can recognise Dylan's contributions here, he does add noticeably to the tracks he worked on – yet, very properly, the final mix merges him in: turns him down rather than up. Particularly on the fine cut 'Blues Stay Away From Me', Dylan's voice is more compelling, more focused and more abrasive than Sahm's – but since the album is no Dylan showcase, it makes sense that he is *behind* Sahm, making the overall effect one of special strength in the vocals. Dylan is behind Sahm in both senses of being back-up.

Similarly, despite the unavoidable fact that thousands of people will have bought the Sahm album because there is a new Dylan song on it, if that song – 'Wallflower' – had been a major work, or a significant marker of a new Dylan direction, then the Sahm album would not have been the place to give it its debut. It finds its appropriateness on the album precisely by virtue of its unremarkableness. Dylan The Artist, in other words, *is* the wallflower.

Undistinguished. And the less vulturous to express it would be to say that Dylan just fits in. No dazzlement: minor enhancing; fitting in. Session work.

[3] *Doug Sahm and Band*, recorded NYC, October 1972, released Atlantic SD-7254, US, 1973, CD re-release Collector's Choice, US, 2006. On '(Is Anybody Going To) San Antone' Dylan sings harmony vocals & plays guitar; on 'It's Gonna Be Easy' and 'Faded Love' he plays organ and on 'Poison Love' guitar; on 'Wallflower' he sings lead vocals & plays guitar, on 'Blues Stay Away From Me' he shares vocals & plays guitar, and on 'Me And Paul' he plays guitar & harmonica. Outtakes included 'On The Banks Of The Old Pontchartrain', 'Hey Good Lookin', 'Please Mr. Sandman' and 'I'll Be There' (all Dylan on guitar), 'Columbus Stockade' and 'The Blues Walked On In' (piano & organ) and 'Tennessee Blues' (harmonica); these were included on Doug Sahm's *The Genuine Texas Groover*, Rhino Handmade RHM2 7845, US, 2003.

That Come-Back Tour
(1974)

Published in The Guardian *on 3rd January 1974: the first time I'd managed to get anything about Dylan into a mainstream broadsheet newspaper rather than just in the music press. Mainstream papers were only then beginning to write about what had been 'pop music' as if it might be an art form, and as if their civilised readers might have heard of one or two of these people. So it's necessarily a rather basic Bob career summary. As we know, it was the last time he toured with The Band, and it duly yielded the double album* Before The Flood: *a release no Dylan aficionado has ever said they much admire. But as we also know, the following year brought us the more exciting first Rolling Thunder Revue.*

Dylan has been recording and writing distinctive songs since before The Beatles emerged from the city cellars of Liverpool, and it is arguable that he has altered the course of popular music more fundamentally than ever they did. Yet he remains a shadowy figure, and for two main reasons: he has, since the mid-sixties, guarded his privacy zealously; and he has changed and changed again his musical territory and his public persona.

The fragile, choirboy-minstrel of 1961, who had to be persuaded to turn his attention from the Woody Guthrie dustbowl America towards the burgeoning problems of the 1960s, and who then dashed off anthems like 'Blowin' In The Wind', 'The Times They Are A-Changin'' and the apocalyptic 'A Hard Rain's A-Gonna Fall': this fugitive from cold and empty Minnesota became the acme of New York City hip, and a performer who could switch one convincing voice for another at will. He could write love songs that accorded women dignity, and, concurrently, vividly surreal, stoned city songs redolent of America's turmoil.

He attracted the turmoil to himself: 'I accept chaos; I am not sure if it accepts me', he once wrote and by 1966 it was becoming unmanageable. That year, Dylan toured America, Australia, Scandinavia, France and Britain, backed – for the first time – by a loud, dynamic rock group. Everywhere, Dylan's 'folk' audiences booed, catcalled and walked out on him. He stood in one auditorium after another, hurling his new music at his listeners in an exhausting reversal of the showbiz maxim 'Always give the public what it wants'.

The tour was insanely long, and that July, with a further 60-odd concerts to go, Dylan reportedly broke his neck in a motorcycle crash in upstate New York.

That is when the guarding of his privacy began in earnest. While most popular recording artists issue two or more albums a year, Dylan issued nothing between the spring of 1966 and January 1968; neither did he make a single public appearance in that period.

When he did return to performing, it was to make a brief contribution to a Woody Guthrie Memorial Concert, clearly given for Guthrie rather than the audience. Bob Dylan's changes of image continued, in spite of the lack of public appearances, and they continued to fly in the face of all the trends, via a series of infrequent new albums.

1968 was a year of unprecedented excess in rock culture: the love generation was indulging its new-found flower-powerlessness and soppiness beyond its own wildest dreams; and at the same time The Beatles' *Sgt Pepper* album had triggered off a barrage of electronic gimmickry and pseudo-symphonic music. In sober contrast, Dylan's first album after the motorcycle accident two summers previously was a stark recall to the simplicity of a folk-music sound combined with a poetic economy entirely new to, and more mature than, rock conventions. That album, *John Wesley Harding*, remains his masterpiece. The city superhip had become the stern ascetic.

Later, dodging his still-carnivorous audience again, he produced, in *Nashville Skyline*, a stunning and mellow celebration of country music: the music habitually despised by almost all but the redneck Midwestern working classes who were for Richard

Milhous Nixon and against the generation that the earlier Bob Dylan had so deeply affected.

With the release, in 1970, of the double album *Self Portrait*, which had Dylan plus strings and girl-choruses and songs like 'Blue Moon', the unpredictable became, for many, the finally unacceptable. 'What is this shit?' screamed the opening sentence of *Rolling Stone* magazine's review of the record. Dylan's stock plummeted. He was no longer anti-hip, he was unhip. Finished.

It looked as though, instead of bringing the customary widening of his own scope and of his audience's tastes, that album was simply a big mistake. Yet Dylan's conduct since then has suggested a very deliberate pulling down of his own stardom: more calculated than any of his earlier dodges or risks. For since 1970, Dylan has done little. Except for a largely instrumental soundtrack for Peckinpah's *Pat Garrett and Billy the Kid*, in which Dylan took a bit-part, he has not put out a single album (although the record company he has finally quit has just scraped one together from old material).

He has appeared on stage just three times: unannounced at the Concert For Bangla Desh in August 1971, unannounced during the encore of a concert by The Band on New Year's Eve the same year, and once, anonymously, playing harmonica behind newcomer John Prine in a New York coffee house.

The tour which begins this evening in Chicago is therefore a dramatic reversal of Dylan's habits since the mid-sixties. It is also remarkable for its scale as a comeback: a scale which has set the music business gasping. When it was first announced, some weeks back, that a total of 600,000 seats would be involved, most observers felt that Dylan's charisma had taken too great a battering since the 1960s to pull in that kind of crowd. The organisers felt otherwise, arranging that (except in Montreal) only postal applications, franked after midnight on 1st December, would be accepted, and that no applicant could purchase more than four tickets (at prices ranging from $6.50 up to a high $9.50).

In San Francisco, these instructions resulted in a major traffic jam in the early hours of Sunday morning, 2nd December, as people tried to mail their applications immediately after the midnight deadline. By the Tuesday, the tour promoter had received nearly two million letters, mostly requesting the maximum of four tickets at the highest price; after that, all post offices were requested not to deliver further mail, and the huge residue was stamped 'Return To Sender'.

It was a record-breaking rush, easily exceeding even the clamour for tickets to the much-ballyhooed Rolling Stones' 1973 American tour. Something like six million people, in spite of all Dylan's image demolition and his three years of virtual silence, wanted to catch hold once more of this most mercurial American artist. And that is perhaps the single most surprising development yet in what has been a career of continual development.

Blood On The Tracks
(1975)

From the April 1975 issue of the UK monthly Let It Rock. *I took the necessary body parts to bring them back to life in* The Art of Bob Dylan, *again in* Song & Dance Man III *and yet again in* The Bob Dylan Encyclopedia, *but all those books are out of print — and this, the original review, was a rare example of my hearing immediately an album's significance, which I rarely do and in this case few critics did until later.*

I don't know how, but some adjustment in our consciousness must now follow from the fact that it is Bob Dylan who has produced, in *Blood On The Tracks*, the most strikingly intelligent album of the seventies.

That seems to me to change everything. It transforms our perception of Dylan — no longer the major artist of the sixties whose decline from the end of that decade froze seminal work like *Blonde On Blonde* into a historic religious object which one chose either to put away in the attic or to revere perhaps at the expense of today's music. Instead, Dylan has legitimised his claim to a creative prowess as vital now as then — a power not, after all, bounded by the one decade he so much affected, but capable of being directed at us effectively for perhaps the next thirty years.

Changed too must be our blueprint of how rock music moves forward. This has been that artists come and go in relatively short time-spans, with new people emerging to make the major changes. Careers are presumed to peak early and then slide into inevitable decline.

Blood On The Tracks demolishes that pattern. It addresses the seventies and our darkness within, with a whole arsenal of weapons — albeit weapons from Dylan's past. It has as much sheer freshness as his or anyone else's first album; as much genuine urge to communicate; as much zest. Yet it combines them all with a sharp wit and intelligence, and an impeccable judgment, so that the sum of these parts is a greater whole than either the Dylan of the sixties, or any artist since, ever brought to rock.

The album deals, among much else, with the overlaying of the past upon the present, the inexorable disintegration of relationships, and the dignity of keeping on trying to reintegrate them against all odds.

Gone, utterly, is Dylan's recent myopic, wilful insistence on eternal love, on its wholesome cocoon; in its place is a profoundly felt understanding of our fragile impermanence of control.

'Tangled Up In Blue' deals with the way in which many forces – past upon present, public upon privacy, distance upon friendship, disintegration upon love – are further tangled and reprocessed by time. It's a scintillating account of a career and a love affair, and how they intertwine. It becomes a viable summary of the last fifteen years through one man's eyes, and in its realism and mental alertness it offers those of us who believe that (in Dave Laing's phrase) one sugar-shortage does not an apocalypse make, a vigorous alternative to all the poses of wasted decay that most 'intelligent' rock has been marketing in the seventies. (In 'Shelter From The Storm' Dylan takes a direct swipe at these apocalypse-freaks, in this barbed and mocking aside: 'Do I understand your question, man, is it helpless and forlorn?')

'Idiot Wind' covers similar territory. It is less consistently successful than 'Tangled Up In Blue' but far more ambitious, and where it does work fully, it yields truly visionary poetry – the strongest imagery and the greatest sense of life experienced on a razor's edge that Dylan has ever achieved.

Seen first as a sort of 'Positively 4th Street Revisited', it isn't very successful. The too-personal bone-scraping of 'Someone's got it in for me / They're planting stories in the press ... / I haven't known peace and quiet for so long / I can't remember what it's like ... / You'll find out when you reach the top / You're on the bottom' – all of it jars. It also produces, in Dylan, a need to step back from that personal quality somehow: and he does it the wrong way, by stylising the anger so that some of his delivery has the same faked passion that spoils *Before The Flood*.

Yet this is a small element in the song. It deepens into one of infinitely greater emotional range than 'Positively 4th Street'. The idiot wind that blows is the whole conglomerate of things which assail our integrity, and the song locks us in a fight to the death, in a contemporary graveyard landscape of skulls and dust and changing seasons. Destruction and survival again.

The preoccupation with this just-possible survival one must fight for is evoked at its most urgently eloquent in this unsurpassable half-stanza: 'There's a lone soldier on the cross, smoke pourin' out of a box-car door / You didn't know it, you didn't think it could be done, in the final end he won the war / After losin' every battle.'

That is matched, later in the song, by the extraordinary tugging wildness of this – a triumph of poetic strength: 'The priest wore black on the seventh day, and sat stone-faced while the building burned / I waited for you on the runnin' boards near the cypress tree while the springtime turned / Slowly into autumn: / Idiot wind, blowin' like a circle around my skull / From the Grand Coulee Dam to the Capitol...' (And what a rhyme!)

The 'you' is an ever-changing element in the song. It certainly isn't a simple object/victim at which Dylan is directing his venom. In an almost explicit demonstration of this, near the end of the song, he deals with his love affair one more time, and starts with a truly universal cameo of how it feels to live with someone when the wall has gone up between them. 'I can't feel you anymore, I can't even touch the books you've read / Every time I crawl past your door I been wishin' I was somebody else instead.'

That isn't venom or dismissal or blame. From there, Dylan deepens it further with another devastating burst of poetry: 'Down the highway, down the tracks, down the road to ecstasy / I followed you beneath the stars, hounded by your memory / An' all your ragin' glory... / I kissed goodbye the howling beast on the borderline which separated you from me.'

Astonishing stuff.

With *Blood On The Tracks*, without question, Dylan has

decimated utterly the idiot winds of 'Dylan's a fat millionaire pig' and 'Dylan's gone soft in the head'. This album is the work of a man who has never been of sharper intelligence nor more genuinely preoccupied with the inner struggles and complexities of human nature. His sensibility is 100% intact.

This album is also – to cite in passing the balladry of 'Lily, Rosemary And The Jack Of Hearts', the re-write of 'Girl From The North Country' that is 'If You See Her, Say Hello' and the flawless blues of 'Meet Me In The Morning' and 'Buckets Of Rain' – the work of a man who has lost not one iota of his devotion to, nor his expertise with, a wide range of American musics.

Dylan In London & Paris
(1978)

*The first part below previewed this distinctive year's London
concerts for a very general readership, given that Dylan hadn't
toured Europe for twelve years. It seems to have been the piece
of mine Dylan himself said he had liked when, via the London
press office, he invited me backstage 'to say hello' after one
concert. (It was his way of avoiding outright acknowledgment of*
Song & Dance Man.) *The second part below reviewed those
London concerts; the final part recounted arriving belatedly for
the last concert in Paris. All three were published in* Melody
Maker, *on 17th & 24th June and 15th July.*

*Those who dismiss the 1978 Europe tour as 'Las Vegas'
surely weren't there. The pallid* Budokan *album misrepresents
how it was. Even my panting overload of superlatives below
hardly conveys the thrill of sitting way up high in London's
Earls Court (in seats no fan would have dreamt of accepting
as good enough for any later tour) and witnessing the blazing
majesty of these concerts.*

1. Why did I spend eleven hours queueing for four tickets to see this man?

Some people enjoyed all that queuing and crushing and camping
out and deprivation at the Isle of Wight nine years ago. Some
people really like loving everyone to order and pretending to be
hippies pretending to be boy scouts. Not me.

So why was I doing it all over again, nine years older and
ought-to-have-more-sense, queuing for tickets at eight o'clock
on a London Soho Sunday morning in 1978? Why was I standing
there humming the inevitably appropriate Bob Dylan lines: 'Oh
no no, I've been through this movie before', and 'Me I sit so
patiently / Waiting to find out what price / Ya have to pay to get
out of / Going through all these things twice'.

It certainly wasn't nostalgia. I've heard people say since that the Earls Court ticket queue brought back fond memories of that ole sixties communal spirit, and that it was great with all these people playing Dylan songs on battered acoustic guitars. But no thank you. I never did much like other people doing Dylan songs anyway. Not Peter, Paul and Mary, not Joe Bloggs and not the Tom Robinson Band either.

For me, and plenty of others who'd felt just as bullied by 'Peace, Man' in the sixties as by 'Street Violence, Man' in '77, and for the thousands of people in those Earls Court queues who weren't old enough to have been at the Isle of Wight in 1969, what was it about this Bob Dylan that made us stand there so long? Especially since the London of the late seventies was the centre of *very* different music, energy and mores from those Bob Dylan's name called to mind.

I can't answer for the hundreds upon hundreds of queuers who were obviously under 21, for whom the only rock-oriented Dylan album since they'd reached puberty had been *Desire* in 1976. I can only answer for me – and that's difficult enough.

It has to do with Dylan's rarity as someone whose creativity signally affects your life. He came along with an individual voice when everyone else was just trying to go along with the times. He was different not because it was smart to be different, or because the papers need a new thing every week, but because he consulted his own intelligence and had the genuine artist's faith that he could reach people better if he wrote and sang and performed from the first base of his own heart and mind.

He was right. He inspired people because he spoke for himself first and let his songs stand or fall by whether they sparked off that flash of recognition in others rather than crafting professional numbers like other people, who so often aimed only at some imagined lowest common denominator of public demand.

This fundamentally more direct approach had a unique consequence for the pattern of his record releases. Other artists, in 'folk' and what was then 'pop', hung onto what success they achieved in one of two ways: they either made a career out of follow-ups, each single and album more or less the same as the last, or they hopped from bandwagon to bandwagon as fashion dictated. Sinatra made a Twist record; The Hollies (Graham Nash included) made a protest single about over-population and The Bomb.

Bob Dylan, in sublime contrast, risked the loss of his success and audience by changing his music-and-words direction, time and again, independently of trends and fashions. And what often happened, though this was hardly his responsibility, was that fashion came stumbling along behind him.

Dylan stopped singing 'protest songs' after 1963, after feeling he'd been naively reformist in songs like 'The Times They Are A-Changin'' — yet in 1965 the mainstream was churning out 'protest singles' as if the world really was about to end. Barry McGuire made 'Eve Of Destruction', Sonny of Sonny and Cher made 'Laugh At Me' (about being thrown out of a restaurant, a martyr to long hair) and everybody danced to Manfred Mann's record of 'With God On Our Side' on *Ready Steady Go*.[4]

By this time Dylan was creating what was soon labelled Folk-Rock, but which was a revolutionary, devastating fusion of the new electric music and an increasingly menacing, surreal, compelling lyric vision. The 1965 Dylan album *Highway 61 Revisited* was the single most vivid explosion of the music's old limitations since Presley's 'Heartbreak Hotel' a decade and a generation earlier.

The following year gave us *Blonde On Blonde*, which had arguably as great a set of repercussions, and opened the door to acid rock, psychedelic rock and a massive influx of new bands — and showed The Beatles that the facile social comment of 'Tax Man' hadn't really been much of an improvement on 'I Want To Hold Your Hand', so that in 1967 came *Sgt. Pepper* and, much to the delight of the rag trade, the trappings of Eastern mysticism.

Dylan's greatness was in opening the doors; if what got wheeled through them was, on the whole, pretty tacky, that wasn't his doing:

[4] A UK pop music television show broadcast every Friday evening from early August 1963 until 23rd December 1966. It was hosted by radio DJ Keith Fordyce and the far younger Cathy McGowan, chosen for her image as quintessential Mary Quant sixties dollybird (to use an expression from the time). Its appealing slogan was 'The weekend starts here'.

Rolling Stone (1969 interview): Do you think that you've played any role in the change of popular music in the last few years?
Bob Dylan: I hope not.

A year and a half after *Blonde On Blonde*, Dylan issued the *John Wesley Harding* album, which was a sharp rejection of the love generation, the drugs revolution and the over-produced, overblown best-selling albums of the time. (Remember *Their Satanic Majesties Request?*)

Dylan's album was severe, ascetic, a masterpiece of pared-down writing and visionary intensity. As Jon Landau – now Bruce Springsteen's producer – wrote at the time:

> For an album of this kind somebody must have had a lot of confidence in what he was doing ... Dylan seems to feel no need to respond to the predominant trends in pop music at all. And he is the only major pop artist about whom this can be said. The Dylan of *John Wesley Harding* is a truly independent artist who doesn't feel responsible to anyone else...

The same unique stance had given Dylan the conviction and the energy and the nerve it must have taken back in '66 when part of every concert audience in America and Europe booed and slow-handclapped his electric music.

The same stance again – the true artist's mining of his own self first and foremost – allowed him to explore country music toward the end of the 1960s when it was the least cool, most despised kind of popular music possible; allowed him not to panic in the long, comparatively unproductive years from 1970 to 1974; and produced in *Blood On The Tracks* what is probably the most intelligent, emotionally real, resourceful album ever recorded – full-stop.

Bob Dylan was nearer 35 than 30 when he made that album: an insuperable achievement coming after an unrivalled thirteen years of recording and writing repeatedly innovative, creative music.

There is more: there is the sheer charisma of the man, his genius for chameleon-like image-building, his most immaculate tightrope-walk from legend-construction to legend-dodging back again and back again – it's all more than enough reason why I, and thousands like and unlike me, should have been standing in that queue in May 1978.

And if Bob Dylan wasn't Bob Dylan, he'd have been standing there, too.

2. We demanded the impossible...

It is nearly a year since the other God of rock died, leaving only Bob Dylan as potentially the once and future king. Out of the whole pantheon, only these two have ever drawn to themselves a whole generation of people permanently wishing and hoping that the idol's original greatness could be restored to him. In Elvis's case, it never happened. His 1968 TV special brought us a glimpse of him tantalisingly close to it for one brief moment; he seemed to hover on the brink, and then he was gone: to Las Vegas.

But in Bob Dylan's case, his return to the British stage has shown us a return also to all the raging glory of this greatest of artists on dazzlingly peak form. People certainly came back to Dylan, and he stood there and soared like a phoenix, and took your breath away.[5]

He did it. There was no possible comparison with other concerts this year – or pretty well any year. There was no comparison either with the man who came to the Isle of Wight those nine long years ago. Expectancy buzzed; the lights went down; the crowd roared; the music started – and the first triumph was right then: right then when the stage lit up these eight musicians and three back-up vocalists and no Bob Dylan at all. What startled your ears to hear was that the sound was well-nigh perfect.

[5] There had been dates in Japan in February-March, in New Zealand and Australia in March, and then 'warm-up' dates in Los Angeles on the first seven days of June; the European part of the tour began in London on 15th June; this was the first of six concerts on consecutive nights. On 23rd June there was one open-air concert in Rotterdam, followed by two in Dortmund, West Germany, one in West Berlin and one at Nuremberg's Zeppelinfeld (ie. all before the reunification of Germany). Then came the five Paris concerts, on July 3, 4, 5, 6 and 8, followed by two in Gothenburg, Sweden, and, finally, the vast open-air concert at the former Blackbushe Aerodrome, which included among its support acts Graham Parker, Eric Clapton and Joan Armatrading. Starting two months later, the autumn North American leg of the tour comprised no less than 65 dates, ending in Florida on 16th December.

Earls Court was conquered before Dylan even got up there.

The mess of noise, the pessimism, the expectation that you'd be hard put to even distinguish which song was which, nightmare tales of the Stones being destroyed in this hall – all of it was vanquished in the first 16 bars of the instrumental 'Hard Rain'. The song was a fast, adroit checklist, and everything could be ticked off: you could hear the sax, you could hear the mandolin, the keyboards, both sets of drums, the guitar, the bass. Phenomenal clarity way up in the balcony.

And then Bob Dylan was on the stage. A fast gesture of greeting in his darting, cinematic way, and then guitar strapped on and into the opener, the unfamiliar 'Love Her With Feeling', with him looking almost uncannily close to the apocalyptic genie of the 1966 shows: slim, wiry, fuzzy-haired, rocking on his heels, energy-loaded, delivering in a voice like a barbed-wire fence that ripped you both back through the years and forward toward a new explosion that was surely going to come.

This was no re-creation: it was new. This was the phenomenon of a 37-year-old bringing a whole new music back home, more lithe than you'll ever be, pouring more than two hours of remorseless energy and surprises out into a crowd of at least two complete generations. This was our greatest artist, fully at the helm of a phantasmagoric new ship and at the height of his power, stunningly better than his old sixties audience could have dared expect ever to see him again, and showing his solid young seventies audience just exactly what that unique charisma and authority and electrified magnetism could do.

He wasn't messing about this time. The voices he used were concentrated, purposeful, searing and intense. He didn't just yell like he did on the 1974 American tour: he used silence and tension, timing and real feeling. This wasn't *Before The Flood*; this *was* the flood.

All superlatives fade to faint praise in the face of these first four performances. Just to see the man move the way he moved was enough to make your heart dance. He'd lost not one neutron of that utterly alert body-presence, that sexual elegance, that raiding grace we thought we'd seen the last of in the sixties.

That Chaplinesque quality was evident right at the start of his career; it was prominent again, particularly in the opening sequence of *Dont Look Back*; almost so as emphatically in the knife-throwing moment of *Pat Garrett and Billy the Kid*. But there, up on that Earls Court stage, the same unique iridescence of movement came flashing back time after time in the darting of the arm as he said 'Thank you!'; in the swaying stance, hand on hip and one foot tapping, as he stood guitarless at the mike for 'Love Minus Zero/No Limit'; in the puppet-doll dips and nods and head-shakes; most knowingly and rejoicingly in the panache of his hands in 'I Shall Be Released'; and in the supreme triumph of theatre in 'Ballad Of A Thin Man', where he acted out the surreal circus-master-of-ceremonies world of the song with a devastating persona that brought the full original power and intent of the song together with an extrovert self-confidence of which he would not have been capable before.

This question of how he moves is not mere detail in Dylan's case: it is at once a symptom of the total alertness he brings to the stage and a significant extra dimension in his arsenal of communication.[6]

And precious few could have anticipated that this would have been so much intact and so much utilised in a 1978 performance. It must have been an eye-opening initiation for the people there who were under 25. And there were plenty of those in audiences that took in everyone from punks to the Minister of Education. Earls Court tube station at midnight on Saturday was full of breathless amazed teenagers – so don't believe it when you read jibes about the crowds being only old hippies. Since these gentlemen of the press could find, to their chagrin, nothing to fault in the concerts themselves, they had to snipe at Dylan's audience instead.

That's their problem. It certainly isn't Dylan's. He has been an embattled artist throughout his career. Now the circle has turned again. Only six weeks after the headlines were crowing

[6] Fifteen years later, a remark of mine in a *Daily Telegraph* review of a Dylan concert, that the way he moved his left leg was worth more than all the novels of Anthony Burgess, was picked up by the Pseuds Corner column of *Private Eye*. I stand by it.

about *Renaldo & Clara* flopping, Dylan has scythed his way ferociously back through that massive undergrowth of scepticism and hostility, of being labelled a burnt-out sixties myth and an irrelevancy in the late seventies.

With songs that truly have been re-born (some 16 years old, some three, some 10, some 12, some new) he has achieved a total artistic and popular success.

From the spine-tingling power of 'Tangled Up In Blue' and 'I Want You' to the wild cathedral evening of the new 'Like A Rolling Stone' and 'The Times They Are A-Changin''; from the messianic intensity of 'Shelter From The Storm' and 'All Along The Watchtower' to the radiant knock-out of 'Baby Stop Crying' and 'Sooner Or Later (One Of Us Must Know)'; and from the chilling beauty of a dozen others to the rock'n'roll glory of more besides, it was never a suspect highway revisited, never just a nostalgia-ride home.

Against impossible odds and beyond what any sane person would have thought achievable in this world, Bob Dylan rode into our cynical, divided camp and brought two generations of music fans together – at a time when they have been more widely gapped than ever before in the history of rock'n'roll.

He gave fully and openly and committedly and hard (and clearly enjoyed it all) and he pulled off a historic, unmatchable coup.

We demanded the impossible of this man for years and years, and at Earls Court he fulfilled our demands. It is his millstone that this will only intensify our expectations in the future; but it is his triumph, unassailable and without parallel in music's history, that he pulled off so superlative a return from the past. In the 1978 Bob Dylan, as surely as in the 1965-6 Bob Dylan, we have our greatest living artist.

3. Dylan in Paris

The assignment sounded simple: go to the last of Bob Dylan's five Paris concerts and review it. Let's not be parochial, after all. Why stop at Earls Court?

And anyway you should be slipping into something resembling a routine by now, with all six London dates plus the open-air gig at the Feyenoord Stadium Rotterdam, behind you. So just nip over to Europe's most civilised city and catch up on this Rolling Wonder Revue's Paris gig as a preview of what's likely from Dylan at The Picnic. Educated guesswork only takes you so far and it's a dangerous business with someone so adept at the art of surprise as Bob Dylan.

Yes, the set was a little different in Paris: few clues, just maybe, about the Blackbushe prospects there. But what really needs saying is just how very fine Dylan's gig was at the Pavillon de Paris, la Porte de Pantin, on Saturday 8th July.

For me it was the sublime end to a ridiculous day. I'd had to miss watching all but the start of the Borg-Connors Final on TV, and resented it. Wimbledon is as good a surrealist microcosm of capitalism-in-action as the rock business, but takes up much less of one's annual time. There's the chorus of suave gentility that Dan Maskell provides with effortless restraint – that well-bred flow of honeyed interpretation – while down in the pits the lone gladiators battle it out, eyes glinting with greed and desperation, their high-tech rackets thrusting and lunging, as they pull off the humiliations of the lob and the drop-shot, and close in to the nets for the kill. And there it is for two short, tantalising weeks: the clear message that individual skill and lone effort are all you need to get to the top; that people divide into winners and losers; that the ruthlessness of competition brings out the best in us… but that of course it helps to be born rich and white, and that women must expect smaller prizes than men in this world.

And here was a final that was the ultimate summary of it all, to be played out when all the peripheral distractions of the tournament were out of the way (like Ilie Nastase, the last great romantic of the game, doomed to sideline eccentricity in the new age of computerised concentration). Borg, the robot garden gnome, versus Connors, the bubblegum pretender – the one playing with all the immovable coldness of Johnny Rotten contemplating Janet Street-Porter, and the other engaging all the fanaticism of Billy Graham pitched alone against the International Communist Conspiracy.

Tremendous stuff – hard to walk away from, even to catch a

plane to Paris. And then, at Charles de Gaulle airport, in a hurry by this time to make the start of the concert, I caught a bus that didn't go into town at all but went in circles round the terminals and ended up at a train station. Panic setting in. Was it possible for someone who speaks as pitifully little French as me to actually fail to arrive at the Dylan concert altogether?

The station produced a train and the train stopped at inconceivably small wayside halts, where no-one got in or out, but finally strolled into the Gare du Nord.

Horrific queue for taxis. Where was the Pavillon? I had no idea. I needed to hand this problem urgently to a cab driver. Ten minutes walking in the rain. A cab. The driver didn't know where the Pavillon was either. Got out his evening paper and looked through the ads on the entertainments page. Dylan unlisted.

Other cab-drivers consulted, and at last a glimmer. As it turns out, the problem is simple: the venue actually, technically, is called Pavillon de Paris, but everyone knows it so well by an entirely different name that they've all forgotten its proper title.[7] Off, then, at the sort of hideous pace that only Parisian cab-drivers can manage, up into the 19th Arrondissement, arriving at 8.40pm for what I'd been told was an 8.30pm concert; thrusting improbable bunches of notes into the driver's hand; running asthmatically across the cobbles to the CBS caravan; finding – it always comes as a vague surprise – that the tickets waiting in my name are actually there waiting.

Then being shown into the hall to find that the concert had already been going half-an-hour and that Dylan was midway through the magnificent 'Tangled Up In Blue.' In fact, the first half of the concert – right up to the intermission – was unchanged from Earls Court. So I'd missed 'Love Her With Feeling,' 'Baby, Stop Crying', 'Mr. Tambourine Man', 'Shelter From The Storm' and 'Love Minus Zero/No Limit'.

[7] It was known by its previous name, Les Abattoirs, from before it was a concert hall; yes, it had been a slaughterhouse, and for far longer than its brief spell as a concert venue, which was only 1975-80.

And what followed was a quite superlative 'Ballad Of A Thin Man', with Dylan using as an extra prop the legendary pair of dark glasses (as he did, thereafter, throughout the set), then 'Maggie's Farm', that wonderful shuffle-beat 'I Don't Believe You', the best 'Like A Rolling Stone' I've heard on this tour, the nothing-short-of-exquisite 'I Shall Be Released' and a 'Going, Going, Gone' that was much tighter even than it had been at Earls Court.

The intermission allowed time to look at the venue. It looked as if it had been built in about 1910, entirely of ironwork, and that its original purpose had been as some kind of large flower-market. I'd guess it held about 7,000 people – certainly well under half the number in Earls Court, so that the stage was much closer to the average punter and binoculars weren't necessary.

It was a weird shape though, with most of the audience clustered on sloping ramps, as if on the wings of some giant iron butterfly-cake. The only thing missing, of course, for those who saw Dylan in 1966 and have never quite got over it, has been the tension of that historic spectacle – of the artist locked in combat with his audience, of Dylan battering against the walls of his own audiences' prejudices with the combined power of his music and his own inner conviction and courage.

Perhaps Dylan embarked on this tour with almost a similar sense of risk, to forget that possibility with the hindsight of its total success. He couldn't have absolutely known it was going to be that way. Certainly it seems probable that the week he did in Los Angeles before embarking on Europe was intended as a testing-out. After all, the LA gigs were pretty much unnecessary if you judge them by the financial criterion that we've heard *so* much about from people who earn their own money in much easier ways. But in any case, that tension, that incomparable flash of psychic energy that charged the 1966 gigs, was bound to be unrepeatable.

In its place, on the 1978 tour, there has simply been the music itself: the quite magical combination of songs, arrangements and musicianship, and Dylan's utterly undiminished alertness and resourcefulness.

The final ingredient, which was certainly missing in 1966, has been the sheer quality of the sound: and this was even better in Paris than in London. In Earls Court, the sound was great in spite of the hall; in Paris the sound was so excellent that regardless of the look of the place, it seemed as if the acoustics of the venue itself must have been OK to begin with. It was just terrific (I'm sorry if you think these superlatives are stupidly olde worlde, but they last longer than your vogue ones. Remember 'groovy'?) And because the sound was so well-transmitted, the band came across far stronger, both as individuals and as a unit.

After the intermission came the first of the changes in the set. The instrumental intro/excerpt from 'Rainy Day Women #12 & 35' was followed not by 'One Of Us Must Know (Sooner Or Later)' but by one of the finest of the songs from the new *Street Legal* album, 'True Love Tends To Forget', sticking closely to the album's arrangement but with Dylan himself adding devastatingly simple asides after the repeated chorus phrase 'True love': delivered with that as-if-casual timing of which he is so much the master, and showing with throwaway ease how thorough is his own steeping in the traditions which songs like this one at once utilise and re-work.

The biggest surprise was yet to come: would you believe Dylan unstrapping the electric guitar, putting on harmonica-holder and acoustic guitar and performing a totally solo 'Gates Of Eden'? Then, instead of 'You're A Big Girl Now' came, with largely fresh lyrics, a poised and fine version of 'The Man In Me' (which he'd apparently done in LA and which is the only number so far on the whole tour to be taken from the *New Morning* album).

That was followed by a return to the Earls Court pattern: 'One More Cup of Coffee' then 'Blowin' In The Wind' – with that incredible Duane Eddy guitar-work: an example of how Dylan's greatness partly consists in his ability to laugh out of sheer admiration of his panache; 'I Want You'; 'Señor (Tales Of Yankee Power)'; that triumphant version of 'Masters Of War', of which it isn't reductive to suggest that it would make a disco single to wipe the likes of the Bee Gees off the planet; and 'Just Like A Woman' treated vocally rather differently from the Earls Court performances.

It was after 'Just Like A Woman' (a highspot in the use of the back-up vocals) that Dylan varied the next number each night at Earls Court. It was the one variable slot in the show. First night: the reggae 'Don't Think Twice, It's All Right'. Second night: a comparatively so-so version of 'Oh Sister'. Third night: a dignified 'Simple Twist Of Fate' with the lyric much closer to the Rolling Thunder Revue version than to the *Blood On The Tracks* original. Fourth night: 'Don't Think Twice' again. Fifth night: a breath-snatching performance of the beautiful 'To Ramona', with quite the most awesome use of vocal harmonies I can ever remember hearing in my life. Sixth and final night at Earls Court: 'Don't Think Twice, It's All Right' once more. (At Rotterdam it was 'Don't Think Twice' also.)

On Saturday night in Paris I was sitting there banging my fists against iron railings, willing it to be 'To Ramona'... and it was. There's just nothing finer. It's it.

After that variant the set went back to that violin-virtuoso showcase of 'All Along The Watchtower', the carnival-churn of 'All I Really Want To Do', the introduction of the band (the singers had stopped being his cousin / first cousin / childhood sweetheart / country girlfriend / fiancée etc), plus the best version I've heard on the tour yet of that darting, flashing 'It's Alright, Ma (I'm Only Bleeding)' and then 'Forever Young'. And then off and the long wait for the encore.

A sartorial and linguistic note: instead of the white pants with the dark electric-lightning side-seam, the Parisian Dylan wore black pants with a silver lightning-flash; and instead of the 'thank you's, to the amused delight of the crowd, laughing at themselves for responding at, and being given, such corn, came 'merci's and even a couple of 'merci beaucoup's and a final 'bon soir!'

The encore provided the final surprise. At Earls Court it had been kept down to the one number each night: 'The Times They Are A-Changin''. In Rotterdam when Dylan and the band returned to the stage, they'd preceded 'Times' with a decidedly odd interpretation of 'I'll Be Your Baby Tonight', which, while a good bonus, was a quick, comparatively easy throwing in of an extra song. In Paris, in quite some contrast, Dylan preceded

'Times' with a far from quick or easy bonus: a tremendous, complex and lengthy version of 'Changing Of The Guards'.

A great concert.

It's fairly safe to assume that Blackbushe will produce a similarly excellent sound quality, allowing for the eccentricities of the great outdoors; and to assume the very high all-round musicianship and unity of the band; and that Dylan, in spite of, I think, disliking open-air gigs on the whole, will be burning up more energy per minute than those journalists can comprehend who have only concerned themselves with specious calculations as to what he'll earn per minute.

But as for whether the set he did in Paris will be close to what Blackbushe holds in store – your guess is at least as good as mine.

'Sixteen Years...'
(1980)

Written for the little book Conclusions on the Wall: New Essays On Bob Dylan, *home-published by editor Elizabeth M. Thomson/Thin Man Ltd., 1980; the other contributors were Robert Shelton, Suzanne Macrae, Wilfrid Mellers, William T. Lhamon, Christopher Ricks, Gabrielle Goodchild, Patrick Humphries, Mike Porco, Louis Cantor, Steve Turner and Paul Cable.*

There's a dark flash and up low in the sky, that London rain comes down. The room glowers and the stereo takes me back down the years, because That Voice is on again. But this isn't 'Diamonds And Rust'. This is my story.

I can't claim any Dylan pedigree back beyond 1964. I was at the bright and burgeoning new University of York, heavily disguised with self-assurance, protected by English Literature and a sarcastic elitism. It was somewhat at odds with my love of rock'n'roll.

I'd been writing my own song lyrics a lot the year before – writing them in my head as I walked home after dates with Diana Nicholas. She was my Echo, and sixteen. She salvaged the end of my schooldays. She must be 32 now, and I haven't seen her since.

Naturally, we listened to Radio Luxembourg, on a big old radiogram in her parents' front room. So I got to York having never been inside a folk club (and, all things considered, I'd like to keep it that way).

The pop music I spent my time with instead was pretty dire by then, of course: all the Johnnys and Bobbys before the stumbling beginnings of such local groups as the Big Three and The Beatles. So, not caring much for them, I clung to my loyalties – to Elvis, Buddy Holly and Little Richard.

This astonished Linda Thomas, a first-year student I could

never get off with. She couldn't believe that I could be listening to clapped-out old pancakes like Presley when there was this Bob Dylan person in the world.

The very notion that something *bigger* than Presley was possible struck me as fundamentally daft, so my resistance was high even before I heard this whining Walter Brennan voice and his lifeless, moralising songs that were too long, too slow and too flat.

But Linda Thomas was sure she was right, and she was very attractive and more intelligent than me… so I didn't hold it against Bob Dylan that the Junior Common Room was full of sociologist bloinks trying to play their own doomed versions of 'Masters Of War' and 'Corrina, Corrina'. (The only version *I'd* known of 'Corrina' was the pop one by Ray Peterson – he of the original 'Tell Laura I Love Her'.)

For Linda I spent a good part of the next twelve months making myself listen to *Another Side Of Bob Dylan*. I disliked that one the least because it had alienated the worst of those student Okies. It had love-songs on it – anathema to them and a halfway step toward the familiar themes of pop music for me.

I finally got it: that Dylan hook in me that's been there ever since. In East Sheen I heard *Bringing It All Back Home*; in a record-shop in York Linda and I listened to *Highway 61 Revisited*; from the stalls of Liverpool Odeon in May 1966, when he brought on the Hawks, I saw a concert that has yet to be topped; and in a stifling apartment off the Broadway end of Harlem, two months later, I experienced *Blonde On Blonde* for the first, unsettling time. Back in London, in a restaurant where *OZ* editorial dinners usurped the contributors' fees, someone played me the Basement Tapes. In York again, in a seminar room, I coped with *John Wesley Harding*.

Those were the years of peak Dylan intensity, so far as his output and its effect on my own life were concerned. On acid with friends in the summer of '68, hearing the bootlegs of things like the fast version of 'It Takes A Lot To Laugh, It Takes A Train To Cry' and 'Number One'. The whole initial acid experience was inseparable from soaking up Dylan and the careening zing of his genius. And the acid come-down was like the Isle of Wight Festival – travelling to Portsmouth in the back of a Triumph

Herald, all the way to that god-awful three days of mud and ritual abjection.

After that, I spent a year and more writing *Song & Dance Man*. We were living in a cottage in Tawstock, North Devon, where I was teaching English at the local grammar school. Sue (Tyrrell) was trying valiantly to adjust to suddenly not being on a campus, to having a new baby to look after, to neighbours who talked only of the weather, and a husband who, before her very eyes, had turned into someone who went out to work every day and then spent each evening locked unsociably in battle with this sprawling, fanatic manuscript.

People were dropping away from The Maestro around that time. Furrowed brows at *Self Portrait*; uncomfortable laughs at 'I just wouldn't have a clue' and 'the birdies' on *New Morning*. 'Bob Dylan's Confident New Music', Richard Williams declared it to be in *The Times*, as if to convince himself. Hmmmm, I thought.

My book came out in 1972. Shortly after that, I was sitting upstairs in the study when the phone rang.

'Michael Gray?' questioned a rich American voice.

I agreed.

'This is Robert Shelton.'

I am not, by nature, excitable, but this produced no small adrenalin rush. The man who'd written that *New York Times* review reprinted on the back of the first album! It was like a Born Againer being telephoned by John the Baptist.

He soon put me to work, making me lash together some sensible overview from a vast assemblage of Antipodean newspaper garbage thrown up by Dylan's 1966 Australian tour, for his own (forthcoming) mighty tome. Unlike the editors of *OZ*, he paid me for my labours, and when he could ill-afford to.

By then, I'd been back to New York, to stumble around radio stations on the modest self-constructed promotional stomp for the US edition of my book. The Hidden Dylan Book, Ralph Gleason called it. And it's true that they managed to sell fewer copies in the whole of America than in either Britain or Japan.

Those radio interviews were weird. One man on a late FM show in Manhattan was too laid back to ask me any questions at all; I doubt if he even switched on my microphone. Not so the elderly speed-freak in Philadelphia who *really* wanted me to let him know for the listeners whether Dylan was a homosexual.

I moved around New York a lot on that visit — staying with friends in Brooklyn, in Queens and in the Village — so I kept leaving different phone numbers with Dylan's office, because they were very nice and *almost* sure that Bob would want to talk to me when he got back to New York from filming in Mexico. Only of course he went up to California and I went home to the Malvern Hills.

For me, and for a lot of people I knew, things somehow went downhill in the period that followed. The relentless awfulness of the times was starting to press in hard on both sides of the Atlantic. The music revolution was as dead as the student revolution, and Richard Nixon was making the world safe for fascism.

I heard my advance copy of *Planet Waves* the night before I heard that my father had died. I felt let down. They'd both copped out, and at a very bad moment. Now, the fact of that intermingled bitterness gets a bit close to the bone and shows something radically amiss. Six years on, I still can't properly disentangle it all. *Planet Waves* is one of my favourite albums these days too.

I finally met Bob Dylan backstage at Earls Court. I took my son and he dared ask Dylan for his autograph. It was the summer of '78 and my son was almost nine by then.

Those gigs were terrific. I saw all of them — plus Paris, Rotterdam and Blackbushe. This year, on 8th May, I caught yet another Bob Dylan concert, one of his religious revival meetings, in Hartford, Connecticut. Afterwards, I stood outside on the sidewalk and watched his bus drive away down the road.

How was it? It was fine. But for me, the real revival came with *Blood On The Tracks;* the surprise and pure honed excellence of that album still stand as the ultimate.

Dylan has done plenty of resourceful and imaginative things since and I wish I could say the same. But right now it feels OK to be left behind this time around. Because I would rather keep on feeling buried in the hail, poisoned in the bushes and blown out on the trail than wake up tomorrow morning feeling Saved.

And I agree with Autumn: '...while the universe is erupting, she points to the slow train & prays for rain & for time to interfere...'

Which it will. One of these tomorrows, Bob Dylan is going to wake up feeling different yet again.

When The Never-Ending Tour Was New (1988)

Published in The Independent, *21st October 1988*

Bob Dylan's star spent much of the eighties fading into space. This week has seen its incandescent reappearance in the New York night sky. Last night at Radio City Music Hall, 'the showplace of the nation', Dylan completed a remarkable four-night run of concerts.

It was a dramatic comeback for an artist who, always keen to keep off television, has this decade been kept off radio and the charts as well by market forces. Few people have liked his recent records – not even him. Few watched the irrelevant and weary *Hearts of Fire*, the Richard Marquand film Dylan made so unenthusiastically in 1986. And at Live Aid, the previous year, he managed the feat of reducing his audience even while performing to over a billion people.

That concert was, writ large, what he has been doing in live performance for the last ten years or so. He has avoided both the compelling intimacy of folk performance and the lure of the avant-garde, in favour of a tacky rockism that half-fills stadiums and excites no one.

But just as a generation of Elvis fans fantasised that one day they might rescue Presley from Colonel Parker and stick him in a studio after reimmersion in his Sun recordings, so the dream of Dylan fans has been for this consummate champion of 'a lone guitar and a point of view' to bid farewell to what he once called the stadiums of the damned, and to return to the simple drama of a white spotlight on the dark stage of the concert hall.

Life is never like the dream, but something close has been witnessed at his New York shows this week. Bob Dylan at Radio City marks both a return to the concert stage and a powerful bid to put himself back in the vicinity of critical attention and contemporary life.

He has mounted this effort with typical eccentricity: choosing an ironic but high-profile venue, fronting his smallest band since he first 'went electric' 23 years ago, and making a sustained, magical acoustic section the centrepiece of his show.

Dylan must be enjoying the incongruity of seeing his own icon-loaded name in lights in the citadel of Judy Garland movies, Christmas Spectaculars and The Rockettes. At the same time he is facing up to the neo-traditionalism of the times, in a move that takes the ex-hippy portion of his audience into an elegant designer environment far away from concrete-bunker decay.

To attempt all this with a repertoire of old songs would be disastrous if, like a Chuck Berry, Dylan were presenting them as a scrapbook of nostalgia. Yet, while he may have no option but to face down his current writer's block by firing off a barrage of his sixties material, he is doing so with a conviction of its power still to transfix, exhilarate and hit home.

Opening with the wit of the thundering riff from Hi-Heel Sneakers as the intro to 'Subterranean Homesick Blues' (never sung live by Dylan till this year), with Christopher Parker on drums, Kenny Aaronson on bass and the marvellous G. E. Smith on guitar, Dylan delivered, with a clear intensity lit by his unique spontaneity of phrasing, a catalogue of songs that again and again addressed the nation on the issues of the moment, a timely three weeks before it goes to the polls.

Dylan has never told people who to vote for, but he chose songs that potently addressed, among other things, Reaganomics ('Bob Dylan's 115th Dream', again never sung live until this year) and the murderous vapidity of super-patriotism. This was done both with an electric resuscitation of his unreleased and rather dreadful 1963 song 'John Brown' and with an impassioned acoustic 'With God On Our Side', made riveting by the addition of a clear-sighted sorrowful verse about the Vietnam War.

In G.E. Smith Dylan has found by far his best guitarist since Robbie Robertson. Thanks to him, the old fumbling around between songs is gone, as are the any-old-endings and the dull automatic bash. Dylan is fully engaged again on stage, with no more lazy dropped verses and no fluffed lines. Via the alertness of the music, it is made clear anew what a mastery of words is here displayed – not least in the sheer volume of material that its author has committed to memory. It is a tour de force.

And it has been some tour. Dylan began with West Coast dates back in June, and in the course of his travels has sung more than 90 different songs: yet it has all been, till now, so underpublicised and has slipped through such weird and previously untrodden venues, that the whole tour has functioned as a mere warm-up for these in-from-the-cold New York shows.

The bad news is that this in itself puts an accident black-spot up ahead on Dylan's road. The speed with which he gets bored works against him when he is still on the road. It is probably just as well that Radio City is his final venue, because signs of impending boredom with his excellent line-up already hover around the edges of his interaction with them. So, even as he achieves this week's rescaling of the heights, Dylan looks restlessly inclined to jump off again.

Still, if G.E. Smith's inspired playing has been a big factor in Dylan's current performing success, that success is due also to an old power Dylan has rediscovered within himself, as his fiery emphasis on pre-electric material shows. The long acoustic part of his set has been its highpoint, and it has seen Dylan re-embrace the strengths of traditional folk songs.

After burning 1988 performances of 'Man Of Constant Sorrow', 'On The Trail Of The Buffalo', 'Pretty Peggy-O' (all unperformed since 1962), 'Barbara Allen' and the thrilling 'Eileen Aroon', Dylan's avid alignment with such material, for the first time in more than two decades, holds out tantalising possibilities as to where he might land next time he jumps.

Grubbing For A Moderate Jewel:
Belle Isle
(1989)

This started from research I did in St. John's, Newfoundland in 1985, prompting a piece in fanzine The Telegraph *No.29, Spring 1988; that grew into the piece below, published under the long title given here, in* Canadian Folklore canadien, *the Journal of the Folklore Studies Association of Canada, Vol. 8, 1-2 (one issue), officially dated 1986 but in fact published 1989.*

I. Introduction

When I arrived in Newfoundland in September 1985 for a three-month working holiday, all I knew of the song I called 'Belle Isle' was that it had always been a favourite track on Bob Dylan's much-derided 1970 double-album *Self Portrait*; I had always been drawn to its mystery and atmosphere – its rainy strings, its surreal Celtic mists – and, as yielded by Dylan's recording, to its tantalising contradictions: that odd combination of extravagance of language with vagueness of storyline; its gauche floweriness yet its whispered erotic tension; its confident melodic flow, yet its obscurity; its obscurity yet Dylan's knowingness with it.

I tried to set down why some of this was so attractive in a book of mine fifteen years ago,[8] but in a crucial respect I was wrong about 'Belle Isle'. Knowing no better than to believe the record-label, I thought it was a Dylan composition.

As given on his recording of it, the song went like this:

> One evening for pleasure I rambled to view
> The fair fields all alone
> Down by the banks of Loch Erin
> Where beauty and pleasure were known

[8] Michael Gray, *Song & Dance Man* (London: Hart-Davis, MacGibbon, 1972); 2nd edition published as *The Art of Bob Dylan* (London: Hamlyn, 1981; New York: St. Martin's Press, 1982).

I spied a fair maid at her labour
Which caused me to stay for a while
And I thought of her, goddess of beauty
The blooming bright star of bright isle

I humbled myself to her beauty
'Fair maiden, where do you belong?
Are you from Heaven descended?
Abidings in Cupid's fair throne?'

'Young man I will tell you a secret,
It's true I'm a maid that is poor
And to part from my vows and my promise
Is more than my heart can endure

Therefore I'll remain at my service
And go through all my hardship and toil
And wait for the lad that has left me
All alone on the banks of Belle Isle.'

'Young maiden I wish not to banter:
'Tis true I come here in disguise
I came here to fulfil my last promise
And hoped to give you a surprise;

I own you're a maid I love dearly
And you've bin in my heart all the while
For me there is no other damsel
Than my blooming bright star of Belle Isle.'

Of course, it sounded like a folksong too – or rather, it sounded like a folksong except for some suspiciously high-flown vocabulary. 'I wish not to banter'; 'are you from Heaven descended?'; 'abiding in Cupid's fair throne': these phrases couldn't readily be imagined tripping off the tongues of rural peasants or industrial workers in the hostelries of old.

My assumption, therefore, was that this was pastiche on Dylan's part – a good-natured playfulness with folksong by the ex-folkie whose tastes, aside from rock'n'roll, had always been for narrative ballads: either those of mystery, which as Dylan himself stressed is 'a traditional fact ... traditional music is too unreal to die', and so yields 'all these songs about roses growing out of people's brains and lovers who are really geese and swans who turn into angels',[9] or else tales of horses and daughters and hangings, exile and injustice.

'Belle Isle' seemed something Dylan had constructed from all these elements, with a humour that gently mocked his own affection for such stuff and yet embraced (as so often when Dylan gently mocks) an intelligent respect for the milieu he was playing with.

II. 'Belle Isle' As Newfoundland Folksong, Part 1

Within a fortnight of arriving in St. John's, I happened upon three references to 'Belle Isle' (a snowstorm of information, considering that I don't think I'd seen or heard mention of this relatively obscure item in Dylan's repertoire for many years beforehand).

First, a new issue of *The Telegraph* came through the mail, containing an article by Rod MacBeath about Bob Dylan's use of folksongs.[10]

Here I read that 'Belle Isle' 'came from Ireland to Canada, where it was adapted to its new environment … The basis was supposedly "Loch Erin's Sweet Riverside" … probably a variant of "Erin's Green Shore", the lyrics to which can be found in John [Way]'s piece ["Flutter Ye Mystic Ballad"] in ER6.'[11]

A week or so later, I received through the post, thanks to the editor of *The Telegraph*, a photocopy of the John Way piece. Though this covered some of the same territory as the MacBeath article, on 'Belle Isle' it was less help than I'd hoped. But it suggested to me the intriguing notion that there might still be a real mystery to be solved about this song: that maybe it wasn't just that *I* didn't know its lineage: perhaps no-one else did either.

[9] Bob Dylan & Nat Hentoff, interview in *Playboy,* March 1966.

[10] Rod MacBeath, 'I Know My Song Well Before I Start Singing', *The Telegraph* #21 (Bolton, Lancashire, UK) Autumn 1985. *The Telegraph* was a well-established critical quarterly devoted to studying the work, and to some extent the life, of Bob Dylan. It published original work by many distinguished critics including Christopher Ricks (UK) and David Pichaske (USA). A book of pieces selected from the first five years' issues of the magazine was published in 1987: Michael Gray & John Bauldie, eds., *All Across The Telegraph* (London: Sidgwick & Jackson, 1987; Futura Paperbacks, 1988).

[11] John Way, 'Flutter Ye Mystic Ballad', *Endless Road* #6, (Hull, Yorkshire, UK) 1984. *Endless Road* was a critical fanzine devoted to Bob Dylan published irregularly in the UK in the early 1980s and no longer extant.

I got my first hint of this possibility from John Way's article, because (comically, from my point of view) he began his discussion of the song by quoting my own attribution of it to Dylan, intending this to confirm his own hunch about its composition. He too, then, had concluded that Dylan had created something which was, as he phrased it, 'almost a distillation of the hundreds of sentimental ballads to come out of Ireland in the 18th and early 19th centuries'.

Way went on to quote some of the lyrics of 'Erin's Green Shore', which was supposedly, via the off-shoot 'Loch Erin's Sweet Riverside', the Irish original for Canada's 'Belle Isle': and the more I read them, the less they seemed to have in common with 'Belle Isle' at all. In the end, the theories offered by Way and MacBeath seemed to cancel each other out.

Then, I met blues guitarist and folklorist Dr. Peter Narváez[12] (a man who had seen Bob Dylan's first Carnegie Hall Hootenanny appearance back in 1961...) and he asked me if I realised that Bob Dylan had not composed 'Belle Isle' at all – that in fact it was a *Newfoundland* folksong. It was not a song he'd ever had cause to study personally, but he had no reason to doubt the accepted (Newfoundland) view of it as belonging to Newfoundland's vibrant folk culture. As for me, I stood gladly corrected, and felt kicked by curiosity, granted the rare opportunity my being there afforded me, into seeing how similar or different Dylan's version of the song was to whatever traditional, ethnic versions its home terrain might offer.

I imagined that a good rummage through books of folksong in Memorial University's libraries would yield up 'Loch Erin's Sweet Riverside', supposedly the missing-link song – the Irish love song behind the Newfoundland ballad – and that the local

[12] Dr. Peter Narváez is Associate Professor, Dept. of Folklore, at Memorial University of Newfoundland. He is also an American émigré from the Vietnam War era, to note which is, for Europeans like myself, to be reminded that Canada has had an honourable special function for generations of American dissenters, including those who were engaged with the civil rights-New Left movement with which the whole folk-revival/'protest' renaissance was enmeshed. That Canada did offer refuge and an alternative political milieu in these times explains why there was so active an exchange of folksong repertoires between the young of these two countries, so that while in mainstream cultural matters Canada has had little impact outside her own borders, Canadian folksongs and folkie singer-songwriters have been extremely successful and influential in the US.

data on 'Belle Isle' itself would clear up any remaining mystery as to its origin. It didn't turn out that way at all.

I looked up 'Belle Isle' in *The Encyclopedia of Music in Canada*, an authoritative work published by the University of Toronto Press in 1981,[13] and found, first of all, that the song's proper title is actually 'The Blooming Bright Star Of Belle Isle'.

The encyclopedia entry then states confidently:

> Newfoundland adaptation of an old Irish love song, 'Loch Erin's Sweet Riverside' … First published in Greenleaf and Mansfield's *Ballads and Sea Songs of Newfoundland* (Cambridge, MA, 1933). 'The Blooming Bright Star Of Belle Isle' is also included in *The Penguin Book of Canadian Folk Songs* (London, 1973) by Edith Fowke…

I got frustrated by these constant references to 'Loch Erin's Sweet Riverside'. It began to seem a suspiciously invisible song. John Way hadn't quoted from it; Rod MacBeath hadn't quoted from it; no-one seemed to know it. Yet why should it be so very elusive, especially if its relevance to 'Belle Isle' was strong and well-established? Perhaps this too was dubious rather than definite terrain.

Eventually, the penny dropped. First, it seemed likely that MacBeath's assertion of the link between 'Loch Erin's Sweet Riverside' and 'Belle Isle' came straight out of Edith Fowke's *Penguin Book of Canadian Folk Songs*. Second, the writer of the encyclopedia entry was also Professor Fowke. It finally occurred to me that the source for this 'Riverside'-'Belle Isle' link-up was *always* Fowke. Everyone trotted around happily repeating this – yet no-one except Professor Fowke had ever actually heard, or read the words to, 'Loch Erin's Sweet Riverside' at all!

This was to prove an object-lesson in the dodginess of second-hand research. I never came across 'Loch Erin's Sweet Riverside' in any of the books of Irish songs I searched: and, as it turned out, no wonder. I phoned Professor Fowke at home in the end, to ask about this invisible Irish song of hers, and with irreproachable

[13] Kallmann, Potvin & Winters, eds., *The Encyclopedia of Music in Canada* (Toronto: University of Toronto Press, 1981).

straightness she backpedalled vigorously on her encyclopedia entry. Subsequently she wrote to me to explain:

> 'Loch Erin's Sweet Riverside' is a song I collected from a traditional singer in the Ottawa Valley. It is obviously Irish, and I had assumed it would be known in Ireland...[14]

Back, then, to 'Belle Isle' itself: and as it happens, I found that it was also misleading of Fowke's encyclopedia entry to say that the Elisabeth Greenleaf and Grace Mansfield book *Ballads and Sea Songs of Newfoundland* gave first publication to 'The Blooming Bright Star Of Belle Isle', and in 1933. (Striking that such a prominent minority of the folklorists of that generation were women – and incidentally Greenleaf & Mansfield were students at this time.) They were pre-empted by that rich and resourceful Newfoundland businessman, Gerald S. Doyle, in the 1920s.

Doyle, who owned the island's pre-eminent drug company and whose folksong publications and radio broadcasts advertised his wares, was nonetheless a genuine enthusiast for Newfoundland folksong. His 'free' songbook printed lyrics and carried adverts for Doyle merchandise into homes in both St. John's and the outport communities. The first edition of this songbook, *Old-Time Songs and Poetry of Newfoundland*, was published in 1927.[15] A second edition followed in 1940, the third in 1955 and the fourth (posthumously) in 1966, the year that mainland commercial record companies finally realised there was a market for the island's indigenous song culture.

The point about the Doyle songbook and its importance to Newfoundland was that in the 20th century, in this British colony, so tight-knit by shared deprivation that it kept a thriving and distinctive folk culture yet one derived mainly from Britain and Ireland... here, the Doyle songbook functioned just like the broadsides hawked around those 'Old Country' islands centuries earlier. And actually, broadsides were themselves sold in Newfoundland right through the 1920s and beyond.

[14] Edith Fowke, letter to the present writer, dated 8th November 1985.
[15] Gerald S. Doyle, ed., *Old-Time Songs and Poetry of Newfoundland*, (St. John's, Newfoundland: Family Fireside for G.S. Doyle, 1927).

III. Bob Dylan And Broadside Balladry

The crucial thing about a broadside, of course, is precisely that it *was* put about *on paper*. All its other pros and cons come from this one basic characteristic.

Shakespeare honed in unerringly on why this makes some people's hackles rise. Country wench Mopsa, in *The Winter's Tale*, remarks: 'I love a ballad in print ... for then we are sure they are true.'

This is just part of an wholly pertinent scene – between The Clown, the aforementioned Mopsa, a second country wench (Dorcas), and the broadside-seller Autolycus, with the bard enjoying himself on the subject of folksong in general:

> **AUT:** Here's another ballad, of a fish that appeared upon the coast on Wednesday the four-score of April, 40,000 fathom above water...
> **DOR:** Is it true too, think you?
> **AUT:** Five justices' hands at it; and witnesses, more than my pack will hold ... Why should I carry lies abroad?[16]

Actually there were objections from folk performers themselves to the setting down in print of any ballads at all. One Mrs. Hogg gave the following dressing-down to Walter Scott after he'd used some of her repertoire in his book *Minstrelsy of the Scottish Border*:

> There was never ane o' ma sangs prentit till ye prentit them yoursel' and ye hae spoilt them a'thegither. They were made for singing and no for reading, but ye hae broken the charm now and they'll never be sung mair.

---

[16] It might strike you that Shakespeare's mockery here is not directed only at the commercial rip-offs he implies that broadside collections tended to be, but also at that element of the fantastical common to many a genuine folk ballad. Yet it is just this characteristic that Dylan refers to in that remark, quoted earlier, about traditional mystery, and songs that are 'too unreal to die'. There might be compelling parallels between this 'unrealism' in the traditional folksong of neo-medieval rural Britain/Ireland and the 'magical realism' in the heavily folk-cultured fiction of modern South American writers like Gabriel García Márquez. It's my belief that the marvellous, unreleased 1981 Bob Dylan song 'Angelina' is an attempt at a sustainedly South American creation: a work which experiments with the evocative poetic effects of that 'magic realism' in its natural context – and that Dylan finds those effects attractive in the same way as he finds attractive 'roses growing out of people's brains' and 'lovers who are really geese'.

And the warst thing o' a', they're nouther right spell'd,
nor right setten down.[17]

This is in interesting contrast, of course, with commentary by
F.J. Child, who was adamant both that the setting down in print
of the old traditional ballads was a good thing, and that equally
the phenomenon of the printed broadside was a bad thing:

'

> Popular poetry cannot lose its value. Being founded on
> what is permanent and universal in the heart of man, and
> now by printing put beyond the danger of perishing, it will
> survive the fluctuations of taste, and may from time to time
> serve ... to recall a literature from false and artificial courses
> to nature and truth [whereas broadside ballad collections
> are] veritable dunghills, in which, only after a great deal
> of sickening grubbing, one finds a very moderate jewel.[18]

A quick think back over some of Bob Dylan's early repertoire
reveals, as you'd expect from a staunch anti-purist, a cheerful use
of the dunghill format, with its 'come gather round' sales pitch.
As early as the third song in his chronologically-ordered collected
work, in fact: 'Hard Times In New York Town' begins with:

> Come you ladies and you gentlemen, a-listen to my song
> Sing it to you right, but you might think it's wrong.
> Just a little glimpse of a story I'll tell
> 'Bout an East Coast city that you all know well.[19]

There is the market-stall sales-pitch intro indeed – and I like
the way that this 1962 Bob Dylan used the implication that he
was just a local performer as a selling point, wrapped inside that
confident claim in the fourth line. Similarly, his 'Rambling
Gambling Willie' opens with this exhortation:

[17] I have taken the Scott and the Shakespeare quotation, plus much else on the subject
of perceived differences between orally-transmitted song and song in print, from Leslie
Shepard's excellent book *The Broadside Ballad* (Hatboro, PA 19040, USA: Legacy Books;
East Ardsley, Wakefield, Yorkshire, UK: EP Publishers [a very profitable small company,
for which I worked, for a pittance, through the winter of 1968-9; the Dickensian tyrant
who owned it also ran a builders and funeral parlour from the same premises], 1962; 1978).
[18] *Ibid*.
[19] Bob Dylan, *Lyrics, 1962-1985* (New York: Knopf, 1985).

> Come around you rovin' gamblers and a story I will tell
> About the greatest gambler, you all should know him well.

A more diffident spiel opens 'Man On The Street' ('I'll sing
you a song, ain't very long/'Bout an old man who never done
wrong': not a commercially compelling opener)[20] but we return
to the conventional broadside intro for 'North Country Blues':

> Come gather 'round friends
> And I'll tell you a tale

And though Dylan here turns the salesman–narrator into the
first-person heroine of the song by the start of the second verse
('In the north end of town/My own children are grown…') he
has still not, by this point, completed its initial scene-setting.

Dylan's two most interesting 'come gather round' intros
are those where this conventional opening address is not used
conventionally, as a sales spiel for the song. They give Dylan,
instead, a quick way in to finger-pointing and hectoring 'the
accused', rather than drumming up business among (dis)interested
bystanders. Inverting the traditional function of the format intro,
Dylan uses it to attack rather than attract his audience. We find
the broadside style purloined in this way for Dylan diatribes in
'The Times They Are A-Changin'':

> Come gather 'round people
> Wherever you roam
> And admit that the waters
> Around you have grown
> And accept it that soon
> You'll be drenched to the bone

No way to sell trinkets, this. And still more pared down here:

> Come you masters of war

Yes you! I'm talking to you!…

---

[20] 'I'll sing you a song / Though not very long / Yet I think it as pretty as any / Put your
hand in your purse / … And give the poor singer a penny'; quoted from *Dean's New
Gift Book of Nursery Rhymes* (London: Dean, 1971): and a nice reminder, this, of how
the sales-pitch relates to sheer begging.

You that build all the guns
You that build the death planes
You that build the big bombs
You that hide behind walls
You that hide behind desks

One final observation, arising from the inter-relationship between Bob Dylan's work and different categories of folk ballad, is this: in apparently stark contrast to those of his songs which employ broadside intros, to whatever effect, we also find in Dylan's early repertoire songs which, because derived from or created in the manner of the Child Ballads, open with a 'plunge right into the action'.[21]

'Seven Curses', for example, does this brilliantly:

Old Reilly stole a stallion
But they caught him and they brought him back

And from then on the action never lets up. But consider that most well-known Bob Dylan composition, 'A Hard Rain's A-Gonna Fall'. This is based on a Child ballad, 'Lord Randal' (No. 12); yet the opening lines of both songs, though not using the sales-spiel intro characteristic of the broadside, do employ a similar delaying device interposed between start and start-of-action. As with those Victorian ghost stories which begin with old buffers sitting around clubs after dinner asking each other to tell ghost stories, so the far more ancient 'Lord Randal' begins, in one variant at least, with the same story-within-the-story delay, thus:

O where ha' you been, Lord Randal, my son?
And where ha' you been, my handsome young man?[22]

Echoed closely, of course, by the opening lines of the Dylan song:

[21] Edith Fowke, quoted on the subject of the characteristics of ballads of oral tradition and, in contrast, those of broadsides, in Bill Usher, ed., *For What Time I am in This World* (London: Peter Martin Associates, 1977). The book is of short contributions, often transcripts of taped conversation, by performers and folklorists present at a Mariposa Folk Festival.
[22] Quoted in Betsy Bowden, *Performed Literature* (Bloomington, Indiana: Indiana University Press, 1982).

Oh where have you been my blue-eyed son?
And where have you been my darlin' young one?

Betsy Bowden shows most entertainingly how here too Dylan twists the old ballad ingredients to his own purposes. She begins, for the reader unfamiliar with 'Lord Randal', by summarising the answer to the question posed in the lines just quoted:

> [H]e has been off in the woods being fatally poisoned by eels, usually fed to him by his treacherous true love. A listener … can feel in 'Hard Rain' added ominousness: the contrast between modern society and the olden days, when death by poisoning came to one person at a time … and [was] preventable by precautions (such as eating only Mom's cooking).
>
> Furthermore, the line-by-line scene shifts in 'Hard Rain' make it resemble a Child Ballad being run through a projector too fast, for a Child Ballad characteristically leaps – but stanza by stanza – from scene to scene of dramatic and emotional intensity. Lord Randal could have spent hours dying, while telling his mother who was to blame. In October 1962, we would have had only seconds…[23]

IV. 'Belle Isle' As Newfoundland Folksong, Part 2

Such considerations, concerning kinds of distinction and kinds of *blurring* of distinction between basic ballad types, were in my mind when I came back to the process of sifting through the Newfoundland data on 'The Blooming Bright Star Of Belle Isle' itself, and thereby into the terrain, apparently, of that other ballad type, the Native North American ballad.

There was nothing odd *per se* about the first known publication of this song having been in a broadside collection in 20th-century Newfoundland: Doyle's *Old-Time Songs and Poetry of Newfoundland*.[24]

I found it there in the first (1927) edition, on the same page as the most popular ballad in Newfoundland's history, the lovely 'The Star Of Logy Bay', topped and tailed by adverts for Doyle's merchandise: 'Sanitol is the Best Tooth Paste', 'ALWAYS

[23] *Ibid.*
[24] As Note 15.

REFRESHING – LIFE SAVERS' and 'P. & G. is the most Economical Soap'.

One of the grounds for objection to broadsides, that they were inaccurate, was illustrated at once by the song title being given throughout as 'The Blooming Bright Star Of Bell [sic] Isle'. (Incidentally 'Loch Erin' was here spelt 'Lock Erin'.) This seemed an odd mistake: I paid it no attention when I first came across the material, but it soon became one among many things which began to hint that perhaps 'Belle Isle' wasn't the Newfoundland song it was supposed to be at all.

A whole series of these clues began to crop up. For one thing, it didn't seem very well-known or popular in Newfoundland. Doyle had published it in 1927, and again in the 2nd edition of his songbook in 1940, but I found that it had been dropped from the third edition (1955) and had not been reinstated in the last (1966) edition, even though this had, as noted, been published at a time of revived mainland interest in the regional folksong of the island. The perennial point behind the Doyle publications was to reach the widest possible popular market: yet 'The Blooming Bright Star Of Belle Isle' had been dropped.

Then, reading through Michael Taft's *Regional Discography*, I was struck by this: Taft wrote that 'some traditional Newfoundland songs have been put on record *only* by non-Newfoundlanders'. He put 'some' songs – but the only one he could cite was, yes, 'Belle Isle':

> …the song 'Blooming Bright Star Of Belle Isle' has not been sung on record by any Newfoundlander, but has been recorded by at least three mainlanders: Bob Dylan, Joyce Sullivan, and Ed Trickett. One can only guess at where these singers learned the song.[25]

[25] Michael Taft, *A Regional Discography of Newfoundland and Labrador 1904-1972* (St. John's: Memorial University Folklore & Language Archive, 1975). Taft is my folklorist hero, for his immense work on blues lyrics, *Blues Lyric Poetry: An Anthology* (New York: Garland Publishing Inc., 1983) and its companion volumes, 'a series of contextual concordances': an amazing compilation of blues lyrics from the 1920s to the 1940s, assembled at the Center for Computer Research in the Humanities, at the University of Colorado at Boulder. Taft has also written invaluably on, and taken a long-term collector's interest in, the recordings of Blind Willie McTell.

Indeed. But *that* area of speculation could wait.[26] What about the arresting fact that this great Newfoundland song had never been recorded by a Newfoundlander in all the years covered by Taft's discography (i.e. 1904-1972)?

It was time to look up Belle Isle itself – the place – and then to look through Greenleaf & Mansfield and whatever other books offered texts of the song, to check out what comments they might yield.

John Way had suggested that Loch Erin was Lough Erne, County Fermanagh, Northern Ireland; but Rod MacBeath had backed up his report that the song was 'Canadian' by referring to the Straits of Belle Isle as lying, of course, between Newfoundland and the Canadian mainland. How could the most beautiful girl from these geographic parts be down by the banks of anywhere in Northern Ireland? Far more likely, surely, that Belle Isle itself featured somewhere with a similar place name?

But it didn't. First clue on this one: at the Memorial University library's Centre For Newfoundland Studies (from inside which you can look up from a huge map of St. John's harbour and ocean to see the harbour and the ocean themselves in the distance) there is no listing at all under *Belle Isle* in the index. It just says 'See *Straits of Belle Isle*'. Under that entry there are studies of the huge geographic area this term encompasses, ranging from a French account of exploration published in 1758 through to a 1979 historical study of population and ecology.

What this meant was that Belle Isle itself is an *uninhabited,* forbidding lump of rock that holds so little human or other history that beyond getting it mapped, no-one has ever troubled to study it. Was this really the setting for so beautiful a song about so beautiful a maiden waiting in service for the return of her lover in a terrain of 'fair fields'? Was there a Loch/Lock Erin there?

No. There is a Three Brooks Cove, a Scotswood Cove and a Green Cove – even a Beauty Cove. But the more characteristic island names are Wreck Cove, Black Joke Cove and Misery

---

[26] Ed Trickett's version is on *The Telling Takes Me Home*, Folk-Legacy FSI-46, US, 1972. This small Vermont company had a big influence on the folk-revival movement of the very early 1960s. However, I've been unable to trace or date the Ed Trickett recording and therefore don't know whether it pre-dates Bob Dylan's 1970 recording on *Self Portrait*.

Point. And though in the heyday of whaling, people used it as a temporary stop-off point where they could store mid-season supplies, Belle Isle has never, ever been anybody's home.

What's more, aside from in 'The Blooming Bright Star Of Belle Isle' itself, there is only one tiny mention of Belle Isle in the entire Newfoundland folksong repertoire. This occurs in 'Concerning One Summer In Bonay', and I'd guess uses Belle Isle in the sense of the whole straits area; that seems discernible from the opening line's use of the more specific term 'our island' to mean Newfoundland:

> The boys in our island have nothing to do…
> To tell all their names it would cause you to smile
> We'd Ham, Shem and Japhet – belonged to Belle Isle.

Neither does it work to assume that the blooming bright star of Belle Isle was the pre-eminent beauty of the whole vast ocean-and-tundra terrain encompassed by the *straits* of Belle Isle. There's no Loch/Lock Erin (or Lough Erne) anywhere there either.

Yet when I turned to the other books that published 'The Blooming Bright Star Of Belle Isle' after Doyle, I was back with, if anything at all, the usual litany as to its background… except that some commentators seemed not only to mention the likelihood of an Irish antecedent but to express a cautious folklorist hunch that 'Belle Isle' might actually be, lock stock & ballad, an Irish song itself.

V. 'Belle Isle' As Irish Folksong, Part 1

Greenleaf & Mansfield said nothing, beyond stating their own sources for the song: i.e. 'Air from Patrick Lewis, Fleur de Lys [Newfoundland], 1929' and 'Words by permission of Gerald S. Doyle, St. John's'.[27] The spelling of the title was here correct, and Doyle's 'Lock Erin' was amended to 'Loch Erin'. Then in *Folk Songs of Canada*, by Edith Fowke (again!) and Richard Johnson, there is this background paragraph given:

---

[27] Elisabeth Greenleaf & Grace Mansfield, eds., *Ballads and Sea Songs of Newfoundland* (Cambridge, MA: Harvard University Press, 1933; reprinted Hatboro, PA: Folklore Associates, 1968).

There are many good folksongs extolling the charms of Newfoundland girls, from 'The Maid Of Newfoundland' to 'The Star Of Logy Bay', but this ['The Blooming Bright Star Of Belle Isle'] is one of the finest. The words suggest a relationship to the many songs about an absent lover who returns in disguise to test his sweetheart's faithfulness, and it may well be descended from an older Irish ballad.[28]

This write-up must have pre-dated Ms Fowke's encounter with the much-cited 'Loch Erin's Sweet Riverside'. She continued:

Wherever it originated, it has spread fairly widely throughout Newfoundland ... recorded by Kenneth Peacock in 1952 at King's Cove near Bonavista, while twenty-three years earlier Mrs. Greenleaf had recorded it at Fleur de Lys, nearly two hundred miles closer to Belle Isle...

Kenneth Peacock, referred to here, himself published three volumes of *Songs of the Newfoundland Outports* (1964-5), and Vol. 2 offered 'The Star Of Belle Isle' [sic], plus, incidentally, a version of 'Erin's Green Shore' field-collected at Joe Batt's Arm in 1952 from a Mrs. John Fogarty, who also provided 'The Green Shores Of Fogo' – another 'native love lyric written ... by a sailor' and 'patterned on the old Irish song "The Country I'm Leaving Behind".' On 'Belle Isle' itself Peacock said:

This lovely lyric is generally considered to be of local origin, possibly because of its reference to Belle Isle. Although I have done no sleuthing, I would strongly suspect an Old World original for this Newfoundland variant. The dialogue form and rather flowery language is pure eighteenth, or perhaps late seventeenth century ... see 'Bright Phoebe' as one of many lyrics of this type.

He went on to mention, after also comparing 'Belle Isle' with 'another Irish-inspired native love song "The Green Shores Of

---

[28] Edith Fowke & Richard Johnson, eds., *Folk Songs of Canada* (Waterloo, Ontario: Waterloo Music Co., 1954).

Fogo"' that the Fogo-Joe Batt's Arm area of Newfoundland was certainly 'strongly Irish'.[29]

Finally, in the authoritative *Native American Balladry* by G. Malcolm Laws (revised edition 1964),[30] he catalogued 'Belle Isle' and added: 'This is a Newfoundland product in the English or Anglo-Irish broadside tradition. For similar stories see [a group of *fifteen* songs] in *American Balladry from British Broadsides*.'[31]

Lots of things seemed promised by all this material. Regardless of whether I should ever find 'Loch Erin's Sweet Riverside', a search would be well worth undertaking among all these other comparable songs: 'The Green Shores Of Fogo' and the localised version of 'Erin's Green Shore'; Laws's fifteen 'American ballads from British broadsides' with similar stories to that of 'Belle Isle'; Peacock's 'Bright Phoebe' or some of these other apparently plentiful songs sharing with 'Belle Isle' its 'dialogue form and rather flowery language'; plus any of Edith Fowke's many other 'songs about an absent lover who returns in disguise'.

Regardless of what specific clues such songs might turn out to hold, the general drift their hovering presence urged upon me was inescapable: that is, it seemed ever less likely that the lovely 'Belle Isle' should have sprung up in Newfoundland, or should celebrate an inhospitable, uninhabited, barren rock in the middle of a sea that is too cold to bathe in at any time of the year, especially since it had hardly ever been sung there, other than by a handful of people in a partly Irish outport area.[32]

[29] Kenneth Peacock, *Songs of the Newfoundland Outports Vol. 2* (of 3 volumes). Vol. 2 is National Museum of Canada Bulletin No. 197, Anthropological Series no. 65, Queen's Printers, Ottawa, 1965.

[30] G. Malcolm Laws, Jr., *Native American Balladry* (Philadelphia, PA: American Folklore Society; revised edition, 1964).

[31] G. Malcolm Laws, Jr., *American Balladry from British Broadsides* (Philadelphia, PA: American Folklore Society, 1957).

[32] Collector Melvin Firestone also field-recorded it at Savage Cove (in the Straits of Belle Isle) by John Crane of Pine's Cove in 1964 (Memorial University of Newfoundland Folklore & Language Archive [MUNFLA], tape C131/64-17). Incidentally it felt very strange to sit listening to this tape of John Crane, unmistakeably a very old man at the time of the recording, singing (to a completely different tune) words so very nearly identical throughout to the ones I'm used to hearing from Dylan. It emphasised also, for me, the foolishness of trying to be precise about 'accuracy' and 'authenticity' in these matters. Where Crane's lyrics differed from Dylan's, this was *in each case* through error: either a mistake or mishearing on Crane's part ('I thought her the goodness of beauty'),

Of course it is impossible to say how widely or otherwise the song really has been sung on the island as part of its living folk culture; but no more than five field-recordings seem to exist (nor do any Newfoundland commercial or demo cuts); and whereas the university folklore archive has just *one* field-tape of 'Belle Isle', this is one out of what was, when Taft's discography was published in 1975, a total of 'several thousand examples of folksongs on approximately 1500 tapes and in 1200 manuscript collections'.

Wasn't there an unavoidable cumulative message from all these clues – that it's far more likely that 'Belle Isle' was, whether amended by its emigration to the New World or not, *essentially Irish itself*? And of course if John Way was right all along in urging that 'Loch Erin' was Ireland's Lough Erne, then any amendments must surely have been minimal, since that place-name's pronunciation had survived intact.

Then I found that something else in the song which had survived intact further pressed home the case for its (Northern) Irish location. Recognising that it might have been a shaky assumption on my part to dismiss a line like 'I wish not to banter' as inauthentic, I looked up 'banter' in Joseph Wright's *English Dialect Dictionary* (1898). Eureka! While 'banter' had widespread and disparate dialect meanings in different parts of the British Isles, Ireland and America in the 19th century, only one such meaning – 'tease, taunt' – made clear-cut sense within the song: and the only place where 'banter' carried that meaning was in Northern Ireland!

Moreover, if it were true that 'Belle Isle' was an Irish song, this would further reduce the puzzle quotient of the song's 'unfolkie' ornateness of language. This seemed to have been partially explained away already, either by the song's having descended from a broadside ('written by a hack journalist, for money') somewhere along its line, or by its being 'pure eighteenth century' in mode (and anyway there need be nothing mutually exclusive

or on the transcriber's ('Lock Erin' again) or on Dylan's (that 'blooming bright star of bright isle' and the misheard-&-repeated 'Cupid's fair throne' instead of 'throng'). It was clearly borne in on me that there's no way to establish such a thing as a correct text across several centuries of oral transmission, between people who mishear each other, misunderstand each other's dialects, change bits deliberately, forget bits, religiously pass on other people's errors, and so on.

about these two explanations; indeed in the *19th* century a lot of these songs also got fancified and genteelised by well-meaning clergymen with literary pretensions).

Then, while wading through books in the Memorial University Library in search of all these other comparable songs, and cursing Professor Fowke the while because of course none of these books *ever* included her 'Loch Erin's Sweet Riverside', I re-read the short piece by Fowke herself which had contained her distinction between the action-packed traditional ballad and the hack-worked broadside, and this time found there a comment I could apply to this 'flowery language' question.

Her observation comes in the course of a short summary of the whole history of folksong in Canada, the main lines of which run as follows: the first and largest stock of Canada's folk songs came with the pioneer settlers of New France. These songs were a legacy from the jongleurs of medieval France. Even songs reflecting artificial court life survived in the incongruous setting of rural Quebec — *'so that the pioneer clearing his land with an axe could still be singing about knights and princesses, and damsels in old Rochelle'* [my emphasis]. Then came the English-speaking settlers, bringing with them the traditional ballads of England, Scotland and Ireland. And by the time they came, the Child Ballads were tending to be replaced by the broadsides...[33]

I came across other confirmatory comments elsewhere. In the section of *Songs The Whalemen Sang* (by Gale Huntington) titled 'Parlor Songs That Went To Sea', Huntington reprints a song found in the logbook/journal of the ship *Cortez* in 1847, called 'Adieu To Erin' (this song title one of many which reconfirmed that 'Erin' very commonly popped up simply as an old or 'poetic' word for Ireland). The song isn't relevant except in the most general sense: its narrator *dreams* of a revisit to his love in

---

[33] As in Note 21. Fowke also notes here that 'songs of the returned lover are by far the most popular of all the plots of broadside ballads in Canada ... probably because there were so many separations in the early days. Men would come over here and try to find work and get settled, and sometimes their wives or sweethearts were left at home in Britain [/Ireland]. Or men would go west to California during the gold rush, or to the Yukon or the Prairies. This made the theme of lovers remaining faithful – usually for seven years – very appealing.'

Erin, but is standing on the deck of his ship at the time – but the book's compiler remarks that 'Although the words seem literary it is sometimes hard to tell with Irish songs'.[34] And in Tomás Ó Canainn's 1978 book *Songs of Cork*[35] he reprints the song 'The Banks Of Sullane' with the comment that this ballad was one of the most popular in West Cork, and that, 'The language is flowery and somewhat artificial – typical of many such ballads composed in Irish-speaking areas over the last century.'

Now that very title, 'The Banks Of Sullane', seemed to promise some resemblance to the lyrics of 'Belle Isle' (just as had the title 'The Star Of Logy Bay', from the Newfoundland folksong repertoire). It seemed time to go back to the lyrics of 'Erin's Green Shore' too: had I been right to think that essentially they bore *no* real resemblance to 'Belle Isle'?

The lyrics John Way had quoted were as follows:

> One evening of late as I rambled
> On the banks of a clear purling stream
> I sat down on a bed of primroses
> And gently fell into a dream
> I dreamt I beheld a fair female
> Her equal I ne'er saw before
> So she sighed for the wrongs of her country
> As she strayed along Erin's green shore.
>
> I quickly addressed this fair female
> 'My jewel, come tell me your name
> For here in this land you're a stranger
> Or I would not have asked you the same.'
> She looked like the Goddess of Freedom
> And Liberty's mantle she wore
> And she sighed for the wrongs of her country
> As she strayed along Erin's green shore.
>
> 'I know you're a true son of Grainne
> So my secrets to you I'll unfold...'

[34] Gale Huntington, *Songs The Whalemen Sang* (New York: Dover Publications, 2nd edition, 1970).
[35] Tomás Ó Canainn, *Songs of Cork* (Cork, Eire: 1978).

Her eyes were like two sparkling diamonds
Or the stars of a cold, frosty night
Her cheeks were like two blooming roses
Her teeth of the ivory so white
She resembled the Goddess of Freedom
And green was the mantle she wore
Bound 'round with the shamrock and roses
That grow along Erin's green shore.

The resemblances between all this and the lyrics Dylan sings on the *Self Portrait* version of 'Belle Isle' seemed to me scanty rather than strong. It's true that the two songs share an approximate outline of story (male narrator encounters beautiful female walking the water's edge) and of descriptive convention ('Goddess of...', 'goddess of...'; 'my secrets to you I'll unfold', 'I will tell you a secret') – but the divergences are far more striking than these sparse parallels. In 'Belle Isle' the narrator returns to his homeland from overseas. Once there he heads for his old romantic stamping-ground and, in disguise so as to test her faithfulness, looks up the girl he'd left behind. When her dialogue with this 'stranger' proves her true, he reveals his identity, and the faithfulness of both parties is rewarded. The lovers are happily reunited.

Obviously, there are many old ballads sharing this theme – some also sharing the 'Belle Isle' dénouement and some offering different classic endings: the maiden proving 'false', or her parents forbidding their marriage, and so on. But 'Erin's Green Shore' conspicuously doesn't fit any of these scenarios! Its narrator, not troubling to convey familiarity with the terrain where he rambles, conjures up his Goddess in a dream; she is neither real nor known to him of old. She is neither his true nor his false love. Their relationship isn't the point of the song, in fact.

So what is? What is the function of this unknown, unreal damsel? The extravagance of that 'Goddess of...' gives the answer. Not 'goddess of beauty', as in 'Belle Isle', but 'Goddess of Freedom'. What we have here is not a love song but a *political* song. The 'fair female' is a symbol, an emblem, not a lover. She sighs not with the loneliness borne of years of keeping her vows and her promise, but 'for the wrongs of her country'; she isn't wearing the working clothes of the maiden still in service, but the green mantle, 'bound 'round with the shamrock'.

A quick check of the lines John Way omitted clinches it; they include:

> I'm a daughter of Daniel O'Connell
> And from England I lately came o'er.
> I have come to awaken my brethren
> That slumber on Erin's green shore.[36]

This puts beyond doubt that 'Erin' in this song simply means Ireland, and not a specific location at all.

Besides – move over, 'Erin's Green Shore': 'The Banks Of Sullane' includes this:

> …and a damsel of queenly appearance
> Came down by the banks of Sullane.

> I rose with great joy and amazement
> And accosted this damsel so fair:
> For to me she appeared like Venus
> Adorned with jewels most rare

Moreover, it rapidly became clear that 'The Banks Of Sullane' had no special relationship here. There was obviously a whole genre of these songs: songs with some real sisterhood to '(The [Blooming Bright] Star Of) Belle Isle'.

[36] O'Connell, Daniel (1775-1847): Irish Catholic barrister; founded the Catholic Association in Ireland (suppressed 1825; O'Connell then turned it into the Order of Liberation) to campaign both for Catholic emancipation (which came in 1829) and repeal of the Act Of Union. Known as 'The Liberator', he developed strong links with English middle-class radicalism and was a powerful enough orator to address a 200,000 crowd in Birmingham (and without a microphone) in 1833. As a counterpoint to this article's main associative thrust between the Irish and a lot of flowery ballads about maidens mooning about on riverbanks, I note that '… a mass of immigrant Irish labourers, who poured into England in large numbers in the 1840s – … one fifth of the population of Manchester was Irish – were potential revolutionaries … they were absorbed into the new economic system as "navvies" and casual labourers or … tossed here and there continuing to harbour their national grievances. So long as O'Connell lived … most politically-minded Irishmen stood aloof from Chartism, but in 1847 and 1848 they were so prominent in the movement that *The Times* could call the Chartism of 1848 "a ramification of the Irish conspiracy".' (From Asa Briggs, *The Age of Improvement: 1783-1867*; London: Longmans Green, 3rd impression, 1963.)

The number of songs I came across with equivalent titles was large, for a start. The following are culled solely from Ó Canainn's abovementioned *Songs of Cork*:

> The Flower Of Magherally
> The Maid Of Bunclody (and many other maids)
> The Phoenix Of Erin's Green Isle
> The Star Of Donegal
> The Little Rose Of Gartan
> The Flower Of The Vale
> The Snowy-Breasted Pearl
> The Blazing Star Of Drung

Plus another of dissimilar title but entirely the same approach called 'Dobbin's Flowery Vale', and – of course – *of course!* – 'The Lily Of The West' (of which, more later).

If there was a whole list of songs with titles akin to 'The Blooming Bright Star Of Belle Isle', there was also an extravagant number of songs available from the English/Scottish/Irish ballad tradition with parallel opening lines. Far too many to list; but I noted down the following just from one catalogue (of an English collection of folk ballads held at Sheffield University):[37]

> One evening as I walked
> One evening by a chance as I strayed
> One evening of late as young Colin I met
> One ev'ning not very long ago
> One lovely morning I was walking
> One morning as I went a fowling
> One morning as I went a walking
> One morning for recreation
> One morning ranging for recreation
> One morning very early, a strange thought came into my head
> One night as I lay sleeping
> One night as Polly Oliver lay musing on her bed (my favourite)

Plus:

---

[37] Peter W. Carnell, ed., *Ballads in the Charles Harding Firth Collection* (Sheffield: Centre for English Language and Tradition, 1979).

One night as the moon luminated the sky[38]
One night at ten o'clock
One night of late, I chanced to stray, all in the pleasant
month of May
One night sad and languid I went to my bed
One night sad and languid I lay on my bed
One night the north wind loud did blow

And to those can be added a good many more which belong to
the same genre (and offer the same theme) but happen to begin
with 'As I' instead of with 'One day/evening/morning/night';
these include 'The Lovely Maid Of The Shannon Streme':

As I walk'd out of a summer's morning

and 'Mantle So Green':

As I walked out one morning in June
To view the fair fields and meadows green

while 'Bonny Labouring Boy' begins:

As I roved out one evening being in the blooming spring
I heard a lovely damsel fair most grievously did sing.[39]

Now some of these plentiful songs of half-sisterhood to 'The
Blooming Bright Star Of Belle Isle' are openly presented in the
old Irish songbooks as 'new' songs. This tends to mean both that

[38] I see a parallel between this marvellous, vigorous use of the word *luminated* (which is,
after all, only 'illuminated' chopped down, yet works incomparably better: 'as the moon
illuminated the sky' would be prissily mundane, but ellipsed into 'the moon luminated
the sky' it is poetry; another similar song has the appealing, if less vibrant, 'the moon
illustrated the sky') from traditional English balladry, and the occurrence in 1920s-30s
American blues lyrics of a similarly vivid ellipsed use of the long word turned inside out,
as it were. Consider this wonderful line from Blind Lemon Jefferson's 'Fence Breakin'
Yellin' Blues', recorded in Richmond, Indiana, on 24th September 1929: 'He must be
desperated, I don't know nothing else it could be' (taken from *Blues Lyric Poetry: An
Anthology*, Michael Taft, as in Note 25).
[39] This made me notice that one song Bob Dylan certainly did write, *John Wesley Harding*'s
under-attended 'As I Went Out One Morning', is modelled on this same genre (and as
with 'The Lily Of The West', thus offers a connection with 'Belle Isle' in his repertoire).
In this song the narrator walks out 'to breathe the air around Tom Paine', placing it closer
to the 'Erin's Green Shore' category: i.e. it holds a political connotation.

they are plagiarised from older ones, and that their re-writes are hopelessly florid and ungainly: so much so that a 'new' song can be spotted a mile off, and can be guaranteed not to have survived off the page. There is all the difference in the world between the lyrics of 'Belle Isle' and this sort of excruciating imitative parallel ('A new song call'd the Maid of Ballymoat'):

> One day as I chanced to go rovin'
> Convenient to sweet Ballymoat
> I met with a charming young fairy
> Hard by her own rural abode;
> I thought she was Juno or Venus
> On whom Paris the apple bestowed
> Or the devil consel'd in legions
> That Pluto from Sicily stole.

The same disease, the priest or the man of letters showing off his classical education, and hang the consequences for comprehensibility and poetry, is rife all through the genre. Here is the second verse of 'a much admired song call'd The Lovely Maid Of The Shannon Streme':

> I then accosted this lovely fair one
> To tell her name and her dwelling place
> Or was she Hebe or lovely Seres
> Or Vulcan's bride whom the apple gain'd,
> She then made answer I am no goddess
> I am no proud or immortal dame
> My appealation [sic] I must leave mysterious
> I live convenient to the Shannon stream.

When, however, all this well-nigh unsingable pap is stripped away,[40] we are still left with a whole body of work that closely resembles 'Belle Isle', some of it Irish folksong and some of it of Newfoundland currency: and what it shares includes what might be called the discretionary power of poetry. The language may still be 'flowery' but the floweriness, including the pseudo-classicism, is always minimised, and a counteractive simplicity of expression

[40] This folk process of streamlining broadsides and making them singable is discussed at length in Laws: see Note 31.

is always there too. What's more, there is always, in these genuine songs, some idea or some flash of vivid imagery which commands direct, timeless appeal. Thus, in Newfoundland's 'The Star Of Logy Bay' we still get the intrusion of mythology (the maiden is compared with 'Venus') yet not only is it a fleeting mention but even this is mitigated at once by the song's also offering a more earthbound, rurally accurate comparison:

> O Venus was no fairer
> Nor the lovely month of May

Followed at once by this inspired, poetically uniting, felicitous extravagance:

> May Heaven above shower down its love
> On the Star of Logy Bay

This is inspired because it is *almost* a stock couple of lines – almost the same, that is, as you'll find at the end of any number of the ballads within this genre: yet here the stock formula is beautifully minimally warped into something individually apt for this song. It is poetically, deftly integrated.

The stock phrase actually does occur at the end of 'The Star Of Logy Bay'. That lovely 'shower down', carrying such marvellous extra evocativeness from its coming straight after the conjunction of 'Venus' and May's benign weather, is dropped at the song's end in favour of the standard, formulaic

> May Heaven above send down its love
> On the Star of Logy Bay.

I dwell on this because, as I found early on in my researches, 'The Blooming Bright Star Of Belle Isle' itself owns one such standard ending, giving it a verse or two more than Bob Dylan's version offers.

This ending varies slightly between other versions, though not, unfortunately, because any variant offers inspired poetic flash.

Essentially, as in Greenleaf & Mansfield, Dylan's ending:

> For me there is no other damsel
> Than my blooming bright star of Belle Isle

is followed by these extra eight lines:

> Now then this young couple gets married;
> In wedlock they both join in hand.
> May the great God of heaven protect them
> And give them long life in the land!
>
> May the great God of heaven protect them
> And loyalty be theirs all the while!
> And honey will sweeten their comfort
> For the blooming bright star of Belle Isle.

Allowing for minor performance error, the version on tape sung by John Crane of Pine's Cove is the same, and so is the one published by Doyle.[41] In Kenneth Peacock, where, incidentally, the title is given as the shorter 'The Star Of Belle Isle', this tacked-on, repetitive, formulaic, hack-journalistic, bathetic ending is to a small extent mitigated and improved by changes which, though minor, are at least more internally alert:

> This couple they both got married
> In wedlock and soft unity
> May the great God above them protect them
> And give them long life in the land.
>
> May the great God above them protect them
> And loyalty be theirs all the while
> And honey may sweeten their comfort
> Along on the banks of Belle Isle.[42]

[41] So it is too in the version in the popular songbook collection by Omar Blondahl (an outsider who has turned himself into a kind of Newfoundland version of Burl Ives), *Newfoundlanders, Sing!* (St. John's: E. J. Bonnell Associates [sponsored by Robin Hood Flour Mills Ltd.], 1964).

[42] 'Erin's Green Shore' is one of the songs to use this stock ending, which gives it a further superficial resemblance to 'Belle Isle': 'May the great God of heaven shine on her/ For I know I shall see her no more/ May the great God of glory shine on her/ As she strays along Erin's green shore'.

This ending still reduces the song's power by drawing back from the protagonists to no narrative purpose; but at least the Peacock version manages something a bit more fibrous than the others with that 'In wedlock and soft unity', which in turn sets up some kind of resonance with the otherwise marooned note struck by 'honey'; and at least this version's final end, to use an apt Dylanism, is not sheer gibberish.

There is another Newfoundland song, quite similar to 'The Star Of Logy Bay' and using the same tune, called 'Down By Jim Long's Stage', which serves to emphasise both that the songs in this genre can be robust even when flowery, and that variants need not be dishonest imitations. Here are its familiar yet graphic and distinctive first five lines:

> As I roved out one day in June
> 'Twas down by Jim Long's stage
> I met my true-love's father
> All in a frightful rage
> His eyes shot blood and slaughter

Similarly, a variant of 'The Blackwater Side', one of the timeless Irish songs in this genre, opens with a lyric that within two lines takes us beyond the standard and familiar by the power of its graphic simplicity:

> As I roved out one evening fair down by a shady grove
> I little thought I would be caught all in the chains of love.

The sisterhood to 'The Blooming Bright Star Of Belle Isle' is never lost, though, in these other songs. The variant just quoted continues:

> Returning to my dwelling place a charming girl I spied
> She's the blooming rose of Erin's isle
> Down by the Blackwater Side

While the standard 'Blackwater Side' itself opens like this:

> As I roved out on a fine Sunday morning
> To view the fair streams as they gently did glide

And though the popular, and spasmodically powerful, 'Down By The Tanyard Side' starts out as though the 'Belle Isle' mode were not close, and rattles through this sturdily independent second stanza:

> Her lovely hair of tresses rare lies on her snow-white neck
> And the tender glances of her eyes would save a ship from reck
> Her two red lips beguiling and her teeth so pearly white
> Would make a man become her slave
> Down by the Tanyard Side

It skids without pause straight back to familiar territory indeed:

> I courteously saluted her and fixed was my gaze so
> I said 'Are you Aurora bright descending here below?'
> 'Oh no, kind sir, I'm a maiden poor' she modestly replied...

Another song that similarly swims in and out of these same waters, as may be guessed by its title, is 'The Maid Of Lough Gowna Shore'. It stands out here because its version of the heroine's speech raises that other great theme of Irish drama, religion, bringing the topic up as extra grounds for demurral at the 'stranger's' initial proposition. This maiden, sacrificing poetic flow to denominational scruple, pipes up:

> Kind sir, I am but a poor female,
> For riches indeed have I none,
> Besides, we are not one persuasion
> My heart lies in the Church of Rome.

Finally, and perhaps rising above all these other similar, peculiar hybrids, at least in terms of helping to get the measure of 'Belle Isle' itself, I came across another Newfoundland song with strong Irish roots: 'The Green Mossy Banks Of The Lea'. This had been collected from one Pat Moloney in the outport of King's Cove in July 1951, and published by Kenneth Peacock in his *Songs of the Newfoundland Outports* in the mid-1960s.[43]

[43] As in Note 29.

Clearly it belongs with 'Belle Isle'. It shares as many parallels of vocabulary as any other one song in the genre:

> One evening I carelessly rambled
> Where the clear crystal fountain do flow
> It was down by the banks of Lock Erin
> Where the sweet running waters do flow.

> 'Twas there that I spied the fair damsel
> She was most modest appearing to me
> As she rose from her seat near the water
> On the green mossy banks of the lea

Yet what is also clear is that this is a song both addressing the subject of, and itself bearing the scars of, transposition across the Atlantic – which is, of course, the theme implied but unmentioned in 'Belle Isle' itself. The lines just quoted are not from the *opening* verses of 'The Green Mossy Banks Of The Lea', as are their sister-lines in 'Belle Isle'; they are the third and fourth verses, and are preceded by these two:

> When first to this country a stranger,
> Curiosity caused me to roam
> Over Ireland in exile I wandered
> Far from my American home.

> Till at length I arrived in sweet Erin
> In the land where I longs to be
> My footsteps were guided by fairies
> On the green mossy banks of the lea

If there seems some confusion here, with one end of the journey as 'home' and the other as 'where I longs to be', it is par for the course, and shows how the transposition process itself acts on the songs which have it as their theme. 'The Green Mossy Banks Of The Lea' is not alone in this.

VI. Atlantic Crossing: Songs Of Transportation

In retrospect it was obvious that in amongst the mists of passage in a genre with a main theme of separation and return across from one side of the ocean to the other, and where the songs themselves get taken across that ocean too, and where then they either remain faithful or else marry into a new and different situation, and where all this adaptation is going on amid songs there were always many versions and variants of, not to mention as well the conscious 'literary' 19th-century abductions of many of these folksongs by would-be poets ... with all this going on in the world that 'The Blooming Bright Star Of Belle Isle' is a part of, there was bound to be some striking transposing done, with girls' names left the same and place names altered, and names retained for rhyming's sake yet warped by shifts in the old names' applicability.

For instance, the traditional English song 'The Barley Mow' is sung in Newfoundland – where, since agricultural harvesting is non-existent, the name means nothing and is therefore 'The Baltimore'![44] I should not have found it especially odd, then, to come upon an Irish version of another North American ballad I was previously familiar with: 'Lily Of The West'. Indeed I was familiar with this in its Yankee ballad form primarily from its having been recorded by Bob Dylan. As he sings it, the song opens thus:

> When first I came to Louisville
> Some pleasure there to find
> A damsel there from Lexington
> Was pleasing to my mind
>
> Her rosy cheeks, her ruby lips
> Like arrows pierc'd my breast
> The name she bore was Flora,
> The Lily of the West.

Now, stepping shyly from the pages of a number of the Irish songbooks, came Erin's green version, as follows:

> When first I came to Ireland some pleasure for to find
> It's there I spied a damsel fair, most pleasing to my mind
> Her rosy cheeks and sparkling eyes, like arrows pierc'd my breast
> They call her lovely Molly O, The Lily of the West.

[44] All the more remarkable, then, that in 'Belle Isle' the pronunciation of 'Lough Erne' (as 'Loch/Lock Erin') has never received this kind of warping for local applicability's sake.

It was a surprise to see it there, so familiar yet so wholly relocated, with 'the West' as serviceable in the one context as in the other, yet its meaning so geographically different in each case; and likewise, instead of hearing 'Lily' as a brash American western saloon name, to recognise it, suddenly, as part of that great catalogue of flowers of here and stars of there and maids of down the road. This made the song at once recognisably in the same tradition as 'Belle Isle' and riddled with evidence of that process of transposition which all this balladry is heir to.

Robert L. Wright, in his 1975 work *Irish Emigrant Ballads & Songs*[45] reports that there are many such songs that specifically mention this transposition process; he quotes a song called 'Dear Old Ireland', which opens with 'Deep in Canadian woods we've met, from one bright island flown' and ends, with the sort of future-gloom Hank Williams would have enjoyed, thus:

> But deep in Canadian woods we've met,
> and never may see again
> The dear old isle where our hearts are set,
> and our first fond hopes remain!

And similarly there are many many songs of departure. As a matter of fact, 'The Star Of Donegal' is one of them, and begins:

> One evening fair to take the air, alone as I chanced to stray
> Down by yon silv'ry stream that ran along my way
> I spied two lovers seated by an ancient ruined wall
> This fair maid's name was Mary or The Star Of Donegal
>
> He pressed her hand and softly said, 'My darling I must go
> Unto the land of Stars and Stripes where peace and plenty flow
> But give me your faithful promise that you'll wed none at all
> Until I do return to you, bright Star Of Donegal.'

You might think this is setting us up for a less than happy ending, and that the blooming bright star of Belle Isle enjoys better luck than many of these hapless young couples, torn asunder by

---

[45] Robert L. Wright, ed., *Irish Emigrant Ballads & Songs* (Bowling Green, Ohio: Bowling Green University Popular Press, 1975).

all this poverty-induced relocation: but actually Mary or The Star Of Donegal has a superior, less passive solution, persuading her young man to marry her *first* and take her with him when he goes.

Another transposition: earlier in these researches, while still looking in vain for 'Loch Erin's Sweet Riverside', either alongside or separated from 'Erin's Green Shore' (there was an adjacent song in the Robert L. Wright book, called 'Erin's Blooming Jane'), I did find mention of one *'Dixie's* Green Shore' [my emphasis]: apparently one of 600-odd 'Ballads and Folk Songs of the South West' that were collected in Oklahoma in the 1950s and 60s.

The crucial point, always reasserting itself, seemed as if it must be this: that regardless of the particulars of a song's storyline or setting, regardless of how those born in the Americas might re-write European narrative songs, songs of transposition would always obey the primal force of history. That is, they would begin with the Old World and the New World would come after. Even their recurrent rapture about 'the land of Stars and Stripes where peace and plenty flow' is the *emigrant's* rapture, its politics born of repression and poverty back in the old country.

In other words, the conclusion urged on me as to the origin of 'The Blooming Bright Star Of Belle Isle' was, as ever, that it must be Irish – and that this would be the case even if, by the time we found it lurking obscurely in Newfoundland, its theme of exile and return had become, as it were, geographically *reversed,* as with that 'Lily Of The West' with its 'when first I came to Ireland', or as with that 'Over Ireland in exile I wandered / Far from my American home' in 'The Green Mossy Banks Of The Lea'.

VII. 'Belle Isle' As Irish Folksong, Part 2

By the time I'd got thus far through wrestling with all this, it was getting close to Christmas, and I didn't have long left in Newfoundland. Then, just as nothing very conclusive seemed ever likely to arise, I got a note from Edith Fowke:

> I have discovered that 'The Blooming Bright Star Of Belle Isle' is not merely an offshoot of Irish ballads – it *is*

an Irish ballad. John Moulden, a collector and scholar in North Ireland [sic] told me of two versions collected there in different areas...[46]

I phoned Dr. Fowke for John Moulden's address, and then wrote to him at once. His reply came speedily and was of considerable length. He had been seriously interested in the song for years.

He confirmed that he had indeed come across two different versions of 'Belle Isle' in Ireland itself – the first collected by Len Graham from one Hugh Tracey of Boho (pronounced *boe*, as in *oboe*) in County Fermanagh, in July 1972, and the other a manuscript dating from about 1910, written down by a sailor who had learnt his songs around 1870. John Moulden had acquired this document from an antiquarian bookseller in Ballynahinch, County Down.

While this all appeared to confirm the Irish origin of the song, and certainly to confirm John Way's supposition that Loch Erin was Lough Erne, County Fermanagh, John Moulden's testimony also served to emphasise yet again how complex can be the ins and outs of these songs of transposition. For the curious thing was this: while the locations retained in the version known in, and assumed to be native to, Newfoundland are *Northern Irish*, the two versions eventually located in Northern Ireland itself *introduce the apparently Newfoundland place-name St. John's!*

The version Len Graham collected in the field from Hugh Tracey's performance ran as follows:

One evening as I strayed out for pleasure
Where beauty and love do resort
It was down by the banks of Lough Erne
I wandered for pleasure and sport

Where the maidens do sing at their labour
Through hardships and trouble and toil
There I met with a beautiful fair one
Called the lovely sweet Star of Belle Isle

---

[46] Edith Fowke, letter to the present writer, dated November 1985.

I instantly stepped it up to her
She approached me right there with a smile
Saying I am no lady of honour
But a poor working maid of Belle Isle

Oh Mary resign from your labours
And come to the town of St. John's
'Tis there many pleasures await you
And servants all at your command

Oh I'll not resign from my labours
Through hardships and troubles and toil
I'll wait for the lad that has left me
Here alone by the banks of Belle Isle

So now I've a story to tell you
I'm only a maid that is true
But to break the fond vows that I made him
Is a thing that I never will do

I ne'er thought that Cupid would win me
But beauty it did me beguile
For seven long years I've been wandering
For you lovely Star of Belle Isle

Now I heard that this couple got married
In wedlock they have joined their hands
For him she crossed over the ocean
Far away from [sic] the town of St. John's

May the great King of Glory protect them
May liberty shine on their toil
May Johnny find comfort for ever
With his beautiful Star of Belle Isle

How engaging the similarities and dissimilarities are between
that lyric and the New World one Bob Dylan found himself singing
in a Nashville studio a couple of years earlier – the comparison
repays much attention, and shows graphically how the whole
process of folksong works, as it is passed from hand to hand. I find
it rather a distraction from this, to have to grapple instead with the
almost irritating specific of why this Irish version introduces, as

it were perversely, the non-Irish place-name St. John's, when the Newfoundland versions of the song all managed without it.

John Moulden's letter took up this point:

> [T]he introduction of the additional place-name was worrying, and I have only, as I have been writing to you, thought of a possible way round ... previously I was, without conviction, offering the town of St. Johnston in Donegal, not that far from Belle Isle, though probably too far for sense, since the Irish scale of distance is still very limited and would have been more so earlier.[47]

Moulden's fresh solution, built on the very reasonable assumption that we were dealing here with essentially an emigration song, arose from learning that anyone emigrating from County Fermanagh in the 19th century would have left Ireland through the port of Derry, and that on the other side of the Atlantic it was the port of Saint John, New Brunswick which was 'the cradle of Derry trade with North America and the destination of great numbers of emigrants for Canada or in transit to the United States'.[48]

This solution seemed to me doubly plausible. First, the confusion of Saint John, New Brunswick, and St. John's, Newfoundland, is unsurprising and perennial. As if to confirm the point, while I was in the latter, several hundred South Korean football fans, keen to see their national team play Canada's in the World Cup qualifiers, were prevented from doing so because their travel agency booked them a flight to the New Brunswick city instead. Second, it would then be reasonable indeed that the versions of the song home-grown in the British colony of Newfoundland should retain no place-naming of an Irish emigrant port of entry many hundreds of miles away along the frozen coast.[49]

[47] John Moulden, letter to the present writer, dated 26th November 1985.
[48] Quoted by John Moulden from Sholto Cooke, *The Maiden City and the Western Ocean* (Dublin: Morris; no date but © 1955). Moulden calls this the standard work on 19th-century emigration from the port of Derry (i.e. Londonderry), and notes, in 'The Blooming Bright Star Of Belle Isle: American Native Or Irish Immigrant?', *Canadian Folk Music Journal* Vol. 14, 1986, that 'the Maiden City' is 'a poetic appellation for Londonderry'.
[49] I heard it mooted that in the case of Newfoundland an alternative explanation might

The other Irish version, the sailor's 1910 manuscript version, effectively an 1870s version,[50] was a tremendous find – and seemed, really, the end of the trail. It appeared to confirm and clarify that 'Belle Isle' was indeed an Irish song, and a song of transposition – an emigrant song – while also pointing fascinatingly towards the pruned-down, simpler, superior emigrant the song itself was to become by the time that Doyle was publishing it as a native Newfoundland ballad in 1927, 'the lovly swete star of Berlile' [sic]:

One evening as I roamed for pleasure
Where beauty and love do resort
O its Down by the banks of lohern
Where the youl find pleasur and sport
A yong falel tha sang at her laibour
that caused me to stop for A while
and I found her a charming yong Creature
and the lovely swet star of Berlile

I umbeled my self to her beauty
and ask her where did she resid
he says then elope from your perants
and Shortley ill make you my bride
She said im no laidy of fortine
aproshing me then with A smile
She said im A [poor] plain Country girld
and A poor Servant maid from berlile

O mary resine your hard labour
and Com to the [ton] town of saint Jon
Where the flowers ar groing most charming
and servants for you at Comand
I cam to fulfill my last promes
So let us have Brandy and wine
and its now I embrase my old Charmer
Shes the Lovely Swet ... star of Berlile.

lie with the hostility of outport communities towards the big city, which would tend to result in their determinedly omitting mention of it from their own native versions of the song. Such parochialism may be a well-established aspect of the island's life, and have many other manifestations in its culture (to note which is not to suggest that Newfoundland is unusual in this regard) but I do not find this convincing: not least because that far more popular folksong of the outport communities, 'The Star Of Logy Bay', is happy to mention 'St. John's town'.
[50] From the Higgins manuscript of County Down, in the possession of John Moulden (and published in his *Canadian Folk Music Journal* article: details as in Note 48).

VIII. Conclusions

I came back to England that Christmas Eve, with, among other things, a large wad of unsorted notes on 'Belle Isle'. John Moulden went into print with the material he'd given me such a generous advance glimpse of in his letter. Incorporating an array of statistics about Londonderry emigration and ports of entry and so on, his six-page article, 'The Blooming Bright Star Of Belle Isle: American Native Or Irish Immigrant?' was published in the *Canadian Folk Music Journal* sometime in 1986. I discovered this in 1987, when a copy mailed for my attention by Dr. Narváez reached me just as I was writing an earlier version of the present article: a version aimed specifically at a readership of Bob Dylan enthusiasts.

But this piece, 'Back To Belle Isle', published in *The Telegraph* in the spring of 1988,[51] all too unquestioningly followed the Moulden line, partly, I think, because of that ringing, confident endorsement with which it was introduced to me by Professor Fowke ('I have discovered that "The Blooming Bright Star Of Belle Isle" is not merely an offshoot of Irish ballads – it *is* an Irish ballad')[52] and partly because by this point I could no longer see the wood for the trees.

Specifically, I had written that Bob Dylan's version and the version of the song that Len Graham had collected from Hugh Tracey in Northern Ireland would repay close comparative attention, but I had failed to give them enough such attention myself.

Dr. Narváez subsequently scrutinized all this published material and paid attention where mine had lapsed. He wrote a short rejoinder to my 'Back To Belle Isle' for a subsequent issue of *The Telegraph*,[53] in which he argued forcefully for, in effect, his original assertion, as made to me when first we'd met back in Newfoundland in September 1985 and before I had researched into 'Belle Isle' at all: that is, he argued again for Newfoundland as the original, rightful terrain of the song.

[51] Michael Gray, 'Back To Belle Isle,' *The Telegraph* (since issue #26, Spring 1987, publication has been from Romford, Essex, UK) #29, Spring 1988.
[52] As Note 46.
[53] Peter Narváez, '"Sic" As Forced Fit: A Commentary For The Newfoundland Provenance Of "Belle Isle"', *The Telegraph* #31, Winter 1988.

First, citing counter-statistics provided by John Mannion's work,[54] Narváez appeared to trounce Moulden's Irish immigration statistics: 'It is true that the massive out-migrations of Irish during the famines of the 1840s bypassed Newfoundland, but by the 1840s *there already were significant numbers of Irish here.*'

Second, he pointed out that Saint John, New Brunswick is an area where the song has never been collected. Third, in place of my 'uninhabited, forbidding lump of rock' (Belle Isle) he offered a most convenient alternative island:

> The correct Belle Isle is in Conception Bay, only twelve miles from St. John's, today known as 'Bell Island'. This latter name was only made official in 1910. The earliest sixteenth century references are spelled 'Belile' (reminiscent of the 1910 manuscript version [of the song] ... reference to 'Berlile'?). Later spellings are either 'Belle Isle' (1762; 1795; 1801; 1839; 1842; 1868) 'Great Bell{e} Isle' or 'Bell Isle' [no dates given].

Then, drawing our attention back to the special significance of the Tracey variant of the song, he continued:

> Today the visitor to Bell Island is struck by its verdant meadows and *dramatic steep banks*, the 'banks of Belle Isle' still providing a very romantic setting ... In the nineteenth century its inhabitants were Irish and English farmers (the soil is remarkably fertile) who sold their produce to people in St. John's and smaller fishing settlements ... around Conception Bay. The wealthy merchants of Newfoundland lived in St. John's. Thus the *relations of social class* exhibited in the Tracey variant ... not only make ballad sense, given the many songs which exhibit similar situations, but they make historical sense as well, for such relations are in keeping with the given place names.
>
> In my estimation, notwithstanding the date of its collection (1972), the oldest variant of 'Belle Isle' is the Tracey version. Like so many broadsides *it has a convoluted, complicated plot that was later simplified by the folk through oral transmission.* The initial voice of the ballad is that of a

[54] John Mannion, ed., *The Peopling of Newfoundland* (St. John's: Memorial University Press, 1977).

wealthy man from the St. John's merchant class who one evening wanders 'for pleasure and sport'. He then meets a beautiful 'working maid' from Belle Isle whom he attempts to seduce to a St. John's life but her response is that she has promised herself to another. Then *the flashback ends* and the (first person) merchant indicates that seven lonely years have elapsed since that first meeting ... and he has heard that during that time the young beauty got married to her 'Johnny', to whom she was betrothed, and to do that she had to leave and cross 'over the ocean, far away *from* the town of St. John's.' *Unlike Moulden and Gray, I am unable to conveniently turn 'from' into 'to' through the offhanded use of 'sic'!* ... This interpretation is not only reasonable in terms of historical social relations in Newfoundland, but also in terms of broadside piety, since the poor female protagonist successfully resists the temptations of the rich St. John's merchant [my emphasis].[55]

Narváez argued that the other versions are later ones, streamlined down into two-person narratives with the well-known 'lover in disguise tests faithfulness' motif, and thus negating 'the interesting thematic question of *class* ... posed by the Newfoundland broadside balladeer in the original'.

Finally, having tried also to account for the stubborn, perhaps inconvenient, presence of the Irish 'Lock/Loch Erin/Erne' in every known variant of the song, Narváez concluded, in both senses, thus:

> [T]he geographic laws of cultural diffusion are at work again. The oldest version of an orally circulated ballad, originally composed by a broadside balladeer who resided and published his song in nineteenth century Newfoundland, has been collected in the twentieth

[55] In interesting contrast, consider the following, quoted from the retrospective 'Diary' column of Q magazine #18 (London: EMAP Metro, March 1988): 'March 2, 1964. The Beatles begin filming their first movie, *A Hard Day's Night*. One of the production's better kept secrets was the dressing-room /caravan in which the Fab Four would invite starlets to "relax" between takes. Model Patti Boyd, with a small part in the film, quickly caught the eye of Beatle George [Harrison] but declined the offer of a visit to the caravan and even of a proper date, explaining [that] she owed some loyalty to her regular boyfriend. She finally relented when The Quiet One virtually begged her to let him take her to dinner. Asked later where this left her regular boyfriend ... Ms Boyd (who within a month had moved in with George) replied: "I said I was loyal, not stupid."'

century on the cultural periphery of Newfound-land –
Ireland...[56]

So. Did Dr. Narváez's late entry into the quest provide a final
verdict?

Well, no: his intervention was welcome, and much of it
persuasive, not least in its style: a man who has 'the geographical
laws of cultural diffusion' on his side, as immutable-sounding
as gravity, is hard to contradict; but I was no longer prepared,
after all that had gone before, to see anybody's intervention as
adjudicative. Everyone was entering the ring from their own
corner: me, Fowke, Moulden, Narváez. No-one was in a position
to be the referee.

Moulden, after all, had an interest in concluding that the song
was Irish: if it belonged to Ireland, then in a sense it belonged to
him. He lived and worked there, and if he was right, then he was
the person who had discovered/uncovered its Irish provenance.
Narváez, equally, had an interest in the song belonging to
Newfoundland – he lives and works there, and his work includes
advancing the idea of the limitless folkloric richness of the island.

It struck me that as a result of my being English, which the song
most certainly isn't, I might be closest to the objective.

While the Narváez article swiftly disposed of any naive idea
that the Irish provenance of the song was now proven, and used
the variants found in Ireland to keen effect in constructing a more
persuasive alternative territorial claim, there were, nonetheless, a
number of things which still did not dovetail together.

If the first big wave of immigration to Newfoundland was 1811–
1816, and the next 1825-1833, and if Newfoundland broadsiders
were 'probably publishing local broadsides based on Irish and
British models as early as 1817', then if 'Belle Isle' originated there
and then – i.e. in Newfoundland but based on an Irish model and
aimed at an Irish market, indeed one necessarily of people only
newly arrived from Ireland, and circulated in a form itself new
to Newfoundland yet long-established in Ireland – then it seems
mere carping for us to call it a Newfoundland, and not an Irish,

[56] All quotes taken from Narváez, details as in Note 53.

song. And if instead, as seems more probable, the song came into circulation rather later, perhaps during what Narváez quotes Newfoundland scholar George Story as calling 'the golden age of the published Newfoundland broadside', 1850-1914, then 'long established and deep connections' between Ireland and St. John's need be no more significant in themselves than the connections by then also established, as Moulden reported, between Ireland and New Brunswick. In truth, nobody's statistics clinch anything.

As to matters of text interpretation, I must declare at once that I did not, as Narváez complained, use '[sic]' to transform 'from' into 'to': on the contrary, I used it to emphasise the importance of that small word in the original text. I *accept* the sense Narváez thus makes of it, in his useful disentanglement of the three-person narrative, the class-relations contained within it, and the way that this sits comfortably within the traditional broadside mould. However, several things conspire against the edifice he tries to build from this.

First, there is an important drawback to the notion that the version concerned with class relations, the version specifying St. John's and offering a social realism, arose before versions with these elements streamlined out of the song: that is, it asks us to accept that when turned down by the working girl, the rich merchant would abandon his business 'for seven long years' in order to wander around nursing his unrequited love for her. Far more plausible that this element in the song should be there as a left-over from earlier versions in which it was the maid's 'Johnny' who went wandering, of necessity, for the seven years specified by convention in songs of this genre.

Second, everything Narváez says about the song's otherwise accurate evocation of social relations between merchant, working lad and working maid rings as true, and makes just the same sense, and always has done, in Ireland as in Newfoundland.

Likewise, the Tracey variant sits equally comfortably within the traditional mould of the *Irish* broadside as of any Newfoundland one. And as Narváez reminds us, there are very few surviving Newfoundland broadsides, so that it seems reasonable to remember that actually we know rather more about Irish ones.

It follows, therefore, that the conformity of the Tracey variant to a main category of traditional *Irish* broadside can be noted with more certainty than its conformity to Newfoundland broadside patterns.

So, in spite of his illuminating reading of these aspects of the text, we cannot link it exclusively with Narváez turf. Although it all *could* fit, nothing here establishes that the setting for this drama must be St. John's, Newfoundland. It could all take place just as Narváez unravels it, yet centred upon that other, Moulden-propounded city of Irish arrival, Saint John, New Brunswick – near which there is a small town called Belle Isle. And it seems clear from the text of the *sailor's* variant that it too shows signs of having been a three-person narrative, and thus of having reflected the same social relations that Narváez rightly finds in the Tracey variant. In the sailor's variant these three-person elements are vestigial but they are plainly indicated by that switch from 'I' to 'he' and back again in the second stanza, and by the last stanza's combining of two different approaches, i.e. voices: the attempt to lure 'mary' with the promise of servants at her command, and then the switch to a narrator coming back to fulfil *his* promise by embracing his 'old Charmer'.

But what of the special suitability of Bell Island? First, out of fairness to John Moulden, who may be felt to be disadvantaged by having allowed me to publish extracts from correspondence that caught his first hesitant thoughts about some aspects of his thesis, I hope it might be acceptable as a gesture of balance to point out in regard to one of Peter Narváez's contrastingly confident proclamations, his crucial one that 'The correct Belle Isle is ... Bell Island', that while this may turn out to be true, and is certainly an inspired assertion, it is not one so incontestable or so obvious that he had thought of it when I was in Newfoundland researching the song originally with his assistance and discussing with him the puzzles involved. Neither had anyone else.

What's more, Bell Island may be 'only twelve miles from St. John's', but this is no easy stroll. First you have to go right across the Avalon Peninsula from south-east to north-west, over high and wild terrain, and then you have to take a boat. The 19th-century St. John's merchant who 'strayed' over there to eye up the local girls 'one evening for pleasure' would have spent an awful lot of his evening travelling there and back.

And whereas Northern Ireland's Lough Erne does contain an island called Bellisle, let it not be overlooked that Newfoundland's Bell Island neither contains nor sits within any Loch Erin.

This means, not least, that in an Irish setting, the song's apparently careless interchangeability between 'the banks of Loch Erin' and 'the banks of Belle Isle' makes full sense, whereas in the Newfoundland setting it does not. In the latter, 'the banks of Loch Erin' merely reminds us that we have the puzzle of a non-existent town/village/lake. Why doesn't the three-person narrative name a real one, granted its commitment to social realism and its clear citing of a real city and a real island?

If, on the other hand, we now follow Narváez in looking to the sailor's variant, then we note too that the sailor's variant never mentions 'the banks of Berlile' at all: it only mentions 'the banks of lohern'. So talk of the visitor to Bell Island being struck by its dramatic steep banks gets no corroboration here.

What else may or may not be of special pertinence in the sailor's variant? If, as Narváez suggests, we pay attention to, and place some reliance on, its sound-spellings and so on, then surely 'lohern', 'Berlile' and 'saint Jon' all shout for Ireland and Saint John, New Brunswick.

On the other hand, we may prefer not to place much reliance on the sailor's eccentric transcription, but rather, on the evidence, may wish to demur from Narváez's claim that it shows 'a good grasp of word separation' and has significant capitalizations of letters. The use of capital letters is random throughout the text: this is true at the start of lines; for some indefinite articles but not others ('for A while', 'found her a charming', 'with A smile'); and for some small mid-text words that there is no reason to stress ('its Down by the banks...', 'a charming yong Creature', 'and Shortley', 'let us have Brandy and wine'). Even 'Berlile' is also rendered as 'berlile'. If the sailor's variant doesn't, therefore, help the cause of Bell Island, we might feel that to try to use its 'lohern' to abolish the inconvenient Lough Erne / Loch Erin problem by seeing it instead as referring to a 'lochan ... a small arm of the sea' is to flounder on sandbanks of the improbable.

As for New Brunswick being 'an area where the song has never been collected', well which way do we want it? Does the area where a song is collected tend to be its home, as Narváez seems to argue when the location involved is Newfoundland, or does it tend to be collected on 'the cultural periphery' of its home, which may be an ocean away, as Narváez seems to argue when the location is Ireland? If the former, well the song has hardly been collected anywhere, has it? The Tracey variant, discovered in 1972 (or rather, in the mid-1980s effectively), marked its first appearance in Ireland, while in Newfoundland, as noted already, it has almost never been field-recorded, collected, professionally recorded or published. Making evidence out of lack of evidence seems a dangerous business in a case such as this.

New Brunswick, therefore, might well be the home of the sailor's variant, and we might as accurately say that it is an area where the song has never been looked for as one where it has never been found. And if, on the other hand, we can expect a song to turn up, like an old ripple, at the farthest edge of the water, then clearly, that the sailor's variant turns up in Northern Ireland makes it as plausible that it moved there from New Brunswick as that it moved there from Newfoundland. Further, on this notion, I might add that while I understand the reasons for Narváez coming to describe Ireland as 'the cultural periphery of Newfoundland', it still seems rather like calling Mexico City the cultural periphery of Nuevo Laredo. In any case, emphatically, it works the other way round too: Newfoundland is on the cultural periphery of Ireland. So just as surely as the versions found in Northern Ireland may be from Newfoundland, the versions found in Canada/ Newfoundland may be from Ireland.

We are left with this: judging that the versions found in Northern Ireland are older rests upon acknowledging the truth of Narváez's contention that, over time, the folk process streamlines complicated, garrulous broadsides into simpler, easier, less cluttered narratives. Yet how does this sit with the fact that the broadsides were written 'to make money', to appeal efficiently to a market, and were in any case modelled on older songs? These two notions conflict, and yet both enjoy valid currency: which ought at least to suggest that you cannot date variants by length alone. In any case, the Tracey variant is the longest and the sailor's one of the shortest, yet while both these versions have three-person narrative elements, no version found in the New World does.

My conclusion, therefore, must be this: that the Tracey version, mentioning St. John's, almost certainly does exhibit Newfoundland content. Equally, the sailor's version, mentioning 'saint Jon' (Saint John), relates just as near-certainly to that other place of Irish landing, New Brunswick. But that these two versions should have arisen in these two separate far-flung places, versions that are, indeed, the most different from each other of all the variants known to exist and yet which still hold so much in common: this suggests compellingly that both are New World revisions of an older, *Irish* song: a strong romantic song appealing enough for emigrants to take it with them when they sailed to the Eastern Seaboard fearing their poverty-forced exile, dreaming of home and hoping to remain in the hearts of those left behind: a song that spoke to all these desires, that in doing so embraced the seven-years-wandering element far more plausibly than the moonstruck-merchant alternative, and that was set in a place of aeons-old romance and natural beauty, down by the banks of Bellisle (which is connected to the mainland by an ancient bridge, so that all this straying and roaming for pleasure can be managed without boats, which are, you might otherwise think oddly, never mentioned by those visiting Belle Isle or Bell Island or wherever) at the eastern end of Lough Erne. County Fermanagh. Northern Ireland.

And the nearest thing to this original song, with its atmospherically Irish content, is the song that Doyle published in Newfoundland, and *The Penguin Book of Canadian Folk Songs* published in Toronto and London, and Bob Dylan recorded in Nashville, all on the cultural peripheries of Ireland.

As for relating 'Belle Isle' to Dylan, of course, there is still – after all the foregoing – a large question that remains unanswered: where did *Bob Dylan* find the song? Where did he encounter a

song so far from common in the mainland folkie world? He wasn't
going to have found it in Greenleaf & Mansfield, was he?

In a 1961 *Sing Out!* I found a listing of all the songs they'd
published in that magazine's first ten years' issues: and there was
'Blooming Bright Star Of Belle Isle' listed for the Summer 1957
issue. Would Bob Dylan have picked it up from that? Not at the
time, but perhaps from rifling through back-numbers in 1961
or '62, when he was mopping up songs like a sponge(r)? One
of those cases of him keeping things back for years before using
them, as he has been noted for doing with other songs? Yet this
can't be right: I can't believe Dylan would have got the words so
accurately after a 7/8-year gap. Then did he, perhaps, know the
song by heart all along? If so, well again: where from?

One tentative guess, now that 'Belle Isle' may be as much an
Irish ballad as a New World one: could it be that Dylan learnt
it from the man he's called 'the best ballad singer I'd ever heard
in my life' – Liam Clancy? Talking in 1984, in Ireland, about
the impact on him of the Clancy Brothers and Tommy Makem,
Dylan said: 'There was a bar [in New York] called The White
Horse Bar, and they were in there … and they'd be singing …
Irish folk songs. I – actually I learnt quite a few there myself…'[57]

This source – or, similarly, that of the McPeake Family[58] –
would perhaps be more probable if 'Belle Isle' itself had been
well-known in Ireland, which of course (as we've seen) it wasn't.
But even granted its absence from the Irish songbooks and so
on, there is still a beguiling possibility here, if we look at some
remarks of Liam Clancy's made in 1984:

[57] Bob Dylan, quoted from an interview conducted at Slane, Eire by Derek Bailey and
David Hammond for their TV/film documentary *The Clancy Brothers & Tommy Makem*
(London: Landseer Films Ltd., 1984), condensed for publication in *The Telegraph* #18,
1984; reprinted in *All Across The Telegraph* (details in Note 10). As a recent example of
Dylan's ability to file a song in his head for future, often far-into-the-future, use, I note
that on his US concert-tour of 1988 he performed for the first time (at least in public),
a song definitely learnt from the Clancy Brothers, the lovely 'Eileen Aroon'.

[58] John Way's 'Flutter Ye Mystic Ballad' (details Note 11) quotes this from Dylan's
Verona press conference, 1984: *Has Irish folk music had any influence…?* 'Oh yeah, very
much so… The McPeake Family, The Clancy Brothers. Have you heard the McPeake
Family? I used to listen to them all the time.' And also says that it was from the McPeakes
that 'Wild Mountain Thyme' was collected. And NB. the McPeakes were from Belfast,
Northern Ireland.

[A]n American woman ... Diane Hamilton ... was a wealthy woman who was interested in collecting ... I helped lug all her recording equipment around Ireland, and discovered music I never knew existed in our own country...[59]

More plausible, unfortunately for romance, is that (via *Sing Out!* or not) Dylan actually picked it up from the easiest, most mainstream collection in which it has appeared: the standard *Folk Songs of Canada* edited by Richard Johnson and, yep, Edith Fowke.

The very simple, flat fact that makes this the most likely and reasonable source for Dylan's learning 'Belle Isle' is that it is this version's lyric, and this version's alone, that Bob Dylan sings well-nigh word for word.

Even the omissions are identical. We noted earlier that Dylan omits the stock ending. Can it have been mere coincidence of good taste that Fowke, alone among those who published Newfoundland renditions of the song (and with the confidence of one pre-eminent in her field, and with, too, her refined intolerance toward 'hack journalist' elements) had not hesitated to omit the song's reductive closing detritus also?[60]

---

[59] Interviewed by Patrick Humphries, *The Telegraph* #18, 1984.

[60] Since the publication of 'Back To Belle Isle' (details in Note 51) I received, via *Telegraph* editor John Bauldie, the following correspondence from the distinguished Scandinavian 'Dylanologist' Christer Svensson (Molkom, Sweden: letter to John Bauldie, undated but summer 1988): 'a shortcut to the source of Dylan's *Self Portrait* version of "Belle Isle" ... [is] *Reprints From Sing Out! Volume 9* (New York: Sing Out! Publications, 1966)'. Svensson supports the contention that this was Dylan's source for the song by pointing out that the same collection contains three other songs also recorded on the *Self Portrait* album, namely 'Copper Kettle', 'It Hurts Me Too' and 'Little Sadie'.

Because *Broadside* was the new, supposedly irreverent magazine, born of the 'new', Greenwich Village, folk-revival mood of very early 1960s New York, and because Dylan contributed to it from the start, its significance has always been overstressed in the Dylan mythology. The result is that *Sing Out!* gets somewhat disregarded. Yet *Sing Out!* was, both inside Greenwich Village and beyond, by far the more widely-read, substantial and influential of the two publications. One of its important functions was in publishing consistently, down the years, large numbers of folksongs from widely disparate ethnic sources, greatly to the benefit of the revivalist performers and their ingénu contemporaries like Dylan.

Finally, there's a second large unanswered question about Bob Dylan's 'Belle Isle'. The present article has been entirely concerned with the *words* on the *Self Portrait* performance, and these do indeed match, except for slight performance error, those published in *Reprints From Sing Out! Volume 9*: but the *melody* Dylan uses is not as given there at all. Perhaps someone else would like to deal with where he found his tune?

A week before this, Dylan had held a press conference at the National Film Theatre in London to announce that he was going to make the film *Hearts of Fire*, with Richard Marquand directing (Dylan's first 'proper' film since *Pat Garrett and Billy the Kid* back in 1973), and I spent a couple of days just trying to acquire a ticket to get in to it. John Bauldie, editor of *The Telegraph*, came too. Robert Shelton, one of Dylan's biographers, was there also. Dylan was very surly for almost all the time, but gave out a couple of flashes of extraordinarily strong-spirited mischievousness. Another person there was an old friend of mine, a picture-researcher, and she took the opportunity to ask Dylan, on my behalf, where he'd learnt 'Belle Isle' from. Unfortunately she rushed in before I could explain to her that he would only respond if she could somehow put it into a context – wrap it up in noting that part of the film was to be made in Canada, for example, and tip the talk in that general direction. As it was she just asked him, out of the blue, with nothing to show that she was *interested* and not just another journalist with another random dumb question:

'Where did you learn "Belle Isle"?'

Bob Dylan just scowled and muttered '*I* dunno.'

NB. My special thanks go to Peter Narváez for his research assistance and great general help on the project. Grateful thanks are also due to Philip Hiscock of MUNFLA and to Beryl Moore at the Centre for English Language and Tradition at Sheffield University for additional assistance; to John Bauldie, editor of *The Telegraph*, Edith Fowke and John Moulden; and to the following people whose hospitality and co-operation made the present work possible: Sarah Beattie, Diana J. Gray, and Valerie and Ron Lowe (UK), and Cle Newhook (Newfoundland).

NB2. Added 2020: Edith Fowke died in Toronto on 28th March 1996; I drew on her work again later in giving some critical scrutiny to Dylan's album *Under The Red Sky* (1990) in *Song & Dance Man III: The Art of Bob Dylan* (London: Cassell Academic, 1999). John Bauldie died in England on 22nd October 1996. Most of my own work connections with John have been made clear already in the above. Peter Narváez died in St. John's on 11th November 2011; my last published connection with him was a review of his posthumous book *Sonny's Dream* in the Fall 2014 issue of *Journal of American Folklore* Vol. 127, No. 506.

Bobcats On The Road Again
(1989)

First published in The Independent, *6th June 1989. In the thirty years since, nothing has changed except the prices and technology. Streaming has made it almost impossible to make money from records now, so touring gives most performers their main income; in turn, concert tickets have to be yet more expensive – and if anything, Dylan toured Europe even more frequently in the decades since this survey.*

New Model Army goes on tour and another army goes too: those fans keen enough to see not one gig but many – in some cases every date. There are enough such people that the band sells season tickets, paring the cost for fans whose average age is in the teens and who sleep on floors, hitchhike and go hungry to follow the band on the road on the cheap. Many are unemployed, footloose and, within their lack-of-cash limits, fancy-free. Much of their time is spent filling in time, so when New Model Army tours, it isn't complicated to go too. The same is true for fans of most acts on the pop/rock circuits.

It's different for the Bobcats: the mostly middle-aged, mostly middle-class fans who travel round in Bob Dylan's wake when *he* launches into a Euro-tour, as he does with increasing frequency these days. Bobcats have complicated, structured lives – careers, families, mortgages, dinner-engagements – from which they must disentangle themselves to go following Dylan when those jingle-jangle mornings come around again.

There was a time when this disruption was rare: Dylan's concerts in 1978 at Earls Court and Blackbushe were his first string of UK dates in twelve years (and his first performance here at all since the Isle of Wight Festival of 1969).

Since then, things have speeded up considerably. Punters catching his every British gig had to get to 8 shows in 1981, 3 (including Eire) in 1984 and 7 in '87. Now, less than two years on, here we go again. Dylan plays Dublin June 3rd and 4th, Glasgow 6th, Birmingham 7th and Wembley on the 8th.

Making these five shows can be hard and expensive. There are no season-tickets on a Dylan tour, though there ought to be, since he, perhaps above all others, attracts exactly the kind of fervent follower who does want to see every show – and since, unlike most acts, whose 1980s incarnation comprises a slick professional sameness, Bob Dylan in concert is still a mercurial figure who really does offer a different performance every time.

Example: in Birmingham in 1987, those who went only to the first night – including the reviewers – saw a churlish, uninspired performance. Those who also caught the second and third nights saw shows wholly different from the first and from each other: shows alive to the moment, exciting and spontaneous and with only four or five songs performed more than once in the three-night run.

This does not come cheap. At £30 a pair for tickets this year (plus booking fee), each Bobcat couple will be paying £95 just for admission to the three UK shows. Add travelling to Glasgow, staying overnight (double-rooms at the Holiday Inn, not normally synonymous with luxury or extravagance, cost £99), a 300-mile journey to Birmingham next day, and so on: if you live in the provinces and don't have friends in these particular cities, the pair of you are looking at anything from £280 (in B&Bs and an economical car) to £500 – to see three concerts.

For many, however, time is the real problem – not only for the trip itself but for the hustling that comes first. Ray Leng, 40-year-old broker from Carlisle:

> I'm taking three days' holiday: all I can manage. The hassle really is trying to get better seats than the ones you've got. I mean, I rang the credit card hotline for Glasgow the moment the box office was supposed to start selling, and after 45 minutes on the last-number-redial button, I got through. The whole thing had only been a gossip item in one Scottish newspaper the day before: no real announcement, no ad, nothing; yet when the tickets

arrived, they were terrible: and the show was long since sold out. So then you start the real work: nights on the phone, trying different angles...

Or, if you're eminent academic Aidan Day, cursing Dylan for coming during the exams and 'desperately trying to swap round invigilation duties for the mornings after the concerts'.

Then there are the *real* Bobcats, who scorn seeing merely the *British* shows. Before these, Dylan is in Scandinavia (and then in Russia, though that was only a rumour, and proved untrue). After that he's in Ireland, Holland, Belgium, France, Spain, Italy, Turkey and Greece. Christian, 25, his car travel subsidised by Dad (but no plane fares), won't forgive himself if he misses a gig, and thinks he has problems: his Russian visa expires at midnight the night of Dylan's second mythical Leningrad show on June 2nd – and if this will need fine timing, so will getting from there to the Dublin show less than 24 hours later.

Keith Marsh, 35, a systems analyst, has booked his 3-weeks holiday to cover most of the tour.

> I'm starting in Dublin and if all goes well I'll be there till the last Italian show. I was on the phone to Italy last night. You need a contact in each country, to send you the ad when it comes out, to have some hope of getting tickets. I've got the Brussels. For the Hague I've got a number which is supposed to be the box office. I don't know anyone in Spain so all I can do is just turn up there and hope for the best...

And spare a thought for those whose partners *don't like Dylan*! Ah, the trouble and strife in these households, as one half takes the money and runs, leaving the other holding the babies, inventing illnesses for employers and muttering darkly about this extra-marital man with whom life must, inexplicably, be lived.

Some are philosophical about the disruption a new tour causes. The long-term partner of one eminent Dylanologist says: 'I take the piss a lot – all these blokes doing their ticket swapsies...' But she doesn't find it *abnormally* abnormal: 'I'm a football widow anyway, so it doesn't make much difference to me.' On the other hand here's Barbara, 27, aggrieved wife of '80s Dylan-convert Dave:

> It's not just hearing Dylan's awful voice every day; it's this gang of people ringing up all the time. The phone goes and it's bound to be for him: someone's heard a rumour about a new album, or they want their 599th cassette. When there's a tour, well, my heart sinks. There's no end to it then.

True: because of course after the tour itself there's the business of collecting the bootleg tapes of the tour...

Dylan himself, interviewed in 1986, made this comment: 'If something I write gets into people's heads and bothers them, that's nothing to do with me.'

Days Of 49: Bob Dylan's 49th Birthday Party, Manchester, England... (1990)

A shortened version was published in The Daily Telegraph, *29th May 1990, but the bit about the four Dylanologists in the restaurant has been newly added and is true.*

Sachas Hotel, in Manchester, UK, would be bizarre at any time. As you climb its marble staircase, a vast stuffed polar bear looms over you. For some reason there's a patch over its genitals. Above, huge mirrors cover the ceiling, multiplying the gaudy chandeliers. Downstairs, a springing tiger vaults over your breakfast. In the florid corridors this wanton distribution of dead animals becomes commonplace. The bedrooms offer, at random, four-posters, canopies, rooms with post-modernist balconies and rooms without windows. The effect is of an English hotel pretending to be a Las Vegas hotel pretending to be a French bordello.

This past weekend, its oddness has been compounded by 450 guests gathered to celebrate Bob Dylan's 49th birthday (undeterred by his absence) and to spend 48 hours discussing his life and work, watching him on film, attending a Bob Dylan Imitators Contest and buying the artefacts on sale in the weekend-long Bob Dylan Jumble Sale.

People have come from around the world. Two have flown in from Sweden without tickets, confident that enthusiasm will prevail over administrative hassle. A French contingent has an existential fight with the hotel bouncers and has to leave.

There is sometimes a tense divide between two main factions: the lit-crits and the trainspotters. During a panel discussion on the *Oh Mercy* album, I am rebuked for something I wrote about a 1966 song in 1972. Another participant is outraged that a professor from Canada should find on the album allusions to several Robert De Niro films.

The local TV company, running an item on this convention and on Dylan's (loose) connection with Manchester, tells us he once stayed at the Midland Hotel. 'No he didn't!' says a trainspotter. 'Yes he did!' says another. And as a roomful of people peers at silent amateur video footage, possibly of a man on stage in thick fog, someone snaps close-ups of the flickering screen. Perhaps he is the German who is rumoured to be seeking help in placing his Dylan photos with a publisher. If there is a contest for Most Unflattering Dylan Pictures Ever Taken, he's certainly a contender.

John Bauldie, Paul Williams, Stephen Scobie and I, along with my partner Sarah Beattie and our baby daughter Magdalena, retreat across the Muscovite bleakness of the square with the bus station in it, and find the refuge of a small, unhappy Turkish restaurant. Paul ignores everyone but John; Stephen ignores the baby; Sarah ignores the sad cuisine. We all see the stand-up card on each table touting Bull's Blood, and start scoffing. Four Dylanologists, and it's Stephen who comes up with the quote: 'Never could learn to drink that blood and call it wine'.

Saturday night climaxes with the Imitators Contest. This attracts the football-crowd faction. Ray looks a bit like Van Morrison but sounds nothing like Bob Dylan; Derek from Stamford resembles neither. Tony from Rhyl sings a song he's written himself; Mark offers a fair imitation of George Harrison singing 'All Along The Watchtower'. One of the contestants is a woman. There are two 'Hard Rain's and a 'Tambourine Man'. Why do they all choose such *long* songs? And why do they all think Bob Dylan cannot sing?

The convention has been staffed by the silver-haired mothers of the co-organisers.

'I can't believe it,' says one. 'They come in and spend fifty or sixty quid on their little books. I think they're all mad, really.' Yet she is working here, unpaid, till two every morning – and she has no interest in Dylan whatever. Under the lurid chandeliers and the mournful gaze of the polar bear, it can be hard to give an answer as to exactly why any of us are here. But then, Bob Dylan has always had a special talent for prompting that kind of question.

A Snapshot Of Dylan's Busy Working Life 1988-91 (1991)

A blogpost from January 1991.

Bob Dylan launches a West European tour in Zurich on Monday (January 28th) – yet his band was this week still in doubt. Guitarist G.E. Smith has quit and Dylan has reportedly sacked drummer Chris Parker. This leaves bassist Tony Garnier and Dylan himself. Two guitarists have work permits for the tour (unknown John Jackson and Dylan's ex-guitar-tuner César Carrillo Díaz). A pianist has been rumoured.

This is grist to the mill of a career that's been chaotic and eccentric since over a billion people saw Dylan looking and sounding raddled at Live Aid in 1985. Within weeks of that, Dylan appeared at Farm Aid and 1985's Moscow Poetry Festival, sang on 'Sun City' by Artists United Against Apartheid and released a box-set of his work.

Then he contributed to a Martin Luther King memorial; cut a rap track; toured stadiums with Tom Petty, releasing a tour video by Gillian *My Brilliant Career* Armstrong; co-starred in 1986's *Hearts of Fire* film flop; played an Amnesty International concert; issued five albums; played some Grateful Dead shows and début concerts in Israel, Finland, Brazil and Iceland (arriving for the first by public bus from Egypt); helped the Smithsonian Institution buy the Woody Guthrie Archive; did a benefit for handicapped children; charted as a Traveling Wilbury; and made a single to help Romanian orphans. In Paris in January 1990 he received one of France's highest cultural honours, Commandeur des Arts et des Lettres.

And that's been in his spare time... for since June 1988 Dylan has been fronting the Never-Ending Tour, quitting stadiums for small halls, endlessly re-shaping his 1960s material (folk and rock) and using a working repertoire of over 100 songs. Three consecutive shows have sometimes offered almost wholly different sets.

The tour has racked up odd moments. Dylan has been cycling to work, arriving at the stage door as the support act is playing. He has barred photographers, performed in half-darkness (usually without speaking) and twice wore a hooded jacket on-stage. In 1989 he ended concerts by jumping into the audience and disappearing before anyone knew what was going on – including the band, left up on stage playing.

Last year the tour moved on through Canada, summer festivals in Europe (including the Montreux Jazz Festival), and the USA. Since the guitarist quit, would-be replacements have been auditioning up on stage – during concerts!

After his European dates, Dylan returns to the States to receive a Lifetime Achievement Grammy. Meanwhile he and cousin Beth Zimmerman have opened a baby-clothes shop in Hollywood called 'Forever Young'. Bob Dylan will be 50 in May.

Bob Dylan In Glasgow One February Night
(1991)

This concert review was published in The Guardian *on 5th February 1991, three days after the concert.*

Bob Dylan shuffled on stage at the Scottish Exhibition Centre's Hall 3 on Saturday night wearing a tartan jacket and looking drunk. He obviously has a pre-City of Culture notion of Glasgow.

He played an unbelievable set. Strapping on his electric guitar, he began by asserting the strength and relevance of the best of his 1980s repertoire – 'Every Grain Of Sand', 'Property Of Jesus', 'Jokerman', 'Blind Willie McTell', 'Most Of The Time', 'What Was It You Wanted?' and 'Under The Red Sky'. And for once, on the long songs, he didn't miss out verses as a brutal way of getting through them faster.

Then, to the huge delight of the crowd, he moved to the piano for an inspired run through some of the songs he has dreamed out of the keyboard over the years: 'Black Crow Blues', 'I'll Keep It With Mine', 'Dear Landlord', 'Father Of Night' and 'Ring Them Bells'.

Next came a solo acoustic-guitar set of brand-new, unheard songs – one or two with lines as long and pauses as telling as 'Visions Of Johanna' when *that* was premiered to British audiences in May 1966, months ahead of the release of *Blonde On Blonde*.

Then it was back to the electric band for reminders of the peerless 1970s repertoire, including – sung live for the first time – 'Never Say Goodbye' and 'Black Diamond Bay'. He bowed out on the two strong closing numbers from his current LP, 'Handy Dandy' and 'Cat's In The Well'. For the encore, he brought on the Memphis Horns behind the band, to sustain him through a dexterous reading of 'Brownsville Girl' and a valedictory 'Wigwam'…

Actually, none of this is true except the tartan jacket and the looking drunk. The rest is a blueprint for a concert at which Bob Dylan would give generously across the whole range of what he can do. Instead we got what a poor Bob Dylan concert offers today: minimum effort, minimum show and an over-worn greatest-hits collection from the sixties.

He has already abandoned his recent work – there's no chance of hearing 'Jokerman' or 'Brownsville Girl'; every chance of hearing his n-thousandth 'All Along The Watchtower' or 'Maggie's Farm'. Of course he didn't finish with current album high-points (of which, contrary to the modish view, there are several) – he ended with 'Like A Rolling Stone'... The man has been finishing shows with that song on tour after tour for over 25 years!

Dylan has compared himself with Little Richard, Chuck Berry, Fats Domino: people who, like him, just keep on keeping on and who, he says, are as good as ever. This is depressing defeatism. These magnificent people each wrote a comparatively small number of successful songs and then, somewhere along the line in the early sixties, *stopped writing*. Each one has settled, since then, for touring round wearily re-singing the same twenty 'hits'.

It's wholly reductive of Bob Dylan's enormously prolific, decades-spanning work that he should be going round doing the same, as if he only ever wrote this small, rigid bunch of songs that runs from 'Don't Think Twice' to 'Leopard-Skin Pill-Box Hat'.

Muttering into the microphone, hiding in the oblivion of the guitars, under lights so low it was hard to see him even from the front row, Dylan was obviously suffering. 'God knows it's a struggle' was his most heartfelt line last night. It surely doesn't have to be this way.

Buddy Holly, Dylan &
The Aspirated Glottal Stop
(1992)

Published in Andrew Muir's first Dylan fanzine Homer, the slut *in September 1992.*

In a long-lost article I re-discovered recently – 'Wo-Uh-Ho Peggy Sue: Exploring A Teenage Queen Linguistically', in R. Serge Denisoff's journal *Popular Music & Society* (Bowling Green, Ohio, USA, Vol. 2, No. 3, Spring 1973) – contributor Maury Dean concludes that Dylan killed off the aspirated glottal stop – the 'wo-uh-ho' that Buddy Holly patented. But he has to conclude this, having begun by arguing that the aspirated glottal stop first arose in the early rock years to irradiate uninteresting lyrics with a non-language expressiveness: that 'wo-uh-hoes' were born out of need, to compensate for all the obligatory 'please be true's. It must follow from this that, as Dean puts it:

> Where have all the 'wo-uh-hoes' gone? ... From a musical nativity of Hollyesque gimmicks and Shannon falsettos, Dylan moved over to lyric poetry, and so did everybody else. Baroque vocalics evaporated... The aspirated glottal stop dinosaur was hunted down by a tribe of troubadours and poets.

Well of course in one way this was true: or rather, something similar is a truism: namely that Bob Dylan showed rock'n'roll how to grow up and be able to say things about a real world beyond bedroom walls of panting teenage angst. But was it *that* process that killed off the aspirated glottal stop? That would make it seem as if somehow Holly and Dylan were on opposite sides, whereas it's clear how much as one they are in spirit.

The pertinent, disentangling fact here is that before Bob Dylan ever made a record, let alone a rock'n'roll one with grown-up words, the aspirated glottal stop had already switched from being a tiny part of Buddy Holly's immensely resourceful expressive armoury to being an exaggerated device, an impoverished mechanism for insipid imitators. 'Hollyesque gimmicks and Shannon falsettos' can only refer to that in-limbo era after Holly's bodily death and just before Bob Dylan's musical birth.

By 1961, when rock'n'roll but rarely made the charts anymore, the aspirated glottal stop was already uncomfortably implanted in the soggy body of Paramoronic, Vintonised, Tillotsonated, Roed and Berried pop that had replaced rock'n'roll and filled up the charts. Dylan didn't need to kill it. By then it *was* just a gimmick and therefore already deader than Buddy Holly will ever be.

In any case, Bob Dylan, with his rich variety of voices – voices that can carve out syllables as if from stone and make numinous words as 'unpoetically' ordinary as 'dollar', 'road' and 'hand' – is the last person Maury Dean should look to as offering a division between those with vocal style and those who sing 'important words'. No-one who appreciates Bob Dylan *or* Buddy Holly could go along with the idea that someone singing 'poetry', or social comment, should abandon all vocal devices in favour of some sort of unadorned 'straightforwardness'. This is not the Bob Dylan but the Pete Seeger worldview – and Pete Seeger could no more have killed off the aspirated glottal stop than Lee Harvey Oswald.

Columbia Celebrates:
Dylan 30th Anniversary Concert
(1992)

This was written for The Daily Telegraph *straight after the event and published on 19th October 1992. I could wish the comments still applied about Bob's unwillingness to promote his own latest album in concert or to see himself as part of the entertainment industry – but things have changed (and not only those things). I republished it on a blog of mine in March 2014.*

Columbia Records Celebrates the Music of Bob Dylan at Madison Square Garden on Friday night – with a huge roster of stars – must have puzzled Dylan more than the rest of those present.

For four and a half years now his Never-Ending Tour has criss-crossed the back roads of America – with the odd diversion into Europe, South America and Hawaii – with Dylan cycling to work, playing small halls with his anonymous band, refusing to admit press photographers and avoiding any notion of promoting his latest releases. Most of the time, his record company doesn't even know where he is.

In bizarre contrast, it was suddenly decreed from on corporate high that there was to be a Live Aid-Lennon Memorial type megabash to 'celebrate' his 30th anniversary on the Columbia label. That he has not always been on Columbia, that they first signed him thirty-*one* years ago, and that the celebration has come seven months too late to mark the anniversary of his first release – none of this mattered either to the media machine selling the event to TV around the world or to the fans at the 4-hour-plus show.

Many stars rumoured to be coming did not materialise – Paul Simon, Elvis Costello, Van Morrison – and there were conspicuous absentees – Joan Baez, Robbie Robertson – but there were plenty left, one act following another in impressively quick succession, serviced by roadies working like a pit-stop team and a house band led by ex-Dylan guitarist G.E. Smith.

John Mellencamp, loudly unexciting, Johnny Winter, louder and worse, Kris Kristofferson crunching through 'I'll Be Your Baby Tonight' and the record-company president giving a speech – these were the lowlights.

There were others whose sheer presence contributed authority and excitement: Johnny Cash, the man in the short black coat, and surprise guest Stevie Wonder.

The younger acts were a very mixed bunch. Sophie B. Hawkins proved a pale pretender to Laura Nyro territory. Eddie Vedder from Pearl Jam gave a fine folkclub performance of 'Masters Of War' successfully transposed to the 20,000-seater venue, but the song sounded dated and pious. Mary Chapin Carpenter, Shawn Colvin and Rosanne Cash were merely competent on 'You Ain't Goin' Nowhere', while Tracy Chapman managed an odd mix of the powerful and cosy on an anthem with no obvious current applicability, 'The Times They Are A-Changin''.

Where were the *real* young interpreters? Where were Jason & The Scorchers and The Poster Children? The one comparative newcomer whose presence did create real electricity was Sinéad O'Connor – and it was solely her presence that did it. Large parts of the crowd booed, laughably unmindful of the events of 1966 and with real hatred seething through the hall. It was a repulsive indictment of the mob mentality at stadium-rock events.

Neil Young took over with a customarily robust performance. Georges Harrison and Thorogood, Chrissie Hynde, The Band, The O'Jays, Tom Petty, Ron Wood and Roger McGuinn all acquitted themselves well enough, but the heavyweight honours went to Lou Reed, choosing, to his credit, an obscure early-eighties song, 'Foot Of Pride', which was fierce and committed; The Clancy Brothers and Tommy Makem with a gloriously unrockist, moving 'When The Ship Comes In', Clapton with a real reoccupation of 'Don't Think Twice, It's All Right' as a churning blues; and Charles Dickens lookalike Willie Nelson, who was one of the oldest present and chose the newest song, 1989's great, and savagely apt, 'What Was It You Wanted?'.

Then, at the end, after the ballyhoo, on came Bob Dylan – and with the feeling and deft intelligence that created this great sweep of musics and poetry, he chose to begin with 'Song To Woody', stressing that *he* sees himself in a line of figures like Guthrie and Leadbelly: people who took their own roads and didn't serve the entertainment industry.

A couple more songs – a solo 'It's Alright, Ma' and a genuinely celebratory 'My Back Pages' shared with an inner circle of compadres, an inevitably rabble-rousing finale with everyone 'Knockin' On Heaven's Door' and in the final end a solo 'Girl From The North Country': a poignant choice and a subdued performance no more attuned to the demands of the big media event than Dylan ever is.

And next month he releases a new album. It doesn't have one Bob Dylan song on it, it's his first solo acoustic 'product' in 28 years, and it's a mixture of folk ballads and pre-war country blues, with a Stephen Foster song and a nursery rhyme thrown in. Almost no-one who was at Madison Square Garden last Friday night will buy it, and Bob will be back in the small halls.

Waiting For Time Out Of Mind
(1997)

Published as part of my first column in ISIS, *June 1997, this now seems a useful reminder of how things were, or seemed, at the time. We knew* Time Out Of Mind *had been recorded in January '97 but it remained unreleased until the last day of September. (The bit below about musicians' studio enthusiasms was used again as an entry in* The Bob Dylan Encyclopedia, *but the omitted other half of the* ISIS *column comprised no longer useful reviews of three compilation albums.)*

It would have been great to begin this new column with a paean to something wonderful. *Time Out Of Mind*, ideally. I can't remember when a new Bob Dylan album was so strongly yearned for, or had such high hopes riding on it.

This is something to do with how long Dylan has been doing the same songs over and over again ad infinitum, and mostly the very old and obvious ones, so that the passion to hear a whole album of new Dylan songs is almost desperate. And there's the sheer fact of how long it's been since such an album: a longer gap than from *The Times They Are A-Changin'* through to *Nashville Skyline*.

The yearning for *Time Out Of Mind* is also to do with the rumoured length of the songs, and the choice of a producer about whom one may not feel unreserved enthusiasm but whose strengths include making Bob *bother* properly. That Dylan has gone back to him, after years of only giving people one restive try before switching to another modish industry favourite, is surely A Good Sign. And then there's that rumoured total running time of 76 minutes (76 minutes! *Under The Red Sky* was 35). And then there are those enticing Jim Dickinson-generated stories that came out of the studio...

159

Of course no-one should ever believe session musicians. They always come out saying it's Bob's best since *Blonde On Blonde* and then it turns out to be *Down In The Groove*. It's natural that they should be so deluded. First, they're working in the presence of a genius, so they're bound to be dazzled, even if his genius isn't present; second, they've been hearing the playbacks on monumentally expensive speakers and very high-quality drugs; and thirdly, they have in mind the best tracks and the best mixes, which Dylan then deletes before the rest of us are offered the album.

Normally. But this time... well, you just can't help but get your hopes up.

And then again, Dylan's illness has made a lot of us stop moaning about what he's been doing and not doing lately, and glow with warmth in the realisation of how ardently positive we feel about him underneath. You don't miss your water till it turns a funny colour. Not long before news of his illness broke, I had a number of conversations with people who'd been feeling for some months, for the first time ever, that they weren't all that bothered whether they heard, or even received cassettes of, all the concerts on the last leg of the tour, and who were more or less bemoaning having to go to the imminent shows.

How his going into hospital changed all that! Now we've all sorely missed hearing 'All Along The Watchtower' just those few precious extra times. And we've been fantasising about (in some cases planning to be) attending Bob's first post-illness concerts.

The Genuine Bootleg Series Volume 3 (1999)

For a while I wrote a monthly column for ISIS, called 'Searching For A Gem', and this was one of them, reviewing a real bootleg (as opposed to the Official Bootlegs initiated by Dylan's office manager Jeff Rosen); the real The Genuine Bootleg Series Volume 3, *was a 3-CD set of 54 tracks recorded between 1961 and 1997, produced by 'Scorpio'. More generally this column addressed questions about Dylan's creativity and the impact of concert audiences on his work.*

Plenty of gems here, though not always where you might expect. Disc 1 relies heavily on the 'Smith home tapes – 1962': no further information, though these used to be called the McKenzie Tapes. They're in vastly upgraded quality. (The notes are deliberately vague – this is the politics of bootlegging – and some dates wrong. The jolly 'If You Gotta Go, Go Now' is not 'unknown location, 1965' but from the 1964 Hallowe'en concert.)

The *chronology* of Disc 1 starts from the already-circulated 1961 Oscar Brand show performance – just weeks before Dylan recorded his début LP – of 'Sally Gal' and the fascinating 'The Girl I Left Behind'. It ends in the different universe of the Sheffield Gaumont performance on 16th May 1966 of 'Visions Of Johanna'.

Disc 2's chronology runs from the same night's 'Mister [sic] Tambourine Man' through Basement Tapes and early 1970s album outtakes to the John Hammond tribute show performance of 'Simple Twist Of Fate' and 'Oh! [sic] Sister' on 10th September 1975. The last disc begins with Bob and Joan's 'Never Let Me Go' live in Montreal three months later and finishes with a live 'Blind Willie McTell' of exasperating ugliness from 1997.

There are some intelligent minor adjustments made to these chronologies in the running-order, though why begin with a 1962 'Hard Times In New York' [sic] rather than the 1961 'Sally Gal'?

It does make sense that Disc 1 ends with the Liverpool 'Leopard-Skin Pill-Box Hat', two days before Sheffield, simply because in the concerts the electric performances followed the acoustic ones. And what a *rocking* 'Hat'!

It makes delightful sense to start Disc 2 with a live 1966 cut (that golden 'Mr. Tambourine Man'), followed by five Basement Tapes cuts: the jump from the one to the other brings to our attention anew the astonishing creativity of the artist Bob Dylan then was, and the joy-inducing leap he made, a leap no-one could have asked for or dreamt of, in little over a year.

To hear, as we do here, the 1967 'This Wheel's On Fire' straight after the drug-laced genius of Sheffield's 'Mr. Tambourine Man' is to recognise afresh that those 1967 songs were not just a refusal to rest on laurels but a powerful avowal of Dylan's undimmed inventiveness. Just as no-one had ever written a song remotely like 'Mr. Tambourine Man' or 'Visions Of Johanna', so no-one had ever written songs like 'This Wheel's On Fire' before, nor made music as spacey and eerie and eye-of-the-universe, as passion-driven weird, and so transcendently different from their musical miracles of the previous year.

After all the valid, admirable context-setting that has surrounded the Basement Tapes in recent years, from Roy Kelly's 'Bunch Of Basement Noise In G' (*Telegraph* 43, Autumn '92) to Greil Marcus's *Invisible Republic* and the reissue of the Harry Smith anthology – work that stressed the folk roots and whiskery communal origins of those prolific Big Pink sessions – it's exciting, here, to jump into 1967 from a very different perspective, so that what hits you is how *new* these inspired tracks were.

What also hits you is that one of the best things about the acoustic halves of the 1966 concerts is the silence of the audience. In Sheffield, he plays the most astonishing harmonica solos these people had ever heard in his transcendent 'Mr. Tambourine Man', especially the gorgeously *long* solo in the middle (which shows, as no other does, how this spacey, newly-invented way of using the instrument begins its reverie from the Irish jig) and at its consummate conclusion… not a sound, not a ripple of applause, no whoop or holler.

It might be said that if 1999's Bob Dylan produced a solo a tenth as well-executed or inspired, his audience would give itself a mass heart attack, granted the ecstasies into which it throws itself whenever he now manages to blow into the instrument at all. It couldn't happen. One of the reasons why he *can't* offer even 10% on harp now of what he offered then is because the audiences he now courts are so noisy. The tiresome vamping he goes in for, the pandering to the lowest common denominator of inebriated audience mood – never trust the mob – may be more 'fun' for Bob up on stage, but it's cheap fun and distracts the artist in him. The benign silence of the old audience repaid him incomparably better. This silence is audible, in the attention it allowed him to pay to his own playing, so that this became so imaginatively expressive of his most subtle and unfettered feelings, in which crowd-pleasing played no part, so that the solo you hear is at once intensely intimate and wholly open to the moment. It takes you not on a clumping, ineptly played romp across a couple of dully doodling notes fired by a bit of coarse, hey!-rock'n'roll! excitement, but on an infinitely fluid, perfectly executed exploratory journey through the psyche of a great, great artist.

Disc 3 has good and bad chronology slippages. Why, in mid-disc, go from a studio outtake of 'Series Of Dreams' to a Nara City 'Ring Them Bells' from five years later, only to then revert to two 1990 outtakes from *Under The Red Sky*? Why is the Willie Nelson Bash 1993 'Hard Times' placed after two 1994 recordings and after that 1997 'McTell'? Why are the two 1994 tracks – the Jimmie Rodgers Tribute outtake of 'Blue Eyed Jane' [sic] and the Elvis Presley Tribute outtake 'Anyway [sic] You Want Me' – in reverse order? Yet the juggling of dates at the end is in the spirit that Bob Dylan brings to the selection of his albums' last tracks. This ends with the 1995 Sinatra Tribute's 'Restless Farewell'. A nice touch.

One thing, though: this collection is strikingly less necessary than Volumes 1 and 2. One of its compelling inclusions was rumoured to be going to be a superior 'I'm Not There (1956)', which is not in fact here. The corollary is that there are fewer highlights here and an awful lot of stuff we've got already.

Sometimes there's *less* than we've got already: the Oscar Brand Show tracks omit the instructive spoken commentary Dylan offers about finding old songs. Why miss this out? Nor is there any upgrade in audio quality. In the case of the Hollywood Bowl 'From A Buick 6', a concert so recently released in its entirety, the quality is *inferior* here.

Many tracks seem to be here for no reason. How necessary are so-called stereo mixes of the Basement Tapes material, when Dylan's voice is only in one speaker? Why the already widely circulated duet-with-Emmylou version of 'Blue-Eyed Jane'?

There's also a heavy reliance on upgrades of quality to justify inclusions. This is justified with the 'Smith' tapes, and for the 1969 studio recordings of 'Folsom Prison Blues' and 'Ring Of Fire', which have always been in atrocious quality and are here upgraded to merely poor instead. But is such reissue necessary for 'Never Let Me Go'? Certainly we don't need 'Lily, Rosemary And The Jack Of Hearts' or 'If You See Her, Say Hello': they're no different and no better than before.

Tracks that *are* previously unheard are often so marginally different from the familiar that a 2-CD set at a more modest price might have been more reasonable. 'Shot Of Love' is mildly interesting for its upfront piano in the mix; the 'Watered-Down Love' take is simply a drearily inferior one. So is 'Knockin' On Heaven's Door'. 'Sign Language' is another pea from the same pod. Nor can I work up much enthusiasm for the non-reggae 1978 rehearsal 'Blowin' In The Wind' (the reggae version is all too foreshortened: nobody's fault but no big deal either), or for a '78 rehearsal 'Ballad Of A Thin Man'. These weren't exactly top of my list of Unreleased Bob Dylan Wants.

Of course the fanatic inside me can say that any previously unavailable material is 'necessary' – but I don't believe it. You can't hear everything, and when you learn of something that sounds crucial and wonderful, and you acquire it, well, it soon slots in amongst the rest. It doesn't change your life. Bob Dylan has already done what he's going to do in that direction, or you wouldn't be in this position in the first place.

Even if you outlive Bob Dylan by several decades, it's unlikely you'll hear everything he's done. And if you die prematurely, are you really the poorer for never hearing some of these previously unheard works? Someone said to me only today what a shame it was that John Bauldie wasn't around for the unmasking of The Man Who Cried Judas… and I thought, well, maybe… I've often thought along similar lines myself – I wonder how John would have liked 'Not Dark Yet'? What would Allen Ginsberg have thought of 'Highlands'? What would Robert Shelton have made of Bob singing for the pope? When it comes down to it, the fact that these people missed bits of Bob Dylan's work, or that most of us will miss other bits in the end, just doesn't much matter. Being alive or dead matters. And even that only matters to you while you're alive.

Meanwhile, some tracks make you feel more alive than others. I'd never have predicted that the Sinatra Birthday Bash 'Restless Farewell' would be a minor highlight. After the TV spectacle of Dylan performing it with all the presence of a wooden spoon and looking at least as old and awful as Sinatra himself, it's a delight to re-encounter it, in fine quality, as a sustained, considered performance, blotched only once by that posturing gargle he gives us sometimes, which never fails to coarsen things – and its twin assassin, the silly sob, on the title phrase at the end of the first verse.

Throughout the rest, he's careful, discreet, alert to what he's on about: so much so that it makes you conjecture as to how it might have seemed if it were a new song, and on *Time Out Of Mind*. Many's the person who would rush to say what a major work it was – a major work of retrospection. Ironic, since it was not only a work of his youth but always regarded as very minor work. Yet he achieves with this revisit a refashioning that is expressive for the middle-aged artist. One or two of the lines do betray an immaturity, but in general his 1995 performance re-occupies and renews the material. Whoever would have guessed?

Another minor highlight is the *riveting* outtake of 'T.V. Talkin' Song'. Gone is the flaccid, hesitant self-imitation and despite a few inferior lines in what is obviously an earlier draft of the lyric, we get real menace, a genuinely dangerous edge, and a track like no other in his work. Dylan should have had the courage of his conviction – conviction so authentic and audible – and issued *this* version on the album. The ending is still feeble, but as a recording, a dramatic monologue, a creation, it's real, it's got real bite and it sizzles.

Altogether dodgier, but a welcome part of the collection, is the 1994 recording of the Elvis Presley song 'Any Way You Want Me' – one of Elvis's sexiest, most sensuously restless, numinous performances. Dylan, vocally shaky and untrustworthy, might be said to ruin it. I don't feel that. It seems to me totally in the spirit of Elvis, as signalled by the first instrumental noises, before the all-too-early entrance of the other, dumbo musos, who've never heard the Elvis record in their lives and are determined to plonk their heavy-dudeness all over the top of it – but Bob is remembering Elvis with accurate, genuine affection, straight down the years back to Hibbing, 1957.

Another surprise is 'Rita May', not for her main comic body, but for the splendid lines delivered by a girl chorus most uncharacteristic of the *Desire* sessions: 'I like the boys with the dreamy eyes / *Something* sighs / And the football thighs… / Don't think twice / It's so nice!'

The collection's major highlight, however, is the most unpredictable one. Who would have thought that an outtake of 'If Not For You' would be it? Here we have three fascinating tracks from 'New Morning' – a beautifully humane, tentative try-out of 'Went To See The Gypsy', with Dylan on electric piano sounding, in the intro, for all the world like 1970s Nina Simone on keyboards; a 'Sign On The Window' with orchestral overdubs as clumsy and over-larded as at Nara City two decades later – and a rapturously good 'If Not For You' that uses what sounds like a string quartet.

How many tracks received this orchestral treatment before it was shelved? How differently *New Morning* would have been perceived had these gone ahead! Instead of standing in contrast to the string-soaked, much-derided *Self Portrait*, it would have seemed like more of the same. Yet 'If Not For You' argues something else again.

Insinuatingly slow, thrillingly relaxed and intimate, Dylan sounds at peace and at home with the strings, and his spontaneous vocal invention is pressed fully into the service of a warm, expressive love. It makes me appreciate how wonderful a thing his voice was in this period – a period so under-appreciated by the great majority of us who, at the time, were busy regretting his defection from the Planet Cool instead of appreciating the new and different gifts he was bringing.

The song rises to match this vocal generosity: it seems a more substantial creation than we've been allowed to glimpse before: a devotional song, not mere pop. The robins singing – you can hear the point of all that here: it's an intimate, good-humoured confession of how hard it is to articulate *why* somebody feels they'd be less alive if not for their lover. And when he sings that 'The day would surely have to break', you mark the serious pun on 'break', balanced by 'My sky would fall'. Gem is too poor a word – and on that note I'll just say fare thee well.

In Bob Dylan's Minnesota Footsteps
(1999)

A shortened version was published in The Daily Telegraph, *20th November 1999; most of this fuller version formed an* ISIS *column in March-April 2000, and was reprinted in the book* Bob Dylan Anthology Volume 2: 20 Years of ISIS, *2005. Needless to say, Hibbing has changed since this was written, and so has its level of interest in Bob Dylan.*

If you're travelin' in the North Country fair / Where the wind hits heavy on the borderline...

My first glimpses of Minnesota made me think of Newfoundland. The plane came down through heavy raincloud, and by the time we emerged beneath it, we were hovering just above wet suburban rooftops and pointy green trees. At Minneapolis' grey airport, the people waiting to meet arriving passengers stood in dirty pastel padded jackets and nylon anoraks, with collapsing Cabbage Patch Doll faces and a cheerful shared pastiness I remembered from Newfie communities.

The same boisterous underclass crowds the public buses that take you, if you're mad, to Bloomington's Mall of America (the USA's biggest), or else the other way, on the $1, half-hour ride to downtown St Paul, Minneapolis' so-called Twin City. Every time I take a bus people banter on the same two topics: sports teams (the Vikings vs. the Packers) and Clinton's indiscretions. Bob Dylan, who rides in limousines now but knows these people of old, said presciently in 1983: 'America is a divided nation right now. It doesn't know whether to follow the President or the Green Bay Packers.' Plus ça change, as they say up in Canada.

But Newfoundland is poor and white; Minnesota, headquarters of many a Fortune 500 corporation, including 3M and Honeywell, is growing richer faster than most other states, and is 11th in per capita income; and while the state is 94% Caucasian, the Twin

Cities are 12% black and include a significant Hmong community brought here by charitable churches in the early 1990s.

The two downtowns are separated by the Mississippi River, that 'strong brown god', as T.S. Eliot called it, which, upstate from here, begins its epic journey from the frozen north all the way to New Orleans. St Paul is its northernmost port.

Something else divides the Twin Cities, St Paul claiming to be 'the last city of the East' and Minneapolis 'first city of the West', or at any rate the Midwest.

It seems true. Minneapolis, far larger, blasts up at the big sky with ultramodern architecture clustered like gargantuan shining organ-pipes, rising to overlook the beginning of that prairie flatness, that heartland wilderness to the west. Downtown St Paul looks like a compressed chunk of Manhattan, with a core of old stone buildings in big pre-war blocks as wide as they are tall, like the splendidly-named and beautifully-finished Bockstruck's, set on flinty streets with iron lampposts, with smart, dark bars and the elegant ghost of F. Scott Fitzgerald, who was not only born and raised here but moved back again to write *This Side of Paradise*.

The two do fuse, though. Uptown St Paul is west of the Mississippi, its Grand Avenue houses dithering between Eastern and Midwestern styles, while Minneapolis includes the unprairie-like Dinkytown, to walk through which now is like having a nightmare that it's the 1970s again. Litter-blown streets where sordid shops you wouldn't want to go into peter out into a bleakness of suburban villas turned over to being frat houses. The students are mostly about 19, mostly already grossly overweight and with eyes as dead as doornails. You look in vain for anywhere you'd want to have a drink or something to eat. The bar I find is like some bad South London pub taken over by the Bodysnatchers. The 10 O'Clock Scholar is long gone, but the Purple Onion remains. It is indistinguishable from a Howard Johnson coffee shop. The ghost of Bob Dylan is not here.

I was in Minnesota to follow his footsteps, and though he was born in the North Minnesotan city of Duluth, on the shores of Lake Superior, his family moved 75 miles further northwest when he was a child, up into the Iron Range, to the town of Hibbing, site of the world's largest open pit mine ('the biggest hole dug by man'), where he grew up and went to school. Then he endured a while at the University of Minnesota in Minneapolis before dropping out and heading toward New York City, fame, fortune and greatness.

My / youth was spent wildly among the snowy hills an / sky blue lakes, willow fields an abandoned open / pit mines...

Hibbing is the smallest and the most important place in Dylan's Minnesotan past. I hired a car for next to nothing and set off from St Paul up the old Highway 65 to see it. It was November, and snowy. Flat, frozen fields, Dutch-roof barns, loblolly pines and stripped silver birch trees, Lutheran churches, dilapidated fencing, pick-up trucks more frequent than cars. The timeless scenery of telegraph poles and roadside mailboxes, the aluminium-grey road stretching out flat ahead, and signs for Jumbo Leeches and Flathead Worms and snowmobiles for sale.

The sky was bright blue, a beautiful day. Where I stopped to breathe the air outside, a dead deer, bony but immaculate, lay on its side in the snowy grass six yards from the road I stopped at Rob's chalet-style place for coffee. The five men in there, all wearing check shirts or overhauls, were drinking bourbon & soda in ice-filled glasses, with beer chasers. As if on cue, their conversation was immediately about hunting. 'I swear, I lit a cigarette and he's still lookin' at me. It's like he's sayin' I know you ain't got a licence...' A notice proclaimed 'MEAT RAFFLE every Saturday'.

A hundred miles north of St Paul I passed through McGrath, pop. 62, with its Catholic church, Calvary Presbyterian Church and Pliny Graveyard. Then trailer-homes and more white clapboard than before, more and more picturesque old barns, grain elevators like cocktail shakers. On the radio they were announcing a bear-dressing contest.

The closer I came to the Iron Range towns, the narrower and emptier the roads grew, and the taller the trees, and the more the banks of snow pressed in from the verges. The whole hushed place turned into Winter Wonderland – and cocooned inside it, Hibbing shone and twinkled like the set for a *Perry Como Christmas Special*.

It would have been in Canada but for a mistake on a historic map. Deep in snow but easy to move around, it epitomises pleasant, old-fashioned small-town life. It's not such a small town, either. At 186 square miles, its grid of leafy, spacious streets is the state's largest by area. The people are exceptionally equable, and make you welcome. It almost makes you wonder why Bob Dylan ever left.

He lived here from the age of six until almost twenty. To begin with, young Robert slept on the floor in Grandma Florence's house; later, this elder son of Abram Zimmerman the hardware-store owner sometimes went debt-collecting with him in the poorer parts of town. In the front room at 2425, 7th Avenue East, his boyhood home, Bob practised in his first and nameless beat group, survived his Bar Mitzvah party and stared out the window dreaming of escape. It was a mere couple of blocks' walk to Hibbing High School.

And what a school. You'd never know it from anything Dylan's let slip, but iron ore built Hibbing a school of palatial grandeur that cost four million dollars in 1920-23, with a sanitised medieval castle exterior in brick and Indiana limestone, hand-moulded ceilings, a 75-foot-long oil painting in the library, marble steps with solid brass handrails and, in the 1825-seater auditorium, six Belgian crystal chandeliers now worth a quarter of a million each and a stage that can hold the Minnesota Symphony Orchestra.

In 1958, with his group the Golden Chords, Dylan stood hammering on Hibbing High School's 1922 Steinway Grand piano (breaking a pedal in the process) and shouting out rock'n'roll songs at the annual student concert... and got laughed at by some, up there onstage in an auditorium so lavish and ornate, and with such acoustic excellence, that it almost justifies critic Stephen Scobie's conceit that 'Every stage Bob Dylan has played on for the past thirty years has been, after Hibbing High School Auditorium, an anticlimax.'

The hotel manager, Debra Jensen, rings her friend Larry Furlong, one of Bob's old classmates, and he readily agrees to show me around the school. Debby drives me over, and we meet

Larry on the snowy steps outside the school. Thin, nervous, a little morose, Larry neither exaggerates nor underplays his Dylan connections. We walk around inside. I gasp at the sheer size of it all. Imagine how it was when you were new there. We stand in the huge library and Debby tells me she still has nightmares about being little and finding her way around it. One class or activity, she says, would be in the basement and the next on the 4th floor, and they were allowed three minutes to get there.

'Gym class to choir was the killer,' says Debby's brother Denny, who has joined us. He's acting as stage manager for the school production that's in rehearsal. I'm lucky, because this means everything's open and functioning backstage – and he asks if I'd like to see That Piano.

So we go to one side at the back of the stage, and Denny unlocks this long, low cupboard door and we roll out that big black Steinway sideways, until it's right there in front of me, throbbing with history. And I'm allowed to play it for a minute. Some sort of bluesy riff seems called for. It sounds great. I've never encountered so rich and deep a tone. It is a double thrill to play it. There I am, forty-odd years on, standing on that stage, looking out into that impossibly glamorous auditorium, thumping on the Steinway the teenage Bob Zimmerman had played.

Larry offers me a guided tour of town, so we leave the others and the school, whose principal these days is the aptly named Mr. Muster. Larry sits in the passenger seat and says 'turn left here, now first right. OK, see that building, that's where Abe's hardware store was', and so on. You can't beat this kind of helpfulness: it's extraordinary and precious.

a train line cuts the ground / showin' where the fathers an' mothers / of me an' my friends had picked / up an' moved from / north Hibbing / t'south Hibbing. / old north Hibbing.../ deserted / already dead / with its old stone courthouse / decayin' in the wind...

Bobby often explored North Hibbing's ghost town, where everyone lived before they moved them two miles south to dig out the ore they were sitting on. Larry guides me there, and the whole place is just snow-covered ground. I'd never have known a town had been there – I can't even see any remnants. We walk toward the edge of the vast, vast hole far down below us, filled like a lake of iron-brown water, and beyond it the huge orange sun is dropping onto the snowy hills.

Teenage Bob, wannabe Brando & Dean in black leathers, hung around the railroad tracks and roared off on a motorbike with dirty-blonde-haired Echo Helstrom, his first real girl from the North Country.

Hibbing's got schools, churches, grocery stores an' a jail ... high school football games an' a movie house ... corner bars with polka bands ... Hibbing's a good ol' town.

Dylan's mixed feelings about Hibbing are expressed perfectly in that one last line from 'My Life In A Stolen Moment'. And back in the Class of '59 yearbook, he had defiantly stated his ambition as 'To join Little Richard'. Hibbing and Bob Dylan have had a difficult relationship ever since.

In fact Minnesota altogether has a problem with Dylan. They resent his having left; they still resent his rudeness of forty years ago. Minnesotans hear tell he was difficult despite being shown much tolerance; they feel he bit the hand that nurtured him and/or denied his roots. Invoking the stroppy teenager, they're determinedly unimpressed by the great artist.

Thought I'd shaken the wonder and the phantoms of my youth / Rainy days on the Great Lakes, walkin' the hills of old Duluth...

In consequence, to the soul's delight and the professional eye's puzzlement, there is no exploitation of Dylan's incandescent name by the Heritage Industry. Look at how poor Liverpool exploits Beatledom: it's one of the city's biggest revenue sources. Yet Dylan, whose impact has at least arguably equalled The Beatles', is conspicuously absent from Minnesota tourism bumph at state level and as regards Duluth. Even Hibbing's 1991 coffee-table puffery *On the Move Since 1893* manages only this:

> Some contemporary well-known natives include Rudy Perpich; Kevin McHale; Jeno Paulucci, founder of Jeno's Pizza; Bob Dylan, folk musician, songwriter; Roger Maris and Vincent Bugliosi, Charles Manson Trial prosecutor.

35 miles away, the Judy Garland Museum welcomes you to the Garland Birthplace Historic Home, Grand Rapids ('It's a swell state, Minnesota ... We lived in a white house with a garden. It's a beautiful, beautiful town,' quoth Judy in the brochure in my Minnesota press pack). In Duluth, Dylan's birthplace home is disregarded; in Hibbing, the many pilgrims who come to the 7th Avenue house must simply decide whether to ring the bell and disturb the present owner or not.

I spent an hour there, by appointment, attuning to Bob's adolescent ghost inside those walls, and staring out at cold-storage suburbia as he must so often have done. The easy-going owner, Greg French, will soon tire of this sort of thing, just as High School staff will tire of letting people like me stand on their stage and play that Steinway. Quite rightly, Greg restricts visitors to the living-room. You can't go poking around in Bob's old bedroom any more. It's another adolescent's now.

When the Zimmerman house went on sale in 1989, the realtor had enquiries from all over the Dylan-fan world, and thought he'd make his fortune. This came to nothing, and Greg paid $45,000 for the flat-roofed, two-storey, 1940s property (in 'Mediterranean Moderne' style), not because it was Dylan's but because it was the best bargain in the neighbourhood at the time.

Once, a state tourism 'PR specialist' called, to ask Greg if he'd consider doing B&B. Er, that's it. Meanwhile there's nothing but a downtown bar-café called Zimmy's to cater to the swell of Dylan-visitors, a swell that cannot but rise in the imminent future.

This extraordinary non-exploitation might seem bizarrely nose-and-face syndrome: a collective sulking at least as immature as the Dylan who said 'You're boring, I'm off' four decades ago.

This communal hurt is quite misplaced. Those who actually knew him in the past – ex-classmates who gladly gave me their time, like Larry Furlong and Margaret Toivola (who let me look through her now-priceless copy of that 1959 High School Yearbook), feel neither spurned nor uncomprehending of Dylan's quantum-leap away.

More importantly, Dylan has, as we know, written beautifully about these places and their wintry magic, both early on, as in the fine, candid poem 'My Life In A Stolen Moment' and in much later songs like 'Something There Is About You' and 'Never Say Goodbye'. In interviews too, he has often re-affirmed his pride in his formative Iron Range, North Country roots.

I'm that color. I speak that way...My brains and feelings have come from there...The earth there is unusual, filled with ore...There's a magnetic attraction there: maybe thousands of years ago some planet bumped into the land there. There is a great spiritual quality throughout the Midwest. Very subtle, very strong, and that is where I grew up.

Yet for the present, before Heritage strikes, it's bliss to explore these places without encountering a Bob Dylan Experience.

Pleasingly, Hibbing was also the birthplace of Greyhound Buses, and to take the road from there to Duluth, as I did after an all-too-brief two days in Hibbing, was to follow its earliest route. By chance, halfway between the two, I stopped at the Wilbert Café, built in 1922 and the first stopping-off point there ever was for Greyhounds. Italianburger & fries, $3.95. It was one of the worst meals I've ever eaten anywhere in the world.

Duluth itself is a scruffy, tough little city full of whiskery geezers hitting the precipitous streets that tumble down to the industrial waterfront where the wind comes off the water.

Armed with Dave Engel's excellent book *Just Like Bob Zimmerman's Blues: Dylan in Minnesota,* I drove up and down the grid of shabby streets, looking for, and finding almost all of, the apartments and houses through which the Zimmerman family passed in stages when they lived here, becoming Americans and struggling to chase the dream. A tough place to start.

Likewise for Bob. I found the dour, forbidding Nettleton Elementary School where Bob shamed his father by having to be dragged the two blocks there kicking and screaming. The doors were locked. I peered through the dirty windows. It was so ordinary, and so drab. The change when Bob moved to Hibbing High was some upgrade.

There was no blue plaque on the wall for Bob Dylan here either.

Yet for Abe, there was another school to compare these with. Dominating the heights of Duluth is the 19th-century monstrosity that *he* attended as a child, Central High, with its ludicrous 300-foot tower – the whole place looking as though built from giant dog turds.

The lake below is so huge it's like the sea, making Duluth feel like a seaport, with a constant wind, tough people and a slight sense of menace, or at least a sense that you'd better have your wits about you on these colourless and poverty-soaked streets.

The ore from Hibbing leaves here by boat to Chicago and points east. In the opposite direction came the immigrants from Russia, the Ukraine and, as Dylan's grandparents did, from Lithuania, via Liverpool, New Brunswick, Montreal and Michigan and along the Great Lake to Superior, across the bay from Duluth. You can see it all from the windows of the fast-deteriorating house the Zimmermans lived in when Bob was a baby. The alley down its side was strewn with foul rubbish, including big lumps of raw meat the rats hadn't yet eaten.

I drove back down from Duluth to St Paul, deliberately taking Highway 61: a road that, like the Mississippi, runs right down from here to the Gulf of Mexico, a road soaked in the history of the blues and revisited famously by the inspired 1965 Bob Dylan who 'went electric' – a road now so utterly displaced by Interstate 35 that for most of its Minnesota stretch these days it's merely a county road.

It's a delight to drive down, therefore: it runs through real, scruffy towns, not strip cities, and now that it's so under-used except for local farmers' pick-up trucks, the constant eyesore of billboards has vanished. It creeps through long stretches of dolorous, fog-coloured forest, past little lakes with frozen edges and circles of ice around tiny islands of cliff and tree in the water, with small wooden jetties and tied-up boats: Coffee Lake, Moose Lake, Sand Lake. There are 10,000 of these frozen lakes in Minnesota.

Sometimes farmland asserts itself for a while and there are horses and big old barns and log piles; more often the road is a stark, forlorn corridor with olive-green sides. It's always a surprise to find a clearing glimpsed beyond the trees. Inappropriately flimsy houses are camped from time to time along the road, their front-yard junk mixed up with their plastic decorative squirrels and fawns, lions and Santa Clauses. You have to dodge and weave and pay attention to keep a grip on 61 as it keeps getting entangled in interstates.

Across a pretty river lies Pine City, the least piney and largest place since Duluth. There's a whiff of the prairies here, and the other side of town there it is: prairie landscape instead of the Great North Woods. Easy to imagine Bob riding this highway: you can still find, on the radio, on the oldies stations, the very music he would have had blasting out when he came down for weekends in the big city.

Back in St Paul, smart people hurry out of the street's icy wind into the warm Manhattan glamour of The Saint Paul Hotel, smiling as they adjust their overcoat collars. They're excited by winter: by its imminent, welcome drama. These people are proud that they endure this climate. Its heartland ruggedness, they like to think, puts its iron in their souls.

I'm used to four seasons / California's got but one.

Stayin' Up For Days In The Chelsea Hotel (2001)

This was published, in a version stripped of most Dylan content, in the travel section of the Weekend Telegraph *in March 2001. It was written when the legendary Stanley Bard still ran the hotel but was nervously contemplating handing it over to his son. It has changed again since then, and is no longer accepting guests, though it still has long-term tenants in dispute with each other and the management, so that in 2020 the renovations are still unfinished after over 19 years.*

If you go down to the Chelsea Hotel, you're sure of a big surprise. Unless you've been before, in which case the surprise is only that recent 'refurbishment' (nice hotel word, that) has left this elderly Manhattan institution so unchanged.

How unreconstructedly scuzzy the place still is, and how humane. There is no concession to the tourist industry, or to the assumptions of all those taking degrees in hotel management.

The first thing you'll encounter is the hopelessness of the Chelsea's booking arrangements. Fax them in advance and they won't reply. Phone to tell them, in puzzlement, that you faxed them and got no reply and they'll say, as if this explains it, that they didn't know quite what they should say, so they didn't. Phone and try to book a room six weeks in advance and they'll offer the endearing non-sequitur that they don't have a computer so they can't cope with bookings more than a month ahead.

The computer bit is said with the pride of people consciously fighting a noble rearguard action. And that's what the Chelsea is all about.

It even manages to remain in an unfashionable location – quite a feat, for almost all Manhattan is fashionable now. The whole city is cleaner, safer, more polite and just a little bit less distinctive than it used to be, and all those once-impossible areas rather pleased with themselves. The dangerous junkie wasteland of the East Village is ridiculously bijou, its every sinister, stinking corner now an art gallery, coffee shop, bookstore or vegetarian body-piercing salon. In the (West) Village, once the HQ of folkies and their civil rights activist compadres, of jazz musicians, writers and loft-living pioneers, whole blocks are now restaurants, the pavement cafés serve designer beer and there is rocket in every sandwich. The *Village Voice* has become a freebie, with barely any space for articles among its hundreds of pages of ads. And even in the former nowhere just north of the Chelsea and across a bit, the galleries are getting a grip.

The Chelsea Hotel keeps its head down, and its little patch of West 23rd Street, near the corner of 7th Avenue, remains undistinguished, dirty and bleak. The shops are no smarter or better organised than at Elephant and Castle. The hotel's thin, cheap awning, flapping above the warm breeze sidewalk, says look, here we are, we've seen better days, we promise.

And it's true. Built in the 1880s, a hotel since 1905, and belonging to the Bard family since 1940, this red brick and ironwork monstrosity, this inefficient, grandiose, crustacean shell embraces 400 rooms in which an almost impossibly perfect castlist of bohemians of every generation have lived, loved, altered their minds and died. When, briefly, before Broadway, 23rd Street was theatreland, Lily Langtry was always popping in.

Sarah Bernhardt installed herself with her own bedding and the coffin she claimed to sleep in. Mark Twain, O. Henry, Cartier-Bresson, Hart Crane, Willem de Kooning, Jasper Johns, Theodore Dreiser and Nelson Algren all stayed or lived here. Thomas Wolfe wrote *Look Homeward Angel* in Room 831. Alphaeus Philemon Cole, who began his career as a portraitist when Post-Impressionists like Seurat were considered avant-garde, died of heart failure at his home in the hotel when he was 112 years old.

Composer Virgil Thomson had a five-room apartment, now sold off intact; fellow composer George Kleinsinger had a tropical apartment on the upper floors, with monkeys and a waterfall. His ashes were scattered on the roof.

Then there was Brendan Behan, Nabokov, radical/porn

publisher Maurice Girodias, Tennessee Williams, Edith Piaf and eventually Dylan Thomas, whose plaque at the entrance notes that he 'lived and laboured here... and from here sailed out to die' (via the White Horse Tavern, Greenwich Village).

Arthur Miller wrote two plays at the Chelsea; Arthur C. Clarke wrote *2001* here, William Burroughs *Naked Lunch*, and in the 1970s song 'Sara' Bob Dylan claimed to have stayed up for days in the Chelsea writing the 1960s song 'Sad-Eyed Lady Of The Lowlands'.[61]

Other 1960s guests and residents included Allen Ginsberg and arts polymath Harry Smith, Robert Crumb, Joni Mitchell (who was prompted to write 'Chelsea Morning' here), Leonard Cohen (whose less sunny 'Chelsea Hotel No.2' unkindly recalls Janis Joplin giving him a blowjob in Room 104), Jimi Hendrix, Claes Oldenburg and Warhol 'superstars' Viva and Ultra Violet.

Patti Smith lived here with Robert Mapplethorpe in the 1970s. Milos Forman lived here while producing *Hair*. Sid Vicious killed Nancy Spungen here. Quentin Crisp lived here for over 35 years. Dee Dee Ramone lives here still.[62]

The walls ooze this history, and as everyone says, the walls are thick. Walk the dilapidated corridors and you'll hear an opera singer practising scales, or a trombonist barking, or a dog. In the lifts you meet these dogs, or people carrying up hot food from the outside world. The lifts are small and charged with an atmosphere of elaborate politeness, as those brought temporarily together for short, vertical journeys avoid prying. Once inside your room, you can't hear much. You can be private and, if you're a resident, feel that you belong: that big New York may knock you about, and funds may be short, but here is your haven. Your art or other travail is your own business but your artist-persona will be accorded respect.

---

[61] According to Ian Bell's 2012 biography *Once Upon a Time: The Lives of Bob Dylan*, Dylan moved into an apartment in the Chelsea, No. 211, with Sara Lownds and her daughter Maria at 'the end of 1964', and Dylan had a piano installed there. But it could have been 1965: Sally Grossman (a close friend of Sara from before she met Bob) recalls them being mostly either in Woodstock/Bearsville, or in one of the Grossmans' Gramercy Park apartments, and that they were probably at the Chelsea for a very brief time. (2020 e-mail c/o Raymond Foye.) Sally Grossman died 12th March 2021.

[62] Dee Dee Ramone died of a heroin overdose in 2002, no longer in the Chelsea but at his apartment in Hollywood.

As a guest you can feel a privileged temporary member of this iconoclastic club. Not everyone wants to, of course. You won't be long in NYC before someone, learning that you're staying at the Chelsea, will give you a perplexed and hesitant look, and decide right before your eyes not to cultivate you further. Then again, if you're a Chelsea sort of person, this won't matter. After all, you know how much it's costing you. The Chelsea Hotel is no longer especially cheap. Perhaps it never was.

The first time I stayed here was in October 1989, with my wife and one-year-old daughter. We were there to see all of Bob Dylan's concerts at the Beacon Theatre – only his second year of the Never-Ending Tour. It must be admitted Magdalena slept through all four concerts.

For one, we'd arranged to collect our tickets from Jeff Rosen, who was selling them to us, outside the stage door. When I paid him cash he asked me with a smile how I knew he wouldn't just keep the money; I said I didn't but I knew who I'd paid. Alongside me soon afterwards Sarah was rocking Magdalena in her arms when Tony Garnier stepped out, saw them and grinned, saying 'Look – they even bring their babies for him to bless.'

At the Chelsea we had a small, very brown room, mostly seventies furniture, in which, given that no cot was provided, Magdalena slept in an open drawer of the room's large chest of drawers. One day we visited the rather brighter office of resident Raymond Foye, writer, curator, editor, confidante of Harry Smith, Allen Ginsberg and Tiny Tim, and publisher of those tiny Hanuman Books (and author of that *ISIS* piece about the time in 1985 when Dylan called on Ginsberg, and was excited to find Harry Smith staying there – only to learn that Smith refused to meet him.)

Sarah, Magdalena and I used to cross the road from the Chelsea to walk a hundred yards or so to breakfast daily at the Malibu Diner, whose flamingo-pink banquettes were cheerily un-Chelsea vulgar. On another foray we found, in real life, the mural Dylan had used as the cover art for his most recent album, *Oh Mercy*.

I re-enter the Chelsea, without the family this time, after a gap of eleven years. The lobby seems only superficially tidied up. Large canvases still shout from the walls and lolloping art installations, bizarre papier-mâché dolls and agonised metal skeletons, still jostle from the ceiling. The chairs remain ill-sorted and exhausted, the whole place too scuffed and crumbling to respond to even prodigious efforts of vacuuming and polish.

The desk at the far end looks like a 1940s film noir hotel set. The pigeon-holes behind the two elderly, shirtsleeved receptionists are filled with cumbersome, yellowing pieces of paper. A fire extinguisher hangs at eye-level. The dark wood counter is covered with old telephones and newspapers. Standing on tiptoes to lean over it, and speaking in delicate tones, a succession of unshaven men tell the manager that they have not yet received their cheque, but that it is certainly on its way. Some are told they can leave it till next week to discuss it; others are told, 'Well, if you like we could move you to a cheaper room – number soandso is pleasant…'

I had never forgotten the unfailing courtesy of these exchanges, and that they still go on is the certain proof that the Chelsea is unaltered in spirit.

Stanley Bard is the remarkable man who has kept it this way. He's in his sixties and ascribes his beanpole slimness to playing tennis in New Jersey, where he lives, and from where he commutes to become, daily, the abbot of this hushed retreat. It must puzzle many of the hotel's residents that he is not one himself.

I ask how he handles the junkies and the suicides, the rock'n'roll casualties, the Sids and Nancys. He's urbane, long used to coping with celebrity excess. He says quietly, remembering: 'Really it was only bad when the Grateful Dead came in.'

He is anxious that when his son takes over, as he did from his father, things might change too much.

'If profit becomes the main motive,' he tells me, 'if it goes commercial and becomes just a big hotel, it will lose a lot. It will lose the people who live here – who have no legal protection but who are protected, really, by my feelings for them. Creative people.'

You could regard paying for your room at the Chelsea as making an honourable contribution. Otherwise you might feel a bit done. The rooms may have been revamped and the stairwell restored but the corridors remain so astonishingly fleapit that on arrival you're likely to regret that you've come. This is where Goth meets Gormenghast.

For less money, you could stay at one of the new breed of 'budget' hotel where everything is clean and shiny. At the Habitat on E.57th, for example, en suite rooms start at $125 a night.

At the Chelsea, an ordinary double is likely to be $185, and could be $275. (There's a sense, when you're first at the desk, that they make up the price when they see the whites of your eyes.) But you could choose to pay $350 a night, for instance, for the small suite that is Room 822, the like of which you will not find at a Habitat: here, preposterous battered cream and gold Louis XVI meets leopard-skin dining chairs and a 1950s coffee table; repulsive nylon curtains separate bedroom from sitting-room. It feels as if Dylan Thomas and Sarah Bernhardt had a fistfight right here on the floor.

It's very, very Chelsea Hotel. But are you?

Dylan In Stockholm
(2002)

Published in shorter form in The Daily Telegraph *of 13th April 2002; an edited version was also published in that year's April-May issue of* ISIS *fanzine. It elicited much hostility from fans but still seems to me to represent fairly the dispiriting audience experience of many a C21 Dylan concert. For this more substantial version I've gone back to my original notes and reproduced them almost intact.*

Bob Dylan is opening the 2002 European leg of his Never-Ending Tour in Stockholm, capital of Sweden. I've never been before.

There's no sense of his presence in the city: no posters and not even a listing in What's On For April. He's a secret eccentricity, known only to the twilight world of those in their twilight years. In the Time To Hurry CD shop in the Old Town, there is plenty of Bob on sale and on display, but this small room in its crepuscular alley is run and staffed by greyhairs in ponytails serving customers much the same.

Outside in the cold sunshine, another world gets on with its consuming, unaware that Bob Dylan once helped make things the way they are today. (Meantime life outside goes on all around you.)

I left my house in Yorkshire this morning. Stansted was thronging horribly, and the Ryanair check-in hard to find. Gruesome queues for Security. Gates hard to find amid the Shopping Opportunities. Gate crowded. Flight delayed. Try as I might, I had no sense of Sweden calling me.

On the plane, the tall blonde girl sitting next to me smelled so badly of Old Tramp that I had to move seats. This put me alongside an oleaginous Indian businessman who drank three large gin and tonics in no time at all. Rock and roll…

When we arrived at an airport of the 1960s secondary-modern

school school, I sat on the transfer bus, peering out at the concrete and the cold night air, recognising the dead centre of nowhere. We drove for just over an hour through a long abrasion of pallid motorway, its verges a feeble pageant of stunted fir trees, the whole visible world more empty, forlorn and pointless than anywhere I could remember. It's a landscape of frosted pale-brown grass, cold rocks and, like frail old people, spindly trees huddled together to fight off hypothermia. A person could easily die out here, most readily from despair.

At the end of it, the Stockholm we arrived at looked like one gigantic East German housing estate. Of course as we drove further in, the city's streets began to look better: like Paris might seem in a bad dream: too grey, too hard, too eerily brutal.

My hotel is nowhere near where it says it is, and I pay heavily for a taxi to take me there through wretched, howling boulevards from the central bus station. And if this is the Swedes' idea of a 4-star hotel, it's not mine. There is nothing to eat, and all the cafés seen en route have been closed too. I've had nothing since a Peterborough Station sandwich eight hours ago. I give up and go to what is, by some oversight, a truly comfortable bed.

I wake with a phenomenal hangover from dehydration and lose a morning's exploration time without a qualm. Nothing I encounter in the afternoon makes me regret it. I walk the featureless streets, tourist map in hand, take the subway to Gamla Stan (the Old Town) and find there nothing but a lot of blowy waterfront and a hilly, sunless triangle of tiny alleyways and streets despoiled by the internationalising forces of tourism, each picturesque cobbled byway now occupied by 7-Eleven fast fooderies and overpriced boutiques, all with the same brand names you'd find in Rhodes or Miami Beach.

The most interesting thing I see is the way the locals make their electricity-meter boxes into little houses by painting tiny black windows and doors on them. The next most interesting is a man taking his cheery miniature Schnauzer for a walk without its lead on. He orders it about incessantly, making it stop and wait every half a minute, keeping his imperious finger outstretched high above its obliging nose until he permits it to trot on. Its owner, by far the less graceful of the two, is so busy ordering it about and supervising its every footfall that he fails to heed the six-foot-tall metal rubbish cart just being placed outside the back door of the restaurant they're passing, crashes into it heavily and falls over, knocking it on top of him. Wagging its handsome tail with tactless vigour, the dog thinks this a fine joke. I agree with the dog.

I feel marooned. It is as deathly as waiting at a Birkenhead bus stop. Actually a good deal of the Swedish capital makes Birkenhead look bursting with character and architectural merit, and the time spent on the platforms of Peterborough was handy practice for being in Stockholm.

After a lunch of mediocre fish soup and good bread I sit at a bar's outside tables alongside a lot of other people, overlooking a huge concrete bridge that takes the subway trains across the water from Gamla Stan to the next island to the south. Everybody smokes. Vacuous pop music is inescapable. Everybody's mobile phone rings. You can't go one minute without hearing these febrile summonses. Often in the form of pert phrases from the vacuous pop songs. Branches of McDonald's are omnipresent.

The omens for Dylan's concert remain bad. I take the subway to Globen, the stop for the stadium, alighting in a postmodern mega-estate, its blank off-white housing towers and dwarfing plazas looking as if they were built yesterday on an otherwise useless swamp and designed by someone inspired by the dimensions of *Metropolis* and the styling of Novotel.

It is a first for me to seek solace inside a shopping centre, yet here is comparative warmth and comfort, in an atrium of metal walkways. It might be Birmingham in here, or the Dumfries Designer Outlet, except of course that Swedes behave better, especially towards their children. Swedish men drink vast quantities of beer all day, but in that what-would-be-more-natural?, pedantic, good-humoured way that Germans do too, rather than in the Brits' malevolent, let's-get-off-our-faces way.

I sit on a bench framed by the Ecco shoe shop, the leather bags shop, the Teknikmagasinet (PlayStations available here), the Klockmäster shop, the Hälsa för alla chemist's and The Blues

Bar. Above my head are some miniature models of balloon flight contraptions, and beyond these five more storeys of metal and glass, and egg-shaped staircases nobody uses because there's a lift alongside them. The vacuous pop is here too, of course, extruding from tinny speakers nestled between the pot plants.

Soon, bizarrely, Bob Dylan will come on stage just one windswept plaza's walk away. There is a vast weight of torpor and too much tat for anything close to excitement to bubble up. Bob, what are you doing here? What am I?

In among the customers for trainers and cosmetics I begin to see blokes with thin, unkempt hair and moustaches, wounded eyes and unclean skin, sporting bellies and grubby jackets, walking in twos and threes. If these men look like poachers, their women look like game old birds. It takes little clairvoyance to know that these are some of the faithful beginning to assemble. As a middle-aged survivor of the sixties with a definite abdominal portliness and no special sartorial finesse myself, these people depress me.

They also depress Bob Dylan. The current concerts are a continuation of the Never-Ending Tour he's been engaged upon for the last 13 years and 11 months. How does it feel for him, night after blurred night, seeing these defeated faces staring up at him in inexplicable glazed agitation?

This year he's done something about it. When tickets went on sale in Britain for next month's UK shows, the promoter allocated priority seats to readers of *Dignity* fanzine[63] – but Dylan demanded that the front few rows not be occupied by the same old faces every night.

Not that all his fans are these bedraggled types, eating bad fast food all over Europe as they follow him around in what, after so much practice, has become indistinguishable from a stupor.

There are at least three other types, starting with the wonderfully mad. Until recently there was an Austrian Dylan fanzine called *Parking Meter,* and one of its subscribers lived in Hawaii. Every quarter, not one but two copies of the latest issue

---

[63] John Baldwin, editor of *Dignity*, also ran the *Desolation Row Information Service*, an e-mail newsline with a relationship with Dylan's promoter that enabled us, via John, to buy priority tickets. John Baldwin died on 29th May 2018.

would be airmailed out there in protective packaging. The editors themselves worked in libraries and computer companies, so it was with a mix of envy and hilarity that they used to picture their customer filing one copy away in temperature-controlled, archival safety, and then sitting on the beach with his second copy, the one he could risk reading.

More famously there was Lambchop – the fan with the *Renaldo & Clara* hat: a man who, regardless of venue, would always somehow manage not merely to be in the front row, but to be in the seat most precisely aligned with Dylan's microphone.

Only Bob himself mattered to Lambchop. Others might prefer some backing bands to others; Larry scorned this as a symptom of dilettanteism: 'Like going to a great restaurant and caring about the lighting fixtures.' In the 1990s he became so prominent that more than once, Dylan addressed him by name from the London stage. No more: for health and financial reasons, Lambchop has emigrated to India.[64]

Then there are supposedly normal fans: the thirtysomething to sixtyish investment bankers and lawyers, academics and accountants, social workers and teachers. Many of these can fly business class to see Dylan in concert. Many more arrange their annual holidays, even their pregnancies, to fit in with what they guess the year's touring schedule will be.

And then there are their children. (And by now, even their grandchildren.)

Sometimes these groups blur together. At half-past six I have a pre-concert beer at The Blues Bar and fall into conversation with a family of three. The man, bearded 50-something with pink skin and brown leather jacket, is tucking into veal and bright yellow chips. He looks after the Stockholm subway's carriages and engineers. His wife, crop-haired and faded blonde by choice, is a costumier for the Royal Theatre Company. Their son, 16-year-old John, a genuine blond with hair down to his nipples, sports a Blind Faith T-shirt, likes Deep Purple, Hendrix and *early* Lynyrd Skynyrd as well as Dylan, and aims to become a carpenter.

---

[64] Larry 'Lambchop' Eden died, back in England, in June 2007.

At the next table there's an American voice. All around me, Bob's bedraggled army is thickening up, and in many cases its children have come along too, looking serious and circumspect.

These children have a heavy weight upon them. They are in the perilous position of sharing their parents' musical taste, and they know that in some wider psychic space they are going to have to account for themselves. And in the meantime they must put up with so much clumsy inebriation, so much middle-age spread. John, born alongside *Empire Burlesque*, is coming to see 60-year-old Bob Dylan. It's as if I'd begged my parents to take me to hear Vera Lynn.

But now, as we file into the stadium, I'm touched and surprised. The well-dressed, suntanned and healthy vastly outnumber the tallow-faced – and the proportion of teenagers Dylan is drawing in is no longer the 8 percent it has been for many years. Now, strange but true, I see that something not far off 40 percent of this audience is in its teens or very early twenties.

Inside the giant red womb of the hall, those behind me include an 18-year-old whose last concert experience was seeing UB40, and his 17-year-old companion, who confesses she has never been to a concert before. A man old enough to have a bus pass is attracting concert virgins. Another young woman has been listening to his records for five years but doesn't expect much tonight. 'I think he just comes here and goes away again: I think that's his attitude. But we'll see.' They promise to let me have their verdicts at the end, and go back to the compulsive text-messaging of youth.

A creditably thin 44-year-old comes along the row to see me, on the hunch that I am, as he puts it himself, 'a Bobcat'. He whispers that the first time he made love to a woman was to a Dylan track. This is more information than I need.

A smell of incense drifts about. It is 8pm. There is no support act, and Bob should have been on half an hour ago, though people were hardly beginning to file in by then and people are still arriving. Classical music roars through the speakers and the lights go down. Shadowy figures creep onto the stage.

Up come the lights, and Dylan and his band strike up with one of their singalong old-timey warm-ups, 'Hummingbird'. Then he starts into 'The Times They Are A-Changin''… and buggers up the lyric immediately. Some of the delivery is compelling but he can never get through the title line without a laughable failure to disguise his failure.

'It's Alright, Ma (I'm Only Bleeding)' is next, and then 'Don't Think Twice, It's All Right' with a much nicer, less throaty voice.

He almost makes this real – that is, makes you sit heart in mouth wondering what might not transpire here – but most of the time the real Bob Dylan is largely missing and he's busier faking it than trying his best. Where once he was so alive, communicating so much quick, creative intelligence so alertly and uniquely, now he snatches at showbiz cliché he once recoiled from. Like repeating half a line en route to the end of it – 'Gave her my heart: gave her my heart but she wanted my soul' – a device so crudely portentous it's always been the preserve of crooners in cabaret. In the end, he's played it too safe and it's gone nowhere and then died, slaughtered in the cheap arena of the circus-stomp ending. This isn't going to amaze anyone.

Then he lights into a tremendous 'Man Of Constant Sorrow' wholly different from the version that was a highlight of his début album, released just over 40 years ago. This time, perhaps chosen only because of the song's revival in the recent film *O Brother Where Art Thou?*, it is treated to a heavy electric slow thud, while members of the band sing echoing lines – 'Perhaps he'll die on that train' and so on – which confirms the *O Brother* inspiration. After that, with no intro, it's straight into a dodgy 'Lay, Lady, Lay' with a pleasing ending. Everyone in the band seems to be standing a long way away from Bob.

'Solid Rock', a surprise, is a smouldering, genuinely moody, felt thing, founded on the solid rock of the drumming. It gives way to a 'Positively 4th Street' pulled out of shape and grunged up, so that by midway through, the insouciant harmonica intro seems to have belonged to a different time and place. The lyrics go awry and too many verses are missed out – yet it ends interestingly and with lovely 'shoes' and parting 'see you'.

The audience sits immobile and polite, and gives 'Tweedle Dee &

Tweedle Dum' indifferent applause. In the middle of 'To Make You Feel My Lurve' the man next to me is text-messaging, and people are coming in and out fetching beer. Dylan fetches old 'Maggie's Farm' and then the new 'Summer Days'. There's a sense of jiving going on all around him and yet when he's at the mike he's barely able to get through the task of singing it, and when he's not, he's pottering about twiddling with the amp like a building inspector. But the crowd loves this one. They're *there* for the first time.

Can they bring Bob there too? He sings 'Sugar Baby', another of the new songs from his wonderful 2001 album *"Love And Theft"*, but it seems to have become mannered already, the growled octave-dropping line-endings wretchedly self-parodic. Yet he pulls it together for the last third, and it's almost OK. Can he really be this bored with it already?

The reworked heavy rock version of 'Drifter's Escape' is nicely anarchic and is followed by a 'Rainy Day Women #12 & 35' that is the closing number, and far more tolerable than usual when it's taken as slowly as this. People rush to the front and my 44-year-old does a splendid piece of spidery dancing as he urges those around him to stand or at least to clap their hands above their heads. They refuse. It goes on forever, enervating everyone except my spidery friend.

Bob Dylan, flanked by cohorts, is enacting his recently developed dramatic device of standing at the front staring out at the audience as if he can't comprehend the phenomenon of applause: almost confronting it like a gladiator, in stillness and silence, while it rolls towards him.

He leaves the stage. Can he possibly wring enough further noise to justify an encore out of this well-behaved, cosy crowd? Of course he'll come on again anyway, and does. 'Things Have Changed'. Yes, 'I'm locked in tight, I'm out of range. I used to care, but things have changed.' Then 'Like A Rolling Stone'. How I wish it would be anything but 'Blowin' in the Wind' next – and it's 'Forever Young', eliciting long but subdued applause. He's *still* not finished: he resorts to 'Honest With Me', the only sub-standard song on *"Love And Theft"*: the one we could all predict he'd perform live because it's the easiest to thrash through, just as

'Everything Is Broken' was doomed to be the song of choice way back when *Oh Mercy* was new (as John Bauldie told me would happen when he first heard that album).

'Honest With Me' in concert has already become the lump of dead rockism it is. Having paid a bit of touched heed to 'Forever Young', young people get back to their text-messaging. Bob can scarcely drag himself through it, and we know the feeling. In the instrumental break, after a bit of desultory knee-bending, he turns his back and pootles around the back of the stage, and it strikes me that he has come to resemble the stage-door jobsworths who used to be so disapproving. And now it *is* going to be 'Blowin' In The Wind', with its jaunty lift-music harmonica intro and its mannered, tottering will-he-won't-he-get-through-it verses and its horrible overblown chorused chorus lines.

Till recently, if you were close enough to see, Dylan's charismatic face was ceaselessly expressive of fleeting subtle emotion and savvy. Now it seems reduced to a handful of clumsy, hammed-up grimaces. Where his concerts were events, in which an artist of genius lived in the dangerous moment, now he plays safe and seems to have no reason to be there. Where once he didn't care what the audience thought because he had his own vision and was ahead of us, now he doesn't care what the audience thinks because he thinks it's a gullible rabble. As Terry from Luton had remarked when we met in the queue for the toilets beforehand, at best 'he treats the audience as if he feels sorry for them for wanting to be there'.

Most of the time. Some C21 nights are thrillingly different – in the intimacy of Portsmouth Guildhall in 2000, for instance – but they're very rare now and more usually the breakthrough of sunlight is confined to one song, or even just one phrase, before a shrivelling cynicism sets in again.

This is, depressingly, becoming the norm. It surely has nothing to do with age and everything to do with sourness, an exhaustion of his resources. No wonder he's given interviews in which he's said he dislikes the long-time fans almost as much as he hates critics. He wants fresh meat: young people who don't remember how incomparably better he once was than he is now.

I thought it would be different after *"Love And Theft"*. This is a work of such excellence, a work so alive and such fun, that I thought he'd be out there revelling in it, re-galvanised and full of unpredictability and purpose.

Not so. He's held in, a little wooden figure supplied with noise on all sides by the hired hands, signalling all the time how unmoved he is by it. He's not so much going through the motions as conveyed along them like a trouser-press on an assembly line.

At the end, everyone around me has loved it. The young woman who expected little says it was 'great'. So do the well-groomed, professional couples and a smart 40-something woman and her 19-year-old daughter, who has now seen him four times. Two 15-year-old girls outside tell me it was 'lovely'. First hooked by the live '66 CDs, they don't mind that his voice is different now, and they adore *"Love And Theft"* for its 'great variety of styles'. They know many young people who like Dylan's work.

It's so weird. Dylan has been riding high (to quote a phrase) for quite a while now. Gone are the bad old days of the 1980s and early 1990s, when he was a laughable old croakhead pilloried as Mr. Sixties Man while the sixties, man, were being blamed for every ill in the western world. Ever since he suffered his temporary heart disease, released 1997's *Time Out Of Mind* and started being pelted with Grammies and Oscars and Lifetime Achievement Awards, somehow he's been walking on Golden Pond. He's praised now for not trying to look eternally youthful. (Don't mention the airbrushed cover photos.) Somehow too, Dylan's concerts are now marvellous for their rawness and their refusal to treat the songs as sacrosanct.

I've written and believed a fair amount of this stuff myself down the years. And what a sufficiency of years they've been. I first listened to a Dylan album in 1964, first saw him in concert in 1966. God knows how many I've attended since. I have long accepted that when you enter the Dylan world, you sign up for life.

Naturally, then, I insisted on Dylan's greatness as an artist all through the backlash decades, and indeed spent most of the 1990s writing a 900-page critical study of his extraordinary, incomparable, massively influential, generous body of work.

I'm not going to renounce all that now. I don't even like the idea of writing bad things about him for a newspaper. But the Dylan of the Globe in Stockholm has been painfully poor. Poor by the very standards of imaginative integrity that Bob Dylan himself threw out into the world.

All the bars in the vicinity of the stadium are playing Dylan records afterwards, and we can hear this spilling out into the streets. The first thing I hear is a blast of 'I Want You' from *Blonde On Blonde* – and in a trice my heart and mind together go 'Ah! *That's* what the real Bob Dylan does...' The contrast between that voice and tonight's, and in how much was being given out, is huge and cruel.

All over Europe people are preparing to take in *swathes* of Bob nights. Many, like me, approach the prospect with heavy hearts, nowadays choosing their venues to allow the compensation of some pleasant dining out on warm, agreeable nights. (In other words, they are going to see Dylan in Italy instead of Sweden.) We expect much less now, and we get it. But we go anyway. Always will.

Note: Not all the concerts on that spring tour leg were poor. After it was over, I e-mailed John Baldwin to thank him for getting me tickets for the other shows I caught that year, saying this:

> I thought the last show (London Docklands Arena, 12th May) was by far the best of those I saw, with Newcastle and London Saturday (11th May) close behind. I didn't agree at all with your *Desolation Row* assumption, gleaned from others, that Newcastle was less good than Manchester. I felt Manchester was trying too hard to be hard rockin', and so tended to be careless, harsh and clumsy. At Newcastle from my vantage-point he seemed in a very attractive mood – not especially good-humoured but very open and fragile, which made for a delicate, contemplative, calm-centred performance. Compare (I'm speaking from memory, not by comparing recordings) the lovely version of 'Love Minus Zero/No Limit' at Newcastle and the

bluffing-through-it version of 'One Too Many Mornings' at Manchester – i.e. two quiet, delicate songs requiring some finesse in the delivery. No contest. But the great middle section of the first night in London was fiercely burning without sacrificing attentiveness, and only the encore seemed too fixed and a bit dreary. The second night in London was pretty tremendous throughout, capped by the dropping of that gruesome nightly 'Blowin' In The Wind' in favour of a 'Knockin' On Heaven's Door' surprisingly true to the spirit of the original. And I don't know that I've ever witnessed him playing the guitar better than that night – acoustic and electric. Seeing him be as good as that, you can understand why he's still up there doing it, and you can be grateful. All four of these concerts were, let me just say, incomparably better than Stockholm.

Ghost Trains In The American South
(2004)

A de-Dylanised and partially blues-pruned version of this was published in the Weekend Telegraph *of 25th September 2004 under the title 'USA: Rail Good Lesson In The Blues'; my brief look at Bob in New Orleans here could have been augmented had it been written later – because in October that year Bob offered a sustained reverie about the city in* Chronicles Volume One, *called it a 'poem', and said this: 'There are a lot of places I like, but I like New Orleans better.'*

The following August, Hurricane Katrina arrived there.

I'm travelling by train, mostly through Mississippi, accompanied all the way by the ghosts of those who sang the blues down here before I was born: those who migrated to Chicago and other northern cities on these trains, and those who stayed behind in the south, in and around the little towns where these trains still stop.

Amtrak's *City of New Orleans* still makes that big migratory journey, 926 miles from New Orleans to Chicago, as it has for over a century – and as it crosses Mississippi it stops not only at Jackson and Greenwood but also at tiny McComb, Brookhaven, Hazlehurst and Yazoo City.

The *Crescent* too pulls out of New Orleans once a day, heading for New York 1,377 miles away, and stopping in small-town Mississippi at Picayune, Laurel and Meridian.

Between them these places embrace where one of the greatest of blues artists, Robert Johnson, was born and murdered, and where the father of country music, Jimmie Rodgers, 'The Singing Brakeman', was born. (Bob Dylan favourites, both.)

These railroads are entwined with music. It was at a station in tiny Tutwiler, Mississippi, around 1903, that W.C. Handy first heard a blues holler and slide guitar – and the words he heard were about the railroads: 'I'm goin' where the Southern cross the Dog...'

Black Americans have always moved north. In the Civil War, 200,000 of them fought with the Unionists. The 20th-century's great migration began around 1915, when booming wartime northern business needed workers and southern cotton was decimated by the boll weevil and by floods.

The annual flooding of the Mississippi River, as of the Nile, had always replenished the land, but with the wilderness cleared, the panthers starved out and the plantations pushing to the river's edge, these floods became disasters.

In 1927 the river overran an area the size of Scotland. Workers were kept in camps at gunpoint to make them repair the levees; blues singers, encouraged by the offer of $500 for the best song, were called in to help a propaganda effort to persuade people to come to do flood-relief work. The winning song was Bessie Smith's 'Back-Water Blues'. (Dylan performed it at New York City's Carnegie Chapter Hall in 1961.)

As everywhere, desperate people moved from the countryside for the promise of the city. A black wage in 1940s Chicago was four times its Mississippi equivalent. A quarter of the black population left. Trains, more than the long, slow highways, were the means of that escape.

Not everyone who rode them went all the way up north. The *City of New Orleans* goes to Memphis before it leaves the south; the *Crescent* goes via Atlanta. Both these southern cities drew a share of migrants from the countryside, among them many of those blues artists who lived in penury but whose names are now revered, and whose voices echo in my head as I ride the rails they once knew. Some such voices came to me directly, and some came, yes, via Bob Dylan: the artist who knows and loves so much of this music and has smuggled the poetry of the blues so creatively into his art.

I begin on the *Crescent*, heading southwest from Atlanta across Alabama to Mississippi, where I plan to stop overnight in small-town Laurel, yellow-pine capital of the world. Why Laurel? Only that it's small and obscure, and therefore typical.

Eleven coaches long, shining silver and huge, 20 hours out of New York, the *Crescent* pulls into Atlanta soaked in its own romance. I climb aboard and I'm shown my sleeping compartment by Mr. Turk, a smart, ebullient man much given to shaking hands: there's a fold-down basin, lavatory, movie channels, reclining seat, fold-down table with chessboard top, air-conditioning, blinds, call button to summon free orange-juice, coffee and more. This is not the style in which my migrant bluesmen travelled.

We roll southwest through woodland, dead brown kudzu draped over the trees. It's winter. Occasionally there's a town (Tallapoosa, 'the Dogwood City'). We run alongside a road lined with trailer homes, tattoo parlours, pet shops and a Showers of Flowers supermart. Mostly it's a patchwork of piney woods and bungalows where old cars litter the grass.

We cross a time zone. Alabama looks just like Georgia. On the platform at Birmingham, Mr. Turk takes delivery of two fat paper bags of hot boiled peanuts. Then we snake on through immense woodlands, crossing swamps and vast fields where cattle stand knee-high in juiceless grass. The locomotive's powerful whistle blows with mournful pride. We gain Mississippi. There are green valley floors, gentle hills, many lakes. The sandy soil has turned a greyish white. It's an epic ride.

At Meridian, built on a rise, the track crosses a wide street that climbs to the town centre's elderly multi-storey buildings. This is the birthplace of Jimmie Rodgers, the tubercular white singer who invented the Blue Yodel and died at 35 in 1933. But Meridian holds more than that. On a tip from H.C. Speir, the pre-war Sam Phillips, record producer W.R. Calaway brought Charlie Patton here after getting him out of jail in Belzoni. They caught this train to New York so that Patton, 'the leadingest musicianer in Mississippi', could record. All these names are numinous. Being here is an honour.

Back then also, a woman on the concourse at Meridian would sing out the trains' destinations. Speir wanted her to make records too. She refused. The station, like the culture, has changed since then.

The train rattles on to Laurel. Few other people alight. The station is like a colonial bungalow with lawns and a low fence. It's a January afternoon; I step off the train to feel the air soft and warm. Peggy, the Laurel Inn's landlady, has decided to meet me. 'There used to be a taxi man,' she says, 'but I think he musta died.'

I'm driven straight to oak-lined suburbs of Belle Époque houses, the town's core asset. As we pull into her driveway facing the park, Peggy says 'I hope you like dawgs.' It'd be a bit late if I didn't. 'They're Great Danes,' she adds, opening the door so I can be frisked by Elvis and Hazel.

I intend walking into town. With 18,000 citizens, 55% of them black, it's surely buzzing on Friday nights. 'Oh no!' says Peggy, 'You cain't walk around after dark!' She insists on driving me again. We find closed buildings on featureless, empty streets.

Peggy sticks close as a dawg. The café is shut. The downtown bar is hopelessly redneck. We get baleful looks because we're strangers. We leave.

The restaurant is open and serves alcohol (though not on Sundays). Looking around, I abandon all hope of spotting a single black person downtown. Peggy says there's a new black club near the station. She doesn't know if we'd be welcome but she's willing to find out. She says she lived in New Orleans for years and never found blacks a problem. Not like those Mexicans coming into town now, who take over a house and have thirty people come live in it...

A man she knows passes our table and she asks on my behalf if there's anywhere in town where whites and blacks mix. He answers, with mild manners and crazed eyes: 'No there isn't: and I hope there never will be.' He whispers that the new black club is already having problems with druhhhgs and the police. Peggy decides we won't go after all. We try the Ramada's bar out on the strip instead. Closed. We return to the Inn. Elvis and Hazel are thrilled.

No blues singers exalt Laurel's history, but there is much to be blue about. A pioneer of the Women's Liberation movement, Bella Abzug, a lawyer, headed the appeal in the case of Willie McGee, a black man convicted in 1945 of raping a white woman in Laurel and sentenced to death by an all-white jury who deliberated for only two-and-a-half minutes. Abzug lost the appeal and the man was executed. Today, the town has below-average wages even for Mississippi, above-average crime, and the usual lack of public funding for health, education and welfare that makes so much of the USA a third-world country. Laurel's only colleges are the Southeastern Baptist and the Mississippi College of Beauty Culture.

Next morning we visit a black neighbourhood store where the mostly-empty shelves hold a few self-improvement booklets amid the groceries. Peggy is immediately approached by a young woman saying, 'Ma'am, excuse me but you look like a person who owns property. D'you have anywhere for my baby and me?' Meanwhile I read this in the Ward 6 newsletter: 'When you encounter a black male child, ask him how is he doing in school? What college he plans to attend? What are his career interests? The odds are against him but you can make it easier by asking these simple questions … begin his thought process operating.'

Back at the station, I'm humming Jimmie Rodgers's 'Waiting For A Train'. Mine is running six hours late (atrocious weather up north) and arrives at 10pm. Police cars, lights flashing, are parked all round that new black club.

It's 3am as we pull into New Orleans. Through dark murk I see giant waterside iron girders, heavy metal bridges, sluice gates, iron bollards – the Big Easy is a serious port. It's also the final southern destination of both the Mississippi River and Highway 61.

It seethes with backstreet spirits too, like that of One-Legged Duffy, whose lover stove her head in with her own wooden leg, and Buddy Bolden, the first jazz cornet player and band leader, who went mad at 31 and lived in the asylum for 24 more years. It was home to the deeply obscure blues singer James Wayne, who first recorded 'Junko Partner' and used the phrase 'knocked out loaded' within it, and to Billy Mack & Mary Mack, an obscure vocal duo who cut 'You've Got To Quit Your Low Down Ways' for OKeh way back at the beginning of 1926.

New Orleans gave us the great Richard Rabbit Brown, the first and most important New Orleans folk singer to record, whose dramatic guitar-playing was almost as strong as his resonant voice, who cut only four sides and yet managed a masterpiece with one of them, 'James Alley Blues', some of its lyrics alluded to in Dylan's song 'Mississippi'. Richard recorded it in early 1927; the real place was Jane Alley, a notorious gang-fight patch of New Orleans. Brown had been born in poverty there in about 1880, and died in poverty in the city just ten years after his beautiful recording. It's also where Louis Armstrong came from, and where Mahalia Jackson found she could sing.

The spirit of the younger Bob Dylan is here in New Orleans too, staggering away from Room 103 and running down Rampart Street, and then in real life in 1964 as part of his cross-country road trip, arriving in the city in his road-manager's blue Ford station wagon during Mardi Gras, a small group of young men who came to rest there five nights in a whirl of people, festivity, wine and grass. New Orleans, too, is where we find a Dylan older than that by 25 years, recording his fine album *Oh Mercy* there in March and April, 1989.

But on this trip my own visit was fleeting: I could stay just one night. I was only here to change trains, and next afternoon I missed a rarity: a real New Orleans funeral parade, for long-serving jazzman Tuba Fats. Its three-hour march around the French Quarter began as my *City of New Orleans* pulled out, starting its long haul up to Chicago.

Almost immediately the upper-level Observation Car, with armchairs, gave fine views over the staggering immensity of Lake Pontchartrain and its swamplands grandeur: a vast, thrilling wilderness of brown grass, glowing chlorophyllic weed and strange grey tree stumps rising from vast black water. Teflon-coloured turtles clambered and basked; herons stalked and cranes swooped; there were coots, hawks and guillemots. The train halted here, and it was like sitting in a tree-top game lodge – a luxury bubble overlooking a primeval scene.

Roosevelt Sykes, an important blues pianist up north in the 1930s, who often had to play with patches in his pants, came fishing with his wife on this lake when he retired in the 1960s. Rabbit Brown worked out here as a singing boatman. 'Seen better days but I'm puttin' up with these...' he sang, in his voice of molten chocolate.

The train left the lake behind, passing strawberry fields and neat, old-fashioned little Louisiana towns, and reaching Mississippi at teatime. A brief stop in McComb, another in Brookhaven. This was farm country once again – old houses, brown fields, brown cows. No-one wanted to get off or on at Hazlehurst, Robert Johnson's birthplace, so we thundered through it and all I could see was the station building with that magic placename on its decaying signboard, two huge trees on the grass facing a few old wooden buildings, and in the distance the usual Strip City.

I stopped overnight in Jackson, a city of 185,000 rich in blues history. Its station is so renovated it looked new – unlike the fabled King Edward Hotel across the cold and windy street. Twelve storeys high and now long derelict, it must have seemed enormous in its day. And grand. ('It's a chicken coop now,' the bartender in the far from grand Edison Walthall told me.) Once upon a time, black and white artists made records within its walls: One Leg Sam Norwood, Uncle Dave Macon, the Mississippi Sheiks, Bo Carter and Charlie McCoy. Almost 100 sides were cut here.

Here too Jimmie Rodgers heard the marvellous Tommy Johnson and Ishmon Bracey out on the street and brought them up to the hotel roof to perform to his own white audience.

What a moment! Small distinction, then, between recording artist and busker. Sidekick Ishmon and tall, thin Tommy, who cut the seminal 'Cool Drink Of Water Blues' but would die from drinking Canned Heat; whose influence was huge but whose records were so few; whose falsetto was half angel's, half ghost's – a black ragamuffin act plucked off the street, bemusing a supper-club crowd.

Not that these performers could have stayed as guests, of course, even if they'd had money. When Jackson was segregated, Louis Armstrong and all the other big-name black entertainers (Nat King Cole, Ella Fitzgerald) had to stay across town at the little redbrick Summers Hotel, which I found, now half-demolished, while searching by taxi with a nice old driver called Bill. Sour punks scowled from the sidewalks.

'These young men like to look very threatening,' I said.

'They gonna need a lotta firepower to git us,' answered Bill. He had a gun under his seat. He's not supposed to but all the drivers do, he said. 'They do if they got common sense.'

All my heroes' houses were gone. A bungalow sat where Elmore James once roomed, near an older building still proclaiming 'No Trespassing, No Cigars'. Downtown they are gentrifying Farish Street, where Lillian McMurry ran Trumpet Records and H.C. Speir had his music store. Within this bulldozed shrine, the spry genius Skip James auditioned! Here in 1935 the youthful Robert Johnson himself made a test recording.

Peache's [sic] Café was still at 327 North Farish, with 'SINCE 1961' on the door; its neighbour was the lovely little Art Deco Alamo Theatre. In the foyer was a photo of a very old black man at the projector, captioned 'Ed Henry: he remembers when KNEES were scandalous'.

Bill dropped me off back at the King Edward Hotel, and asked if I knew why it had closed. He said it was when integration came. The owner chose to close it rather than let the blacks in. I had took a walk all around it; it must have seemed a *huge* building in its day: twelve brick storeys plus the roof garden; four sets of twin pillars holding up the stone portico. Eleven pairs of double windows across both front and rear, and nine along each side. The oil barons' Petroleum Club used to meet there. It's all fenced off now, every window smashed, green mold on the ground-floor brickwork, and a fallen tree blocking the sidewalk between the entrance and the street.

Next morning, down the block, I found the Mayflower Café, a perfectly preserved 1930s diner, with models of fish and old photos on the walls, brown banquettes, white linen tablecloths, four women staff waiting on nobody, three or more in the kitchen, terrible coffee. I chatted to an old man who'd been in the café the first day it opened, in 1935; it had been run by his uncle, and he'd been there ever since. A woman came out of the kitchen and told the waitresses, 'No lasagne or catfish today.'

When I left the Mayflower, I sought out the still-surviving home of Medgar Evers, Field Secretary of the Mississippi NAACP, born 1925 and assassinated on his own front lawn by a white racist in 1963. Strange to stand there.

'Only A Pawn In Their Game', Bob Dylan sang about it: his most radically left-wing song, and a very great one. The house is a tiny museum now. It's a small, neat, brick bungalow with metal windows and 1950s decorative touches, with a driveway but no garage, in a respectable suburban street of neat bushes and an absence of litter.

As it happened, I was there on Martin Luther King Jr. Day, a national holiday for another murdered African American. Where better to pay homage than Jackson, Mississippi?

I felt lucky to witness the laying of a wreath by a quiet circle of perhaps 45 or 50 people, some of them white, all holding hands around the little monument called Freedom Corner. There was a photograph of two men alongside each other: King and Evers. We were alongside an anonymous stop lights junction across from a Church's Chicken shop.

Back at the combined Greyhound & Amtrak station later in the afternoon, I waited in freezing weather for my train. After a while I was accosted by a testy, dishevelled and middle-aged white guy called Tony from Leland, Mississippi, who told me more than I needed to know about his slightly interesting if implausible life, and rather more about his medical history and current condition. He produced a pile of fifteen CDs in an astonishingly scruffy state, their silvery skins flaking off – and in the end I paid him two dollars to go away.

Naturally the *City of New Orleans* was late, so that we passed in darkness through Greenwood, where Robert Johnson was poisoned and died: a murder devoid of political import but incalculable consequence. He'd been uncelebrated in his lifetime, but risen to posthumous pre-eminence in the blues world, and a main force in enriching the rock music that grew up in the 1960s and has never died. The man who signed Bob Dylan to a record deal in 1961 then compiled and issued *Robert Johnson, King of the Delta Blues Singers*, the album of Johnson's work that so thrilled the postwar Folk & Blues Revival world. Where might the composer of 'Hell Hound On My Trail' have taken the blues had he survived? Singer Johnny Shines said this: 'He was playing stuff then that they're only catching up to now.'

My train pushed on out of Mississippi, heading north, escaping the Delta. I reminded myself that not all Mississippi is the Delta, and not all blues is from Mississippi.

It takes a lot to laugh... Many a ghost from throughout the Deep South, and fragments of song from Bob Dylan, kept me awake late that night as the train rattled its slow, historic way up towards Chicago.

A Bob Dylan Encyclopedia Promo Trip (2006)

From my long since abandoned blog, September & November 2006

The same week I collected my bus pass, I gave a talk at the Rock & Roll Hall of Fame in Cleveland, Ohio. It was the first gig on my American promo trip in support of *The Bob Dylan Encyclopedia*.

We travelled an average of over 1000 miles a day for the 17 days of the trip. Shocking carbon footprinting.

Greatest disappointment: Woodstock. It's been a magical name in my imagination since 1967, and when we got there we found what seemed a pretentious dump full of self-regarding phonies pretending to be green and caring. The groovy bakery/coffee-shop, Bread Alone, is about as green as McDonald's: paper plates, paper cups with plastic lids, plastic knives and spoons. No wonder the lyric to that Dylan–Clapton co–composition includes 'There at the bakery / Surrounded by fakery'.

Staying in what everyone said is the best place in town, The Wild Rose Inn, we felt marooned. It wasn't an inn at all, of course, but a B&B. Nice old house cutesified to death, no phone in the room and almost never anyone there to run the place either. Clearly they weren't letting their business interfere with their lives. This near–total absence was PR-ed as 'our make-yourself-at-home policy'. Yeah, right. It wasn't helpful in a town where you can't get a cellphone signal, where it rained all the time that we were there yet there were no umbrellas for sale (the airline had lost our luggage en route, and took three days to find it again), and when we wanted a taxi back through the deluge from an overpriced restaurant we were told it would cost $27 to take us a mile – because no Woodstock taxi wanted to work and the one they could get had to come from another town miles and miles away. This just about summed up its spirit of place. Woodstock 2006 – we're so laid back we can't be arsed with anything.

The other lowspot was Powell's Bookshop in the beautiful city of Portland, Oregon, where the guy running my event claimed – and I know this was a blatant lie – that he'd never been given a list of the sound equipment he was supposed to have ready for the soundcheck we'd had scheduled for an hour ahead of time. He claimed he'd only been told he needed 'an LCD player and a projector', yet he hadn't bothered to have even these things set up – and when he and two colleagues finally rounded them up, they spent the whole hour failing to find out how to connect the two. Nor had he heard of the posters the publisher had had printed and sent to them. In the end I had to give the talk with no film or sound at all, and to the smallest audience I've ever addressed: a handful of punters of saintly fortitude and patience. This was at 'the world's biggest bookstore'. They have so many author appearances: several every day. Clearly, writers are ten a penny and that close to worthless.

Greatest highs? First, the Rock & Roll Hall of Fame itself: kind people, and unexpectedly ultra-competent; thoroughly decent archiving, a tremendous, knowledgeable audience and a great theatre to speak in, with a brilliant sound system and a suitably huge screen – on which the footage of the complete Newcastle '66 'Like A Rolling Stone' was heart-stoppingly thrilling. This was part of a special new one-off version of a talk called 'Bob Dylan & the History of Rock'n'Roll', which in a previous incarnation six years ago was the first talk I gave after *Song & Dance Man III*'s publication. At the end, they were selling copies of that book as well as of the *Encyclopedia*.

Then there was the Dylan exhibition happening right there at the Hall of Fame: an extraordinarily well-curated, wide-ranging assemblage, full of encounters with shimmering, numinous artefacts.

The next high: just an hour or two after my talk, walking down the street, my wife and I happened to go into a bar called the Fat Fish Blue, where there was a septuagenarian group playing, including several sax players. There was no cover charge, and the place was busy. A couple of drunk white women were dancing with embarrassing enthusiasm, looked down upon with merited disdain by the leader of the group – and then they announced

'Once again, ladies and gentlemen, the great Robert Lockwood Junior!'... and this immaculately dressed, sharp-suited old gent with excellent co-respondent shoes and a more modest smile walked slowly across the front of the band, up a couple of steps to a stool, sat on it, was handed his electric guitar, plugged in, and gave a strong performance, including some forceful and dexterous guitarwork: a far better set than such an old man could have been expected to deliver.

We got talking to the bandleader afterwards, and when I told him I was writing Blind Willie McTell's biography he insisted on introducing me to Mr. Lockwood, saying that he would be able to tell me stuff about him from way back when. Privately I doubted this, since McTell had no Mississippi connections, but I was very happy to meet Robert Lockwood Junior – and he was lovely: a warm handshake, an easy manner and a much-appreciated straightforwardness. 'I never met the man,' he told me à propos of McTell.

The next high was the New School gig in NYC, organised by Bob Levinson and professor and poet Robert Polito: a tremendous audience, place packed out, with people in the stairwells and corridors.

And then there was Austin, Texas – the first time I'd been in this beguiling town since 1979. Again, a packed-out hall and a marvellous audience, plus civilised considerate people all over town, including radio DJ Bryan Beck, who drove us from his studio to the campus to save us having to get a taxi, and Dylan-enthusiast classics professor Tom Palaima, who had organised the event. He had met us at the airport when we arrived at *1am* on a direct flight from New York, and, with his wife Carolyn, he threw a fine reception for us at their home just ahead of the gig and let us unwind there again afterwards. Here we stayed at a real B&B: Woodburn House: a lovely old wooden home that was being looked after, not smothered in pastiche, and where the guests were looked after too.

Other memories: the security queues at airports being less of a pain than in the UK (better organised and less under-staffed); travelling up and down Manhattan on water taxis; being in a taxi in Austin that crashed into the side of a pick-up truck at a traffic-lights (both sides to blame); the pleasantness of City Lights bookstore in San Francisco; the unpleasantness of Booksmiths bookstore in the same city, on boringly scuzzy old Haight Street, where we met Bob Dylan's old Dinkytown pal Dave Whitaker, who came to my talk but was only there in body (and only sporadically in that: he kept getting up from his front-row seat, pacing around at the back and sitting down again).

Much more pleasant was meeting Tony Glover at the end of the Dylan talk of mine at a bookstore in Minneapolis. 'That's an interesting thing that you do,' he told me.[65]

We were grateful, too, for the kindness and interesting mind of the manager at Black Oak Books in Berkeley, Lewis Klausner, with whom we drank beautiful old-vines Zinfandel a few doors down the street, at a wine bar run by people who are actually interested in wine – which made me register that in England this is more or less unheard of.

There was, too, the delightful refuge of Jack's Restaurant (formerly Jack's Oyster Bar) and its ex-London Eastender head waiter whose accent was a weird mix of East Coast US, Australia (where he'd grown up) and cockney, in the handsome state capital of NY, Albany, when we had escaped from Woodstock.

Home in North Yorkshire, with winter coming on, I went to my computer one morning and learnt of the death two days earlier, on Tuesday 21st November, of Robert Lockwood Junior. He had died in hospital of respiratory failure after suffering a stroke on 3rd November in Cleveland, where he had been based for many decades. He was 91.

His death severed almost the last direct link with the pre-war Mississippi blues world. His father had disappeared when he was young, and his mother had taken up with Robert Johnson, who was only four years older than Junior; Johnson had taught him guitar, and they had played together live many times.

Mr. Lockwood had first recorded when Bob Dylan was two months old.

[65] Tony Glover died in St Paul MN on 29th May 2019; he was 79.

I'm Not There
(2007)

I was commissioned to write about Todd Haynes's film I'm Not There *by* Sight & Sound *magazine, which meant I was able to attend a preview in hushed ultra-comfort in central London and a long time before it might have reached any big screen near my North Yorkshire home.*

It is, for a start, the perfect title for a film about Bob Dylan – and must have been the perfect title for Todd Haynes to have proposed to Bob Dylan in the first place, to secure his blessing and the rights to use the songs. For if there's one thing totally predictable about Bob Dylan, it's his desire to maintain his unwavering career-long stance as the artful dodger.

The idea of representing some of the crucial manifestations of Bob Dylan with six different actors was simple but ingenious and beguiling, and no doubt appealed at once to the current version of Bob Dylan, who seems today, at 66, to be so very interested in his own artistic history, instead of being the man whose motto was once *Dont Look Back*.

(There was, with pointless defiance, no apostrophe in that phrase when it was the title of the gorgeous cinéma-vérité film by D.A. Pennebaker which documented Dylan's 1965 visit to a Britain that still *was* black and white, or at least foggy monochrome, with an industrial north full of smoking chimneys and street urchins on cobbled back alleys far from Swinging London – two worlds bridged only by the moptop Beatles before Bob Dylan descended as from another planet, to be photographed levitating amongst ragamuffin scousers and staring out the grimy window of a steam train crossing the Pennines, as well as holding a giant light bulb and chain-smoking through the London Airport mêlée and the Savoy hotel press conference.)

You might say, too, on the evidence of Haynes's earlier film

Far from Heaven, that here is the ideal director for any film set in a past recent enough for its distinctive period look, and the way it photographed itself at the time, to be recognised at once by those of a certain age. *Far from Heaven*, as narrative, declines into an implausible so-what?, but as a long, long stare into the undergrowth of a specific era, rendered with all the hushed curiosity of David Attenborough peering through the bushes at soon-to-be-extinct gorillas, it is heart-stoppingly beautiful.

With *I'm Not There*, Haynes has decided not to bother about narrative plausibility, instead letting his masterly gift for period jump around the time zones of Dylan's first two decades of creative work. We move recurrently from black and white to colour and back again as we encounter – and certainly not in chronological order – the Wannabe Guthrie boy with the chubby cheeks and the fantasy CV; the protest singer; the amphetamine genius of 1965-66; the *Basement Tapes* country drop-out who crashes his motorbike and saddles up a horse, morphing into Peckinpah's Billy the Kid along the way; the philanderer whose art created *Blood On The Tracks*; and the sartorially challenged live performer-preacher from *Saturday Night Live,* 1979-style.

The viewer who, like me, knows all Haynes's Dylanesque allusions off by heart, has no difficulty whatever in following the story (a standard postmodernist fusion of fact and fiction) through all these episodic set pieces, no matter that not one on-screen character is named either Bob or Dylan, and no matter that they are played, among others, by a black youth (Marcus Carl Franklin), an Englishman (Christian Bale), a woman (Cate Blanchett), and a raddled and slightly paunchy Richard Gere. The unexpected upshot is that while all the hype about the film shouts that this is as far from the tired old conventional biopic as possible, for the Dylan aficionado it works *exactly* like a biopic.

Like a biopic, it gets some things more right than others, and some more wrong. Like a biopic, it tries to touch upon the main dramas of the life and the career (and it would be rare, even within the most plodding film of the genre, not to point up the tussles between public success and private failings). It tries to get close to its subject, while relying on the shorthand of whatever handy myths are to be found blowing around; and it asks one star to try to impersonate another.

In general, surely, films of this kind try to be compelling, and contemporary in their telling, by a seductive kind of suprarealism, and by tougher scripting than in Hollywood's golden age. I don't much go in for biopics myself, but I was dragged along to see James Mangold's *Walk the Line*, on Johnny Cash, and submitted voluntarily to Taylor Hackford's film *Ray* (re Charles, as it were) and admired both. Watching *Ray*, I often forgot that Jamie Foxx wasn't Ray. Watching *Walk the Line*, I found Joaquin Phoenix and Reese Witherspoon more convincing than their real-life counterparts.

Unlike a biopic, though, with *I'm Not There* you just have to know the subject's story before you watch the film. That may not limit the audience for this film too much anymore. In choosing Bob Dylan, at this time, Haynes comes running along behind Martin Scorsese's *No Direction Home,* which itself gobbled up footage from Dylan's widely-unseen and previously-obscure *Eat the Document* while simultaneously putting Dylan up there in the mainstream pantheon at last. Up there, that is, no longer just as the very famous minority-taste fixation of an ageing generation but as an authenticated All-American 20th-Century Hero alongside Brando, Monroe and Presley. Besides, Bob Dylan continues to pull in wave after generational wave of new young people, drawn to him usually by the work of his youth – especially by the clarity and continued aptness of the pre-electric socio-political songs so long taken for granted and largely ignored by the original baby-boomer audience who had been so excited by Dylan's going electric instead.

Oddly, perhaps, it was Scorsese whose film drew out the magic not only of the solo acoustic young Dylan but of the whole Greenwich Village bohemian scene, while Todd Haynes, who was born the same year Dylan began recording, is clearly entranced only by the electrified, wild mercury mid-60s Dylan.

This is where the film begins, and where it loves to linger and admire. This Dylan dies in the motorbike crash at the start, only to rise again in three minutes and in a thrilling, brief sequence, to inhabit the viewer – as I watch the film, I am that wild mercury Bob walking onto the stage in a blur of adrenalin rush to join the Hawks, who are straining at the leash but in a whirl of bewilderment, as I take up my position ready to invoke all that shouting and outrage.

If nothing else in the film quite matches the exceptional vividness of that moment, Todd Haynes's real love of his own medium – his powerful understanding of *how film looks on the big screen* – yields comparable drama many times in what follows.

There is mesmerising footage early on of black and white New York City and dazzlingly coloured rural America running alongside Dylan's studio sides of 'Memphis Blues Again' and 'Nashville Skyline', running into 'Moonshiner' (a resourceful bumping-together of different Dylans in itself).

There is a scene set to 'Simple Twist Of Fate', Dylan kids playing in the park, so it's the early 1970s, and you know this instantly because what we see, affectingly, is exactly the colouration we have at home on all the colour prints of our own lives snapped at the time. He is surely unmatched at this fond precision: we are plunged, in the blink of a frame, *into* the early 1970s.

In interviews Haynes has seemed to rush to forestall the anticipated nitpickery of Dylanists (like me). He told Sean O'Hagan in the *Observer Music Monthly* that 'To me, it's like the ultimate misunderstanding of Dylan to try and pin him down by collecting and endlessly analysing everything he does.' Whereas *he* 'wanted to track Dylan's creative imagination and where it took him and how his life mirrored that imagination, or propelled it, or followed it'. (Oh, is *that* all?…)

For me, at least, the inaccuracies and tweakings of the Dylan myth are thoroughly untroubling. The only times I want to demur are in those very few places where the filmscript's interventions serve up something less effective for the film itself than a closer reading of Dylan's own script would give them.

Why re-write the perfect Manchester Free Trade Hall *'Judas!'* moment? Cate Blanchett's Dylan has that word shouted at her twice instead of once, and then replies far less succinctly and alertly than Bob did. He said 'I don't believe you. You're a liar.' It was anti-showbiz in a trice: personal, open, brief, clear, and direct dialogue: unprecedented. Cate's response is a stumbling, blurred and tired generalisation: 'You're all liars.' A hopeless substitution.

A different foolish move is to take some of the speech out of the mouth of the marvellously wise-beyond-his-years Bob Dylan who is only 23, and suddenly the hippest person alive, and yet who talks in earnest honesty to the hapless Horace Judson, the hack in a mac from *Time* magazine, telling him that since each of us might die at any time, each must decide how seriously to take that, and should know our purpose in the world.

When Judson asks Dylan, 'Do you care what you sing?', Dylan's riposte – 'How could I answer that if you've got the nerve to ask me?' – is, in context, restrained, almost like a mentor guiding a child toward enlightenment. Haynes says he marvels at Dylan's interviews of the period as performance art, and he's generally right: one of the many ways that Dylan dragged us into the contemporary world was (like Mandy Rice-Davies's explosively truthful retort in court at the trial of Stephen Ward two years earlier), by breaking the rules of the game – in this case the game whereby even the daftest of media questions was answered with dull solemnity by every celebrity. Rebellious 1950s Elvis had said 'Yes, sir' and 'Yes, ma'am' to reporters. Dylan's technique of countering a dumb question with a more acute one of his own comes across as desirous of direct communication. Taken out of context in the film, it is reduced to being a part of Blanchettbob's spoilt-brat petulance.

These falls into clumsiness are a small price to pay for the film's exuberant visual richness, for the pay-off we get from the fact that in the end, Haynes is more wholly in love with film than with his iconic Bob Dylan.

To Dylan people it's a small surprise, but no transgression, that Haynes shoots 1966 in black & white as well as 1965 (we're used to *Dont Look Back*'s 1965 bursting into the colour of *Eat the Document*'s 1966).

There's the larger surprise that while Charlotte Gainsbourg plays a French painter who's an amalgam of Sara Dylan and Suze Rotolo, this superficial fictionalising allows Haynes to get away with peeking quite long and hard at the real first Dylan marriage and its breakdown. As I watched these scenes between Gainsbourg and the Heath Ledger Bob (we know it's him by the sunglasses), I thought of the way the Bob'n'Sara divorce settlement bound her to life-long silence, and wondered how she might feel to see this Dylan-endorsed Hollywood movie sprawling their lives across the screen.

Again, it's not long since Dylan's lawyers were leaning firmly on the filming of George Hickenlooper's *Factory Girl*, to try to stop anyone playing Bob Dylan in a story suggesting that he and Edie Sedgwick had a relationship; yet in *I'm Not There*, he's there: the long sequence in Warhol Factory op-art New York has Blanchettbob and Edie centre stage, the warring cool couple, young and thin and beautiful, but in a relationship, plain as studio lighting.

It's inspired to conflate the going-up-the-country of the Woodstock years with the Durango outlaw milieu of Dylan-as-Alias in *Pat Garrett and Billy the Kid*. It's truly inspired that there's a sudden correspondence created by the temporal impossibility of moving from this rural-retreat reclusive country-rocker and hunted-outlaw Dylan jumping onto a boxcar to find the Woody Guthrie guitar of the young hobo-dreamer Dylan who had hung around in Minnesota and Colorado before ever he came to New York City.

It's some kind of cyclical salvation, but in its way it admits a truth the film largely appears to deny: namely that these Bob Dylans are not, at base, disparate or separate characters, but differing stages in the growth of a man and in the ebbs and flows of a great artist. One Dylan can very often be seen turning into the next. Certainly it seems a redundancy that Haynes splits into two the Dylan of the late 1965 press conferences (Ben Whishaw as the Arthur Rimbaud Bob) from the Blanchettbob of 1965-66.

Yet these largely-separated Bob Worlds are all portrayed with vigour and with what often comes across as a Dylanesque kind of instinctive intelligence – as when Whishaw's press conference Dylan is questioned not by reporters but by what seems to be some kind of House Un-American Activities Committee.

I had qualms only about the world of Dylan and The Band 1967-8, the world so memorably dubbed by Greil Marcus as 'the old, weird America'. The use of records as the soundtrack is powerful and celebratory from start to finish in the film (it's striking how central *Blonde On Blonde* is) and it's hugely gratifying to find Dylan's own spooky oft-bootlegged recording of the title song out here officially for all the world to hear, but even the piercing beauty of Dylan's 1967 song 'Goin' To Acapulco', sung by Jim James with Calexico, can't quite redeem this stageyness (which, like all the scenes with Richard Gere, lacks the certainty of the rest). This particular weird America all starts to look a bit too much like the unconvincing marketing-job that was the front cover of the official *Basement Tapes* double-LP suddenly come to theatrical life.

But this is to collide again with an unease about Dylan's own shift toward a deliberate reprocessing of his own legend. There's a hint of unseemly re-marketing exercise about this. If it began with that *Basement Tapes* front cover, it reached its apogee with the dreadful *Masked and Anonymous* of 2003, a hopelessly ponderous film mostly about Dylan's mystique.

There's nothing ponderous about *I'm Not There*. It's a highly-charged, celebratory rejoicing in film itself. Todd Haynes didn't have to rearrange their faces and give them all another name – but he's done it with style and grace. It doesn't even matter, in the end, that one of the things the film can't help but show is that none of these star actors comes within striking distance of the mid-60s Dylan's charisma and beauty. So perhaps it's a fan's touch on Haynes's part, in the final end, that he reaches for some more of that *Eat the Document* footage – a slice that Scorsese didn't trust the audience enough to show, of Dylan conjuring his most inventively intimate harmonica on stage in 1966, the camera lingering in close-up on a real Bob Dylan.

A Tell Tale Signs 1-CD Personal Best-Of (2009)

In 2009 I compiled, just for my blog, a 1-CD shortlist of the best tracks from the 3-CD Dylan release Tell Tale Signs, *ruling out the live tracks. It's not given best-track-first etc, but as they seem to make the best running order. Essentially it begins at the most acoustic folk-and-blues end and swells from there.*

1. Mary And The Soldier
(Disc 3)

2. 32-20 Blues
(Disc 2)

3. Most Of The Time
(Could almost be a *Blood On The Tracks* outtake, Disc 1)

4. *Red River Shore*
(Disc 1)

5. Can't Wait
(The slow version from Disc 3)

6. Mississippi
(The different-words version, so surely the earliest, Disc 3)

7. Mississippi
(The folksiest version, Disc 1)

8. Mississippi
(Lovely prowling, stylised voice, almost a bit 1966ish, Disc 2)

9. Dignity
(Disc 2)

10. God Knows
(Surprisingly appealing, unlike on *Under The Red Sky*, Disc 2)

11. Can't Escape From You
(Disc 2)

12. Ring Them Bells
(Disc 3)

13. Marchin' To The City
(Definitely Disc 1)

14. Can't Wait
(Disc 1, with some lovely alternative words)

About that version of 'Dignity': well, first of all despite Bob being too low in the mix, I like the bounty of so many different words – not better ones, but highly interesting: and sometimes funny, as when he sings of getting off the train and it starting to rain and then adds a reference to 'somebody with water on his brain'. Another moment I like comes after his looking east, west, cursed, blessed, when he adds the neatly self-mocking and undercutting 'askin' everybody like a man possessed' (also a resourceful rhyme to throw in). And then I also think he sings 'land of the midnight sun' even more beautifully than usual.

Then when I was driving along one time, the motion of the car made me register the rhythm differently. Some tracks work better in the car than in the house. In the same way, some tracks need to be heard on headphones while others sound best from a whole room away from the speakers.

'Duncan And Brady' nearly made it to the list above; I still dither about ''Cross The Green Mountain'. I don't dither about 'Tell Ol' Bill', 'Born In Time', 'Dreamin' Of You' or 'Huck's Tune': no no no. And while Disc 2's 'Ain't Talkin'' has the advantage of comparative brevity over the *Modern Times* take, it was never going to make any shortlist of mine: it's just risible that a song claiming the singer 'ain't talkin'' has him talkin' for such a very long time.

Meeting Bob Dylan's High School English Teacher (2009)

Adapted from a blog entry of 31st July 2009.

I was very sorry to learn of the death of Boniface J. Rolfzen, Bob Dylan's high school English teacher for two years in the 1950s. He was born in April 1923 and died, aged 86, on Wednesday 29th July 2009. He had retired from teaching in 1985, and until illness required him to live in a nursing home, he and his wife Leona had long lived on East 24th Street in Hibbing, Minnesota. My own encounters with Mr. Rolfzen were limited but memorable (on my side, anyway). He came to my talk in Hibbing Public Library in April 2001, and though he wasn't one of those who came up and spoke to me afterwards, I heard later that he had delivered a most complimentary verdict about it. Then on 24th March 2007, as a busload of us arrived in Hibbing for lunch at Zimmy's Atrium & Bar Restaurant, on the trip to town organised as an optional extra for speakers at the University of Minnesota's three-day Dylan Symposium, I was among those who met and chatted to both BJ and Leona.[66] He was alert and gracious.

By then I had been able to send him a copy of *The Bob Dylan Encyclopedia*, and in return he gave me, and inscribed, a copy of his self-published *The Spring of My Life: A Memoir of Growing Up in a Small Town in Central Minnesota During The Great Depression Years 1923-1941*. It was an interesting story, and scrupulous in avoiding stretching his story past 1941 to big up his connection to Dylan.

Yet his contribution *was* big: many of us were rescued, as schoolchildren, by having one inspirational teacher, and Boniface J. Rolfzen was that teacher for Bob Zimmerman. He surely

[66] Leona A. Rolfzen died 7th April 2015.

contributed hugely to us all, by educating and helping to develop Dylan's strikingly early self-confidence in and around English and American Literature. That's quite something.[67]

PS. After I wrote the above about Mr. Rolfzen just after his death, I was contacted by 'Alex from Grand Rapids Minnesota', who reported him as having told her this about when Dylan was in his class:

> Robert was shy. I can see him coming through the door of classroom 204. I remember it distinctly because he was always doing the same thing. He always came in to class alone. He always sat in the same chair, three seats from the door in the first row. Right under my nose for two years.

Got to get up near the teacher if you can, if you wanna learn anything...

---

[67] Late in life, Mr. Rolfzen co-operated with Hibbing's annual Dylan Days (and would listen to Dylan at home: see https://www.minnpost.com/community-voices/2009/08/bj-rolfzen-legacy-words-and-dreams/ written August 2009).

Muldoon, Carmichael & Dylan
(2009)

From a blog post of December 2009.

In a *London Review of Books* September issue, in a letter from an Anthony Paul in Amsterdam, I found this terrific statement from the poet Paul Muldoon, from his 'Author's Note' to his *Poems 1968-98,* pursuing the logic of feeling that there is a mystery, or visitation, or transcendence, at the heart of poetic creation:

> I have made scarcely any changes in the texts of the poems, since I'm fairly certain that, after a shortish time, the person through whom a poem was written is no more entitled to make revisions than any other reader.

I love that. When it comes to poets who *did* feel free to revise their texts substantially, the first who spring to mind are the alliterative William Wordsworth and Walt Whitman; but when Muldoon calls himself 'the person through whom' the poems were written, I think of Bob Dylan saying he felt his early songs seemed to exist in the air and that he was just the person who wrote them down.

Dylan seems still to feel sometimes that a song can simply 'arrive', as it were, as when he said this of Hoagy Carmichael on *Theme Time Radio Hour:*

> One of the most famous songs Hoagy every wrote was 'Stardust', and like many songwriters he wasn't sure where it really came from. This is what he had to say the first time he ever heard a recording of 'Stardust': 'And then it happened. That queer sensation that this melody was bigger than me. Maybe I hadn't written it at all. The recollection of how, when, and where, it all happened became vague as the lingering strains hung in the rafters in the studio. I wanted to shout back at it

"Maybe I didn't write you, but I found you!'" Hoagy Carmichael on 'Stardust'. I know just what he meant.

All this relates to a basic fact about art: the artist can only know about the work done by the conscious part of his or her mind, and not about the undoubted contribution of the unconscious: so the artist is no more of an authority on the work than the rest of us, provided that we're interested, receptive and attentive.

This is why had I been writing a biography of Dylan, an interview might have been helpful, but in writing books about Dylan's *work* I've felt no need to try to interview him. People have often expressed surprise when I've said this; Paul Muldoon would not be surprised.

Christmas In The Heart
(2009)

Reviewed on my blog, 20th December 2009.

I love and admire it. From very first hearing, it earns its place in the Christmas canon, along with the Phil Spector album and the Elvis one. It works, as Peter Doggett suggests, not least because (and this is in strong contrast to *Modern Times* particularly) 'its intentions and aims are so modest, and its pretensions are so few'.[68]

Everything people have written about its authenticity of spirit, its clear sincerity, seems exactly right. And though this sincerity means, for the 68-year-old Bob Dylan, harking back to the musical heralds of the 1940s-50s, there is no big orchestra, no florid choir, no grandiosity. Hence the carols on the album are a particular and complete success. I don't know *how* it works to combine/alternate, as Dylan does, the clear and clean-cut, scrupulous 1950s background (and sometimes not so background) voices with his own decrepit vocal struggles, since the two evoke such utterly different eras and atmospheres, but it *does* work. It can only be modesty of size on both sides that gives this unity.

The still small voices on, for instance, 'Hark The Herald Angels Sing', sounds nothing like the Ray Charles Singers or any massed choir; they remind me, if anything, of the voices at the beginning of 'Take A Message To Mary' on *Self Portrait*; both have a kindly tone and gentle intimacy, as if explaining the story to very young children. (The *blend* of male and female voices is also exactly what Roy Orbison was aiming for on the dum-dum-dum-dum-bee-doo-wahs of 'Only The Lonely' – a record from 1960 but which shimmered with the same lovely aural richness captured by the valve equipment that made 1950s records glisten so distinctively.) In inspired parallel to the singers, Dylan and the two (just two)

[68] Peter Doggett, probably a review in *Record Collector*, which he edited.

violins, the plain piano and their unobtrusive support are small-scale too.

Their valiant straightforwardness is an affecting enactment of humility – and unlikely as this is, the picture it conjures in my mind is of a little rural church in the English Middle Ages, with a small congregation of ardently believing peasants, back before church organs replaced the music-making that made the worshippers participants. In this way it's close to folk music, and to semi-pagan hymn singing inside draughty, bucolic, poor church walls, not far from the stables and the cowsheds and the inn. This is so much fresher and more vivid than the approach we could have expected from the Bob Dylan of 2009.

Similarly, on 'The First Noel', which ends so bravely, rather than replicating some Hollywood Cathedral on Capitol Records 1955, the solicitous choral voices emerge like a small huddle of carol singers, careful and polite at the lamplit snowy door. So strong is the effect of simplicity in all this that it survives even the rather grander upward key-change toward the end of 'O Little Town Of Bethlehem', which declares itself with a more artful tip of the musical hat, a retrospective throat-clearing glance as Dylan pulls back to reoccupy his more customary starring role and thus to give us that 'Amen' that ends the album. And it is *the* most charming 'Amen' you'll ever hear, and so one of the very best signings-off he's created at a Dylan album's end.

The rest all offers the same straightforward attentiveness and artistic sincerity. The particulars that come to mind include these: the lightly sinuous guitar or mandolin figures on 'Do You Hear What I Hear?', the lovely piano on 'I'll Be Home For Christmas' and the many pleasures of his singing, despite it all. Not least: the appropriately fleeting way his voice goes away on the phrase 'gone away' on 'Winter Wonderland'; the delicate vocal shepherding of the little lamb on 'Do You Hear What I Hear?'; the terrific way he sings 'now---' before the second bridge on 'Have Yourself A Merry Little Christmas', and the empathy he radiates as he sings 'their treasures' on 'Silver Bells' (enacting the way a child might value toy 'treasures'); the vocal ease on 'The Christmas Blues' and 'Christmas Island';[69] the pleasure of hearing him sing 'sinners reconciled' – the original text, as it were, from which an earlier Bob Dylan had spun his variation within 'Lord Protect My Child'; the funny panache with which on 'Must Be Santa' he sings 'who laughs this way: "ho ho ho"?' in a way no Santa Claus will ever better on record or in magic grotto;[70] and that other enactment, in which his voice strains to reach 'the highest *bough*---' on 'Have Yourself A Merry Little Christmas'.

There's one moment where he doesn't, if you will, sing the song quite straight – the one diversion into noticeable vocal improvisation – but since it is one moment, it's beguiling rather than disruptive. It comes on the same song when, the first time around after 'Next year', he phrases 'all our troubles will be out of sight' as a precipitate wandering-off (that briefly reminds me of his wonderful route through Elvis's 'Can't Help Falling In Love' all those decades ago).

There's also the quiet way he keeps faith with the context in which 'I'll Be Home For Christmas' and 'Have Yourself A Merry Little Christmas' were written, in that part of the early 1940s when even the Americans had joined in the Second World War and soldiers were wistfully far from home. And what Dylan sews through these songs is the consequent sense that it's *death* that might or might not – 'if the fates allow' – keep the singer from the Christmas hearth.

And then, Dylan's voice adds in a hint of his knowledge that death must come relatively soon for him too, not as wartime soldier but as frail, growing-elderly man, conscious that after all those Christmases which quintessentially feel timeless, time is running out and there will inevitably be a Christmas for which he cannot make it home.

[69] The first time Dylan played on a recording of a song called 'Christmas Island' was when he put harmonica on the Dick Fariña song of that name, 14th-15th January 1963, cut at Dobell's Jazz Record Shop, London and released on *Dick Fariña & Eric Von Schmidt*, Folklore Records F-LEUT-7, 1964 and CD, Solano Records 1772, July 2007. On the *Christmas In The Heart* album, it's a different song, written in 1946 by Lyle Moraine (1914-1988).

[70] When I blogged this, a reader commented 'Let's hope there's another video.' I said let's hope there *isn't* another. 99% of videos are reductive, and the one for 'Must Be Santa' elbows aside the universal feel of timeless, fun muscularity and the blurry-edged, rambunctious red and gold glow of the audio for a pallid and tedious scene as from some hopelessly Californian TV series, drained of lifeblood and zest.

Just as Andrew Muir said of *World Gone Wrong*, this is a collection of non-Dylan songs that adds up to an authentic Dylan album.[71] (And of course that means these days that it's a relief not to have to wonder which parts of the lyrics he's stolen or borrowed from elsewhere.) But to reverse the emphasis, it's partly so terrific because the songs, these non-Dylan songs, are mostly so very good. So enormously, strikingly better than those on *Together Through Life* or for the most part on *Modern Times*.

(A couple of small demurs here: it doesn't speak to anyone looking for political commentary on that little town of Bethlehem of course, and as wife Sarah has pointed out, 'Here Comes Santa Claus', cheery and catchy though it is, palpably lies when it tells children it doesn't matter if you're rich or poor, Santa loves you just the same. This might be true of Jesus, but not of Santa, who has always given blatantly better presents to the children of the rich.)

On the whole, though, these are very strong songs, and built to last. Like Dylan's early songs – like 'Blowin' In The Wind' and unlike 'Ain't Talkin'' – the repertoire he offers here can speak to anyone in our culture. Not one of them is by Cole Porter (though it's true Mel Tormé co-wrote 'The Christmas Song') and not all are from Tin Pan Alley. 'Here Comes Santa Claus' was co-written by Gene Autry. 'O Come All Ye Faithful' was written in the 18th century by English hymnist John Francis Wade, exiled from England for his Catholic beliefs; 'O Little Town Of Bethlehem' by an Episcopal priest (Phillips Brooks) in the 1860s; and the English carol 'The First Noel' was probably written in the 12th or 13th century: rather earlier than Tin Pan Alley (or even *Hamlet*).

Yet with *Christmas In The Heart* it isn't just the songs but the interpretation. It isn't just the songs but the *album*. It already feels as if I've known it all my life yet sounds entirely fresh. It's all so *accurate* and perfectly in the best spirit. No contamination by knowingness or soppy ingratiation. No fakery. A real Bob Dylan album.

---

[71] Andrew Muir, *Troubadour* (Bluntisham, Cambridgeshire, UK: Woodstock Publications, 2003), p.191.

Bob Dylan In Concert, Brandeis University 1963:
The Liner Notes
(2010)

Dylan's office asked me to write liner notes for this Sony-Legacy release. The one change to the notes insisted on by Dylan's office was to delete my clear attributing of 'Honey, Just Allow Me One More Chance' to Bob Dylan & Henry Thomas – the credit given on the 1963 album, and given again 40 years later on the 2003 CD. The revised version (below) takes Henry Thomas off the credits other than in the most sidelined way. I made the change reluctantly, being in no position to decline the assignment but disliking the way that in recent Dylan decades, shared songwriting credits – and therefore monies – get denied to pre-war originators and links in the chain.

That said, it is not an important item in Bob's catalogue, but it catches him at a tipping-point career moment, and the liner notes place that in context. On the vinyl version they are spread across the back cover, which is designed to look as if the whole thing had been issued back in 1963.

It's a small miracle this recording exists. In 2009 a collector found a tape box labelled 'Dylan Brandeis', in faint pencil, among material collected over a lifetime by the late great music critic Ralph J. Gleason. Clearly a professional recording, it had survived 46 years in Gleason's house in terrific condition. The Bob Dylan performance it captured, from way back when Kennedy was president and The Beatles hadn't yet reached America, wasn't even on fans' radar.

It reveals him *not* at any Big Moment but giving a performance like his folkclub sets of the period: repertoire from an ordinary working day – and very much of its time…

It's early May 1963, and Dylan is low on the bill on the opening day of the Brandeis University Folk Festival. The weekend's stars are Jean Redpath, Jean Ritchie and Pete Seeger. Bob is 21 years old. His début LP, *Bob Dylan*, released fourteen months earlier, has proved a commercial flop. Recording sessions for a second album have been happening fitfully for over a year, ending less than three weeks back.

Dylan has leapt a creative canyon with this material. His first LP features only two of his own songs; this second album will be full of them.

Strange, then – yet typical of Dylan – that tonight's short Brandeis set offers nothing from the album that's out there, and only *one* major song from this bountiful, newly completed collection.

No 'Girl From The North Country'. No 'Don't Think Twice, It's All Right'. No 'A Hard Rain's A-Gonna Fall', though its eerie brilliance and poetic power have enthralled all those who've heard it in performances stretching back seven months.

Brandeis doesn't even get 'Blowin' In The Wind' – a song 'hot off the pencil' more than a year earlier, and which Albert Grossman has hawked around established acts. The Chad Mitchell Trio's cover has been out two months. Peter, Paul and Mary's is coming. Bob's version will be out in 17 days' time: the new album's opening track.

Tonight, Dylan chooses only 'Masters Of War' from among these big songs. What *do* we have on this new CD from almost 50 years ago?

1: 'Honey, Just Allow Me One More Chance' is closest to the material on Bob's first album, and to fitting his description in Brandeis' magazine *Justice*: 'one of the new and most exciting blues performers'. Negligibly based on the obscure 'Honey, Won't You Allow Me Just One More Chance' by Henry Thomas – a song which is firmly in the folk music songster tradition – cut in Chicago in 1927, which Bob hears on a 1961 reissue, it will become a minor *Freewheelin'* item.

2: 'Talkin' John Birch Paranoid Blues', the first of three talking blues tonight, mocks America's frenetic anti-communists. Bob published it in the launch issue of *Broadside* magazine back in February 1962. He's recorded it, and performed it before. It goes down well tonight, but two days later Bob will turn up at the TV studio for his big slot on the *Ed Sullivan Show...* and walk out when the studio won't let him perform it.

3: 'Ballad Of Hollis Brown': a major song, and one already frequently performed – yet won't see release until the *third* Dylan album, *The Times They Are A-Changin'*, in 1964.

4: 'Masters Of War' closes the first half, leaving a crowd audibly excited by Dylan's purposive freshness and clarity as a singer, musician and wordsmith.

5: 'Talkin' World War III Blues', more topical commentary, previews another minor song to surface on *Freewheelin'*.

6: 'Bob Dylan's Dream' does likewise, using an old folk melody to forge a new song of great reflective eloquence about camaraderie, time and loss. This may be the set's latest composition.

7: 'Talkin' Bear Mountain Picnic Massacre Blues' is surely the oldest. It's Dylan at his closest to Woody Guthrie, and he's been performing it since June 1961, when he was still emerging from his Guthrie jukebox phase.

This is the last live performance we have of Bob Dylan before he becomes a star. Within weeks, *Freewheelin'* is issued; Peter, Paul and Mary release their 'Blowin' In The Wind', which sells two million; and in late July Dylan arrives at the Newport Folk Festival as a newcomer and leaves as its stellar success. A month later comes the March on Washington. Everything seems transcendent with hope, warmed by communal consensus and the politics of change.

That November, President Kennedy is assassinated. Dylan's political certainties unravel. He expands his gloriously long exploration of the possibilities of song.

Benjamin, De Quincey, Auster & Dylan (2010)

Unpublished; written in 2010.

Dylan harks back to the blues, 1940s radio, pre-1960s Hollywood and the non-commodified beginnings of rock music in much the same way as the grand old man of cultural studies, Walter Benjamin, looks back at what was the recent past to him. As Angela McRobbie puts it, it was:

> [T]he discarded ruins, the recent remains, the small trinkets and souvenirs of consumer capitalism and modernity which interested Benjamin ... [he] sought out the older shops and café corners and the crumbling arcades of the cities in which he lived, rather than the magnificent boulevards or great buildings which so clearly expressed the bold modernist confidence of their architects. From watching and walking ... he developed a cultural vision of the city as layered and labyrinthine ... It is this circumspect, convoluted and sometimes seemingly perverse mode of analysis which makes Benjamin a figure to whom writers on postmodernity have recently turned back ...
>
> For Benjamin the task was to unravel the meanings of the discarded items lying in these dusty corners.
>
> The Paris arcades, already in Benjamin's time well past their 'sell-by date' ... could be looked to as a 'precursor of modernity' ... the arcades become emblems, icons of an 'unmastered' past moment not yet defined as historical ... their cathedral-like ceilings, the dim light from the glass and windows, and their long passageways like church aisles, flanked on either side not by small chapels but by chapels of consumption, demonstrated exactly what Benjamin recognized as ... *the tendency to incorporate at some unconscious level familiar and comforting reminders of those things which new technology ... social progress and ... the new object itself makes redundant.* This looking back to the non-contemporary signifies not simply nostalgia but rather a stirring of discontent or dissatisfaction with the present

which cannot be extinguished even by the brilliance, luxury and the apparent mass availability of the new.[72]

De Quincey seems to have chosen to wander the streets of London in a comparable way, partly for its randomness of experience and its cavalcade of faces, but also for the resonance set up between external and internal change: between experiencing the loss of old buildings and alleyways as grand new buildings went up, and the stirring of memories of personal loss.[73]

All this is recognisably a significant part of what impels Dylan's recurrent interest in rifling through the old acoustic blues while writing songs, in insisting upon thrusting the whiskery past – the old, weird America, in Greil Marcus's phrase – and even in his habit of shuffling around cheap neighbourhoods at odd hours of the night while on tour, and how he makes lost pasts feel like lost loves, or else, more commonly, insists upon the continued *presence* of the past.

You might also feel that the very first page of Paul Auster's novel *City of Glass* takes us into terrain where Walter Benjamin and Bob Dylan seem to meet. Auster describes his detective (Quinn) in his home terrain of New York City:

> More than anything else, however, what he liked to do was walk. Nearly every day, rain or shine, hot or cold, he would leave his apartment to walk through the city – never really going anywhere, but simply going wherever his legs happened to take him.
>
> New York was an inexhaustible space, a labyrinth of endless steps, and no matter how far he walked, no matter how well he came to know its neighborhoods and streets, it always left him with the feeling of being lost. Lost, not only in the city, but within himself as well...[74]

[72] Angela McRobbie: 'The Passagenwerk and the place of Walter Benjamin in cultural studies: Benjamin, cultural studies, Marxist theories of art'; *Popular Culture Journal*, Vol. 6, No.2; London: Routledge, 1992. Also published in McRobbie's *Postmodernism & Popular Culture*, 1994.

[73] *Confessions of an English Opium Eater*, Thomas De Quincey, 1821. But see also 'Romantic London and the Architecture of Memory' by Christine Lai, 2013; https://doi.org/10.1111/lic3.12047.

[74] Paul Auster: *City of Glass* (Los Angeles: Sun and Moon Press, 1985). There is a further discussion of postmodernist connexions between Auster and Dylan, plus a brief note on Benjamin, in *Song & Dance Man III: The Art of Bob Dylan*, 1999 (pp.259-60).

Listening to Dylan songs from 'She's Your Lover Now', 'Visions Of Johanna' and 'Three Angels' to 'Dignity', 'Series Of Dreams' and 'Highlands', you can hear each as depicting a protagonist pottering and wandering in that Benjaminian way, in that labyrinth of steps, or else like De Quincey or Auster, 'Lost, not only in the city, but within himself.'

Dylan's very inventing of the *long* song – his determination that, as with a poem, a song can be six minutes, or nine, and why stop there? – gave him the *form* within which to enact just such wanderings within his music, in the tales he spins.

Dylan At 70
(2011)

This was published in the Tokyo-based English-language newspaper The Japan Times *on 22nd May 2011; three days later it appeared online on Bob Dylan's website, the only Dylan Turns 70 article put up there. I had adapted some of it from the final section of* Song & Dance Man III.

Bob Dylan, the single most important artist in the history of popular music, will be 70 years old on May 24th.

He was born Robert Allen Zimmerman in the flinty, scruffy city of Duluth, Minnesota, which teeters on the hills that plummet down to the shores of Lake Superior – a lake so large it has tidal movement. But when he was six years old, his parents moved further north and west to the iron-ore town of Hibbing: so far north that but for a cartographer's miscalculation it would have been in Canada.

Iron ore built the town, and built the remarkably lavish Hibbing High School that Bob Dylan attended: a school whose concert hall has a hand-plastered, hand-painted ceiling from which crystal chandeliers imported from Belgium are lowered three times a year for cleaning, and a stage large enough to accommodate the entire Minnesota Symphony Orchestra.

This is the hall in which Dylan the schoolboy first performed, on piano, with his rock'n'roll group The Golden Chords. He hammered out Little Richard numbers on a 1922 Steinway Grand. And when he was leaving school in 1959 he wrote in his high school yearbook under 'Ambition': 'To join Little Richard'.

But by the time the young Bob had spent a semester at the University of Minnesota, and then dropped out, Little Richard wasn't really available to be joined. He had renounced secular music for the gospel, and the rock'n'roll of that generation of artists – Elvis, Chuck Berry, Jerry Lee Lewis – was being pushed off America's airwaves by nervous advertisers, and replaced by a milksop kind of pop that held no interest for Dylan. In any case, by this point he had encountered the pre-war blues recordings of Leadbelly, the campaigning songs of Woody Guthrie, acoustic folk guitarists in Dinkytown, the bohemian enclave of Minneapolis-St Paul, the writing of Jack Kerouac and more besides.

All this made sense to him, and with his usual impeccable timing, he arrived in New York City's Greenwich Village at the very beginning of 1961 – a 19-year-old already making up romantic stories about his past – just in time to take part in the most exciting period in the rise of the folk revival period. A fearless performer, a charming urchin and a pushy, slippery youth, he soon got attention: an attention he held by the striking, forceful songs he began writing so prolifically.

'How many years can a mountain exist / Before it's washed to the sea? / Yes, 'n' how many years can some people exist / Before they're allowed to be free? / Yes, 'n' how many times can a man turn his head / Pretending he just doesn't see? / The answer, my friend, is blowin' in the wind…' It's hard to feel this now, but at the time 'Blowin' In The Wind' was a wholly new, exciting song – and in a time of racial struggle and conflict across America, a time, too, of general repressive restraint, this 'protest song' spoke out, articulating what so many young people felt. When black gospel-turned-soul star Sam Cooke heard it, he was rocked back on his feet. 'How come it took a little *white* boy to write this?' he asked – and in response he was moved to write his own great anthem 'A Change Is Gonna Come'.

It's a long time ago. While we're not looking, everyone in popular music moves from symbol of youth to senior citizen, unless they fulfil the callow wish The Who once hurled at us: 'Hope I die before I get old.' Ask Pete Townshend or Roger Daltry how they feel about that now. They'll say, er, maybe old is better than dead after all.

Bob Dylan obviously thinks so. He's seen innumerable contemporaries – musicians and colleagues and friends – fall by the wayside; but he's a survivor. And not because he's looked after himself. His attempts at doing so have been fitful at best, and somehow always incongruous, from giving up smoking to taking up fitness-training, boxing, cycling to work… even playing golf, having been introduced to this most unDylanesque hobby by country star Willie Nelson.

Nor has Dylan made much attempt to keep on looking youthful. He's consented to one or two howlingly obvious airbrush jobs on album cover photos, but not many: certainly not for him the eerie reconstituting of the visage like Cher or Michael Jackson.

Dylan usually looks his age (and the rest); he's often appeared on stage stiffened by corsetry, not to pull in his stomach but to support his back; and it's been ten years now since, accepting an Oscar for the *Wonder Boys* film-soundtrack song 'Things Have Changed', he launched the innovation of a small pencil-moustache, the effect of which has been to make him look oddly like Vincent Price, and at least as sepulchral.

No, the secret of Bob Dylan's ability to keep on keeping on is nothing to do with our general clamour to put on an ageless front. He grows old, he grows old, but he stays alive because he's always been ready to die.

This is a philosophical position, a spiritual stance, and one acquired early. It doesn't emerge with the sometimes disconcerting 1980s-90s Bob Dylan who licks his lips over an imminent apocalypse. Nor does it date only from the Born Again period of the late 1970s when the Jewish Bob Dylan (born Robert Allen Zimmerman) converted to Christ and started evangelising at us with alarming venom. 'Are You Ready?', he demanded to know back then, clearly implying that we weren't and he was.

If this alone were the quality and provenance of Dylan's readiness to face death, it wouldn't perhaps be up to much, or explain his continued unconquerable insistence on ploughing his own furrow.

But look back, for a moment, to *Dont Look Back*, the documentary film of his 1965 visit to Britain, when Bob is young and beautiful. Here he is, just turning 24, with the world of celebrity and glamour kissing his feet and cooing in his ears. He is the most perfectly hip creature on earth. Imagine how you'd cope with this. Even ten percent of it would turn your head. But Bob Dylan does cope, telling the man from *Time* magazine:

> You're going to die. You're going to be dead. It could be twenty years, it could be tomorrow, anytime. So am I. I mean, we're just going to be gone. The world's going to go on without us. All right now. You do your job in the face of that, and how seriously you take yourself you decide for yourself.

That is the Bob Dylan stance. Forty-six years on, he's still all alone in the end-zone, determinedly unimpressed by the clamour he's engendered and endured throughout.

After the babble of 1960s approbation, initially for the power, articulacy and originality of songs like 'A Hard Rain's A-Gonna Fall', 'The Lonesome Death Of Hattie Carroll' and 'Masters Of War', Dylan felt trapped by his reputation as 'protest-singer, spokesman of a generation'. He went electric, and after the booing stopped, he was lauded far more widely for the brilliance of his fusion of poetry and electricity and a run of peerless albums from *Bringing It All Back Home* through *Highway 61 Revisited* to *Blonde On Blonde*. Here were records that broke down the walls of song – liberating all of us and making it possible for every other musician and singer to seize that creative freedom.

They could be as unlike Bob Dylan as they wished: but he made their liberation possible by his revolutionary insistence that popular song, rock music, could handle all subjects and the whole range of human emotion and the life of the mind – and by writing songs and making records that proved it.

But you weren't supposed to be crass enough to ask him what his songs were about. When *Playboy* magazine asked, the answer was this: 'Oh, some are about four minutes, some are about five minutes, and some, believe it or not, are about eleven or twelve.'

But then came the motorcycle crash of summer 1966, rural seclusion and recovery in the New York State countryside around Woodstock, the ascetic challenge of his next album, *John Wesley Harding*, which in its beautifully pared-down instrumentation and thanks to the mystery and gravitas of its songs, effectively rebuked all the excesses of the new rock-star world: a post-*Sergeant Pepper* world of self-indulgent, drug-induced guitar solos and hippy-dippy lyrics sprawled across lavishly-packaged double-albums.

Impossible now to describe the thrill of being there then, hearing these seminal Dylan records when they were new – and when each one was so different from the last – and when Bob's extraordinary voice, or rather, voices, offered so subtly nuanced and so direct a communication that he seemed to be expanding your mind when he opened his mouth.

After *John Wesley Harding* came the dramatic switch toward warm simplicity and a pretty voice on 1969's *Nashville Skyline* – and then the falling off the pedestal that was *Self Portrait* at the start of the new decade. Not only was this a provokingly unhip album, but in the inevitable early-1970s backlash against the 1960s, Dylan became perceived as a passé pariah, the very embodiment of the decade now being spurned.

In the mid-seventies, Dylan's fortunes revived, thanks to a vast North American tour with The Band – six million people applied for 600,000 tickets – and then the more street-cred and intimate Rolling Thunder Revues, on which a troupe of entertainers, fronted by Dylan, re-captured some of the spirit, the troubadour ethic, of their folkier youth.

More crucially came a huge renewal of admiration (and sales) thanks to the mature masterpiece that is *Blood On The Tracks* and to its successor, *Desire*. Then came the giddy success of a World Tour of concerts in 1978, after a 12-year absence from the capital. By this time it was the height of punk, and punks still regarded Bob Dylan as that loathsome thing, an Old Hippy – yet in London the police had to supervise nationwide, all-night queues for tickets for Dylan's concerts at Earl's Court, which were followed by an extra performance at Blackbushe Aerodrome, for which British Railways laid on special trains to handle a crowd of some 300,000. A live album from this tour was recorded when Dylan reached Budokan, Japan.

That was, as it turned out, the last gasp of Dylan's superstardom, which petered out little by little over the next twenty years. First, unhappy with his personal and artistic life, Dylan became a Born-Again Christian. Disconcertingly, the man who had warned us 'Don't follow leaders / Watch the parkin' meters' was now admonishing us with 'There's only one authority / That's the authority on high'. After a couple of albums in this vein, he began to retreat from the evangelising but reverted to struggling to find his artistic feet. He stumbled through most of the 1980s, selling only modest numbers of records and performing for smaller audiences. His wretched, inebriated appearance at Live Aid in 1985, along with a series of poor albums – *Empire Burlesque*, *Knocked Out Loaded* and *Down In The Groove* – was enough to get him roundly dismissed once again as a figure from the past: an aging star of no contemporary cultural significance.

This was the received wisdom for almost two decades. Dylan was regarded with a kind of automatic knowing contempt. He began the Never-Ending Tour in June 1988, but his own record-company didn't bother to keep tabs on where he was, and the general public went back to thinking of him simply as the man who'd come up with 'Blowin' In The Wind' and 'The Times They Are A-Changin''.

That's how it was – while in truth his more than forty albums offer a 50-year exploration of, and make a large creative contribution to, every form of American popular music, while offering a range of literary explorations too. There's his use of poetry from Blake and Browning to Eliot and the Beats. There's his imaginative ear for the poetry of traditional folksong, its dark balladry and weird jump-cut narratives, and for the evocative word-power too of blues lyric poetry – especially that of the pre-war blues, with which Dylan is uncannily au fait. Not least, and winding through all the rest, is his career-long intimacy with, and adept deployment of, the King James Bible.

Up on stage, he still lives in the moment, making his concerts events, not mere shows. The result is that he can still surprise even those like me who have been to see him dozens of times. In 1989 I watched in delight as he ended a New York City concert by jumping from the stage into the audience and dodging out by a side staircase – in effect calling down his own bolt of lightning to escape by – and leaving his band as surprised as the crowd.

At his two début performances in Israel in 1987, years after he had retreated from Born-Again evangelising on his albums, he chose to give his Tel Aviv and Jerusalem audiences several Christian songs each. At the same time his repertoire was wholly different the one night from the other. Who else could, or would, do that?

More often the unpredictabilities are to do with his mercurial, fleeting moods and his daring to risk where they take him – sometimes in mid-concert, even in mid-song, and certainly from one night to the next. In 2000, I could scarcely believe that the man who performed so badly, so unwillingly, in the hell-hole of Sheffield Arena could offer such transcendent greatness two days later in Portsmouth.

When he's on form, he's still untouchable. There's simply no doubt, as you stand there, that you're in the presence of genius, however wayward it might be.

Yet despite all this, and despite his writing and recording numinous songs in more recent decades (isn't 'Blind Willie McTell' the best song of the 1980s, by anyone?), he still remained perceived in the general public mind as a left-field figure, a charismatic maverick who operated on the sidelines of our culture. But times really do change.

For Dylan change seemed to begin with a rush of warm re-appraisal when, in 1996, he was taken ill with a heart disease. Even the people running the arts sections of the broadsheet newspapers suddenly imagined the prospect of Dylan's permanent absence: and were surprised to find themselves feeling some regret over this.

And then in 1997, with *Time Out Of Mind*, Dylan's first collection of new songs in seven years, he succeeded in reminding people of how striking and unique the artist in him was and is and always will be.

He even picked up a set of Grammies and a Kennedy Center Award, presented to him by President Clinton. But it took the *New York Times* bestsellerdom of Dylan's carefully crafted memoir *Chronicles Volume One* in 2004 and then the 2005 Martin Scorsese film *No Direction Home*, before Dylan was rightly elevated to the rank of mainstream American icon, alongside Brando, Monroe and Presley. Or Whitman. It followed that in 2006 his new album, *Modern Times*, topped the US charts: the first time he had done so in 30 years, and at the time the oldest living singer ever to reach that position.

The media blitz around his 70th birthday confirms this seachange in the way he's now perceived. He was always somehow minority-interest, even though he had revolutionised popular music. Today, he's a grand old man of American Letters – and at the same time far more commercially successful than ever before.

So now there's a snowstorm of Grammies and Oscars and lifetime achievement awards and, every year these days, an argument about whether Dylan deserves the Nobel Prize in Literature. He may turn up and accept these awards now, but he knows better than to be swayed by the excessive giving of honours and titles.

He knows that such things generally come to artists, if they come at all, when they're felt to be safe and over the hill. There's nothing he can do about that. He keeps on going and he hasn't finished yet.

At the centre of all this renewed hubbub, Dylan remains a mystery. He is a mystery because what drives the man is the artist, and he *is* an exceptional artist: a true original of risk-taking range and bravery, who has never been satisfied with finding a popular niche and settling in it. The important thing about Bob Dylan, as we look back, prompted by the occasion of his turning 70, is what has always been important: his enormous and variegated body of work.

If you want to know who Bob Dylan is, why perfectly sane people continue to find him compelling, and why he keeps on drawing in intelligent young people, in wave upon generational wave, it's easy. Listen to his records.

High School Confidential
(2012)

A March 2012 e-mail exchange in which a Samantha H at Bucks High School in Philadelphia PA, asked me for answers to help with a project on Dylan. I added that I retained copyright in my answers but that she was free to use them as she wished for her project.

1. When did you first hear Dylan singing, and did you like him immediately, or did it take time to really get into him?

Not the voice, no: it took a while – but the fact that he was so different: I liked that as soon as I realised it.

2. You are giving Dylan discussions in your home and travelling to talk about him and have also written several books, so it's clear you are a huge fan of his; has your outlook on life been altered or changed in any way because of him? In other words, how has Dylan personally influenced you in life?

Yes, but more because he changed the whole consciousness of a generation in the 1960s than because he had a measurable personal impact on anything like whether I learnt to play guitar, or whether I wanted to get married, or whether he altered my religious beliefs.

3. Bob seemed to go in many different directions in the sixties, changing from folk to electric to ending up doing recordings in Nashville – which part of Bob's career in the sixties was the most influential to the decade in your opinion?

The druggy electric rock – the marrying what Christopher Ricks calls 'the force of poetry' (I think it's a book title of his) with the power of progressive rock music, plus the sheer cool of his persona and the biting intelligence of his words. I don't mean here the genre of Prog Rock, but that the music he and the Hawks were hurling at concert audiences in Europe in 1966 was radical, challenging, thrilling, pioneering: and he was hurling it whether the audiences wanted or understood it. So brave, so unerring, so sure of himself, so right.

4. The folk community in the sixties seemed really affected by Bob; do you think that whole area of culture would be drastically different if he had not come along? If so, in what way?

Yes, it might simply have stagnated. Though if Phil Ochs hadn't died young, he might – might – have given it a kick in the pants regardless of Dylan. Yet that begs the question: would Phil Ochs have written any (or any decent) 'protest songs' if Dylan hadn't come along? Also, many of the folk scene's old hands didn't believe in *writing* songs – they were aiming only to try to play the oldest, supposedly purest versions of traditional songs that they could – while others simply didn't write many: whereas Dylan was amazingly prolific in those early days. Oh, and also, some of the folk scene people were very rigid about what genre they performed – if they sang southern mountain songs then they wouldn't sing sea shanties, for example – and Dylan came along with a rock'n'roll attitude that wouldn't put up with, or take seriously, that kind of rigid 'purism'. And this stance of his, plus his strong songwriting, and strength as a performer in those clubs (as Dave Van Ronk testified) plus his general pushiness, meant that he was noticed quickly and had a big impact.

5. As a quick, more personal opinion question – when it comes to the famous motorcycle crash, what are your thoughts on it? I've heard some speculation about whether or not it was as bad as it was made to be. I've read Bob may have exaggerated it so that he could get some down time, do you think this could be true?

I don't really care about this. I'm glad he took a vacation.

6. If you had to pick an album or a set of songs that have most influenced and affected you personally, which would you pick?

One album? Impossible, but the answer would have to be *Blonde On Blonde*. Two? That and *Blood On The Tracks*.

7. Bob to me seems to be great at the art of fame, by changing his music styles frequently he's remained in the public eye, if Bob had never gone electric, do you think he would have remained relevant? How much did the sixties benefit from albums like Highway 61 Revisited *and* Blonde On Blonde*?*

Impossible to say – the whole future would have been different, for all of us: or at least all of us with any interest in popular music or modern culture. How much did the sixties benefit? Hugely.

8. When I was talking to Howard Sounes, he mentioned that he feels those in the UK and continental Europe have always held Dylan in a higher regard than the US has, whether it be the sixties or present day – do you find this true as well?

Yes – but then I think the UK has always been more reverent about musicians. In the UK people still revere Eddie Cochran, a pioneer rock'n'roll star who died in 1960; no-one in the US gives a damn about him. Even Buddy Holly, who was crucial to the whole creation of the scope of rock music, and died in 1959: he's only cared about or remembered by US musicians, not the US public, whereas everyone in Britain over the age of about 30 is aware of who he was, even though they were born more than 20 years after he died. And it was the British who brought blues greats like Howlin' Wolf and Muddy Waters back into American popular consciousness (via Cream, Eric Clapton etc.) And Jimi Hendrix became recognised as a star and guitar genius in Britain, long before he made it in the States.

9. Have you ever met Dylan? If so what was like, if not do you know what you would say?

Yes, but I haven't time (ie inclination) to tell you about it, except to say that he doesn't do small talk, and while he can be ferocious with anyone he thinks is a journalist or PR person etc., he tends to be gentle and kind with people he perceives as vulnerable, including children: and when I met him (which was because he'd invited me to 'come backstage and say hello' at one of his London 1978 gigs) I took my 9-year-old son with me. So he was nice to my son and OK with me.

10. What was the most surprising thing you've learned about Dylan over the years? Is there anything that stands out?

It surprises and disappoints me that he's become so keen on money at the expense of principle, as I see it: that he issues a record through Starbucks, and has done TV ads for Victoria's Secret and for Cadillac, and allowed his music to be used in ads for the Bank of Montreal. All that stuff surprises me. So does how little he bothers, now, when he's onstage. OK so he's 70 years old, and he doesn't *have* to perform live at all – but he chooses to do about 100 concerts a year, yet doesn't try to have the best band he can, nor to sing as best he could.

Another Self Portrait?
(2013)

Unpublished; drawn partly from personal correspondence with other Dylan aficionados at the time.

Another Self Portrait has given us further hints of the Dylan voice Bonnie Beecher said Bob used to sing with: the voice we glimpse in that 1959 recording of 'When I Got Troubles' (the first track on the *No Direction Home* Bootleg Series release) and on that St Paul Minnesota 1960 tape. And inevitably, the new release has provoked a re-evaluation of the album we'd had the first time around. So much so that as the critic Andrew Muir commented when the new tracks began to circulate, suddenly *Self Portrait* was everyone's favourite album.[75]

The first to re-write history, though with an opposite thrust, was Bob Dylan. In *Chronicles Volume One,* in 2004, he claimed to have been deliberately recording terrible material to get people off his back. This was strikingly disrespectful to all the other musicians who'd been involved, a downright lie about who he was at that time, and less about *Self Portrait* than about what a calculated liar he was in *Chronicles Volume One,* the very title of which probably misleads by implying that there'll ever be further volumes.

And then along with *Another Self Portrait* came Greil Marcus's brochure notes, weasel-wording that he'd only opened his *Rolling Stone* review of the original album with that notorious 'What is this shit?' to reflect what everyone had been saying. No, Greil: it was what *you* were saying, and you probably wrote it before almost anyone else had managed to obtain a copy.

All that said, *Another Self Portrait* has ushered in some welcome

---

[75] Muir's comment came in an e-mail to me, 17th July 2013, cited here with his permission. However, some of us liked plenty of *Self Portrait* all along. There is a sizeable passage of considered praise for it in the 1972 first edition of *Song & Dance Man.*

appreciation of the original album, albeit over 40 years late, and in itself it gives us a scattering of tremendous outtakes, revealing even more than the 1970 album (or even than *Nashville Skyline*) what conventionally lovely vocals he was capable of. Weirdly, therefore, much of *Another Self Portrait* seems part of an alternative history, like a sci-fi plot: 'the universe where Dylan never got phlegmy...'

A clear highlight in this respect is 'Pretty Saro', showcasing Pretty Bob. One critic whose work I respect said his initial reaction was that this track is 'Sublime. With the possible exception of "Sad-Eyed Lady Of The Lowlands", this is the most beautiful recording Bob Dylan has ever made.' I can't go that far, but it's wonderfully touching, and was wholly unexpected.

Other highlights begin at the beginning, with what we're told is the demo of 'Went To See The Gypsy': the lyric is not yet tightened up, but the performance is so felt. The version on Disc 2 is also interesting, and a fine vocal, but a nasty electric piano sound.

Yet I always love Dylan's piano work on a real piano, and I especially love versions of 'Spanish Is The Loving Tongue' when that solo piano is dominant, so the version on Disc 1 is another fine gift on the collection. It is less alive here than the one we first heard on the B-side of 'Watching The River Flow', on which twinned with the rich vocal tone that piano is so sumptuously recorded and Dylan plays it with all his unique expressive panache – yet vocally the take on *Another Self Portrait* Disc 1 enfolds the most tender moments – moments of affecting apparent shyness. Those moments are more sustained in 'I Threw It All Away', and this scrupulous, loving song deserves them. It's as good as the version on *Nashville Skyline*, and, for that matter, the version he sings with such immaculate attention to every phrase, live at the Isle of Wight (re-mixed and re-mastered on the very expensive additional Disc 3 here, along with the rest of that 1969 performance).

Hard not to like the sly humour of 'Annie's Going To Sing Her Song', while the vocal on 'Wallflower' (a minor song already familiar from that great *Doug Sahm & Band* album) is tremendous here: one of his most authentic country-music performances. He makes me like 'Country Pie' too: he seems more *there*, and more expressive, than on *Nashville Skyline*.

The same is true in droves on the demo of 'When I Paint My Masterpiece', which seems to me quite close to *being* a masterpiece, with its plush virtuoso piano, played as only Bob could, and a thoughtful and beautiful vocal. And yes, he should have retained its Victrola line – a great rhyme for gondola but also such a sharply witty confession of his love for, and knowledge of, the world of the pre-war blues (when 78rpm records were bought and played on the Victor company's relatively affordable Victrola wind-up gramophones/phonographs). The surprise and delight of his impulsive allusion to it here is not from his *knowing* these things but from his springing it on us in the middle of a song that isn't remotely a blues itself.

When we attend to the tracks where *Self Portrait*'s overdubbed strings and backing vocals have been stripped away, well, these sometimes work and sometimes don't. For me the only one that works equally well either way is 'All The Tired Horses', which I liked all along and now like all over again.

The ones that really succeed are 'In Search Of Little Sadie', which gives yet more prominence to David Bromberg's immaculate guitar, and 'Days Of 49': it's a strong track anyway but works better without the overdubs; and so does 'Belle Isle'. The two tracks that seem to me very *badly* served by abolishing the overdubs are 'Wigwam' and 'Copper Kettle'. I hope Stephen Scobie won't mind my reporting that his first response to the stripped down 'Wigwam' was that it made it sound as if it belonged on the soundtrack of *Pat Garrett and Billy the Kid*, which I hadn't thought of but recognised as helpful and true[76] – and that's all very well, but the version we've known since 1970 does more. It has always sounded transcendent and celebratory, a joy to hear and a surprise to spring on other people – and all the more to be savoured for being utterly unique in his canon. No need to impoverish it now.

In the case of 'Copper Kettle', always a daring and imaginative

[76] E-mail exchange with Stephen Scobie, his dated 31st August 2013.

counter-folkie version and the absolute stand-out track on *Self Portrait*, it strikes me still more forcibly that the stripping away of the overdubs weakens what remains. I always felt that part of what made his incomparable vocal so good-humoured and humane was the illusion it gave that he was *hearing* the violins and the women as he sang. He gathered them in, he welcomed them in as co-conspirators in his sweeping away of the po-faced folk-revivalism the song itself usually had to suffer, at the very same time that he was being *so* respectful, syllable by syllable, of the song's real strengths. What's been swept away is that imaginary dialogue between Dylan and those bootleg-assisting women.

And all those other folkie/non-Dylan songs on *Another Self Portrait*? Mostly I feel like giving the answer Dylan gave to The Science Student in *Dont Look Back*, when asked what he feels first when he meets someone new and he replies 'I don't like them'.

'Little Sadie' is ho-hum here, and so is 'Tattle O' Day'; 'Railroad Bill' and 'These Hands' are just about OK; but 'Thirsty Boots', given inexplicable prominence by its additional issue as a Record Store Day single, is unDylanesquely too 1960s and too cute. And though 'This Evening So Soon' sounds moderately marvellous, just revisit Dave Van Ronk's studio version: it leaves Bob's sounding pallid and insincere.

In contrast, there are a couple of bonuses in the folkie song category: one is a Dylan song and one not. The performance of his own 'Only A Hobo' – a song I've always disliked for its hectoring soppiness – yields a sweet voice in place of the grit-loaded one we're accustomed to, and this almost redeems the song by distancing him from that didactic tone. Somehow this makes it sound more like a half-decent Woody Guthrie song than when Dylan was being Guthriesque. The other surprise, to me at least, is that song of obscure origin, 'House Carpenter'. At first I disliked the strained vocal, but as I've listened more, and that voice has become a reminder of the great Roscoe Holcomb, it's won me over.

Further surprises lurk in the outtakes of several *New Morning* songs not yet mentioned. There's the unpleasant surprise of 'Time Passes Slowly' twice over: the silly la-las obtrude pointlessly on

Disc 1, and on Disc 2, its frantic pace and arrangement is in destructive combat with the words. The best version by far is the one on the original album, and it's no wonder these outtakes were rejected 40-odd years ago.

There's also the horror of the *added* strands on a couple of other tracks. After all those excisions of overdubs, why abuse a track as directly beautiful as 'Sign On The Window' by adding anything, let alone these ghastly strings and the final insult of that *harp*?! It's truly dire. Nor is what Al Kooper has been allowed to do to the original album's title track any better. This is Kooper reverting to his Blood, Sweat & Tears tendency, and makes a pleasant minor song into a horribly dated one that doesn't sound as if Dylan could have written it at all.

Praise be that others are unexpectedly *cheering* surprises. *Another Self Portrait* gives us a touching, intimate version of 'If Not For You'. In 1970 you heard people ask if, with its 'wouldn't have a clue', it was a joke. Not here, where he makes it a real, heartfelt song. And 'If Dogs Run Free' is *far* better this way. That loping pace!: so *New Morning*, and so much closer to 'Three Angels', until it explodes into that soulful chorus, its back-up singers fused with Dylan in canine delight.

It's matched – and again this is unexpected – by 'Bring Me A Little Water', a song many of us may first have heard on the *Tribute to Woody Guthrie and Leadbelly* album (Folkways Records, various artists, 1988). There, titled 'Sylvie' and by Sweet Honey In The Rock, this black southern work song was offered more as sweet honey than anything approaching rock; and if we knew the song long before, on its recording by Leadbelly himself, we'd heard it as a one-minute-long throwaway, perky and trivial. Dylan seizes it with rock flair, giving it chiselled verses, dusting the whole thing up with relish and a gloriously harsh pizzazz.

In the end, though, there's one big hole in *Another Self Portrait* – a gaping, mysterious absence that, had it been filled, would have made all the other strippings and separations of layers insignificant beside it. To put it as the Greil Marcus of 1970 might have done about this 2013 release, *where the fuck is 'The Boxer'*?

The year before the official issue, when some of the outtakes were rumoured among the avid, I asked about 'The Boxer' of a man who told me about what would be on it and what wouldn't but who swore me to secrecy on pain of death – and he told me it wouldn't be included. And he was right.

It is the greatest, most regrettable missed opportunity. Hugely more interesting than a stripped-down 'Days Of 49', for example (which was never that stripped up in the first place), or the 'Wigwam' that is exactly how you knew it would be without its multi-coloured, pantheistic brass, the most *needed* revisit was always going to be to that Dylan recording of 'The Boxer'. What was and still is needed is to hear it separated into its two real constituent parts: the track that has him singing in his 'old' voice – the 1963, pre-electric voice – and the other track, on which he sings with his 'new', *Nashville Skyline* voice – the one so close to the pre-pre-electric voice that Bonnie Beecher had heard way back in 1960.

Don't Give Dylan The Nobel Prize In Literature (2013)

This was written for, and delivered on 13th May 2013 at, an Einstein Forum Workshop entitled Einstein Disguised As Robin Hood *in Potsdam (Germany), devoted to whether Dylan should receive the Literature Prize. Mine was, I believe, the lone talk arguing against. I argued with conviction… but of course, being human, and an admirer of his work for over 50 years by then, the moment I heard he'd won it (in October 2016) I was thrilled…*

The first question is: who hands out this monumentally prestigious prize? A committee of the Swedish Academy, called to order by a permanent secretary. Nominations come in from far and wide – but only from those the committee has selected and approved, including from other national bodies that are just like the Swedish Academy!

Not one of its committee members is a distinguished literary critic, so what sense does it make that this Clerisy decides who merits the accolade of Great Writer?

And as it is, the committee is a nest of vipers and the negotiations a mix of right-wing politicking, partisan prejudices and risible conventions about etiquette. They awarded the 1908 prize to Rudolf Eucken: 'in recognition of his earnest search for truth, his penetrating power of thought, his wide range of vision, and the warmth and strength in presentation with which in his numerous works *he has vindicated and developed an idealistic philosophy of life*' [my emphasis].

Eucken was an admirable philosopher. But he was given the prize because he '*vindicated*' a particular form of idealism that the Swedish Academy wanted to enhance itself by approving.

104 years later, in 2012, winner Mo Yan's acceptance speech

thanked the Swedish Academy: 'I want to take this opportunity to express my admiration for the members of the Swedish Academy, who stick firmly to their own convictions. I am confident that you will not let yourselves be affected by anything other than literature.' Yet the chair of the Nobel committee, Per Wästberg, had praised Mo Yan for writing 'a convincing and scathing revision of 50 years of propaganda … instead of communism's poster-happy history'.

Days earlier, Mo Yan had been called 'a patsy of the regime' by Salman Rushdie because he'd declined to sign a petition asking for the release of Liu Xiaobo.

In 1962, halfway between that long span of dates, they gave the prize to John Steinbeck – while thinking his work rather poor. He got it because committee member Henry Olsson wouldn't consent to Robert Graves, being reluctant to award any Anglo-Saxon poet the prize before the death of Ezra Pound, believing that other writers did not match his mastery but that they couldn't give the prize to Pound because they'd have been widely berated over his political stance.

It follows from all such horse-trading that there are many, many people who have been awarded the Nobel Prize whom nobody now reads. A number of them – surprise! – have been Swedish.

The converse is that there's an unnecessarily swollen list of writers of real literary importance who have never been offered the prize. To name a few: Tolstoy, Chekhov, Ibsen, Zola, Mark Twain, Proust, James Joyce, Nabokov, Strindberg, Brecht, Allen Ginsberg, Ed Dorn, John Osborne, J.R.R. Tolkien, Flannery O'Connor, Kathleen Raine, Sylvia Plath, Edna St. Vincent Millay, D.H. Lawrence, Auden, Thomas Hardy, Philip Larkin, Iris Murdoch, Hilary Mantel, Mervyn Peake, Anthony Powell, William Carlos Williams, Robert Frost, Sean Casey, Michael Ondaatje, Thomas Keneally, George Szirtes, Dylan Thomas, F. Scott Fitzgerald.

None of this neglect affects the special kudos attached to the Nobel Prize all the same, so that despite its corrupt genesis, its corrupt procedures and its deeply mediocre record as a judge of literary greatness, people don't refuse it. Yet there is an admirable history of people refusing other important honours for reasons of conscience or integrity.

Consider the Egyptian writer Sonallah Ibrahim, born in 1937, author of the powerful novel *That Smell*, which is about being imprisoned and tortured by Nasser and then released. He wrote his book, had it banned, and survived to recoil when Sadat turned non-aligned, socialist Egypt into a country in hock to the US and its consumerism and allied to Israel. I quote from Adam Shatz in the *London Review of Books* (7th March 2013):

> While [Naguib] Mahfouz held court at his weekly salon at the Café Riche in downtown Cairo, Ibrahim barely left his desk … Those who knew of [his] disdain for Egypt's rulers were surprised when, in 2003, he turned up at a ceremony to receive the Ministry of Culture's Arab Novel Award. But they were even more astonished by his speech, an unbridled denunciation of the Mubarak regime of a kind that few at the time would have dared to make. He couldn't accept the prize, he said, because the government 'lacks the credibility to bestow it'.

That's brave. That's taking a stand instead of a bauble.

Consider too the case of Sinclair Lewis, whose novels *Main Street, Babbitt* and *Elmer Gantry* had so much impact on American consciousness. He declined the Pulitzer Prize, saying:

> All prizes, like all titles, are dangerous … The Pulitzer … is tending to become a sanctified tradition. There is a general belief that the administrators of the prize are a pontifical body with the discernment and power to grant the prize as the ultimate proof of merit …
>
> Only by regularly refusing the Pulitzer Prize can novelists keep such a power from being permanently set up over them. Between the Pulitzer Prizes [and] the American Academy of Arts and Letters … every compulsion is put upon writers to become safe, polite, obedient, and sterile. In protest, I declined election to the National Institute of Arts and Letters some years ago, and now I must decline the Pulitzer Prize.

> I invite other writers to consider the fact that by accepting the prizes and approval of these vague institutions we are admitting their authority, publicly confirming them as the final judges of literary excellence, and I inquire whether any prize is worth that subservience.

Does Bob Dylan fit? Is his body of writing of sufficient substance, originality and influence? Yes, without question. I said so over 40 years ago, in the first book to discuss him alongside Bunyan, Blake, Browning and Eliot. I also looked back, in that book, to a far earlier period in our arts, when words and song were inseparable. But I also wrote, on the very first page, that Dylan's words were not poems for the page, but parts of songs and parts of *performance*.

He is essentially a songwriter, musician, recording artist and performer. Does he fit the candidature profile? Is he really to be defined as a literary figure? No. He's crucially a cross-disciplinary artist who is, by best personal example and by his own canon, resistant to the categorisation, the force-fitting required to reshape him into a Nobel Prize in Literature recipient.

I say 'by *best* personal example' because in old age he has been through an unbecoming phase of displaying his Oscar on top of an amplifier on stage every night at his concerts. Unseemly. Tacky. Shallow. He knows his own importance in the history of contemporary western culture; it's been visible over and over again in waves of public success and in the constantly attested unique affection and respect he's been afforded by his creative peers. It's demeaning and risible to show off his Oscar, as if *that's* what proves his worth or assures his place in history. You might think perhaps this says something in itself about the effect of receiving things like Oscars.

In his earlier, better phases, he specifically scorned these glass beads. In *Dont Look Back* we see his own record company trying to offer him a Silver Disc, and he says he doesn't even want to *see* the thing. Not only was he instinctively clear that these awards were bullshit, he was *teaching that attitude* back at a time when accepting bullshit was all of a piece with the old rigidities – all of a piece with not challenging authority.

He was so much younger then. Yet even sixteen years later, he was holding to the same values in his own lyrics. In 'Lenny Bruce', he sings, very pointedly, that Bruce 'never did get any Golden Globe award…'

The suggestion, there, is not just that it doesn't affect Bruce's worth or real reputation one jot, but that part of his value, his power to disturb, meant he never would have been given one of these supposed honours.

Dylan had said in his liner notes to *Bringing It All Back Home*, why Allen Ginsberg wasn't chosen to read poetry at the White House 'boggles my mind'. It hadn't boggled his mind at all. He'd been making the same point: the Lenny Bruce point.

As the British singer and DJ Cerys Matthews tweeted in 2013, 'I think I must be dead. I've received two award nominations this morning.'

And what happened to Sinclair Lewis, so eloquent in 1926 about why writers should decline such prizes? In 1930 he *accepted* the Nobel Prize in Literature – after which he lived for 21 more years and wrote eleven more books, none of which is remembered today.

One person alone has had the courage to decline the Nobel Prize itself. Jean-Paul Sartre refused it in 1964, saying that 'a writer should not allow himself to be turned into an institution'.

Bob Dylan, meanwhile, as *Rolling Stone* reported in March this year, 'has been voted into the American Academy of Arts and Letters, marking the first time a rock musician has been chosen for the elite honor society. Officials in the Academy – which recognises music, literature and visual art – were unable to decide if Dylan belonged for his words or his music and instead inducted him as an honorary member.'

So what does it say about Dylan that he is now in this 'elite honor society', the American Academy of Arts and Letters? It surely says that the award is a farce, requiring a change in its own criteria to accommodate this misfit when the supposed constancy and rigour of those criteria are claimed to be their raisons d'être.

What will it say if Dylan wins the Nobel Prize in Literature? It will say that Dylan is a safe artist: 'he's one of us'.

Of course there is a multiplicity of Bob Dylans, and there are great songs, great recordings, made through every decade since the 1960s – well, at least up to and including the 2000s – but the songs that didn't win official blessings, the performances that disqualified themselves from any award nominations, because they were challenging, because they broke the rules and were disruptive – 'A Hard Rain's A-Gonna Fall' in *1962*, 'Like A Rolling Stone' in 1965, the 1966 concerts: *these* are the ones that define Bob Dylan's achievement, by his re-defining the possibilities of song and by his delivering his art via a defiantly original, mercurial persona.

We know all this, just as we know that Marlon Brando was a great and innovative movie actor. Did he get a Grammy? Who, now, cares?! We know that Little Richard and Buddy Holly were crucial figures in the vibrant creation of rock'n'roll. It doesn't matter a damn whether they've been inducted into the Rock & Roll Hall of Fame, or some other self-appointed Hall of Fame. It's their work that mattered and matters still – while the kind of people who like to sit on awards committees are exactly the kind who would have killed rock'n'roll at birth if they'd been able to.

So I suggest that these things are profoundly irrelevant – except that the giving and receiving of them contaminates. Because of the inevitable tendency of such things to err on the side of caution, to choose the culturally and politically conservative, they offer a poisoned chalice.

In pushing for Dylan to be given the Nobel Prize, enthusiasts think they are shouting for his importance to be recognised, but his importance already *is* recognised, and what would be achieved would be the opposite: the Prize would solidify the assumption that Dylan is no longer of any real pertinence but just another effigy owned by AmericanDream.org.

To put it less clamourously, I quote Benjamin Kunkel, from a *London Review of Books* in 2010:

> A basic feature of dialectical thinking is the liability of
> subject and object to turn into each other, for the way a
> thing is looked at to become part of the look of a thing

> ... The status of landmarks is ambiguous. Does a statue confirm the living influence of a man, or only that he belongs to the past?

As Arlo Guthrie said in 1998, when his father's image was placed on the US 32-cent postage stamp, 'for a man who fought all his life against being respectable, this comes as a stunning defeat'.

Give the Nobel Prize in Literature to a novelist or a poet who is quintessentially a novelist or poet and who can use the security of the prize money. Don't give it to the superlative artist and creative maverick who encompasses so much more.

Professing Dylan
(2016)

This was written as the Foreword for, and published in, the collection of essays Professing Dylan, *edited by the late Frances Hunter, US paperback, 2016: essays by university and college teachers. The print run was just 100 copies. As it happened, the year it was published turned out to be the year Dylan finally won the Nobel Prize in Literature. The book's publication date was 15th November, so the editor's secretary just had time to mention the award on the back cover.*

For the longest time, the academy was loathe to recognise Bob Dylan's work as worthy of attention. Princeton broke rank in 1970 when it bestowed an honorary degree upon the 29-year-old – and perhaps only an institution that sure of its unassailability could have dared do so then.[77] Louis A. Renza, one of the contributors to the present volume, first taught a course on Dylan at Dartmouth's progressive liberal arts college a couple of years later. It was another *twenty-five years* before Tino Markworth convinced Stanford faculty member and actor Rush Rehm to teach a Dylan course (not a course students could take to gain a credit), which led to the 1998 Stanford Conference on Dylan, the first to focus on this artist – more than thirty years after his great mid-1960s work.

I was prompter than that, but I was outside the academy (and have remained so).[78] My *Song & Dance Man: The Art of Bob Dylan* was the first critical study of Dylan's work. It came out in Britain in late 1972, and in the US in January 1973, in both cases from mainstream publishers.

[77] I forgot, when I wrote this, that Princeton gave Dylan this honorary doctorate because the students had a vote and had used it to choose him: it was not because it came down on high from a progressive literature or music department.

[78] With one brief exception: for the spring term 2005 I was, by invitation, at Girton College, Cambridge, as the Mary Amelia Cummins Harvey Visiting Fellow Commoner. I loved it! Some early research for *The Bob Dylan Encyclopedia* was done in the college library.

I'd started wanting to write it, and made tentative beginnings, as an undergraduate in York (England) in 1967, when I was being trained to pay close-to-the-text attention to literary works that were firmly in the canon, and felt that the extraordinary first five years' worth of Dylan's work included much that could bear the weight of the same order of critical scrutiny. Only a book could accommodate what I wanted, which was simply to write about Dylan's work at length: to achieve something on a different level from mere album reviewing.

In the early stages of writing, I was helped by one or two of Greil Marcus's articles in the 'underground press' – in the *San Francisco Express Times* – and encouraged by one tutor, the late R.T. Jones (a George Eliot specialist); but my lone task was to carve a way through to the crucial fact that Dylan was creating not poems on the page but *songs* – and that for me the works of art were his *recordings* of his songs.

I also had to be able to afford the music-publisher permission fees for my quotations from 115 songs, *and* to argue for being allowed to quote what we actually heard on the records. Assuming we heard that aright. Dylan never published lyrics on his album sleeves – those luxuriously large sleeves of 12-inch vinyl albums – and, true to the spirit of rock'n'roll, didn't always sing each word decipherably; but this was a fight I had to win. The lyrics Dylan handed to his music publishers were not those he stuck to when he went into the studio to record, and it was obvious to any listener which sets of words were those that mattered; but back then it was a struggle to get music-publishing professionals to concede this. The smell of old Tin Pan Alley still lingered: that decaying whiff of the time when sheet music had been the dominant form.

Anyway, that first book came out, and since then Dylan Studies has become a significant academic industry, and growing all the time: more than 83,000 academic papers on Dylan's work exist, and in a recent issue of the long-running fanzine *ISIS* a Danish aficionado offered for sale his collection of 900+ items on Dylan, with half the books in English and the rest in 25 different languages – including Farsi, Finnish, Greek, Japanese and Turkish.

Yet the difficulty of arriving at reliable lyrics to scrutinise has remained. The official books of lyrics have never been trustworthy – which might astonish the outsider. The enormous and expensive 2014 book *The Lyrics: Since 1962*, with (some) annotations from Christopher Ricks, was expected to yield, at last, reliable transcriptions of the song lyrics. It doesn't.

Bob Dylan isn't alone in this instability: there is, for example, still no reliable edition of the poetry of Robert Burns, and now it's nigh-impossible ever to achieve one – to strip away all the errors and corruptions. This is the fate that awaits Dylan's canon if his office doesn't sort it out.

For teaching purposes, lack of trustworthy printed lyrics might be alright, given that the recordings themselves are so readily accessible, if college classrooms and lecture halls offered even half-decent audio and audio-visual equipment. My experience of sitting in on classes suggests that this is rare.

There's another difficulty in teaching Dylan's work to undergraduates: as Walter Raubicheck writes in his exemplary essay in this collection, 'to them, Dylan is … not a representative of their own popular culture … He is a figure of the past.' Indeed. I remember, in a school class of fellow-16-year-olds in the early 1960s, our disbelief when we found that the Modern Novel we were to be offered at last, D.H. Lawrence's *Sons and Lovers*, had been published in 1913…

The problem is, if you will, Charles Dickens Syndrome. Beware putting people off for life. Realise how young they are. Those who plan and construct *courses* on Dylan's work need to avoid making that work into something dull. There's little so dispiriting as seeing a class of the largely stultified, most eyes glazed over, or fingers texting away beneath the desks, while an earnest professor asks everyone what they think Dylan means when he sings that 'death is not the end'. That is a kind of death, and the end.

Yet Dylan can still make himself accessible, getting through with exuberant panache and a biting eloquence. He has attracted bright students generation after generation. A great deal of his work is quick-witted, alert, and more of an enticement than a difficulty. He's very bright and he appeals to the bright. So can Dylan Studies, done right.

The genuinely wide range of approaches described in these [*Professing Dylan*] essays prove that there are many different ways to do it right. You'll find here, among other things, John McCombe's candid account of agonising over whether, as a young faculty member, he dared to teach Dylan (in 2005); James Cody's fine account of how to use Dylan's work to teach mythology; and Alex Lubet's extraordinary, sustained examination – and from a Music rather than the usual lit-crit perspective – of one rather minor song and the minor album it comes from. There's David Gaines's warm memoir of teaching Dylan in Texas, and Andrew Wainwright's terrific account of being a fan before Dylan went electric, of talking to Dylan himself in 1964, and then of teaching classes on him decades later: classes in which that third of the students who could quote the songs and felt they knew about the 1960s nevertheless 'welcomed the opinion of someone who had been there and still had reasonably long hair'.

Bob Dylan himself has long been ambivalent about critics, but has always kept an eye on the academy. He mentions 'the green pastures of Harvard University' on his début album in 1962, and 44 years later sings (perhaps thinking of those academic papers on his own work) that 'the world of research has gone berserk / Too much paperwork'; yet he accepted that honorary doctorate from Princeton, and, judiciously, just one other: from the venerable St. Andrews in Scotland.

I'll finish by citing one more contribution you'll find here, Nina Goss's brilliant and sprightly essay 'Why Teach Dylan?', in which she skips nimbly through the green pastures of criticism, and appropriates this quote from the late great critic Frank Kermode:

'The cause is a good one. And pleasure is at the heart of it.' Amen to that.

The Cutting Edge, The Sad-Eyed Ladies
(2016)

This is most of the talk I delivered at the Salon, Vienna, in 2016. (I've omitted only the introduction, which discussed Dylan's various kinds of radicalism, because that is better discussed in the later talk at the University of Southern Denmark Dylan Conference, included in this volume.)

What's here begins with a very brief response to The Cutting Edge *box-set in general, followed by a detailed look at the takes of one song. Since in essay form we can't hear this together, I've printed the Take 1 and* Blonde On Blonde *verses adjacently, italicising the words of Take 1 that Dylan chose to alter after.*

So much for the idea that Bob goes into the studio and if it doesn't work within a couple of takes, he gives up and moves on to the next song. I'm not sure I want to hear 20 attempts at 'Like A Rolling Stone' (specially when Take 4 has turned out to be perfect). Just now and then I do get 'sick of all this repetition' – but mostly I just thrill to the invigorating, incontestable genius of it all: how radical, how brave, how *new* it all was, and how fresh it still sounds.

Naturally, the tiny changes, and the larger ones, fascinate. They are so unfailingly beguiling and often touchingly sweet. And this applies both to words and to music.

On the *Highway 61 Revisited* tracks, to my ears, the one clear overall shift he makes when he chooses the versions he releases is in playing down or reducing the rather conventional prettiness of the musicians' contributions.

The issued tracks are far more effective for the prettiness being *retained but minimised*. Over and over, when you hear the outtakes, the piano and the prettier guitars are offering far more of-their-time conventional riffs, which, had they been on the album, would have lessened the innovative thrust of the whole.

Listen, for example, to Take 2 of 'Queen Jane Approximately'. Or try Take 5 of 'Just Like Tom Thumb's Blues': it's almost a country lullaby.

I want to look at just one of these songs in detail now, and it's the long one that comes right at the end of *Blonde On Blonde*.

Just as we've often been told that Dylan only has the patience for one or two takes of a song, so too we've often been told that for this album (among others) Dylan spent hours writing reams in the studio and yet the songs weren't ready, so that he changed everything from one take to the next.

In the case of 'Sad-Eyed Lady Of The Lowlands', the only changes are, by any standard of revision, tiny.

It was recorded at the third Nashville session for the album, on 16th February 1966, and there are just three full takes of this song (Takes 1, 3 and 4) plus Take 2, which is a 'rehearsal' and lasts only 2 minutes 7 seconds. There's no take of the song at all on the 2-CD *The Best Of The Cutting Edge* (an omission that gives the lie to the title immediately); Take 1 is on the 6-CD *The Cutting Edge – DeLuxe Edition*. All four are on the full *18-CD* set *The Cutting Edge – Collector's Edition* (Columbia 88875124402I8).

The take on the original *Blonde On Blonde* album is a very slightly cleaned up Take 4.[79] But let's listen closely to Take 1: for here we have a marvellous first take, and I hope to show, by paying it attention, both that tiny changes matter, in words and melodic line, and that at the same time, this song was *very* close to fully realised from the very start.

It's a long song, but actually it has only five verses – each of eight lines – plus, after each verse, a five-line chorus.

---

[79] The first *Blonde On Blonde* was in Canada, Columbia C2L 41, comprising earlier mono mixes. This used the original Take 4, on which in verse 4 Dylan sings: 'How could they ever have…uh…'suaded you?' For the US album, this verse was corrected by splicing the line from Take 1: 'How could they ever have persuaded you?' This spliced version is used on all subsequent pressings, including on *The Cutting Edge*.

With your mercury *eyes* in the *months that climb*
And your eyes like smoke and your prayers like rhymes
And your silver cross, and your voice like *the* chimes
Oh who *among them could think he* could bury you?
With your pockets well protected at last
And your streetcar visions which you place *out* on the grass
And your flesh like silk, and your face like glass
Oh who among them could think he could carry you?

With your mercury mouth in the missionary times
And your eyes like smoke and your prayers like rhymes
And your silver cross, and your voice like chimes
Oh who do they think could bury you?
With your pockets well protected at last
And your streetcar visions which you place on the grass
And your flesh like silk, and your face like glass
Who could they get to carry you?

On Take 1, only the opening line is strikingly different, with 'in the months that climb', perhaps meaning that the months are mounting up, and/or that an urgency to reach the sad-eyed lady is being introduced. It's taken up later in every version of the lyric, with 'waiting in line', and 'at last', and the 'wait' that ends every chorus. As an invoking of time as interesting for its own sake, though, if it's a theme suggested there at all, it is never developed as the song progresses.

That opening line aside, the changes in verse one are minimal. The fourth line's economical question, 'Oh, who do they think could bury you?' had begun as the wordier 'Oh, who among them could think he could bury you?' on Take 1 (and on Take 3, as it happens). The official bobdylan.com version, never a reliable replicant of the words we all hear on the albums, has the similarly less brief 'Oh, who among them do they think could bury you?'.

The change he makes in line six, from placing her streetcar visions out on the grass to merely on them, strikes me as not for the better; out on the grass is less neat but more vivid: it captures a more physical action, so that we see it, instead of hearing it as a line poetical yet vague. (Take 3 has it as 'which you *put out* on the grass', the worst of both worlds.)

The last line of every verse is a match to its fourth line. Take 1 repeats its 'Oh who among them could think...', while *Blonde On Blonde* parallels its own far shorter formulation.

Then we come to the first time around for the chorus:

> Sad-eyed lady of the lowlands
> Where the *prophets say* that no man comes
> My warehouse eyes, my Arabian drums
> Should I *leave them at* the gate?
> Or, sad-eyed lady, *must* I wait?

> Sad-eyed lady of the lowlands
> Where the sad-eyed prophet says that no man comes
> My warehouse eyes, my Arabian drums
> Should I put them by your gate?
> Or, sad-eyed lady, should I wait?

Take 1's prophets are immediately *plural* – and they seem preferable: one prophet, mainstream religion or not, is a bit too mystical-guru-man. *Blonde On Blonde*'s version is quick to agree: it gives us plural prophets on all four subsequent choruses.

Take 1's, though plural from the start, are not yet sad-eyed. In fact they don't become sad-eyed on this take until the *fourth* chorus.

Perhaps, too, this Take 1 first chorus choice of 'must I wait?' is more touching than 'should I wait?': the former sounds more a humble(d) and respectful question, and the latter closer to a pressurising, though in life it could as easily be the other way round. It surely works as it does in the song because, as sung (and that is always key), 'must I' sounds saddened, as if the expected answer will doom him, whereas 'should I' sounds more neutral, less personal: more like a delivery driver's question.

We're naturally disadvantaged by looking at all this in print instead of listening: yet in one respect, it helps. The punctuation that print allows clarifies meaning in the choruses. As noted, it's perilous to trust the official lyrics, but let's put some faith in the comma we find in the printed line 'My warehouse eyes, my Arabian drums'. That comma means the two things cited are the eyes and the drums. Without it, 'eyes' might be a verb and not a noun, so that the two things cited could as easily be the *warehouse* and the drums. It can cross your mind that way, too, on some hearings, not so much because it seems the more likely way to make sense of the line but because, for a trice, you picture the warehouse eyeing up and wanting rid of the drums, the narrator having to shift them, to leave them at the lady's gate. The comma rescues us from this foolishness.

The second verse:

> With your sheets like metal and your belt like lace
> And your deck of cards missing the jack and the ace
> And your basement clothes and your hollow face
> Who among them *could hope* to outguess you?
> With your silhouette *in the sunlight that dims*
> Into your eyes *like mirrors* where the moonlight swims
> And your matchbook songs and your gypsy hymns
> Who among them *could hope* to impress you?

> With your sheets like metal and your belt like lace
> And your deck of cards missing the jack and the ace
> And your basement clothes and your hollow face
> Who among them can think he could outguess you?
> With your silhouette when the sunlight dims
> Into your eyes where the moonlight swims
> And your matchbook songs and your gypsy hymns
> Who among them would try to impress you?

That's a verse replete with surprising similes, yet in which four lines out of eight remain entirely unchanged from first take to 1966 album release. Unchanged, that is, as you see them on the page. On the recordings, though, Take 1 has a most beautiful falling melodic line as the voice reaches line seven – 'And your matchbook songs and your gypsy hymns' – and this holds a musical beauty we soon lose. We lose it not only on the later takes, but even in the equivalent lines before the end of this take. He remembers it in verse three, singing 'And your cowboy mouth and your curfew plugs' with the same lovely melodic descent – but after that, it's gone. Dylan has forgotten it already.

The text changes in this second verse are very small. *Blonde On Blonde*'s 'When the sunlight dims' is leaner than the clumsy early version, and by losing an unremarkable image, the eyes like mirrors, we gain an economy of line. Yet we also lose 'who ... could hope to...?', and it's surely no improvement to switch to 'can think he could...?' and its less cleanly matched 'would try to...?'

The second chorus yields only a single new amendment between takes:

> Sad-eyed lady of the lowlands
> Where *the prophets* say that no man comes
> My warehouse eyes, my Arabian drums
> Should I *leave them at* your gate?
> Or sad-eyed lady, should I wait?

> Sad-eyed lady of the lowlands
> Where the sad-eyed prophets say that no man comes
> My warehouse eyes, my Arabian drums
> Should I put them by your gate?
> Or sad-eyed lady, should I wait?

Take 1's earlier 'must I' has already shifted to *Blonde On Blonde*'s 'should I' (though he goes back to 'must I' on Take 3) and, similarly, 'the gate' has now shifted to 'your gate'. As on the first chorus, Take 1 has 'leave them', but *BOB* has the more prosaic 'put them'. It's an ill-advised change, and perhaps simply a slip, because on all three later choruses, *BOB* reverts to 'leave them', allowing the voice to stroke the word, to express regret in the lingering curve he gives to 'leave them', holding onto it fractionally, as 'put' cannot be held onto, and so allowing 'leave' to whisper a reluctance to leave.

Verse three (and as it happens, on this verse more changes occur on Take 3 than from Take 1 to *BOB*. They're not significant):

> *Ah,* the kings of Tyrus with their convict list
> Are *all* waiting in line for *the* geranium kiss
> And wouldn't you know *it*, it would happen like this
> But who among them really wants just to kiss you?
> With your childhood flames *and* your midnight rug
> And your Spanish manners and your mother's drugs
> And your cowboy mouth and your curfew plugs
> Who among them do you think could resist you?

> The kings of Tyrus with their convict list
> Are waiting in line for their geranium kiss
> And you wouldn't know it would happen like this
> But who among them really wants just to kiss you?
> With your childhood flames on your midnight rug
> And your Spanish manners and your mother's drugs
> And your cowboy mouth and your curfew plugs
> Who among them do you think could resist you?

That change from waiting in line for 'the geranium kiss' to waiting for 'their geranium kiss' improves that surreal phrase. I'm not sure the same is true of the shift from the casually conversational 'And wouldn't you know it' to the less open and clear 'And you wouldn't know...', which we may feel sounds more, well, knowing.

The third chorus offers no new variants. Take 1's prophets are still not sad-eyed, and the singer's eyes and Arabian drums are still *at* rather than *by* that gate:

> Sad-eyed lady of the lowlands
> Where *the prophets* say that no man comes
> My warehouse eyes, my Arabian drums
> Should I leave them *at* your gate?
> Or, sad-eyed lady, should I wait?

> Sad-eyed lady of the lowlands
> Where the sad-eyed prophets say that no man comes
> My warehouse eyes, my Arabian drums
> Should I leave them by your gate?
> Or, sad-eyed lady, should I wait?

Verse four brings us down from kings to farmers and businessmen, and while 'the blame for the farm' is possibly the one intrusively obscure allusion in the song, the one we cannot, and cannot be expected, to grasp, the questions asked in these lines carry a new plainness: the plainness of sounding more urgent, more agitated. The first question, and it's almost petulant, as from frustration or panic, comes early – not on the expected fourth line, but, breaking the song's pattern, on the third. It piles in as an extra question, nipping in ahead of the fourth line question – and it's in there right from Take 1, word for word:

Now the farmers and the businessmen, *they did* decide
To show you *all the dead angels that they did hide*
But why did they pick you to sympathise with their side?
Oh, how could they ever mistake you?
They wished you'd accepted the blame for the farm
But *the sea was at your feet*, and the phony false alarm
And the child of the hoodlum wrapped up in your arms
Oh, a-how could they ever have persuaded you?

Oh, the farmers and the businessmen, they all did decide
To show you where the dead angels are that they used to hide
But why did they pick you to sympathise with their side?
How could they ever mistake you?
They wished you'd accepted the blame for the farm
But with the sea at your feet and the phony false alarm
And with the child of the hoodlum wrapped up in your arms
How could they ever have persuaded you?

The Take 3 start to this verse is telling, too, about the more personal, agitated edge that escapes into the narrative: 'Oh, the farmers and the businessmen, *I see* they did decide / To show you all the dead angels that they used to try to hide' [my emphasis]. That 'I see' marks the sole moment when an 'I' bursts into any of the verses, and it burns with animus. It's withdrawn by *Blonde On Blonde*'s Take 4.

The hidden angels are also improved by the later formulation, but when the narrative has calmed down from those doubled questions, then Take 1 offers that lovelier 'But the sea was at your feet'. Its expressive tranquillity, and its inherent recognition of that tranquillity being newly gained, is lost on *Blonde On Blonde* when we hear, instead, the less felt 'But with the sea at your feet', that 'But with' having a touch of debating, rather than feeling, about it.

We reach the fourth chorus, and the Take 1 prophets are sad-eyed at last, though curiously, the bobdylan.com version of the lyric is alone in still having a solo prophet at this point, and the *Blonde On Blonde* version's next line now has them saying no man *has* come instead of the usual 'no man comes':

> Sad-eyed lady of the lowlands
> Where the sad-eyed prophets say that no *man* comes
> My warehouse eyes, my Arabian drums
> Should I leave them *at* your gate?
> Or sad-eyed lady, *must* I wait?
>
> Sad-eyed lady of the lowlands
> Where the sad-eyed prophets say that no man's come
> My warehouse eyes, my Arabian drums
> Should I leave them by your gate?
> Or sad-eyed lady, should I wait?

The final verse:

> With your sheet-metal memory of Cannery Row
> And your magazine husband who one day *had to go*
> And *with* your gentleness now, *which just can't* help but show
> Who among them do you think would employ you?
> Now *with your thief, you stand* on his parole
> With your holy medallion and your *fingers* now that fold
> And your saintlike face and your ghostlike soul
> *How could any of them destroy you?*
>
> With your sheet-metal memory of Cannery Row
> And your magazine husband who one day just had to go
> And your gentleness now, which you just can't help but show
> Who among them do you think would employ you?
> Now you stand with your thief, you're on his parole
> With your holy medallion and your fingertips now that fold
> And your saintlike face and your ghostlike soul
> Who among them could ever think he could destroy you?

I hear Take 1's omission of the 'you' in the third line there, giving us a gentleness 'which just can't help but show', as kinder and fonder than 'which you just can't help but show': in the former, her gentleness is there whether she knows it or not; in the later version she's aware of it herself (and perhaps tries to hide it), making it a less natural, because self-conscious, quality. Maybe this double edge is better poetry, but I like the simpler Take 1 line.

Another change I prefer within the first take comes in line six, where her *fingers* fold, either around the medallion or independently of it – that allows either gesture – whereas finger*tips* folding are harder to credit, envisageable only if they're holding that medallion.

It's striking that the finishing end of the song's verses, their final line, is the one Dylan has most trouble settling. Every version – the bobdylan.com, the *Blonde On Blonde* and each other complete take – is different. As we see there, Take 1 has an oddly short line, and one that leaves its meaning rather more ambivalent, holding as it does, the suggestion that perhaps it can happen, or even might have happened already. And while the whole song is riddled with ambivalence ('riddled' in both senses), it's clear from the re-takes that this one was unintended. Destroying her becomes unthinkable or impossible in all these other versions, and the rhetorical nature of the question is given primacy.

Take 3 has the line as 'Who among them could think he could destroy you?' – not 'ever think' but just 'think'; on bobdylan.com we're given 'Oh who among them do you think could destroy you?' (with that surprising 'who … do *you* think…?') and, as we see above, *Blonde On Blonde* settles for the longest, clearest and most satisfying version, 'Who among them could ever think he could destroy you?'

The final chorus holds no final variant or surprise:

> Sad-eyed lady of the lowlands
> Where the sad-eyed prophets say that no man comes
> My warehouse eyes, my Arabian drums
> Should I leave them *at* your gate?
> Or sad-eyed lady, should I wait?
>
> Sad-eyed lady of the lowlands
> Where the sad-eyed prophets say that no man comes
> My warehouse eyes, my Arabian drums
> Should I leave them by your gate?
> Or sad-eyed lady, should I wait?

This unique song ends, then, with a version of the chorus in which only one word is changed between the very first take and the last.

Not only that, but when, back on the first chorus, he tries more of a departure with Take 3, he veers straight back again for *Blonde On Blonde*'s Take 4. The Take 3 lines he tries, and then abandons ever after, are these:

> With his warehouse eyes, his Arabian drums
> You think I should wait,
> Sad-eyed lady, at your gate?

Here, just the once, the warehouse eyes and the drums belong not to the teller of the story but to one of the prophets; and the tentative question that follows is simply whether *he* should wait at the gate. In itself, that phrasing 'You think I should wait…?' has an appealing vulnerability, but it doesn't fit with the thrust of the song, in which the voice we hear is by no means simply at the sad-eyed lady's mercy or disposal: rather, the narrative is full of sharp appraisals of how she stands in relation to others, and alive with suggestions that she and he already have a relationship with history. He's been near enough to her to offer a catalogue of observations. He knows her well, he knows something of her past. Some change has happened 'at last' (verse one); he's touched her bedclothes 'like metal' (verse two); he knows about her 'childhood flames' and something quite personal about her mother (verse three); he's been around to see a child 'wrapped up in' her arms (verse four); and her gentleness is there 'now', after her husband has gone (verse five). It's only fitting, then, that the timidity, the outsiderliness, of 'You think I should wait…?', tried once, is promptly ditched.

One final difference between Takes 1 and 4 is musical: Take 1 comes to an end without Dylan's harmonica – but with a fleeting few moments of Hargus 'Pig' Robbins's lovely piano-work. The other musicians on all takes are Charlie McCoy (guitar), Joe South (guitar, bass), Al Kooper (organ) and Kenneth Buttrey (drums).

'Sad-Eyed Lady Of The Lowlands' has often been dismissed as a pretentious or meaningless lyric set to a corny waltz tune, and when I was young I was hard on it myself: not on the music but the words. I don't feel at all like that any longer. I recanted my snobbishness about it nearly twenty years ago in *Song & Dance Man III*. And it seems to me now that whichever take of the recording you prefer or favour, you're hearing a song of sustained purpose: a creative expression of prolonged supplication, a hymn of devotion, a distinctive and imaginative love letter.

We're given to feel, straight away, in this opening verse, an undercurrent of religious devotion both towards the sad-eyed lady – the hushed purr of the voice, the incantatory long unspooling of the music – and how she is seen: her prayers and her silver cross are in the opening description of her. Intentionally or not on Dylan's part, there's a flickering moment when the image of a Catholic statue of either of the sacred Marys might pass across your mind. And in the choruses we find the further religious touch of the prophet(s).

All this is balanced in later verses by the presence of 'angels', albeit hidden and/or dead, and more directly in the song's final verse, where she has a 'saintlike face' and a 'ghostlike' (perhaps holy ghost like) 'soul'. It's one of the many counterbalances Dylan builds into the song, as when the closing verse's 'sheet-metal memory' carries an echo of the second verse's 'sheets like metal', and when the kings of Tyrus are replaced by farmers and those recurrent villains in Dylan songs, businessmen.

All through the song, the assessment of the sad-eyed lady modulates between the devotional and, undercutting it, sharper descriptions: perhaps especially of her face. The final verse, as noted, calls it saintlike, but in the first verse it had been 'like glass' (smooth, fragile, transparent – in itself not always a compliment – but also hard, fixed and inflexible), and in the second verse it's a 'hollow face'. The dual nature of her qualities is never far away, and is suggested neatly in that single word 'hollow' as Dylan sings it, his voice giving the aural pun of touching on 'hallowed'.

Perhaps we were given a hint of crime as an extra element in the song back on that first-verse line 'With your pockets well protected at last', but in any case it's made explicit in the third verse with its 'convict list', picked up in the next by 'the hoodlum', and picked up again in the final verse with 'thief' and 'on parole'. Who gains or loses by this criminality isn't clear, but the sad-eyed lady is seen to be caught up in it. The effect of these mounting allusions is to augment the sense that things are not safe, that the desired relationship is hanging in the balance. If, having routed the magazine husband, the farmers and the businessmen, it's the storyteller himself who is the thief, they are on his parole together – giving the strong suggestion that their relationship, tentative and not to be assumed, despite its history, is what is 'on parole'. Reinforcing, of course, the recurrent thrust of 'must I/ should I wait?'

One more thrust breaks into that final verse. It begins, in every take, by offering what many will recognise as directly biographical details, albeit obliquely stated: confirming, for anyone interested, that the real-life lady being addressed is Dylan's wife Sara.[80] For those who know or care nothing for the personal background stories – and that is the cleaner way to be open to any work of art – the opening lines of this last verse engage the imagination by the striking (and alliterative) phrase 'your sheet-metal memory', and regardless of real-life background, 'your magazine husband' sounds a neatly Dylanesque dismissive summing-up of a rival, despatching one rival for the sad-eyed lady's love. Who else may still be 'waiting in line'? What future might there be? What does the lady want? We're left, at the end, still uncertain. It's the uncertainty that is, in the end, the subject of the song.

Whether you hear Take 1 or the take we've known for fifty years, you're hearing an extraordinary track, the like of which had never been encountered before, a song sustained over nearly ten minutes of gentle bombardment: a purred assailment of the

[80] Dylan's wife Sara Lownds's first husband was magazine photographer Hans Lownds, and her father ran a scrap-metal business in Wilmington, Delaware. See the entry *Dylan, Sara* in *The Bob Dylan Encyclopedia*, Michael Gray (London & New York: Continuum International, 2006 & 2008), pp. 201-203.

I note that in the poet David Cameron's review of Emma Swift's album *Blonde On The Tracks*, he welcomes biographical knowledge in the song, using it to counter attacks on Dylan's gender politics: 'This is another of Dylan's songs that can be criticised from a feminist perspective: isn't it a projection of male fantasies (about Woman as Muse) onto a living, breathing woman? … But in the song's lyric, the mythical and the personal are interwoven so well that we feel both the awe of Dylan's adoration of Woman and his connection with this real woman, who was Sara Lownds (just a 'la' short of 'lowlands') when they met.' (https://intocreative.co.uk/blonde-on-the-tracks-emma-swift/, seen online 2020.)

imagination and a courageous love song – one of those Robert Reginio called 'the exploded and reconstituted love songs' of *Blonde On Blonde*[81] – its uncertainties delivered with a defiant amorous languor.

We're lucky to have been given (well, sold) the outtakes of such a song. 'Sad-Eyed Lady Of The Lowlands' repays every morsel of the attention the outtakes demand we give them. As when we hear Dylan in concert, so too when we have such access to earlier drafts of a song,[82] we're given the gold of the *process* that lies behind, but also enriches, the long-familiar original release.

---

[81] This quote was added in 2020, my having being able, by then, to read and quote from Professor Reginio's essay 'Listening to the Other: Bob Dylan and Empathy' in the collection *New Approaches to Bob Dylan*, edited Anne-Marie Mai (Odense: University of Southern Denmark Press, 2019), pp.273-296.

[82] Another 2020 footnote: The Dylan archive in Tulsa, Oklahoma, has exponentially increased what we can see and understand of 'the *process* that lies behind, but also enriches' this incomparable artist's work – all across his long working lifetime.

Bob Dylan's Affective Symphony
(2018, 2019)

This paper was the opening keynote speech at the University of Southern Denmark's conference 'New Approaches to Bob Dylan' in October 2018. It was published in the book of the same name (Odense: University of Southern Denmark Press, 2019). The title alludes to affective theory.[83] My aim was to give a brief personal scrutiny of how it was, emerging into young adulthood as a near-contemporary of Bob Dylan, to hear that lapidary run of albums from Another Side Of Bob Dylan *through to* Nashville Skyline *as they emerged, one after the other, at the time, in the 1960s. It was written over 20 years after that other personal retrospective piece, 1997's 'Bob Dylan, 1966 & Me', and almost 40 years after the 1980 piece 'Sixteen Years…' Perhaps some repetition was inevitable. Perhaps it can be forgiven.*

I am just five years younger than Bob Dylan, and first encountered his work as a student in 1964, when *Another Side Of Bob Dylan* was his most recently released album – and the fact that this was the last time his record company had the power to choose the titles of his work is itself indicative of a significant shift that was happening in the boom economy of the 1960s. We were witnessing in the air all around us the push towards abolition of the gulf between 'high culture' and 'popular culture', and one of its consequences was that the serious singer–songwriter genre Bob Dylan had more or less invented was beginning to earn him recognition as an artist rather than 'just' a folk or pop singer. And in being accorded the status of artist, he had to be allowed artistic

---

[83] That is, I'm touching in part on how Dylan's work yields possibilities of 'Joy/Enjoyment' and 'Excitement', defined as 'primary affects' in Silvan S. Tomkins's *Affect Imagery Consciousness: The Positive Affects* (1962) and discussed in Donald L. Nathanson's *Shame and Pride: Affect, Sex and the Birth of the Self* (1992).

control. His being capable of wresting that power from a major American corporation was quite something: a sign that the times were a-changin'.

I had heard Bob Dylan briefly before becoming an undergraduate: a friend and I (who were spending much of our adolescent free time listening to singles by everyone from Elvis Presley to Howlin' Wolf and from Little Eva to Clarence 'Frogman' Henry) had shared a laugh at hearing, on the radio, Dylan's vocals and, we thought, his incompetent timing on 'The Times They Are A-Changin''; and I had probably glimpsed his own 'Blowin' In The Wind' as it drowned among the commercially viable cover versions by Peter, Paul and Mary and others. Only as a student reading English and History did I encounter a whole Bob Dylan album – and indeed the notion that he was an 'albums artist'.

His voice was a difficulty at first. I was not a folk fan: I had grown up force-fed the crooners of the 1950s and the philistine mores of a very traditional school, and it was rock'n'roll that had rescued me from both – opening another, wider, more joyous, anarchic world. Bob Dylan sounded like none of it. He challenged both equally forcefully: for me, an unimaginable other universe.

Of course the hook dropped inside me and I have never wanted to be free of it. That much-criticised voice, so crude on first uneducated hearing, became in my judgment the most superbly subtle one, capable of communicating, with darting quick intelligence, a largely unexplored range of feelings and of thoughts. And in speaking so directly, in assuming in the listener some adequate corresponding intelligence, this voice achieved something else: it abolished the traditional gulf between performer and listener.[84] It was a living demonstration, in the broadest sense, of W.S. Graham's contention that 'A way of speaking, if it is any good, as it persists creates its understanders.'[85]

---

[84] I would find, in later years, that in the pre-war blues, there was no such gulf: the songster was embedded in his or her local community and served its needs.

[85] Graham, W.S., *The Nightfisherman: Selected Letters of;* (Manchester, UK: Carcanet Press, 1999).

In registering this, I was among many contemporaries in confronting the fresh ways in which this mysterious and youthful Bob Dylan was deploying voice, audible breaths, stance, clothes and a self-invented hip grace as well as words and music to be creatively radical. This was a process of ever-replenished discovery as the rest of the 1960s unfolded.

To add, first, to the matter of the voice itself: there were so many voices! Think of the very different sounds that mouth of his makes. Think of it on 'The Times They Are A-Changin'' and then on 'All I Really Want To Do'. Then recall the voices of 'She Belongs To Me' and on 'Subterranean Homesick Blues'. How different again on 'Like A Rolling Stone' and how different yet again on, say, 'Temporary Like Achilles'. Think through 'As I Went Out One Morning' to 'Peggy Day'.

No-one else did that! No-one had. Crooners' voices had grown deeper as they'd aged; rock'n'rollers had mellowed at the edges as they took on 'ballads'; but that was all. Yet here was an artist capable of an astonishing ventriloquism of voice.

When I first went to a Bob Dylan concert – Liverpool Odeon, 14th May 1966 – I found of course that there was a comparable feature to his live performances. Outside of jazz, with its emphasis on the creativity of improvising, everyone else tried to sound as close as possible to their recordings (and if American rock'n'rollers failed to manage this in the UK it was because, for reasons of cost, the meanness of promoters and the obduracy of the Musicians' Union, their back-up musicians were locals picked up at the last minute, instead of the real thing). Dylan's stance, uniquely, was a deliberate refusal to replicate himself. In this we were witnessing him define, and then redefine, the singer-songwriter: and he would soon go beyond transforming songs by reshaping them in live performance to the public re-writing of the words of songs after their initial publication or first round of performances (as poets, of course, were wont to do).

Along with these innovations and the uniquely apparent ever-changing voice, and most apparent in live performance again, were the clothes and the hair and the slouch and the pencil-thin androgyny that in silent defiance challenged the dominant image of the clean-cut all-American youth and the besuited, glossy-haired pop idol. When Dylan wore a suit, it was a parody of a suit. He could hardly have looked more different, either, from the contemporaneous Beatles, all dressed like matching bank clerks. Even the Hawks look as if they have proper jobs when they're behind him in 1966. Watch him walk on stage for the solo first half of each concert, without showbiz flummery. He peers out and tiptoes in through the centre parting of the curtain at the back of the stage, all bony knees and hair from Mars, stands there saying nothing and spends a good couple of minutes tuning his guitar before he's ready for *that* voice to rise through the hall.

All of it, with that calm centre of self, maintained while challenging so many of the rules we hadn't even recognised we'd been in hock to – all of it was above and beyond the songs themselves: the works of art on offer.

Tellingly, it wasn't only in Britain, where I grew up, that he was showing us a kind of hipness as well as new kinds of song. Listen, if you can, to the audience response in Santa Monica in March 1965 when they hear, five days after its release on album, his 'Love Minus Zero/No Limit' in concert. Richard Goldstein once wrote, back in that era, that 'Dylan approaches a cliché like a butcher eyes a chicken'[86] – and this process itself is so unfamiliar to the crowd that they *laugh* with pleasure at the anarchic freshness of 'talk over situations / draw conclusions on the wall'.

They – we – also got the same pleasure, the same electric *charge*, from the radical nature of those 1964-5 songs in the arena of (what no-one then called) sexual politics. In remembering his supposed retreat from the politics of the New Left – politics he had articulated in so much of his work of 1962-1963 – I note what Mike Marqusee writes about Dylan's paralleling the Student Nonviolent Coordinating Committee women's internal struggle:

> About the same time Dylan was writing 'My Back Pages' ...
> a group of SNCC women activists issued a historic challenge
> to sexist practices within SNCC itself: and came up against

[86] Gray, Michael. *Song & Dance Man: The Art of Bob Dylan;* 1972 op.cit. p.216, quoted from a *Village Voice* review, n.d..

a barrage of male mockery. Many of the criticisms made by the SNCC women echo Dylan's grievances against the movement: it did not practise what it preached, it exploited its adherents, its leaders were trapped within their own egos. Like Dylan ... the SNCC women were redrawing the boundaries between the personal and the political.[87]

Thus, perhaps oddly in retrospect, given that Bob has been somewhat of a reactionary in relation to women for most of his career, this early phase of radical anti-politics brought a radical recognition of women's equality to his love songs. Crucially, these yielded, when new, a highly positive Affect response. We all, whatever our sex or sexuality, felt excited recognition of a liberation that was ours for the taking and that freed us from the restrictive sexual mores of the older generation. This was a giddy response quite outside of any lit–crit assessment of the songs per se.

Rock'n'roll, it's true, had by its very nature encouraged us towards a bodily wildness – and perhaps a couple of Elvis Presley tracks had expressed in primitive form what Dylan's new songs articulated so clearly now: 'A fair exchange bears no robbery / and the whole world will know that it's true... If you wanna be loved then you got to love me too', sang Elvis, and 'Why make me plead / For something you need?'[88] – but essentially love songs had always been about the primacy of monogamous love, about wanting to find that special one after chasing and prizing the hottest girls, or taming the bad boys into husbands, or pleading for male infatuation to be reciprocated, or needing to fight off rival guys in order to claim ownership of the coolest girl.

(An extreme case, though no pop fan demurred at the time, was Britain's Cliff Richard with his chart-topping single 'Living Doll': 'Gonna lock her up in a trunk / So no big hunk / Can steal her away from me'.)[89]

[87] Marqusee, Mike. *Chimes of Freedom: The Politics of Bob Dylan's Art* (New York, New Press, 2003) p.203n.

[88] 'One-Sided Love Affair', words & music by Bill Campbell; recorded by Elvis Presley NYC, 30th January 1956; released 1956; and 'Give Me The Right', words & music by Fred Wise & Norman, recorded by Elvis Presley, Nashville, 12th March 1961; released 1961.

[89] 'Living Doll', words & music by Lionel Bart, recorded by Cliff Richard & the Drifters, London, April 1959; released 1959.

What Dylan created, in merciful contrast, was a genre of songs in which the singer could be saying 'All I Really Wanna Do (Is Baby Be Friends With You)' or even 'No, no, no'. At the time it was a highly radical notion to hear him refer to 'a lover for your life and nothing more'; and just as arresting to make a joke of pretended indifference ('If You Gotta Go, Go Now'); and still more so to suggest that the loved woman sleeping with someone else could be contemplated with equanimity ('Mama, You Been On My Mind').

And of course to address women in this way was to treat them as equals: as people equally capable of autonomous lives.

We register how striking all this was to contemporary audiences when, again, they laugh at first hearing some of Dylan's new material in concert. They laugh *even in California in 1965* at the very idea of jesting about a girl's virginity or lack of it! ('It's not that I'm asking / For anything you never gave before / It's just that I'll be sleeping soon / An' it'll be too late for you to find the door.')[90] Or perhaps they laughed in shock recognition of something every young person knew but that had never been said in song before: that virginity was just not a big deal anymore.

In 'Love Minus Zero' we hear Dylan advance a clear corollary argument here, like a teacher of moral philosophy, as to one aspect of this new shared liberation and its respect for the autonomy of others: 'She doesn't have to say she's faithful / Yet she's true like ice, like fire'; and 'People carry roses / Make promises by the hour / My love she laughs like the flowers / Valentines can't buy her'.

From here what our young ears encountered in the 1960s was Dylan's further revolutionising of popular song by making it grown up – by bringing into it the poetry of literary movements – of the French symbolists, the Blakes and Whitmans, and the Beats – and, crucially, adding his own lyrical romanticism; hence the rapture of 'Lay Down Your Weary Tune'. And while The Beatles were singing 'I Want To Hold Your Hand', Bob was singing 'To dance beneath the diamond sky with one hand waving free / Silhouetted by the sea...' etc.

The retrospective impact of this whole affective symphony, of

---

[90] 'If You Gotta Go, Go Now', Bob Dylan, Santa Monica CA, 27th March 1965.

this magnificent work, cannot be the same, or felt to be the same, as when it was new. These albums can only be heard differently now – because in retrospect we're hearing them from within a culture that Dylan's work itself significantly helped to re-shape; when they were new, they were only just starting to bombard that culture.

And besides, like Bob Dylan, we were so much younger then, we're older than that now.

Farewell Bob Willis
(2019)

An unpublished tribute. A number of reasonably famous people have proved themselves so keen on Bob Dylan's work that they have even come to talks of mine about him over the years, including racing driver Graham Hill and singer-songwriter P J Harvey, but the one star I've known personally, and known to be keenest on Dylan, was Bob Willis, who died at age 70 on 4th December 2019.

There aren't many sane people who legally change their name to include 'Dylan' simply because of a devotion to Bob, but the great England cricket player Bob Willis, full name Robert George Dylan Willis, was one.

I knew him through his brother David, a student friend at York in the mid-1960s. I liked Bob a lot – he was a fascinating presence, volatile yet rock-solid at the same time. He was shy but powerful, and he was stoical but took no shit.

I don't remember when I first met him, but it must have been at the end of the sixties or the start of the seventies. Certainly I remember watching the 1972 Wimbledon Men's Final at his flat in Harborne, Birmingham, made miserable by the then-great Ilie Nastase losing to the always-boring Stan Smith, having been persuaded, disastrously, not to play his own magnificent, erratic game of inspiration and flair but to 'play sensibly'. I was the only one in the house watching the match, sitting in Bob's 'listening chair': one of those big wing-backed armchairs with a speaker built into each wing to feed the sound straight into your ears.

He'd bought the chair to listen to Bob Dylan in comfort. He had the albums but by the mid-1970s he also started assembling his own selections of tracks on cassette. He was on the dole in England. He'd had knee operations the previous summer and wanted a chance to recover. He made three compilations when *The Basement Tapes* was the most recent album, and others later.

He said he really wanted songs he liked but in a different order. And while he had 'all this stuff on albums', he couldn't take albums on tour, so he had to put them on cassette to take them on cricket tours, and it made sense to pick and choose a bit, and to freshen things up, putting unexpected things together.

There was a time when he took no other music on tour – he played them around the England team in India 1976/7, and then in Pakistan and New Zealand 1977/8. They also made three trips to Australia 1978/9, 1979/80 and 1982/3.

A very big fan, in other words, and always open to new Dylan material, though 'Positively 4th Street' remained his all-time favourite track.

In 1984, meanwhile, I went to the Parc de Sceaux in Paris to start seeing some of that year's European tour by Dylan, later catching those at Wembley and Slane – but in between there was a very special event for me, because I was there in Newcastle with Bob Willis, his brother David and Ian Botham (who seemed a pleasant person at the time). At the end of the concert, the sheer joy of Bob W electrified Botham's car as we all travelled back in it to Yorkshire.

I remember too a weekend at Bob's neo-Georgian house in Birmingham in February 1985 when his daughter Katie Anne was a 1-year-old. And later that year going to Michael Aspel's *Six O'Clock Show* on British television, because Bob was a guest, after which Bob, Dave and I took the train to Birmingham to stay overnight. Next day the three of us went down to Sheepscombe in the Cotswolds for a cricket match, playing an advance cassette tape of *Empire Burlesque* in the car en route.

Just into the second half of the 1980s, the first party I ever attended with my future wife, Sarah Beattie, was also at Bob's house.

When I was editing the first collection of pieces from John Bauldie's fanzine *The Telegraph* for the book that became *All Across The Telegraph*, it was a pleasure to be able to ask Bob if he would like to write a special introduction to the book, and another pleasure to find that what he gave me was so good and – well, so Bob Willis.

Years later I remember Sarah and I going up to Newcastle – it was June 2004 – where we met up with Dave and Bob and after a bottle of wine together we had front row seats to see Dylan at the arena.

At one point near the end of the 1990s there was Bob's venture into the wine business itself, with the Botham Merrill Willis Collection, and also some sort of travel business, and for the latter I remember finding Bob a terrific vintage coach up in North Yorkshire and working out a route for him to take his punters over the hills and down the dales.

The last time I spent any time with him was about a year ago, when Bob, David and a couple of others spent a long afternoon in a rather dark Chinese restaurant somewhere at Elephant & Castle. He was far from well by then, but he could still hold an impressive amount of wine without losing any of his somewhat quirky social grace.

In all the time I knew him across the decades, I never saw a bad side to him, never saw him acting the star, and to me he was always warm, alert and interested.

PS: Prostate cancer, detected late, was the cause of Bob Willis's death. In early 2021, Bob's widow Lauren Clark and his brother David created The Bob Willis Fund for Prostate Cancer Research (BWF for short) - and, uniquely, Bob Dylan agreed to be its Honorary Patron.

Rough And Rowdy Ways
(2021)

Written for this book.

For years now, my thoughts and feelings about Bob Dylan's work have been burdened by a debilitating exasperation. My own problem, I know. But faced with a decades-long bombardment, in print and online, of unsparing adoration for everything Dylan is and does, I have recognised in myself a damaging response both to the cult-like uncritical outpouring *about* him and to how, in a number of ways, Dylan has turned out to be. I've resented the way his great corporate promo machine thrusts him at us now, exactly as if he were a Nespresso machine or a new iPhone; it's on a par with selling his material and personal appearance to any corporation that pays enough, whether it's as tacky as Victoria's Secret – so shopping-mall – or as bad for the planet as a testosteronic Cadillac SUV just as we hit the tipping-point of climate change.

I have also regretted his ponderous literary name-dropping; once done with quick wit and humour, it's now part of building an immodest image, Dylan as serious intellectual polymath. This is risible. The 20th-century songs drop literary names with a sharp, light touch; *Tarantula*, too, is full of fast, sly references to, and a playfulness with, major American literary figures. His more recent equivalents are heavy-handed – and yes, he was caught out using SparkNotes for his Nobel lecture,[91] suggesting, and not for the first time, that some of his literary referencing is designed to impress. I remember an interview many years ago now when he

---

[91] 'SparkNotes, the literary summary site that helps students write essays about books they haven't read. The whale Moby Dick is "the embodiment of evil" in Dylan's speech and on SparkNotes, but not in Herman Melville's prose. Dylan says Captain Boomer "can't accept Ahab's lust for vengeance," SparkNotes says he "cannot understand Ahab's lust for vengeance," and Melville says neither.' ('Bob Dylan Cheats Again?', Spencer Kornhaber, *The Atlantic,* 14th June 2017; https://www.theatlantic.com/entertainment/archive/2017/06/bob-dylan-nobel-spark-notes-plagarism/530283/)

said his favourite poets were Shelley and Keats. This was suspect: as any thoughtful reader of 19th-century English poetry will know, and as critics from F. R. Leavis to Christopher Ricks have pinned down, people take sides between Shelley and Keats, making crucial qualitative distinctions between them: they do not rate them equally and pair them as favourites.[92]

Ever since *Chronicles Volume One* he's been telling us about his wide reading, where once he used to trust us to notice it. He is *not* a serious intellectual, he's a creative artist of genius. Literary pretension is unnecessary from Dylan, and bad enough in interviews and talks, but now it threatens to mar the work. (It certainly doesn't improve *Rough And Rowdy Ways*: but we'll come to that.)

I don't suggest that Dylan *isn't* widely read, or that in *Chronicles Volume One* the reading he mentions (and doesn't mention but draws upon) isn't an absorbing part of his fable. But his literary name-dropping used to be beautifully good-humoured. I especially liked (and so, I imagine, did Ricks) his answer in 1969 as to why he had come to the Isle of Wight: 'I wanted to see the home of Alfred, Lord Tennyson.'[93]

For me, though, the saddest change is that *almost* every live song performance for the last fifteen years has been somewhere between indifferent and dreadful, yet has been received by his crowds as if every one was a thrilling rock'n'roll excalibur. He said when he was young that he wanted, with age, to acquire the dignity of the old blues performers, but he hasn't: he has less now, and less subtlety on stage than when he was in his youthful prime. Who doesn't tire of the cacophony of fans who come out of a 2010s concert claiming online that 'it was the best ever'? They are deluded.

---

[92] See Leavis's chapter on Shelley in *Revaluation*, 1936, which alleges that, unlike Keats's, Shelley's poetry is self-indulgent and declamatory. Ricks makes a comparable point in a lecture on 'Scarlet Town' that is accessible online; referring to 'Ballad In Plain D' and its failure to achieve the 'high impersonality' of which Dylan is often capable, Ricks says: 'It's a wonderful song but it's a song by Shelley and not by Keats ... It wears its heart on its sleeve.' ('The Black and the White the Yellow and the Brown', Boston University, 19th February 2013; see https://vimeo.com/80220193.)

[93] From Dylan's Isle of Wight press conference, 27th August 1969; online text at https://www.interferenza.net/bcs/interw/69-aug27.htm

Yes, there are exceptions – large, beautiful ones, but they occupy a minuscule percentage of song renditions from his huge number of concerts. In 2018 he solidified a set and a way of performing it, and this gave us a few more felicitous performances: some funny re-written 'Gotta Serve Somebody's set to the beat (perhaps ironically) of Presley's 'Baby I Don't Care'; a significantly re-written 'When I Paint My Masterpiece', funny in the Coliseum verse and compelling in the bridge; and in 2019 an inspired re-working of 'Not Dark Yet'. Yet what begins as fresh seldom remains fresh for Dylan.

Take his re-designed 'Don't Think Twice, It's All Right'. In Rochester, New York, on 14th November 2018, the 77-year-old Dylan delivers a sustained, concentrated performance, on (effectively almost solo) piano *and* on vocals. The yearning regret, that sub-text wish the song has always held for a last-moment reunion, is expressed by his singing new, reached-for and held high notes at the end of lines five, six and seven in every eight-line verse, and after each such note, the voice runs without a pause for breath across the first syllables of the line that follows and then takes a quick and delicate drop down on the line's next syllables: '…break of dawn----------- Look out your…' cascading down into 'window', and so on. And in what was always his traditional instrumental space before a final verse, a decent harmonica break, with a pretty (but not too pretty) piano to conclude. I'm sorry he makes it *'all of my precious time'* instead of the original's unelaborated and better-judged 'my precious time', but then, few of his in-performance word changes are better judged than on the original recordings, and in this case it's a very small blemish on a wonderful performance.

The point is, having achieved that, on *one* night in late 2018, he never again stays concentrated enough to do justice to his beautiful re-casting of the song. The deterioration is immediate – and that's how it's been for a long time. His songs so easily become occluded and smudged, as he grows bored with his own lack of inspiration and resorts to those petulant gargled shouts, tiresome showbiz devices (the repeated half, repeated half lines), and mannered exaggeration on a level he never stooped to when he was young and his integrity was more intact.

Even when a *vocal* performance is achieved with that integrity, as on a 'Girl From The North Country' as recently as 12th October 2019 at Santa Barbara, the delicate fondness of his singing of the verses comes between painfully obvious musical interludes, centred around his crudest, most galumphing piano work.

I know I'm by no means alone among Dylan critics and admirers in feeling that there's precious little concert work after 2005 worth playing to oneself, let alone to anyone outside the cult – anyone with a disinterested curiosity and love of music. Sometimes you have to hope he *won't* sing the songs you love the most.

For all his assertions down the years that the albums are less important than live performance – that he only writes the songs to have something to perform – it is his albums alone to which he devotes real care now: being as exacting in the studio as any of us could wish.

Even here, though, I've felt weighed down: troubled by my hostility to the way every album is hailed as a masterpiece, and by Dylan's own bullshit in the interviews he gives ahead of each new release, telling us how to align ourselves with them and what to feel about them. He never used to do this: he used to shut up and trust us to think what we thought and feel what we felt.

How thrilling it was, then, that *Rough And Rowdy Ways* arrived the way it did, with the unannounced huge surprise of 'Murder Most Foul' – introduced with a short online message from its creator asking us to 'stay observant': and we didn't have to be especially observant to notice the double meaning there, or that he trusted us to pick up on it.[94] It truly was exciting to hear this audacious and audaciously *lengthy* song suddenly looming over the radio that morning, an audio experience like no other. (''Twas a matter of timing and the timing was right'.) It was exhilarating

---

[94] The release came with this introduction on bobdylan.com: 'Greetings to my fans and followers with gratitude for all your support and loyalty across the years. This is an unreleased song we recorded a while back that you might find interesting. Stay safe, stay observant and may God be with you. Bob Dylan.' Even here he offers a sharp pun. As Andrew Muir expressed it: '"Observant" is a very Dylanesque touch and "pay attention" is the lesser of its two meanings in play here.' ('Afterword' in the 2nd edition of Muir's study *Bob Dylan & William Shakespeare: The True Performing of it*, Cornwall UK, Red Planet Music Books, 2020.)

that Dylan could so dramatically surprise us after all these years. It was magnificently unpredictable. And then came 'I Contain Multitudes' and 'False Prophet' and the confirmation that these were indeed parts of a new album – a new double album (four sides of vinyl or two CDs).

Listening over and over, countless times, to *Rough And Rowdy Ways*, my long exasperation recedes. I welcome how unlike *Tempest* it is – how little of that album's gargling bravado his voice retains this time, and the surprise of the music's dreamy burble and melodic gentleness. I've heard the music complained about for being virtually absent, but I find it refreshingly not what Dylan album music usually is. I also appreciate how high in the mix his vocal is, for the emphasis it gives the words.

'Murder Most Foul' is, yes, the final track on the album, but the first track we heard, and it remains somehow a separate creature from the rest, and not only physically – the whole fourth side of the vinyl, or an entirely separate CD – but in the uniqueness of its character as writing and sound. It's an extraordinary achievement, partly because it manages such mesmerising power despite including some terrible lines of lyric.

It begins as it means to go on, with a phrase taken from another song: in this case another song about the Kennedy assassination, 'Dark Day In Dallas', written and sung by Tommy Durden (more successfully the co-writer of 'Heartbreak Hotel'). His sepulchral 'Dallas' ballad does begin ''Twas a dark day in Dallas...' but that's where the two songs part company.[95]

It's only to British ears that Dylan's opening couplet

> 'Twas a dark day in Dallas, November '63
> The day that will live on in infamy

is immediately reminiscent of the notoriously bad Scottish poet William McGonagall (1825-1902), whose copious, ungainly broadsheet ballads include the famous one on the topic not of an assassination but of a tragedy, for Scots engineering pride as well as for those who lost their lives, in 'The Tay Bridge Disaster'. It begins:

[95] Tommy Durden, 'Dark Day In Dallas', Sounds S1-152, US, 1967.

Beautiful Railway Bridge of the Silv'ry Tay!
Alas! I am very sorry to say
That ninety lives have been taken away
On the last Sabbath day of 1879,
Which will be remember'd for a very long time.

The real common ground here is the broadside ballad. McGonagall didn't sing his, he recited them, to great contemporary acclaim, in Edinburgh pubs; Dylan, in the world of song – even if 'Murder Most Foul' is essentially recitation – knows that the story of a political assassination is classic broadsheet material.

His monumental song soon reaches far beyond conventional ballad narrative, but it does begin with that traditional opening word *'Twas*. I've seen Dylan's use of it scoffed at, but it's not as if only irrelevantly antiquated songs begin with it. It's there in the ancient but unfailingly popular 'Barbara Allen', one of those traditional ballads Dylan said are 'not going to die' – but it's also the first word of a song from that great Dylan album *Blood On The Tracks*, with 'Shelter From The Storm' beginning ''Twas in another lifetime…': another song that then promptly departs from standard balladic narrative. No-one objected to, or even particularly noticed, that *'Twas*. So little does it draw attention to itself that it's perhaps a surprise to find it in a whole cluster of Dylan's songs: ''Twas down in Mississippi' ('The Death Of Emmett Till'); ''Twas down in Chaynee County' ('John Wesley Harding'); ''Twas then he felt alone' ('Simple Twist Of Fate'); ''Twas there by the bakery' ('Sign Language'); ''Twas then that I knew what he had on his mind' ('Isis'); and ''Twas the fourteenth day of April' in that admittedly dreadful 2012 ballad 'Tempest'.[96]

In most murder ballads – and they're a genre by themselves – it is only the murders that make their perpetrators famous; in 'Murder Most Foul', the perpetrators remain mostly unnamed and the victim is hugely famous long before his death. But

---

[96] A favourite genre-busting imaginative spin-off from ''Twas' is by another C19 Briton, McGonagall's more skilful contemporary Lewis Carroll (1832-1898), whose poem 'Jabberwocky' begins and ends with this: ''Twas brillig, and the slithy toves / Did gyre and gimble in the wabe: / All mimsy were the borogoves, / And the mome raths outgrabe.'

'Murder Most Foul' soon channels not another broadside ballad or 19th-century British poet but a 19th-century American one, as Dylan creates an astonishing, Whitmanesque lament for America, swirling in and out of Kennedy's disintegrating head, his existential consciousness, on this last ride in the long black Lincoln limousine.

Kennedy is first named, and first rides, in the third line of the song, with the neat double meaning of 'President Kennedy was a-ridin' high', with its momentary nod to cowboy ballad and its hint of riding for a fall. Later, when he's shot 'still in the car', that car is named as a Lincoln to cite America's first assassinated president; and this is alluded to again, much later, with the line 'Play it for the First Lady, she ain't feeling too good', echoing the joke we've known all our lives, supposedly said to Mrs. Lincoln after her husband died in the theatre: 'But apart from that Mrs. Lincoln, how did you enjoy the play?'

It's also impossible not to hear, at least for anyone attuned to Dylan's musical taste (and the song specifies plenty about that) a parallel car gliding along – a line *without* Lincoln in it – in the chorus of Presley's track 'Long Black Limousine', recorded for his last album of consequence, *From Elvis in Memphis*: a song about another tragic early death, and often used later underneath the footage of Presley's own funeral cortege. Its key line is 'You're ridin' in a long black limousine'.[97] And more generally, we associate long black limousines with funerals. (There's a very brief poem by Gregory Corso, 'Italian Extravaganza', describing the funeral of a baby, which ends 'Wow! Such a small coffin / And ten black Cadillacs to haul it in' – which, when Allen Ginsberg is telling his father about it in a letter, he writes as the poetic '... and the 10 immense black Cadillacs of sorrow...')[98]

In Dylan's song, that final ride is disrupted both by the killers'

[97] 'Long Black Limousine' (composed Vern Stovall & Bobby George), cut 13th January 1969, issued on *From Elvis in Memphis*, RCA Victor LSP-4155 (US), 17th June 1969.
[98] 'Italian Extravaganza', Gregory Corso, in *Gasoline* (San Francisco: City Lights Books, 1958); he can be heard online introducing and reading it at *http://archives.naropa.edu/digital/collection/p16621coll1/id/2692/*; Allen Ginsberg, letter to Louis Ginsberg, 1958, in *Family Business: Selected Letters Between a Father and Son*, ed. Michael Schumacher, NYC: Bloomsbury, 2001; p.105 in paperback, London: Bloomsbury, 2002.

rifles and by their taunts and threats. Their imagined dialogue with JFK begins as early as line 6, with his 'Wait a minute boys, do you know who I am?' and their retort 'Of course we do, we know who you are / Then they blew off his head while he was still in the car'. In reality of course, his head was not blown off, though a piece of his brain was, and was retained by Jackie, until she handed it to Dr. M. T. Jenkins in the emergency room at the hospital. Until that moment, the doctors, unaware of the smashed skull under his hair, had noted his failing but not yet failed heartbeat – that is, they were still struggling to save him, considering him medically still alive.[99] Naturally the hurried drive to the hospital had been in the desperate hope of his remaining alive and of saving his life. Thus there was, just about, a bodily parallel to Dylan's song-long conceit of Kennedy's extended consciousness.

Unexpectedly late in the song comes another imagined taunting intrusion upon this consciousness by the assassins. Another voice tells Kennedy help in the shape of his brothers is on the way, and following his confused response, the killers butt in with 'Tell 'em we're waitin' – keep comin' – we'll get them as well'. Dylan is reminding us, of course, that Senator Robert Kennedy was assassinated too, less than five years after JFK, and that a year later, in 1969, Edward (the Prince Andrew of the clan) had his career and mediocre reputation killed at Chappaquiddick when he caused the death of a young woman who remained trapped in his car overnight in the river while he swam free.[100]

This allusion comes unsettlingly late on because by then the song has long since slid into its incantatory address to DJ Wolfman Jack. The mesmerising anaphora 'Play it...', 'Play...' has already launched thirty-three lines, with many others naming further song and film titles, before those brothers are thrust into the song. It's an additionally alarming intrusion because most of the dialogue from the killers has come in the very first stanza.

[99] Testimony of Chief of Anesthesiology Dr. M. T. Jenkins seen online 11th November 2020 at https://www.youtube.com/watch?v=DX58vrL5ZiA
[100] US Attorney General and New York State Senator Robert F. Kennedy was assassinated on 6th June 1968. Re Edward Kennedy's July 1969 disgrace see https://en.wikipedia.org/wiki/Chappaquiddick_incident.

Back there, Dylan puts in their mouths almost the worst phrase in the song, 'We'll mock you and shock you...', an example of a writing habit to make anyone wince – a clumping together of internal rhymes he indulged so inadvisedly all through the *Tempest* period[101] and persists in now. When he was young, he could pull it off, as in 'To Ramona' ('they'll hype you and type you'), because in 1964 he was knocking down the walls of popular song and it was part of a vital expansion of the genre's vocabulary. He's older than that now, and indulging this verbal tic in his belabouring, head-cuffing way just makes for woeful versifying. On *Rough And Rowdy Ways* it starts on the opening track, with 'I rollick and I frolic'; he gets away with it only with the quieter 'Wake me, shake me' in 'Mother Of Muses'.

The only 'Murder Most Foul' lines worse than the mocking and shocking one come far later on, and in the mouth of the narrator. 'But his soul was not there where it was supposed to be at', with that laughable 'at', shoutingly redundant other than to give a rhyme, is unforgivably bad – and made worse by a limp, am-dram delivery I'd never have thought Dylan capable of. And this is followed, a few lines later, by 'I'm just a patsy like Patsy Cline'. This is clunky, even if it's intended as a remark from Lee Harvey Oswald: it's so clumsy and dull-witted a line to include. That Ms Cline was 'a patsy' makes no sense. It's just her given name, and that's all. He might have cited her differently in the song (asking Wolfman Jack to play the apt 'I Fall To Pieces', perhaps), and then there might have been a point to our remembering that she too died young, in a plane crash, earlier in the same year Kennedy died.[102]

But set against these small, unaccountable blemishes is a torrent of honed writing, and ideas imaginatively expressed within the song's 164 lines.

---

[101] On *Tempest*, 'Soon After Midnight' is stuffed with them (and stuffed by them), from 'My heart is cheerful, it's never fearful' onwards. In 'Early Roman Kings' we get 'They're peddlers and they're meddlers' and 'They're lecherous and treacherous'; and in the title track 'Leo said to Cleo' and 'They mumbled, fumbled, tumbled / Each one more weary than the last'. Yes indeed.

[102] 'I Fall To Pieces' (composed Hank Cochran & Harlan Howard), Patsy Cline, 1961. In March 1963, her plane home with fellow performers Cowboy Copas & Hawkshaw Hawkins crashed in bad weather near Camden TN, killing all on board.

As we've seen, there's so creative a use of disparate voices within the song. Kennedy himself is given voice long after no such speech or thought could have been a physical reality – after he's 'Heading straight on into the afterlife' – and that voice, that ghost's voice, trying to grasp at the soothing compensation of music, becomes the spine of the song. But other voices join in quite aside from those of the murderers. Some belong to ghosts, as so many gothic ballads do (think of 'Polly Vaughan' or 'Long Black Veil'), or have another kind of disembodied voice, like the prominently invoked radio DJ, Wolfman Jack – a man who had named himself werewolf – but some belong to realist politicians. The song's second line, that 'The day that will live on in infamy' is taken, minutely tweaked, from the voice of an earlier US president in response to another calamitous day for the American psyche. The day after Japan's surprise attack on the US naval base at Pearl Harbor, Franklin D. Roosevelt began his short speech to Congress by declaring: 'Yesterday, December 7, 1941 – a date which will live in infamy…'

Another voice's now-famous quote, here minimally amended, is also woven into the song: that of Idanell Brill Connally, known as Nellie, the wife of Texas Governor John Connally. The couple were passengers in the car with Kennedy. Seconds before the gunshots, she said to him, 'Mr. President, you can't say Dallas doesn't love you.' In Dylan's song, his version is followed by 'Put your foot in the tank and step on the gas / Try to make it to the triple underpass', suggesting neatly, and accurately, that the crucial, calamitous event kicked in right after that remark: the event that instantly made Connally's remark so intensely, fatefully ironic.[103]

As the song then takes us on the hurried route of Kennedy's limousine from Elm Street to Parkland Hospital, another fragment of a speech bobs up almost verbatim, from Kennedy's famous 'And so, my fellow Americans: ask not what your country can do for you – ask what you can do for your country.'[104]

[103] Idanell Brill Connally (1919-2006), First Lady of Texas 1963-69. Her husband John Connally (1917-1993) was also shot during the ride through Dealey Plaza. He was seriously injured.
[104] This was one of the many painfully slick homily-ridden quotes that made up Kennedy's inaugural address, 20th January 1961, Washington D.C..

Dylan intensifies its hollow piety by placing it in the milieux of the desperate and oppressed, of those with nothing to give or lose, as his stricken Kennedy, heading for the hospital, tells us 'I'm in the red-light district like a cop on the beat / Living in a nightmare on Elm Street / When you're down on Deep Ellum put your money in your shoe / Don't ask what your country can do for you'.

That 'nightmare on Elm Street' fuses the nightmare of Kennedy, shot on that very street in Dallas, with the name of the film made by Wes Craven in that later year of ominous reverberations, 1984: another gothic tale of slaughter, which is what you might call 'Murder Most Foul'. But it's the slide into Deep Ellum from Elm ('nightmare on Elm Street / When you're down on Deep Ellum') that is so acute a touch, linking the death of the privileged American 'king' to songs about that once notoriously murderous patch of Dallas – the black part of Elm Street (Ellum a pronunciation much like the Irish turning of 'film' into 'fillum') – where the most downtrodden citizens had to struggle to stay alive, where the bars and entertainment places were, plus what bluesman Will Shade called 'a sportin' class of women'.

The old song 'Deep Elem Blues' (aka 'Deep Elm Blues' aka 'Deep Ellum Blues' aka 'Elm Street Blues') seems to have been recorded first as a blues, in 1929, by Texas Bill Day & Billiken Johnson, and then in the mid-1930s by the (white) Lone Star Cowboys. Theirs sold so well that a more robust cover was rushed out by the equally white Prairie Ramblers. The song has had legs ever since, moving from western swing to rock'n'roll (Jerry Lee Lewis, 1956) to the folk revivalists' repertoire at the start of the 1960s, with Dylan himself performing it at Gerde's Folk City back in 1962 in his inimitably hillbilly style. It usually begins 'If you go down in Deep Ellum / Put your money in your shoe(s)'.[105]

[105] 'Deep Elm Blues', Texas Bill Day & Billiken Johnson, Columbia 14514-D, 1929, issued on *Blues Fell This Morning*, Philips BBL.7369, UK, 1960 (the companion album to Paul Oliver's pioneering book of the same name). 'Deep Elm Blues', Lone Star Cowboys, Victor 23846, 1933 and then Bluebird B-6001, 1935; accessible on https://youtu.be/ I2MZWzSSro4. 'Deep Elem Blues', Prairie Ramblers, Mellotone 5-11-51, 1935 (https:// youtu.be/kx3hB3b1PG8). 'Deep Elem Blues', Jerry Lee Lewis, Sun Records 1956, best on *Jerry Lee Lewis Sun Essentials*, Charly Records SNAJ 737 CD, UK 2006. 'Deep Ellum Blues', Bob Dylan, 16th April 1962, Gerde's Folk City, NYC; *50th Anniversary Collection*,

A stanza later in 'Murder Most Foul' comes one of its most inspired lines, picking up on the reverberations of 'nightmare… street' as those conspirators' voices say the menacing 'We're right down the street from the street where you live'. Most of us so easily feel the potential scariness of hearing that said to us, wherever we live. It lights a touchpaper of fears all the way from the paranoia of suburban Neighbourhood Watch officers to the real dread urban mothers everywhere feel that sons may succumb to local gangs.

Other voices pile into the song too. Wolfman Jack's is called upon, and his repeated 'howl' serves as an echo of the poetic voice of Allen Ginsberg, a sharp critic of Kennedy's politics, whose poem 'Howl' was a founding work of the Beat Generation. It's another cultural marker of the era the song is about, and at the same time a calling back to that other long song on the album, 'Key West', in which Ginsberg is cited by name.[106]

There is the sinister voice Dylan channels early on, intoning 'Rub-a-dub-dub', harking back to a version of the late 18th-century English nursery rhyme, in which, pertinently to the truth of there having been several assassins involved in killing Kennedy (and to the mention of 'three bums comin' all dressed in rags') the rhyme proceeds with this accusatory warning: 'Three fools in a tub / And who do you think they be? / The butcher, the baker, The candlestick maker. / Turn them out, knaves all three.'[107]

Some lines echo other *Dylan* voices, and so other songs of his, too. There are cadences within this song about murders and killing that revisit those from the very young Bob Dylan's 'Who Killed Davey Moore?'. The cadence of that song's 'Don't say murder, don't say kill / It was destiny, it was God's will' resonates under the vocal delivery on 'Murder Most Foul' of lines like 'It

Sony, US 2012. (Here, the composer credit given is Joe & Bob Attlesay [sic]. Joe & Bob Attlesey were the Sunshine Boys and composers of 'Just Because'. The two Attleseys plus Leon Chappelear were The Lone Star Cowboys. They changed their name in 1935 and had a pre- and post-war career as the Shelton Brothers. The first thing they did under this name was re-record 'Deep Elem [sic] Blues'.

[106] *Howl and Other Poems*, Allen Ginsberg, published 1st November 1956, No.4 in the Pocket Book Series, City Lights Books, SF.

[107] Iona & Peter Opie, *The Oxford Dictionary of Nursery Rhymes* (Oxford: OUP, 1951).

happened so quickly, so quick by surprise / Right there in front of everyone's eyes'.

A *verbal* reminder comes in that line 'Play it for me and for Marilyn Monroe': the playful presumption of putting himself together with Monroe yields a reminder that he had named her nearest equivalent European stars and linked them and himself to Kennedy on 'I Shall Be Free', the last track on *Freewheelin'*: 'Well, my telephone rang, it would not stop / It's President Kennedy callin' me up / He said, "My friend, Bob, what do we need to make the country grow?"/ I said, "My friend John, Brigitte Bardot / Anita Ekberg / Sophia Loren / Country'll grow!"'.

More soberly, 'Play it for me and for Marilyn Monroe', heard as coming from Kennedy – and delivered so beautifully by Dylan – yields a neat allusion to Kennedy's affair with Monroe, and the implicit subtexts both of the rumour that he had had her killed, and of the memory of her singing 'Happy Birthday To You' so very publicly to 'Mr. President' (and so giving us, by implication, Monroe's voice too).

Then there is the myriad of voices – singing and on musical instruments – named by Dylan and conjured by his listing of so many records these artists made, starting with The Beatles two lines after the first title phrase and running all the way through to 'Play Love Me Or Leave Me by the great Bud Powell' on the song's penultimate line, making 'Powell' his final rhyme with 'Foul'.

By no means all the songs are so named: frequently Dylan simply slips their title phrases inside his own lines ('let the good times roll', to give one clear example): and sometimes he both names *and doesn't* name a song. The instance that stands out strongly, where a title holds a far greater hinterland of meaning, and relevance, than merely as the *named* song, is here: 'Play me that Only The Good Die Young'. OK, yes, as every early reviewer of *Rough And Rowdy Ways* rushed to say – and only say – it's a nod to the Billy Joel record (Dylan casts a democratically wide net). But that's to ignore the far more important, relevant song more prominent in Dylan's mind here, 'Abraham, Martin And John'. You'd think from the reviews that Dylan had never listened to the very early version of *that* song by Dion (an artist Dylan particularly admires), that it wasn't a song that repeats 'only the good die young' throughout, and that it isn't entirely about significant figures shot down, among them those two assassinated presidents, Lincoln and Kennedy. It's also a song Dylan, on piano and duetting with the admirable Clydie King, sang nineteen times in concert in 1980, a further six times in 1981 and on film in the studio.[108]

In the song's great litany of literature and music, voices from films bubble up too, among them Clark Gable's, misquoted from *Gone with the Wind*, an allusion that gives Dylan, along with his invoking of Lincoln, another of the song's reminders of the Confederate South and the American Civil War, that other national tragedy, its 100-year-old hot reverberations very near the surface on that November day when Dallas confronted its Camelot 'king' – a Texan city descended upon by its privileged northern president at a time of hugely divisive Civil Rights ferment.[109]

We feel the animus of that from Dylan's opening stanza, within the killers' cynical yet spiteful line 'We've already got someone here to take your place', because that someone is a Texan ('Johnson sworn in at two thirty-eight'). The black American song 'Oh Freedom', quoted in Dylan's later line 'Freedom oh freedom, freedom over me', is a song associated with the Civil Rights movement (sung by Odetta and others, including by Joan Baez at the March on Washington in 1963).

Martin Luther King's well-known quote 'I've seen the Promised Land. I may not get there with you' is put into Kennedy's mind or mouth as the parallel 'I'm never going to make it to the New Frontier'; and another voice from the car en route to Parkland

[108] 'Abraham, Martin and John', composed by Dick Holler (also co-composer of the Royal Guardsmen's 1966 hit 'Snoopy vs. the Red Baron'), was first cut by Dion (DiMucci) in 1968, Laurie Records, US; in 2000 it was included on the 3-CD box set *Dion – King of the New York Streets*, The Right Stuff (a division of Capitol Records) 72435 28677 2-1, US: a release *featuring enthusiastic sleevenotes by Bob Dylan!* The film footage of Dylan and King singing the song is on *Trouble No More: A Musical Film*, issued 2017 including as Disc 9 of Bootleg Series Vol. 13, Sony US, 2017.

[109] Jackie Kennedy started to PR his era in office as a new Camelot almost as soon as he was dead. See eg 'Captivating Kennedy Photos That Capture The "Camelot" Era In All Its Glory', Marco Margaritoff, 2020, https://allthatsinteresting.com/camelot-kennedy.

Hospital, perhaps Jackie's, is heard saying 'let's keep hope alive', which was the tagline for Jesse Jackson's famous address to the Democratic National Convention in 1988, a reminder of how barely alive the hopes still were for victory in the Civil Rights struggle twenty years after the killing of Dr. King.

The racism of the South, witnessed throughout that struggle, and which had become a political issue embroiling Kennedy and Johnson, was a strident sign of that larger, unhealed Civil War defeat – a defeat touched on again as 'Murder Most Foul' draws to an end, its penultimate couplet starting with 'Play Marching Through Georgia', that triumphalist Union song, and its final line beginning 'Play the Bloodstained Banner…', a religious song but also the Confederate flag.

So much compression in one song. And so many voices inside 'Murder Most Foul'… and underlying that great sweep of American voices there is the voice of William Shakespeare, *four* of whose plays are cited or alluded to in the song: *Hamlet*, *Macbeth*, *Julius Caesar* and *The Merchant of Venice*.

(You could say Shakespeare's voice is in *every* Dylan song: Dylan/Shakespeare critic Andrew Muir says so in the vivacious interview he gives to the podcast *The State of Shakespeare*, arguing that Dylan heard Shakespearean language when the traditional English ballads came down from the Appalachians – 'language preserved from the Pilgrims' sailing to the New World while the Old World was shifting its ever-changing language further from the Shakespearean'.)[110]

'Murder Most Foul', the phrase itself, comes in *Hamlet*, spoken by the ghost of Hamlet's murdered father, the king: 'Murder most foul … most foul, strange and unnatural' – and Dylan gives us the parallel of our hearing Kennedy's ghost. Muir argues that 'unnatural' there implies the originally Catholic notion of monarchs being appointed by God and a king's murder thus an offence against God – and he reminds us that, as Dylan may or may not be bearing in mind, Kennedy was the USA's first Catholic president. I'm citing Muir here because in the 'Afterword' to his

[110] Andrew Muir, *The State of Shakespeare* podcast interview, 25th October 2020, http://stateofshakespeare.com/?p=7031.

book *Bob Dylan & William Shakespeare: The True Performing of it* he covers so much, and so thoughtfully, about how revenge tragedies, balladry, gothic works and more live on timelessly in our culture, and how some of these intersect with Bob Dylan's song. It's an indispensable work and there's no point my trying to precis its vast amount of information.[111]

Enough, here, to say that the key word 'foul' – last word of Dylan's title, of every stanza and of the song itself – is one that recurs so often in *Macbeth* that it's often assumed it's within *that* play that the 'murder most foul' is denounced – but that's another murdered king, another ghost, another horror: and its initiator is cited in Dylan's line 'Play Stella By Starlight for Lady Macbeth' ('Stella By Starlight' first heard, aptly, in that pioneering 1944 film about ghosts, *The Uninvited*.)[112]

The line that forms the rhyming couplet with that is 'Play Merchant of Venice, play merchant of death', and soon enough Dylan gives us a slightly modified line from *Julius Caesar* too (another play with a ghost and the murder of a 'king'), from Act II Scene ii: 'Seeing that death, a necessary end,/Will come when it will come'. Three lines from the song's end, as if Kennedy's death has not already happened, yet at the same time a reminder that we never know when it's coming, Dylan intones '…and death will come when it comes'. (There's another call across to a different song on the album here too, death coming when it comes balanced by life of a sort, which will 'be done when it's done' in 'My Own Version Of You'; and Julius Caesar himself figures in two other songs.)

Given that Dylan's uses and mentions of Shakespeare go back a long way, it's no surprise that 'Murder Most Foul' is not the only track on *Rough And Rowdy Ways* in which that earlier bard is quoted – but before coming to the album's other songs, I want to add that alongside Dylan's clever, collaged use of quotation

---

[111] Andrew Muir, 'Afterword' in the 2nd edition of *Bob Dylan & William Shakespeare: The True Performing of it*, op.cit.

[112] *The Uninvited*, directed by the Englishman Lewis Allen, with Ray Milland, Ruth Hussey and Donald Crisp, Paramount Pictures, US, 1944; based on the novel *Uneasy Freehold* (UK, 1941) by the Irish novelist Dorothy Macardle, published in the US as *The Uninvited*, 1942.

in layering this lengthiest of his songs, what makes it so likeably absorbing is more than its intertextuality or its cleverness. It's this too: how good, in 2020, to hear Bob Dylan releasing so political a song.

As Timothy Hampton wrote on his excellent blog: 'And now comes "Murder Most Foul", the seventeen-minute song released in late March 2020, in the midst of the Corona Virus Pandemic, against the backdrop of Donald Trump's daily flood of lies and insults from the house where Lincoln, Roosevelt, and Kennedy slept.' Why Obama isn't more worthy than Kennedy there, I don't know, but this doesn't affect the point Hampton makes.[113]

When the song was first heard, a flurry of people wrote that it amounted not to a celebration of music but solely to Dylan's indictment of his generation's failures to deal with the corruption of the culture, distracted from political reality by a love of materialism and of a celebrity culture that has landed us in the age of Trump ('the age of the Antichrist').

It may not be clear, or garner agreement among listeners, as to *when* in the song Dylan switches from alleging that The Beatles' invasion of America and the quickly soured silliness of aspects of the hippie 1960s was that kind of generational failure and led to

---

[113] Timothy Hampton, http://www.timothyhampton.org/blog/posts/36043, 1st April 2020: altogether a beautiful, intelligent read. How he could have assembled his thoughts about the song or written this so quickly I can't imagine. (I agree with everything except his concluding couple of sentences.) For another enterprisingly thoughtful piece, see Anne Margaret Daniel's *Dylan Review* essay, which begins with this: 'In November 1863, as the Civil War blazed on, an eighteen-year-old Baltimorean named David Bachrach traveled in a buggy to Gettysburg, Pennsylvania to photograph President Abraham Lincoln as he delivered what would be known as the Gettysburg Address. The young man quickly made a name for himself as a prominent portraitist in the relatively new medium. Almost a century later, in 1959, David's grandson Fabian Bachrach was hired to photograph…Senator John Fitzgerald Kennedy. Fabian's portrait of Jack would become President Kennedy's official White House photograph … "Murder Most Foul" … uses the Bachrach Studios portrait as its associated image. It's a crop of the portrait, sepia-toned, what one would normally but cannot in this case call a headshot without cringing.' https://www.dylanreview.org/anne-margaret-daniel-murder-foul. For an early more general summary of the song I recommend Seth Rogovoy's 'No – You're wrong…' at https://forward.com/culture/music/443087/no-youre-wrong-bob-dylans-17-minute-song-is-a-work-of-epic-genius/. And for a brilliant, largely musicological essay on the whole album (and from an English Department academic too), see Charles O. Hartman's 'Review' at https://www.dylanreview.org/charles-hartman-rough-and-rowdy from the same issue of *Dylan Review*.

dire political consequence, but at some point Dylan *does* switch. Yes, early on in the song those key post-assassination events of the 1960s are being savaged, and efficiently. The couplet 'Hush little children, you'll understand / The Beatles are coming, they're gonna hold your hand' cleverly matches a line barely tweaked from the children's lullaby 'Hush Little Baby' with the particular Beatles' title 'I Want To Hold Your Hand', so doubling the sneer at public immaturity – and perhaps it's another layer that Dylan is also echoing there the similar bending of the lullaby line he knows from the old song 'White House Blues' by Charlie Poole & The North Carolina Ramblers ('Hush up little children now don't you fret'): a song about another assassinated president, William McKinley, and which Dylan quotes verbatim at the start of 'Key West'.[114]

There may be uncertainty as to *when* Dylan moves across from expressing this distaste for the music of the 1960s after Kennedy's death, but for much of the song he is invoking and recommending some of the valuable, potent creations of the culture in what becomes his long, powerful catalogue (eighty titles, at least).

What's certainly clear too is that Dylan is urging upon us an acceptance that Kennedy's slaughter was a political conspiracy and not, as we were for so long urged to think, the apolitical act of an unstable loner. Nothing sensational in alleging that, but nothing unclear or uncommitted about it either.

I feel a warm gratitude that it returns him to the subject matter of so many of his sharp, compelling early songs: songs like 'Only A Pawn In Their Game' and 'The Lonesome Death Of Hattie Carroll' – and the stately, serious nature of the song makes for a worthy examination of a key moment in American history that happened within Dylan's own lifetime.

I suppose, too, more loftily, the song is a lamentation for the

---

[114] Charlie Poole & The North Carolina Ramblers, 'White House Blues', cut 20th September 1926, released Columbia 142658; CD-reissued eg on JSP Records JSP7734, London 2005. Poole was a textile mill worker in the northern Piedmont area of North Carolina, born in 1892, who headed for New York in 1925 determined to make records, and, as leader of The North Carolina Ramblers, succeeded that same year with 'Don't Let Your Deal Go Down Blues'. He's long been a favourite of Dylan, who mentions him in his Nobel Lecture of 5th June 2017, online at https://www.nobelprize.org/prizes/literature/2016/dylan/lecture/.

spirit of America: it's riddled, as noted, with ghosts; it refers to the afterlife, and Judgment Day, and directly to the soul of the president, symbol of the nation's. All the same, I'm reminded of a comment by Doris Lessing, a Nobel literature laureate like Bob, when she was responding to that far more recent catastrophe for the American psyche, the attack on the Twin Towers: 'Americans felt that they had lost paradise. They never asked themselves why they thought they had a right to be there in the first place.'[115] Yet what could be more topical, after four years of Trump and his rabid divisiveness, than Dylan's complex, crepuscular meditation on the soul of the not very United States of America?

What I further savour in 'Murder Most Foul' is the nifty *detail* woven into it, detail that has the stamp of Dylan's imagination, rather than his enterprising deployment of someone else's.

I love, for example, that immediately after 'Play Moonlight Sonata in F-sharp', surprising us with that specified *key*, the next phrase is 'And a *Key* To The Highway' [my emphasis: naturally Dylan gives it none]; that no-one ever does play 'Moonlight Sonata' in F#; and that Bud Powell never did record 'Love Me Or Leave Me'.[116]

And while it was a fine and penetrating riposte in a great song when Joan Baez answered Dylan's denial of feeling nostalgic with 'give me another word for it / You who're so good with words / And at keeping things vague',[117] it may seem obvious that the Dylan of recent years so often puts two meanings into one phrase or line, using puns to *concentrate* meaning, to double it, as any poet can.

In 'Murder Most Foul' this punning for concentration's sake is part of its detail. There's the adroit pun of 'perfectly executed', and the quieter one on 'gonna flag a ride' (the Kennedy limo was flying the US and presidential flags), which follows the song's earlier 'Pick up the pieces and lower the flags'. And perhaps the

[115] Doris Lessing quoted in *A Reading Diary*, Alberto Manguel (updated edition Edinburgh & London: Canongate, 2006).
[116] The complete, detailed discography of Bud Powell is online here: https://www.jazzdisco.org/bud-powell/discography/.
[117] Joan Baez, 'Diamonds And Rust', recorded January 1975, LA; A&M SP 3233, LA, 1975. By far the best song she's ever written: a great, remarkable love song.

first part of *that* sentence is a pun of double meaning too, the one being the normal non-literal meaning of the phrase and the other Jackie Kennedy's literal retrieval, as noted, of part of JFK's brain.

Less detectable puns – so less successful – are Dylan's sly naming of two men who'd been accused of having had a hand in the assassination. The song's lines 'Slide down the banister, go get your coat / Ferry 'cross the Mersey and go for the throat' may seem nicely poetic phrases (and the second connects to 'The Beatles are coming, they're gonna hold your hand'); but the couplet really exists only to name William Guy Banister and David William Ferrie, the one a dirty-tricks FBI man and fanatical anti-communist, the other a pilot alleged to have been an acquaintance of Lee Harvey Oswald and in Dallas to drive the assassins' getaway car.[118] Dylan's allusions to these men don't help to concentrate meaning unless the listener already knows this background rumour, and even then they hardly yield any *other* meaning because at the surface level they really make no sense.

To British ears, though, there's a likeable but unintended aural pun there, because Americans always pronounce the Mersey as 'mercy'. (It should sound as if the *s* is a *z*.)

Far more successful is 'Play it for the reverend, play it for the pastor / Play it for the dog that's got no master'. On one level the couplet ends with that lovely touch of compassion, an immediate reminder of 'Chimes Of Freedom' with its piling up of lines like 'tolling for the luckless, the abandoned and forsaked' – yet it can also be heard rather differently, with 'dog' used, for the second time in the song, as a pejorative, as someone godless, in theoretical contrast to reverend and pastor, 'the dog that's got no master'.

The song's other virtues include its occasional contrasting plain meaning, as with the brilliant straight-to-the-heart-of-the-matter of 'Thousands were watching, no-one saw a thing'. Another is the Dylanesque aptness of some of his pairings in

---

[118] These allegations were made by New Orleans District Attorney Jim Garrison, who investigated the Kennedy assassination (separately from the Warren Commission). Although this information is of course available on Wikipedia, it may well be that Dylan has derived it and more from the book that was also called *Murder Most Foul* (but with an additional exclamation mark), subtitled *The Conspiracy That Murdered President Kennedy*, Stanley J. Marks, 1st edition hardback published by the Bureau of International Affairs, US, 1967.

the litany of 'Play...' lines – among them 'Play... that Old Devil Moon' straight after '...the Rising Sun', and 'Play Down In The Boondocks for Terry Malloy', the song there a hit single by Billy Joe Royal with the chorus line 'Lord have mercy on a boy from down in the boondocks' (released, as it happens, on Bob Dylan's birthday in 1965) and Terry Malloy being the dockworker in need of mercy, trapped between loyalty and the need to testify truth in *On the Waterfront*, 1954, a part played so burningly by the young Marlon Brando.[119] There's also the way the inspired flash of the line 'Play St. James Infirmary in the court of King James', paired with 'write down the names', is immediately followed by 'Play Etta James...'

And then there are the rhymes themselves, including 'let the good times roll' paired with 'the grassy knoll'; 'Wolfman Jack, he's speaking in tongues / ... at the top of his lungs'; and the rhymings of the title word 'Foul' with 'throw in the towel' and 'wise old owl' – and that's not the last we hear of avians: there's the splendid rhyming of 'All That Jazz' with 'the Birdman of Alcatraz' – and that couplet is deftly placed immediately after the line citing jazzman Charlie Parker, whose nickname was 'Bird'.

There's one final kick of surprise we're given right at the end of the song. His work has quite often been unintentionally postmodern (the shiftings of who 'I' and 'you', 'she' and 'he' are in songs like 'Tangled Up In Blue'; the jumpcuts and the random switches of narrative sequence – unintentional touches of postmodernity so often present in traditional folksong and the pre-war blues); but *this* song – and hence the whole double-album – finishes with an unexpected, deliberate flash of self-reflexive text, that trademark postmodern device, as Dylan's last words are '...play Murder Most Foul'.

The song is a brave and bravura achievement, its structure so formally simple – remorseless rhyming couplets throughout – dependably holding resourceful levels of complex meaning, appropriate to tackling so huge a subject as the still murkily

---

[119] 'Down In The Boondocks' written by Joe South, a hit for Billy Joe Royal on Columbia 43305, NY, 1965; *On the Waterfront*, directed Elia Kazan, Columbia Pictures, US, 1954.

managed slaying of a president and its inter-action with the psyche and soul of the nation. Within this epic Dylan song we have to feel, and we do, the stained weight of American history.

The subject-matter is matched by the overall sound: the music begins with that grave, umami note from the bowed stand-up bass – the pianos and other touches stay quiet and ruminative, sometimes firm, sometimes close to faltering – and always the dark, presiding Dylan voice is so fully at the front. For all the tricks, flourishes and disruptive flashes in the tale as he has so audaciously told it, it makes for a sombre listening experience.

But music, song, is infinitely flexible, and resilient not least through grim days. 'Murder Most Foul' is saying so, while the rest of the album proves it.

Dylan's title calms things down from a *Tempest* to mere *Rough And Rowdy Ways* (a phrase of neatly identical shape and rhythm to 'Long And Wasted Years': perhaps it's an ear-worm rhythm of his) – and in general it's an altogether warmer, more gregarious and welcoming album.

Over thirty years after the release of *Oh Mercy*, I find that what I wrote by way of introducing some scrutiny of it a decade later in *Song & Dance Man III: The Art of Bob Dylan* seems as apt for *Rough And Rowdy Ways*.

I wrote then that *Oh Mercy* is a 'many-layered work, full of openness, new writing, dignity and resonance, offering unexpected pleasures. Such is its cohesion that whatever theme within it, or aspect of it, you discuss, you find yourself drawing on key words, phrases or lines that match each other directly yet come from inside many different songs. Quoting from one, you reach readily for matching, supportive quotations from at least a couple of others too.'

(You might think the same could be said of any Dylan album, though the one 21st-century album that most properly and rewardingly fits the same description prior to *Rough And Rowdy Ways* is the now twenty-year-old *"Love And Theft"*.)

We know now, from everything we've read, or simply from hearing, say, the official Bootleg Series collection *Tell Tale*

Signs, that 'key words, phrases or lines' certainly *can* 'come from inside many different songs'. It's one of the consequences of his scissors-and-paste approach to writing by other people and by him.

Scott Warmuth has been invaluable and assiduous in bringing what some of us may feel is the bad news that Dylan has chopped up bits of dozens of other writers and re-used them, verbatim or almost so, for many years (including, most skilfully, in *Chronicles Volume One*); and the huge amount Dylan has reprocessed from that marvellously rich resource, pre-war blues lyric poetry, was the subject of a 112-page chapter in *Song & Dance Man III* itself.[120]

However eccentric some of the choices in Dylan's cut-up technique, the reach of *Rough And Rowdy Ways* seems to me to give an almost subliminal, pleasurable sense of greater connectedness to past and present worlds. One or two songs even offer a degree of narrative coherence in a conventional way, and without the tiresome occlusions of a *Tempest* song like 'Tin Angel'.

'I Contain Multitudes', as a statement, is pretty straightforward, if more complex as a song, and there's a clear narrative, in its way, in 'My Own Version Of You'. The first is founded upon a famous line from Walt Whitman's 'Song Of Myself': 'Do I contradict myself? / Very well then I contradict myself / (I am large, I contain multitudes)', but whereas Whitman put his phrase in brackets, as an aside, Dylan has it right up front, as title and repeated verse-end line.

Having stated it so plainly, it gives him licence to be as random as he likes with everything else in the song, delighting in throwing in some enterprising rhymes for the last syllable of 'multitudes'. Given American pronunciation – 'oods' – every one is a perfect rhyme except the first, 'feuds', which needs the same chewed 'ee-oods' that in English mouths also works as the perfect rhyme for all except 'foods' and 'moods', including the initiating 'multitudes'. ('Dudes', the singular of which Dylan used

[120] Scott Warmuth scrutinises Dylan's intertextuality very closely indeed on his blog http://swarmuth.blogspot.com/. Michael Gray, *Song & Dance Man III: The Art of Bob Dylan*, op.cit.

so sweetly as an internal rhyme within 'Winterlude' fifty years earlier, is such an American word that English pronunciation would be silly.)

From the freedom to list some multitudes contained stems one of the album's large weaknesses – a sometimes unsatisfying fragmentedness – that is at the same time the major part of its fundamental strength, charm and charismatic appeal, as lines and phrases and fragments from within one song call across to their twins or siblings in other songs, and we can hear them calling and spot their resemblances.

In that opening song, for example, 'I'll lose my mind if you don't come with me' calls across to 'Take me out traveling, you're a traveling man' and to 'I'm going far away from home with her' in the very beautiful fourth song, 'I've Made Up My Mind To Give Myself To You', and to 'Mona baby… / Couldn't be anybody else but you who's come with me this far' in 'Crossing The Rubicon'. (It was Mona who tried to warn him off travel in 'Stuck Inside Of Mobile With The Memphis Blues Again'; she's also the subject of a Bo Diddley track, like another figure cited on *Rough And Rowdy Ways*, Jerome, encountered further on.)

All through each song, too – this is not the sole preserve of 'Murder Most Foul' – there are submerged song titles (printed lowercase in the official though so often inaccurate bobdylan. com lyrics), all of which might well be tracks you'd hear on *Theme Time Radio Hour*. In the case of 'I Contain Multitudes' we have 'Red Cadillac And A Black Moustache' (a self-reference in that Dylan recorded this Warren Smith-linked song himself, and performed it live in 1986); 'All The Young Dudes', a Mott The Hoople hit from 1972; 'Pink Pedal Pushers', a Carl Perkins single from 1958; and 'Red Blue Jeans And A Pony Tail', which is on a 1957 EP from another major 1950s rockabilly-cum-rock'n'roll outfit, Gene Vincent & His Blue Caps. Meanwhile, alongside these vintage singles, plus the literature of Blake and Poe, we also have Dylan's allusion to one of the classics of European cinema, *Les Enfants du Paradis*, in his lovely line 'I live on a boulevard of crime'. (Le Boulevard du Crime is the setting for much of that film, and was the home of vaudeville and variety theatre in 1820s

Paris. It's a place we can imagine Poe might have relished soon afterwards.) Dylan aptly pairs his line with 'Everything's flowin', all at the same time'. Yes indeed.[121]

The song has a couple of less clear-cut, more appealingly odd allusions too. One is the line 'I go right where all things lost are made good again'. This was an immediate reminder, to me at least, of all the mystery of nursery rhyme and fairytale Dylan explored so creatively on the underrated album *Under The Red Sky*. In that context he's suggesting he goes to the moon, for (as noted in *Song & Dance Man III*) the legend has it that everything is saved and treasured on the moon that was wasted and squandered on earth: misspent time, broken vows, unanswered prayers, fruitless tears and unfulfilled desires. We've heard Dylan refer to broken vows decades ago on 'Everything Is Broken', but misspent time is something that very much concerns the persona on this new album. In 'False Prophet' we have 'I'm the enemy of the unlived, meaningless life'; in 'Key West' 'I've never lived in the land of Oz / Or wasted my time with an unworthy cause'; and in 'Crossing The Rubicon' he asks 'How can I redeem the time, the time so idly spent?' – though here his source is Shakespeare (once again), in this case 'Sonnet No. 100', in which the voice implores 'Return, forgetful Muse, and straight redeem / In gentle numbers time so idly spent'.

(Dylan's sweet rhyme for 'idly spent', 'badly bent', may have been taken from a Little Walter B-side with a title giddily appropriate all across *Rough And Rowdy Ways*: 'Dead Presidents', where the line is 'I ain't broke but I'm badly bent'.)[122]

---

[121] Though Warren Smith is the rockabilly artist generally associated with 'Red Cadillac And A Black Moustache' it was first cut by Bob Luman in 1957, Imperial X8311, US, 1957. 'Pink Pedal Pushers', Carl Perkins, Columbia 4-41131, US, 1958; 'Red Blue Jeans And A Pony Tail', Gene Vincent & His Blue Caps, Capitol 1-811, US, 1957. *Les Enfants du Paradis*, dir. Marcel Carné, France, 1945. For an essay arguing the centrality of this film to a huge sweep of Dylan's songs, see the 2020 essay by Howard Davies available at https://www.facebook.com/notes/subterranean-homesick-bob/bob-dylan-on-the-boulevard-of-crime/3189814711075517/.

[122] *Song & Dance Man III: The Art of Bob Dylan*, op.cit., p.686. William Shakespeare, 'Sonnet No. 100', one of 154 sonnets first published together (London: Thomas Thorpe, 1609). Little Walter, 'Dead Presidents', cut Chicago, 5th February 1963, Checker Records 1081, Chicago, 1964. (nb. It was recorded before Kennedy's assassination, and is referring to denominations of the dollar with dead presidents on them, and the singer's general lack of them.)

The other appealing oddity on 'I Contain Multitudes' comes hand in hand with 'Mr. Poe', in the graphic line 'Got skeletons in the walls of people you know', which may refer back to Poe's story 'The Tell-Tale Heart' itself, or allude to another Poe story ('The Cask Of Amontillado') or more generally to the interest Poe had in the subject. Certainly the most striking linkage of these skeletons is to 'The Tell-Tale Heart' itself; in that story the unidentified narrator murders a man, buries him under the floor and then becomes haunted by a repeated inexplicable thumping noise, which he decides is the tormenting, reproachful heartbeat of his victim. Considered in that way, 'Got a tell-tale heart' followed at once by 'Got skeletons in the walls…' amounts to a confession, so that his multitudes may include being a murderer who must always suffer the consequential guilt.[123]

What interests me more is the same line's unintended meaning. We can surely assume he means 'I've put the skeletons of people you know into the walls'; but what the line actually says is 'I've put some skeletons into the walls of people you know', implicitly 'unbeknownst to them'. It gives a more beguiling picture as you hear it that way.

One last fragment of a story comes late on in 'I Contain Multitudes', when the 'I' identifies with the sad, unofficial bodyguard of Lincoln (that first assassinated president), Ward Hill Lamon. Ever concerned that Lincoln never protected himself adequately from the danger posed by diehard pro-slavery Southerners, Lamon is normally reported as carrying pistols and a Bowie knife, but as Shelby Foote's magnum opus *The Civil War: A Narrative* has it, describing an incident in Baltimore as Lincoln was about to travel to Washington D.C. to assume office, Lamon was on the spot clutching, yes, 'four pistols and two large knives'.[124]

Knives, and swords too, are flourished all through the album. 'Show me your ribs, I'll stick in the knife' in 'My Own Version Of You'; 'I climbed a mountain of swords on my bare feet' in

[123] Edgar Allan Poe, 'The Tell-Tale Heart', 1843. Edgar Allan Poe, 'The Cask Of Amontillado', 1846; nb. Poe had also read the earlier story 'A Man Built In A Wall', by Joel T. Headley, 1844 see https://www.eapoe.org/works/mabbott/tom3t030.htm.
[124] Shelby Foote, *The Civil War: A Narrative*, 1958 (a 3-volume history of the American Civil War undoubtedly known by Dylan).

'False Prophet'; 'I'll take a sword and hack off your arm' in 'Black Rider'; and 'I'll cut you up with a crooked knife' in 'Crossing The Rubicon'.

You could feel 'hmm: we used to get more than fragments'. Dylan's songs once gave us clear yet creative narratives, from early work like (say) 'The Lonesome Death Of Hattie Carroll', 'Seven Curses' (with its shrewd observational insight, as when the lustful judge's 'old eyes deepened in his head': Dylan illuminating instead of 'keeping things vague'), running all the way through till about *Saved*; that then, generally, we had short scenarios instead – in songs like, and around the time of, 'Caribbean Wind' – and that now it mostly feels as if what we get is fragments from the ruminative thrashing of his mind. But there have always been diversions from that pattern, and if, now, Dylan has lost interest in telling straightforward tales, it doesn't mean none are there. It means that now he obliges the listener to make the connections to discern the narratives.

Fragments of stories yield glimpses into worlds, into pictures, into moods and states of mind. We could say the same of 'A Hard Rain's A-Gonna Fall'. In *Rough And Rowdy Ways*, too, stories may be fragmentary but he refers to them in several places: 'go tell the real story', in 'Goodbye Jimmy Reed'; 'Man, I could tell their stories all day', in 'Mother Of Muses'; and 'That's my story, but not where it ends', in 'Key West'.

In 'My Own Version Of You', remarkably, Dylan gives us his own statement about this. It's a witty confession of what has been his main working method ever since *"Love And Theft"* and *Chronicles Volume One*. He's gathering bits and pieces to make a new whole.

Ironically this makes 'My Own Version Of You' a highly distinctive song in itself, full of recognisable Dylanesque touches, and reminders of earlier songs, yet without self-imitation. Structurally, it's an oddity, with varying verse lengths, always combined from rhyming couplets yet with each verse postscripted with one separate such couplet. At least, that's the way it's laid out on the bobdylan.com website, where it comprises two 4-line verses, three 8-line verses, two more 4-line verses and then a 20-

line verse before the full-stop of the last separate couplet. As you listen, no oddity of structure obtrudes: you hear it as a more or less unending stream of inventive phantasmagoria.

He comes in with the vivid surprise of that brief yet oddly explanatory 'All through the summers into January / I've been visiting morgues and monasteries' – and how very Bob Dylan it is to refuse the more obvious rhyme of 'mortuaries' for 'January', and instead to give us 'monasteries'. It's the second most resourceful rhyme for January in his canon, the unbeatable one, of course, being his rhyming it with 'Buenos Aires' on 'The Groom's Still Waiting At The Altar' almost forty years earlier. It also prompts a recognition that a perfect rhyme for 'Buenos Aires' *would* be 'monasteries', leaving January as intermediary between these two Dylan songs.

There's also a spirit to the track's playfulness that reminds me of the very different 'Subterranean Homesick Blues', or 'I Wanna Be Your Lover'. It's in his taking 'the Scarface Pacino and the Godfather Brando / Mix 'em up in a tank and get a robot commando' – with that neat pun on 'tank' for his commando: the war vehicle as well as the dastardly container for medico-chemical experiment. (And whether Dylan knows it or not, Robot Commando is also a toy from 1961 and a 1986 gamebook.)[125]

Some of the song's listed ingredients are specific and apply to all of us: 'Limbs and livers and brains and hearts'. That's a refreshing plainspeaking about what the 'I' in the song wants from 'morgues and monasteries', and an immediate four-line placement of the song squarely in the literary gothic tradition – suggesting too, therefore, that we may be entering into, as well as paralleling, Mary Shelley's *Frankenstein* before the song is through.

And we do. The song takes that pioneering work as its model, the narrator building his own monster in the hope of doing 'things for the benefit of all mankind'. The full title of the novel is *Frankenstein; or, The Modern Prometheus*. Shelley and Dylan are re-telling the Ancient Greek myth of Prometheus, a Titan who

[125] Robot Commando from Ideal Toys, USA, 1959/61. There's a great TV ad for it still viewable at https://youtu.be/DJFzi6Gx7SA. Robot Commando (Adventure Gamebooks #22), UK: Puffin Books, 1986.

made humanity from clay and then stole fire from heaven to give us civilisation. In revenge, Zeus had Prometheus chained to a rock where an eagle came each day to feast on his liver, which grew back each night, until he was rescued by Zeus's son Heracles.[126] This lends an extra morsel of frisson to those 'livers' in Dylan's opening verse.

The 'I' in the song fluctuates between being the Dr. Frankenstein figure and the creature. It's the latter who says 'I study Sanskrit and Arabic to improve my mind' – and here Dylan has plunged straight inside Mary Shelley's book as well as into the monster's mind. In Chapter Six, she writes that 'The Persian, Arabic, and Sanskrit languages engaged his attention'. Frankenstein wants to finesse the quality of his creation's sensibility, and these studies are a kind of improving homework. A voice in 'Key West' offers a similar claim to learnedness with 'I know all the Hindu rituals'.

I thought at once of that 'Limbs and livers and brains and hearts' when I read this, from Ellen Moers's article 'Female Gothic':

> In Gothic writings fantasy predominates over reality, the strange over the commonplace, and the supernatural over the natural ... to get to the body itself, its glands, muscles, epidermis, and circulatory systems, quickly arousing and quickly allaying the physiological reactions to fear.[127]

And how thoroughly surprising it was – disconcerting to some – that Dylan should produce, in 'My Own Version Of You', such an, er, full-bodied plunge into this oeuvre. It's his objective correlative (to use a phrase T. S. Eliot made popular), the specific

[126] Mary Shelley, *Frankenstein; or, The Modern Prometheus*, 1818. My brief summary of the myth I take from *The Hutchinson Encyclopedia* 10th edn 1995, Oxford: Helicon Publishing, 1994. As Wikipedia will tell you in some detail, it had been Goethe who first resurrected Prometheus for the Romantic Movement. After *Frankenstein* came Mary's husband Percy Bysshe Shelley's huge *Prometheus Unbound* and the myth has been used ever since in every kind of artwork, including poetry from Kafka to Ted Hughes, and with particular debt to Mary Shelley in the case of films.
[127] Ellen Moers, 'Female Gothic', in *The Endurance of Frankenstein: Essays on Mary Shelley's Novel*, eds. G. Levine & U.C. Knoepflmacher, Berkeley: UC Press, 1974. For my own access to this I'm grateful to Dr. Nick Kennedy's MA thesis 'The African-American Female Gothic', University College, Cork, 1999, which he was kind enough to let me read. It was Dr. Kennedy too who drew my attention to the novel *Cactus Blood* by Lucha Corpi (a fine surname, in the gothic circumstances), (Houston TX: Arte Publico Press, 1995), mentioned later in my text.

imagery on which he can hang so resourcefully his thesis about making things new by assembling and re-ordering the old. It's yet another way to insist on the omnipresence of the past within the present. Some of the times it comes around, 'My own version of you' means a version of the past: of history and of humanity.

As with 'I Contain Multitudes', there's a more weary obviousness to some of Dylan's literary components. Given that on previous 21st-century albums, he used without acknowledgment a poet as obscure as Henry Timrod (on *Modern Times*: and on the same album, extensive borrowings from Peter Green's translation of Ovid's *Black Sea Letters*) and that he used, again without a namecheck, a poem as relatively obscure as John Greenleaf Whittier's 1851 'The Chapel Of The Hermit' (in 'Scarlet Town' on *Tempest*), it seems unnecessarily belaboured that he should add to 'Gotta tell-tale heart' the didactic 'like Mr. Poe' or to add 'like William Blake' to 'I sing the songs of experience', and just as clunky to throw into the tank of 'My Own Version Of You' so well-worn a Shakespeare line as he tweaks to 'Well this must be the winter of my discontent' – especially when he stresses that *my* so audibly, as if that makes it somehow a shrewd usage.[128]

Yet other allusions rest on more enterprising sources. Who knows where he learnt that getting blood from a cactus is a slice of folklore deriving from the fact that a red dye, carmine, is extracted from cochineal, a cactus-dwelling insect? Perhaps he didn't: perhaps he just plucked the idea from knowing of the 1995 gothic crime novel *Cactus Blood* by Lucha Corpi. His 'gunpowder from ice' has a sort of science behind it too, inasmuch as refrigerator ice-packs tend to contain ammonium nitrate, which can in other circumstances certainly be explosive, as the port city of

[128] William Blake, *Songs of Innocence and of Experience*, first printed by Blake himself to combine poems and paintings, 1789. The use of Henry Timrod's verse by Dylan has been widely documented ever since the release of *Modern Times* in 2006; but for the significant use of the *Tempest* song 'Scarlet Town' I'm grateful to the work of Nina Goss, whose talk at the University of Southern Denmark's Dylan Conference in 2018 I heard and have been able to refer back to in its printed form in *New Approaches to Bob Dylan*, edited Anne-Marie Mai, op. cit. Ovid, *The Poems of Exile: Tristia and the Black Sea Letters*, translated Peter Green (LA: University of California Press, 2005). (Andrew Muir remarked in his *State of Shakespeare* podcast interview, op. cit., that Dylan 'quotes Ovid almost as much as Shakespeare [does]. Nobody quotes Ovid as much as Shakespeare.') The Shakespeare line 'Now is the winter of our discontent' opens his play *Richard III*.

Beirut found to horrendous cost in lives and destroyed buildings in August 2020. But Bob Dylan's 'I'll get ... gunpowder from ice' comes from a quirky snippet in Jonathan Swift's *A Voyage to Laputa*, 1726 – not the most readily recollected volume of *Gulliver's Travels* – in which the Balnibarbian capital, Lagado, has a technical school whose projects include extracting sunbeams from cucumbers and, yes, converting ice into gunpowder.

Inevitably the song has weak, perhaps just lazy, lines: 'They talk all night and they talk all day / Not for a minute do I believe anything they say', for example. Who is this 'they', unmentioned till now, and never mentioned again? There's no morsel of interest in that couplet. And 'You know what I mean – you know exactly what I mean': that's mere filler, and we don't.

Yet there are strong lines too, the four together that seem most fully realised, pulling you into a vivid scene of dialogue and action, being 'After midnight if you still want to meet / I'll be at the Black Horse Tavern on Armageddon Street / Two doors down, not that far to walk / I'll hear your footsteps, you won't have to knock'. A further phrase of attractive economy, and comic panache, is 'If I do it up right and put the head on straight / I'll be saved by the creature that I create'. He seemed in more autobiographical voice when he sang 'Most of the time / My head is on straight' (back on *Oh Mercy*), but to sing here, as the Frankensteinian figure, 'If I ... put the head on straight' gives it a nicely bizarre, um, twist.

There's another extraordinary, inspired fragment in the song that surely comes via the creature's voice. I didn't include 'Can you tell me what it means, to be or not to be?' as an overly obvious Shakespearean reference – because it's so brilliant a question for this hapless creature to ask. To be alive or not to be alive is a core question for a man-made creature: what does it mean – am I a living being or not? Dylan has done that very difficult thing: he has created a new life from the bones of English literature's most famous question.

The song is a hugely variegated whole, returning, for instance, to mid-1960s absurdist Dylanesquerie with 'I'm gonna make you play the piano like Leon Russell / Like Liberace, like St. John the Apostle', and with that comparable pairing of St. Peter with Jerome – not St. Jerome, that is, but Bo Diddley's Jerome (though perhaps both) – while at other moments prompting a picture of Dylan/narrator as a very old man, querulous and testy while the music augments his thumping the ground with his walking stick, as he says 'I will bring someone to life, in more ways than one / It don't matter how long it takes – it'll be done when it's done!' And then the agitation disappears as the narrative voice returns to articulating the Frankensteinian mission, the promethean task of making his own version of us – of humanity, that is – and remembers to 'Do it with decency and common sense' and to 'Do it with laughter, do it with tears'.[129]

As he says all through the song, and as we recognise to be his 21st-century way of songwriting, he takes bits and pieces from here and there and re-uses them. But that only works if the re-using is creative, and we're not left suspecting that every attractive phrase and appealing fragment we pick up on might have been lifted verbatim from someone else's work. I found I had to use Google to check, for example, whether he'd written 'The killing frost is on the ground' (at the end of 'Crossing The Rubicon') and 'The healing virtues of the wind' (in 'Key West') himself. Given the history of Dylan's song assemblage over the last couple of decades, we're left having to hope that the best and most memorable fragments are his and not lifted from elsewhere. The British critic Roy Kelly is good and severe about all that heavy lifting, though his review of the album in *The Bridge* seems barely to concern itself with other aspects of the album.[130]

All the same, while there are magpie snippets along with his own, in place of coherent narratives, on this album we do have

[129] Bo Diddley, 'Bring It To Jerome', B-side of 'Pretty Thing', both cut 14th July 1955, Checker Records, Chicago, 1955. St. Jerome (4th-5th century AD) updated the first Latin translation of the Bible, his version becoming known as the Vulgate; it was recognised as the official Latin bible of the Catholic Church a mere 1100 years after his death. Harvard classicist Richard Thomas notes that Raphael Falco, Professor of English at the University of Maryland, suggests St. Jerome may have regarded his translation, addressing God, as 'my own version of You'. (Richard F. Thomas: '"And I Crossed The Rubicon": Another Classical Dylan', *Dylan Review* Vol.2.1, 2020.) (And Bo Diddley, 'Mona (I Need My Baby)', cut March 1957, Checker Records 860, Chicago, 1957.)
[130] Roy Kelly, 'The Songs That Know Themselves', *The Bridge*, No. 67. Summer 2020, Newcastle upon Tyne, UK.

main themes, or worlds, even if explored with less rigour than we might like. One of the characteristics of Dylan's canon is that while other singer-songwriters have tended to explore only their deeply sensitive feelings about their own lives, Dylan has always seemed to speak for all of us, to be contemplating a wider world of history and culture instead of just himself.

It doesn't always work out maturely, especially at those times when he indulges his personal grudges against particular historical figures. We've had his shallow dismissal of Karl Marx before, in 'When You Gonna Wake Up?' ('Karl Marx has got you by the throat, Henry Kissinger's got you tied up in knots'), and now here is that same great thinker of the last two hundred years, back in the feeble evangelical firing line, with 'My Own Version Of You' offering 'Step right in to the burning hell / Where some of the best-known enemies of mankind dwell / Mr. Freud with his dreams, Mr. Marx with his axe...' – and as if this vibration from the rhetoric of hellfire throws him back to that Born Again period, two lines later comes 'Got the right spirit – you can feel it, you can hear it', that last part delivered quickly and sounding immediately familiar. And that's because we *have* already heard it: verbatim, in that foaming 1980 song 'Solid Rock'. An odd diversion, now, from bringing the past to life 'with decency and common sense'.

The past is always with us, and one of the pasts always with Bob these days is the 'classical' world: the gods and poets, soldiers and muses of Ancient Greece and Rome. He's added these layers, these voices, to those of the Bible and Shakespeare and the pre-war blues.

It's his apparent love of this classical world that seems to lead him into lines that bulge with recurrent ugly avowals of physical violence. It began in earnest on *Tempest* and keeps getting unleashed on *Rough And Rowdy Ways*. These boastful, swaggering, violent threats that pop up so often, inexplicably and repugnantly, appear to *intrude* from these ancient worlds that fascinate him, often to deleterious effect, rather than intertextually illuminating the songs. All these threats to hack off people's arms, make their wives widows, cut them up with crooked knives, fight with a butcher's hook – this catalogue of malevolence so often comes at us rasped out irrationally in Dylan's 21st-century songs.

The sore-throated ill temper of 'False Prophet' exemplifies what's deeply unappealing here. The myths and histories of Ancient Greece and Rome are crammed with this cruelty, with gruesome slaughter, avowals of revenge, bloodletting and the turbid horrors of wars. But Dylan lifts them out of context and throws them at our ears, where they arrive sounding fitful and grotesque. Harvard classicist Richard Thomas (author of *Why Dylan Matters*) suggests in his *Dylan Review* assessment of the album, that the belligerent narrative voice in 'False Prophet' is largely channelling Augustus, vowing revenge after Julius Caesar's murder. That really doesn't improve the song.[131]

It's regrettable that the sluggishly volatile 'False Prophet' is so charged with this grating animus, because it begins (again in rhyming couplets – has there ever been an album so coupleted?) with a four-line verse of vivid poetic appeal that could have been delivered as reflectively as its words deserve:

> Another day that don't end – another ship going out
> Another day of anger, bitterness and doubt;
> I know how it happened: I saw it begin
> I opened my heart to the world and the world came in.

The song is all bumpily downhill from then on, lacking coherent conviction, its energy injected only from the music he's taken from a Sun Records B-side recorded when Dylan was 12 years old.[132]

Think how incomparably T.S. Eliot re-inhabits the ancient within, as part of, the modernity of 'The Waste Land'. Dylan exposes how shallow-rooted his album's recruitment of it is when

[131] Richard Thomas, *Why Dylan Matters* (New York: Dey Street Books, 2017); and '"And I Crossed The Rubicon": Another Classical Dylan', op.cit.

[132] Billy 'The Kid' Emerson, 'If Lovin' Is Believing', cut January 1954, released Sun B-195, Memphis TN, February 1954 as the B-side of 'No Teasing Around'. Dylan's track 'sits in the same tempo, and key, as Emerson's song [and] faithfully replicates the rhythm guitar phrase and leans on the same lead guitar line for punctuation'. (Tom Moon, 'Trickster Treat: Bob Dylan's New Song Sounds Awfully Old ... And Familiar', NPR, 12th May 2020, quoted from Fred Bals, 'Credit Where Due: Bob Dylan, Billy Emerson and "False Prophet"', 2020, at https://fredbals.medium.com/credit-where-due-bob-dylan-billy-emerson-and-false-prophet-89c708aa4e1.

we hear it lead him to the specific foolishness of these 'Mother Of Muses' lines:

> Sing of Sherman, Montgomery and Scott
> And of Zhukov and Patton and the battles they fought
> Who cleared the path for Presley to sing
> Who carved the path for Martin Luther King.

Richard Thomas explains that the Mother of Muses, Mnemosyne (or Memory) has the traditional duty, summarised by Dylan in the song's earlier verse, to

> Sing of honor and faith and glory be...
> Sing of the Heroes who stood alone

and that 'The Homeric *Iliad* and *Odyssey*, and Virgil's *Aeneid* ... provide examples of the invocation of the Muses as a prelude to memorializing the fighters of old.'[133] Thomas offers that useful explanation of why Dylan's song has those lines about Sherman et al – using military leaders of the American Civil War and World War II instead of those in battle two thousand and more years earlier – but that provenance doesn't improve Dylan's lines. I had already assumed there was that logic to the song's argument: that his list of these 'heroes' starts with Major General William T. Sherman because his famous burning of Atlanta and subsequent March to the Sea by his Unionist forces helped to end the Civil War and slavery, leading eventually to its being possible for even the southern white working class to hear and respond pleasurably to black music, as Elvis so creatively did – and that since the others (Britain's Field-Marshal Bernard Law Montgomery, USAF Brigadier General and flying ace Robert Lee Scott Jr., Soviet General Georgy Konstantinovich Zhukov, and US Army General George Smith Patton Jr.) were the military leaders who helped defeat Hitler, this defeat of fascism made possible the comparative political freedom that Martin Luther King Jr. and the Civil Rights movement encouraged in the USA. And Dylan is certainly economical and resourceful in squeezing all that argument into four lines. But, Homeric and Virgilian or not, it is

[133] Richard Thomas, 'Review', op.cit.

a *very* old-fashioned, gung-ho view of history: the sort my father learnt at school in the days of the British Empire. Man, I could tell their Boys Own Adventure Stories all day.

(And actually, having said he could tell those stories all day, Dylan doesn't tell us any.)

Not all the album's political thrust is so silly. As with 'Murder Most Foul' it's full of dark, veiled but clear commentary on the contemporary dreadfulness of American political life. You can't hear all these allusions to the age of the Antichrist, violence and political assassination without Trump, his encouragement of fascists and the dangerous disruption of democracy lurking in your consciousness behind what's being said. The album's broader sweep is in itself a creative lesson in history and culture, and gives its many, many listeners a stimulus to look things up — we all have to do that with 21st-century Dylan work. Each of us can say he points to further reading 'to improve my mind'.

Nor, of course, is his fascination with the history and literature of the ancient world as harmful to his poetry elsewhere on the album as with those particular 'Mother Of Muses' lines and those lip-smacking threats of personal violence in the songs. And when Dylan concludes his 2017 Nobel Lecture with 'I return once again to Homer, who says "Sing in me, oh Muse, and through me tell the story"', he is following this up with his song of appeal to the mother of all muses in the album's seventh track — and he knows there is more to Mnemosyne, mother of nine muses, goddess of remembrance and memory, than to encourage singing about military successes. Invoked in the *Iliad* and the *Odyssey*, speakers also call upon her to help them get the words right when launching into performances of lengthy oral-tradition poetry. It can't but cross your mind, though, that when he was young and less concerned for his literary reputation, Dylan was confident he could handle it by himself: 'I'll know my song well before I start singing'. In concert in Ireland and the UK in 1966 it was astonishing to hear that, stoned as he was, he gave faultless word-perfect recitations of all those long songs — 'It's All Over Now, Baby Blue', 'Visions Of Johanna' and the rest. In later concert years, yes, he has often fluffed words, mixed up lines and, regrettably, omitted verses deliberately. In previous incarnations too, he has appealed elsewhere for inspiration – to lovers or to God. Does he need Mnemosyne now, or is this just ponderously fanciful? Some of us may feel that Dylan was more Homeric before he cared to be.

Glenn Gould said something in a 1968 television special, now on YouTube, that I called to mind when I was thinking about this greater artistic self-consciousness of Dylan's. Gould said this: 'Within every creative person there is an inventor at odds with the museum curator: and most of the extraordinary and moving things that happen in art are the result of a momentary gain by one at the expense of the other.' It seems to me that the corollary is that sometimes, for Dylan at least, some of the least creative things happen when the museum curator gains too much at the expense of the inventor.[134]

Yet he makes us forgive the pomposity with this incomparable flash of audacity, of unexpectedness, of wacky logic, later in the same song:

> I'm falling in love with Calliope
> She don't belong to anyone – why not give her to me?

It's as if he's asking in jest for her mother's permission to marry her. Calliope, though, is (only) the muse of epic poetry: perhaps she inspired 'Murder Most Foul', the closest thing to epic verse we've had so far.[135] Yet Calliope is not the muse of music (that's Euterpe), of *lyric* poetry (Erato), tragedy, history, dance, astronomy, comedy nor hymns, and in the next stanza, the song turns its attention

---

[134] Glenn Gould, 'How Mozart Became A Bad Composer', aired by Public Broadcasting Laboratory, USA, April 1968; now online at https://youtu.be/JauII1jCG6Q. It's long, but riveting.

[135] A much earlier connection between Calliope and Dylan was made by Allen Ginsberg, watching the Rolling Thunder Revue from the sidelines; he wrote: 'Dylan ... seems to me to be epitomizing all the Americana poetics from Poe thru Vachel Lindsay thru the poetry-jazz experimenters of a decade ago – He's able to stand up & chant/recite/sing intricately regularly rhymed irregular-lined narrative poems to continuous downbeat & instrumental background, making a combination of music & poetry, with emphasis on the words, that maybe hasn't been performed as theater since the Greeks ... Real poetic genius transcending anything I've seen invented for utterance – tho maybe I've heard better words from Kerouac, but the combination of Terpsichore, Clio (narrative poems), Thalia, Erato, & Calliope among Muses is rare – Dance, history, theater, poetics & music. So the tour has been a poetic vision...' Allen Ginsberg, *Family Business*, op.cit., p.381.

back to the motherlode, the goddess Mnemosyne, and does sound remarkably like a hymn, or at least a prayer:

> Show me your wisdom – tell me my fate
> Put me upright – make me walk straight
> Forge my identity from the inside out.

All through the album it seems that either the gods have replaced God, or at the very least that his Observance is divided.

There are a couple of other touches in 'Mother Of Muses' that draw beneficially on this ancient-world preoccupation. One even occurs in the stanza about Sherman, Montgomery & Co. It's an aural pun, like that Mersey/mercy in 'Murder Most Foul'. Here, when he comes to sing that these military heroes 'did what they did and they went on their way', he makes that second 'did' sound like 'dared'. An apt enriching of his tribute.

There's also the loveliness of the opening verse, in which the line beginning 'Sing of the mountains' ends in 'the deep, *dark* sea', a fresher phrase than a deep blue sea would have been, and perhaps another tip of the hat to Homer and his often-repeated epithet a 'wine dark sea'; and there's a sweet yet comic appeal to hearing Bob Dylan sing of 'the nymphs of the forest' and a quiet delight that he rhymes that with 'you women of the chorus'.

The song ends well too. Its penultimate line, 'Got a mind to ramble, got a mind to roam' brings us back to overlays of many old blues songs, not least among them 'I've Got A Mind To Ramble' by Alberta Hunter, 'Roaming And Rambling' by Tampa Red, and the exquisite 'Got A Mind To Ramble' by The Yas Yas Girl (Merline Johnson). Dylan's line brings us close to his album title too – it's taken from Jimmie Rodgers's 1929 track 'My Rough And Rowdy Ways', in which Rodgers sings that he thought he was settling down but that 'Somehow I can't forget my good old ramblin' days / The railroad trains are calling me always'.[136]

[136] Alberta Hunter, 'I've Got A Mind To Ramble', Tampa Red, 'Roaming And Rambling', cut Chicago, Hallowe'en, 1947, Victor 20-3008, NYC 1947. The Yas Yas Girl And Her Rhythm Rascals, 'Got A Mind To Ramble', cut Chicago 10th February 1939, Vocalion 04885, NYC 1939. (The lovely piano here is by Blind John Davis, and Big Bill Broonzy is on guitar.) Jimmie Rodgers, 'My Rough And Rowdy Ways', cut Dallas TX, 22nd October 1929, Victor 22220, released 3rd January 1930.

In 'Mother Of Muses', the singer does finally come home, or perhaps just promises he will, with the quietly poetic final line 'I'm traveling light, and I'm slow coming home'. (The 'and' there so much better than 'but' would have been.) The line's first phrase brings us another song title: two in fact, though it may be that Dylan is rather more aware of the Leonard Cohen album track 'Traveling Light' (in which the first and last line of lyric is 'I'm traveling light') than the Cliff Richard UK hit single of 1959, 'Travellin' Light'.[137]

Richard Thomas suggests that, as with his Nobel lecture, Dylan seems on this final 'Mother Of Muses' line to have 'an eye on Cavafy's great poem "Ithaca": "Keep Ithaca always in your mind / Arriving there is what has been ordained for you /But do not hurry the journey at all. / Better if it lasts many years."' The gist of the poem, written in the form of advice to the traveller, is that your journey through life should take a long road, to give you as much enriching experience as possible, and therefore not to hurry. (The origin, perhaps, of Robert Louis Stevenson's 'To travel hopefully is a better thing than to arrive'.)[138] When I first played 'Mother Of Muses' to a person in her early 30s who likes a lot of Dylan records, she mocked the wobbliness of his voice on that supposedly sustained last word, 'home-------'. It's possible that he wobbles because he was close to 79 years old when he recorded it, but equally possible that he meant it to be that way, as an aural evocation of doubt: that perhaps he won't in the end reach his Ithaca – that the road has been so long that he has no direction home.

Another benefit we wouldn't have if it were not for Dylan's

[137] Leonard Cohen, 'Traveling Light', cut LA 2015-16; released on *You Want It Darker*, Columbia, NYC, 2016; also issued as a single, 23rd February 2017. Cliff Richard and the Shadows, 'Travellin' Light', cut London 1961, Columbia (EMI Records) 45-DB 4351, London, 1959.

[138] Richard Thomas, 'Review', op.cit. Ithaca the place, a Greek island, was the supposed home of Odysseus, and embraced a rich city; his eventual homecoming, and the island itself, are described in *The Odyssey*. 'Ithaca', the poem by Constantine P(eter) Cavafy, was written in 1911. Cavafy was Greek but was born in Alexandria, Egypt, where he died on 29th April 1933, his 70th birthday. Robert Louis Stevenson, from 'Virginibus Puerisque', London: *Cornhill Magazine*, 1876, then in his first essays collection *Virginibus Puerisque and Other Papers* (London: C. Kegan Paul, 1881). (A version of the same saying is attributed to Buddha, apparently falsely.)

interest in the ancient world is this: it's a witty as well as a clear signpost from song to song when, having given us 'I go right to the edge' in 'I Contain Multitudes' and followed it up in 'My Own Version Of You' with having 'No place to turn – no place at all' he adds that initially surprising 'And I ask myself what would Julius Caesar do'. It's a witty interjection because we know that the answer is to go 'Crossing The Rubicon'. And the mention of Caesar in that earlier song, straight after 'Well I get into trouble then I hit the wall / No place to turn – no place at all', is intertextuality working well. Julius Caesar did feel he had no choice, that he was forced into not just 'going right to the edge' but beyond it: and if we know that the Rubicon marked the boundary of Caesar's province, and that he did feel pushed into crossing it, then it enriches the album for us when we recognise the analogy, on top of the humour, of those dialoguing lines from other tracks.

Meanwhile back in the gothic of the Romantic 19th century, the 'I' that bemoans its getting into trouble, hitting the wall and having nowhere to turn in 'My Own Version Of You' may be either the monster's or its maker's. This is part of the *Frankenstein* story: the monster runs amok, murders the brother and bride of the doctor, who then dies trying to destroy it, and it ends up vanishing forever in the Arctic wastes. Man and creature have both gone both 'right to the edge' and 'right to the end'.

Caesar's end, as everyone knows, comes when he has crossed the Rubicon, kicking off a civil war that dooms the Republic and initiates the transition to the Roman Empire. What the song gives us is a series of glimpses, mini-narratives, of his preparations for imminent departure – Dylan perhaps putting us in mind of the similarly backward move from America's comparatively benign democracy to the violent and frightening autocracy Trump's presidency threatened to make irreversible. Dylan gives us, in any case, an interesting series of different scenes of preparation – preparations any of us might make before taking some momentous step, or embarking on an odyssey – even as you think, as you listen, that they're all a bit random.

Yet actually there's nothing random about the fitness of the early scenes: 'I painted my wagon, Abandon All Hope / And I crossed the Rubicon'. In American English, to paint your wagon has a figurative meaning unfamiliar to the British: it means to get on with doing something, to get a move on. 'Abandon All Hope' presages the enterprise's doom: it is written above the gates of hell in Dante Alighieri's *Inferno*, a common English translation giving it as 'All hope abandon, ye who enter here'. Yet the journey through hell is the first part of Dante's epic masterpiece 'from the fourteenth century', *The Divine Comedy*. Next comes the *Purgatorio* – and in the Dylan song crossing the 'red river' duly brings him 'Three miles north of purgatory – one step from the Great Beyond', the third stage for Dante being his *Paradiso*. Dante fought in battle himself, ended on the losing side of religious warring forces and wrote *The Divine Comedy* in the years after escaping death by going into exile (from his native Florence). In Dylan's song, the singer-narrator is mostly as much Dante as Julius Caesar, his preparations for crossing the Rubicon including praying to the cross, and finding that he soon 'stood between heaven and earth'.[139] There are moments when the testy old feeble gent thumping his stick obtrudes, as on 'Redder than your ruby lips and the blood that flows from the rose', but on the whole the 'I' who paints these scenes and moves from preparedness to action sounds a calm, determined, capable figure who knows what he's doing.

When we hear Dylan touch upon hell, purgatory and 'the Great Beyond' in this song, it might make us recall 'Armageddon Street' in 'My Own Version Of You'. And in turn, when we hear that word 'Armageddon' in Bob Dylan's voice, we're likely to remember it from 'Señor (Tales Of Yankee Power)' – another odyssey; but he has sung it in one other song since, the less remembered 'Are You Ready?', in which a very evangelical Dylan interrogates us with 'Are you ready for the judgment? / Are you ready for that terrible swift sword? / Are you ready for

---

[139] Dante Alighieri, *The Divine Comedy*, dates of composition uncertain but mostly thought to have been 1307-21. He completed it shortly before his death that year. (Born in 1265, more of his life was in the 13th than in the 14th century.) For some of the detail used, I have drawn on *The Hutchinson Encyclopedia* 10th edn 1995, op.cit., and *The Oxford Companion to English Literature*, 6th edition, ed. Margaret Drabble (Oxford: OUP, 2000).

Armageddon? / Are you ready for the day of the Lord?', and as if still interchanging persona in 'Crossing The Rubicon', he sounds like some kind of priest again (a rather kindlier one) in singing 'I poured the cup, I passed it along'.

What a very great deal he passes along.

There's plenty to like within 'Goodbye Jimmy Reed' *and* 'Black Rider'. The first is a jolly, avuncular romp through a tunnel of R&B, though it seems to have very little to do with Reed and a great deal to do with Van Morrison, mostly courtesy of a 2005 biography of Morrison by Johnny Rogan. The details of how closely Dylan's song follows a particular chunk of that book have been logged by Niall Brennan and are best seen on his blog rather than reiterated by me. He calls his post, very reasonably, '"Goodbye Jimmy Reed", Hello Van Morrison'.[140]

I find it disquieting that Dylan is once again heavy lifting from a particular source, albeit prose, and using it essentially to give words to add to his generic bluesy melody; but there are lines that, while they do arise from his strange rummage around in Van Morrison's background milieu, yield moments of different recognition. It's bizarre to hear Dylan sing the word 'Proddy', but it's telling then to include 'For thine is the kingdom, the power and the glory', the one part of the Lord's Prayer added solely by Protestants: the Roman Catholic version is shorter. To it, Dylan adds 'Go tell it on the mountain', another song title slipped in without capitalising its words (though on bobdylan.com, often as random in that regard as in its choices of punctuation, it capitalises the one word 'Mountain'). You could say he's citing three songs there: the original 19th-century African-American spiritual that celebrates the birth of Jesus, the version ('Tell It On The Mountain') that was part of the 1960s alliance of Civil Rights and Folk Revival movements, and that other 19th-century song 'Oh! Let My People Go', these last two both drawing on the Old Testament book of *Exodus*, to implore 'Let my people go!' Black Americans had long been using the Biblical accounts

[140] Johnny Rogan, *Van Morrison: No Surrender* (London: Secker & Warburg, 2005); Niall Brennan, https://www.highsummerstreet.com/2020/07/goodbye-jimmy-reed-hello-van-morrison.html.

of the oppression of slaves in Egypt to voice their own, and 'Let my people go' is also the repeated line in 'Go Down Moses'.[141]

In the vaguest possible way, this may connect to R&B star Jimmy Reed's own attitudes and tastes – we can't know – and though it stretches credibility, Dylan may perhaps have in mind some parallel with the oppression by the 'Proddies' of Northern Ireland's Catholic population. If so, it contributes nothing to our understanding of that painful history, from which the song in any case soon departs.

It does hold out, though, morsels of specific appeal. There is the line that comes straight after 'Go tell it on the mountain, go tell the real story', which is the splendid 'Tell it in that straightforward puritanical tone': an unexpected, somehow very unDylanesque critique, its mocking eye on the severity of Ulster Presbyterianism, which sits rather oddly alongside the hellfire fulminations Dylan himself gave us on *Slow Train Coming* and *Saved*. But I did wonder, given how many times on the album he invokes the world of the gods, whether he meant *those* ancient religions as much as the Judeo-Christian when he sings 'Give me that old time religion, it's just what I need'.

There are also fragments of a couple of earlier Dylan works in the song. It mentions 'this lost land': 'The Lost Land' is the title of the second chapter of *Chronicles Volume One*; and the attractive delivery of 'I thought I could resist her but I was so wrong' half-echoes a line from the awful 'Jolene' on *Together Through Life*, 'People think they know but they're all wrong'.

Here, Dylan's 'I had nothing to fight with but a butcher's hook' seems a line that might actually pay Reed some attention: he once worked in a meat-packing plant in Gary, Indiana, the hometown of the label Vee-Jay that signed him and helped him to success –

[141] The first of these was written by the first black American known to have collected folksong, John Wesley Work Jr. and dates from 1865 or earlier. 'Oh! Let My People Go' is another 19th-century black American spiritual (much associated with the Underground Railroad). 'Tell It On The Mountain' was tweaked from the earlier song by Milton Okum for Peter, Paul and Mary, cut 1963, issued as a single, Warner Brothers 5418, NYC, 1964. The producer credited for this is Albert Grossman, their manager; it is also one of the tracks on their album *In the Wind* – named, of course, after Dylan's 'Blowin' In The Wind', which is also there, as are 'Don't Think Twice, It's All Right' and 'his' 'Quit Your Lowdown Ways': Warner Brothers W-1507 (WS-1507 in stereo), NYC 1963.

and perhaps the normally casual lope of the Vee-Jay house band behind Reed is hinted at in the lope and pace of the Dylan song. And then the very end of it gives us something we can certainly associate with Jimmy: the last three words of Dylan's last line, 'Can't you hear me calling from down in Virginia', form the title of one of Reed's records. 'Down In Virginia' was a single – yet Reed neither lived nor died there (he was born in Mississippi, recorded in Chicago, died in California and is buried in Worth, Illinois), and another of his singles was the more interesting 'Down In Mississippi'. The one begins and ends 'I went down in Virginia, honey, where the green grass grows': the other replaces it with 'Down in Mississippi where cotton grow tall'. (Another Reed title, 'You've Got Me Dizzy', is used on 'Murder Most Foul', fused with 'Dizzy Miss Lizzy'.)

What's obvious, though, is that there's a far closer resonance between a Jimmy Reed track and one by Bob Dylan when you hear Reed's beautiful instrumental 'Odds And Ends' from the mid-1950s and Dylan's great 'Pledging My Time' from a decade later on *Blonde On Blonde*.[142]

If 'Goodbye Jimmy Reed' seems to be a lopsided juggling between looking at Reed and at Morrison, it's characteristic of one of Dylan's abiding interests: he contains not only multitudes but dualities, aligning and dividing them. On *Tempest*, he threw that old blues line 'two trains running side by side' and placed them on the track of 'Long And Wasted Years'; and as Christopher Ricks noted, the same album's 'Scarlet Town' has 'evil and the good living side by side', and in the title song, friends and lovers are clinging to each other 'side by side'.[143] On *Rough And Rowdy*

[142] Jimmy Reed, 'Down In Virginia', Vee-Jay 58-864, Gary IN, 1958; 'Down In Mississippi', cut Chicago, 1962, released Vee-Jay 62-2466, Gary IN, 1964; 'You've Got Me Dizzy', Vee-Jay 56-551, US, 1956; 'Odds And Ends', Vee-Jay 57-667, Gary IN, 1958.
[143] At the Finjan Club, Montreal, Dylan performed Muddy Waters's 1950s number 'Still A Fool'/'Two Trains Runnin', probably based on Tommy Johnson's 'Bye Bye Blues' of 1928, which includes the repeated line 'Well there's two trains runnin', runnin' baby side by side' (though Waters may have heard it first from Robert Petway's debut single). It was almost certainly a commonstock blues line, subject to adaption as well as adoption. 'They's two trains runnin', none of them going my way', for example, a line Muddy Waters barely changes, is on 'Frisco Whistle Blues' by Alabama's Ed Bell (tagged in the Paramount catalogue as The Weird Guitar Player). Muddy Waters: 'Still A Fool', cut Chicago, 1951. Tommy Johnson: 'Bye Bye Blues', cut Memphis, 4th February

Ways we have these dualities in his preponderance of rhyming couplets and the extreme duality of maker and creature in 'My Own Version Of You' (and its pertinent either-or question of 'to be or not to be'). But the song that seems more subtly engaged by duality – by picking the number two and splitting it – is 'Black Rider'.

In *Revelation*, the black rider among the four horsemen of the apocalypse is the figure suggestive of heralding famine, but others have interpreted his weighing scales as those of justice, making the black horseman the 'Lord as Law-Giver'. The common ground there is the scales, their two sides seeking balance: another symbol of a duality. Dylan's 'Black Rider', like 'Ballad Of A Thin Man' or 'What Was It You Wanted?', is a Dramatic Monologue, which on the face of it sounds a solo or singular thing, but isn't: it means you hear one voice addressing another who never gets to answer back in the poem or song. It's a one-sided conversation between *two* people – except of course if, like a Hamlet, he's addressing himself: one person as doubled persona.

You can hear it that way in 'Black Rider'. (Naturally it's written entirely in rhyming couplets.) In some verses the narrator's voice is telling himself/the enemy 'Better seal up your lips', and in others it's 'tell me when – tell me how', which can only sound reasonable if he's issuing these demands to himself. That's how it seems, too, when he sings 'Be reasonable Mister – be honest, be fair / Let all of your earthly thoughts be a prayer'.

It's harder to hear it as self-addressed when we come to the splendid 'Go home to your wife – stop visiting mine'; but it's a beautifully articulated duality. Another is the lovely 'You've seen the great world and you've seen the small', while in the couplet 'I'll suffer in silence, I'll not make a sound / Maybe I'll take the high moral ground' we get a doubling in 'silence' and 'not make a sound', and an implicit dualism in 'the high moral ground' (on which his delivery is so utterly immaculate) since it implies a

1928, Victor 21409, NYC, 1928. Robert Petway, 'Catfish Blues', cut Chicago, 28th March 1941, Bluebird B8838, US, 1941. Ed Bell, 'Frisco Whistle Blues', cut Chicago, c.September 1927, Paramount 12546, US, 1927. Bob Dylan, Finjan Club, Montreal, 2nd July 1962, issued *The 50th Anniversary Collection*, Sony 87564 60722, 2012. Christopher Ricks, op.cit.

lower alternative. It's a fresh line to hear expressed from Dylan, and his variance of the usual phrase – 'the moral high ground' – to 'the high moral ground' makes it sound somehow more strategic, like taking a place to ambush or attack from, rather than a place you have to climb to and preserve. And the quiet wit of 'maybe' he'll take it deepens the hint that it's a more sly, consciously tactical stance and deliberately undercuts any claim to the authentic. High morality is supposed to be trustworthy: it isn't presumed to be optional. (And somewhere underneath it, too, in the listener's mind, there's the duality of 'You take the high road and I'll take the low road'.)

If only the whole song were so good. 'Black Rider' is another song that suffers from Dylan's Ancient Rome Syndrome. One of the poets of the early AD era of the Roman Empire was the satirist Decimus Junius Juvenalis, aka Juvenal: 'the greatest poet of the silver age'. He tended to write ignoble poetry in the style of grand epic verse, and great poetry reliant on blazing rhetoric. He was vastly less prolific than Bob Dylan, with a muscular, dense, epigrammatic style. Dylan may have drawn on English translations of Juvenal before (in the dire 'It's All Good' and in 'Early Roman Kings', perhaps) but here he takes a line and a half from 'Satire 9', which would only seem in context if 'Black Rider' were, to any sustained extent, an angry diatribe of jealousy: whereas aside from the beautifully equable poise of that 'Go home to your wife, stop visiting mine', delivered with elegantly mild politesse, there seems no evidence of jealousy, let alone real animus. The Juvenal passage, in English, reads 'If your stars go against you / The fantastic size of your cock will get you precisely nowhere,' and runs on into a seething, snide tirade. Dylan purloins just this: 'hold it right there / The size of your cock wouldn't get you nowhere'.[144]

That's just a bad line. He makes it, er, stick out. It's an unexplained vulgarity: and so, ironically, the exact opposite

[144] Juvenal, 'Satire 9', probably from the English translation in *Juvenal and Persius*, Susanna Morton Braund, Harvard: Loeb Classical Library, 2004, though he is elsewhere believed to have drawn on Peter Green, *Juvenal: The Satires* (Baltimore: Penguin Books, 1967). I have drawn for additional information on *The Oxford History of the Classical World*, eds. John Boardman, Jasper Griffin & Oswyn Murray (Oxford: OUP, 1986).

of what Juvenal was normally concerned to excoriate, which was the sordid, disgusting and vulgar. In Dylan this vulgarity is reminiscent of only one other moment in his work: when, on his prose piece on the back of the *Planet Waves* sleeve he writes of remembering 'Furious gals with garters & Smeared Lips on bar stools that stank from sweating pussy...' And there, at least it has context: it's in a catalogue of events he 'tried to recall' from 'Back [at] the Starting Point!'

'Black Rider' also includes a differently clunky line, made worse by Dylan's hammy delivery. It falls (in both senses) at the end of this couplet: 'The road that you're on – same road that you know / Just not the same as it was [*hopelessly attenuated pause*] a minute ago'. It's cliché of both writing and timing.

It's the worst example of a stylisation in Dylan's timing that for decades worked beautifully but now doesn't: that is, his patented delay beyond the anticipated moment, beyond the music's moment, of singing the last word or phrase of a line. He uses it with genius on, to take a tiny sampling, 'The Groom's Still Waiting At The Altar' or 'Highlands' or any number of performances of the chorus of 'Mr. Tambourine Man' (actually of almost any song in live performance). It's all of a piece with his thrilling ability to fit as many syllables into a line as possible and still make them fit, even when the same line in another verse of the same song has only half as many. This brings us joy in 'Handy Dandy'. On *Rough And Rowdy Ways*, it becomes regrettably mechanical: heavy-mouthed, as it were, from over-use. It's a sad loss.

As everywhere, there are song titles in lower case, the two here both songs Dylan has himself recorded. 'Black Rider' ends where 'Duncan And Brady' ends, with 'you been on the job too long' – and we might feel, fleetingly, the same about Bob Dylan, given that while mostly we can say he *smuggles* these lines and song titles in, the start of the penultimate line of 'Black Rider' gives us a horribly cack-handed shoeing in of 'Some Enchanted Evening'.[145]

---

[145] 'Duncan And Brady' (traditional song), cut June 1992, Chicago (with Dave Bromberg & his band), issued on *Tell Tale Signs: Bootleg Series Vol. 8,* DeLuxe edition only, Columbia CKC 735797, NYC 2008; Dylan also performed the song live 81 times 1999-2002. 'Some Enchanted Evening' composed Rodgers & Hammerstein, *South Pacific*, 1949.

Musically, though, it's a distinctive recording, and seems the one track that draws on a specific kind of progressive musical theatre – one that, as he writes in *Chronicles Volume One*, he first took notice of when Suze Rotolo revealed it to him, at the Theatre de Lys in Greenwich Village. This, as he writes, wasn't really theatre so much as 'a stream of songs by actors who sang'. These were the songs by Bertolt Brecht (the lyrics) and Kurt Weill (the music). The one Dylan says 'made the most impression' on him was 'Pirate Jenny' – and 'Pirate Jenny' kept coming to mind on my early listens to the album, back in that early adventurous stage when an album is new and you don't yet know which bits fall in which songs. But 'Black Rider' soon became pinned down as the one that brushes 'Pirate Jenny' with a melodic resemblance. It's in a minor key, and while the chords move down and up, Dylan's sung lines ascend, one note at a time, intensifying the import of the words step by step – its 'fevered drama', as Charles O. Hartman calls it – and having climbed, yield at verse end, dropping down to a melodic resolution, even as the lyric, the pay-off line, is sometimes of equally dramatic intent.[146]

In contrast, 'Key West (Philosopher Pirate)', a song about, and not about, an island on the far tip of Florida, exudes a most leisurely ruminative calm, except when, as if out of nowhere, we're thrown into the very brief drama of 'Twelve years old, they put me in a suit / Forced me to marry a prostitute...' This may be a sudden disquieting recollection disrupting the general mood of mumbling contentment from the voice of an elderly sea dog, but it's a greater disruption if, out of the blue, as has been suggested, it's the voice of the elderly Robert Zimmerman choosing to give a hysterical description of being prepared for his 1954 bar-mitzvah, with the *organised* Jewish church, like all others, as corrupt (a prostitute), and that we're to understand that now, all these decades later, like many people brought up in a particular religious tradition he remains attracted to the faith;

[146] 'Pirate Jenny', from *The Threepenny Opera* by Kurt Weill, original lyrics by Bertolt Brecht; this 'play with music' opened in Berlin in August 1928; English lyrics by Marc Blitzstein, 1954. Bob Dylan, *Chronicles Volume One* (New York: Simon & Schuster, 2004), pp. 272-3. (Deplorably, Dylan's book has no index, so I constructed one. See http://www.michaelgray.net/index-info.html). Charles O. Hartman, *Review*, op.cit.

he hasn't abandoned it. He's 'still friends' with it. I don't find this particularly credible, but either way what these lines achieve is a story no-one can take at face value or comprehend, either, as a figurative truth.

Aside from that eruption of old bitterness, recollected by no means in tranquillity but supposedly resolved, this long song, the end of which seems to come around more quickly now than when first played, is largely and pleasantly adrift in tranquil waters. It starts, though, with mention of the first of two further dead US presidents, in this case the one assassinated before Kennedy, the Republican William McKinley, the last president to have served in the American Civil War and the one in office when the US won another war, the very brief Spanish-American, in 1898. He was assassinated three years later, and 'Key West' begins with his death, though this did not take place in Florida.

The first line comes verbatim from Charlie Poole's 'White House Blues', that song we'd already heard him draw on in 'Murder Most Foul'. But Dylan elaborates Poole's opening line into a fuller deathbed scene in the attractive opening verse, bringing in doctor and priest, though clearly making it a fictionalised version of the scene, the old sailor's version of what he thinks he's remembered from the radio news – though McKinley's death was twenty years before the first radio news was ever broadcast. Memory, as ever, is unreliable:

> McKinley hollered – McKinley squalled
> Doctor said McKinley, death is on the wall
> Say it to me if you got something to confess
> I heard all about it, he was going down slow
> Heard it on the wireless or radio
> From down in the boondocks – way down in Key West.

From here the song pootles along, its accordion accompaniment emphasising the nautical setting, while random recollection gives us an often enticing though weird mix of the very general ('Key West is the place to be / If you're lookin' for immortality') and the highly specific ('off of Mallory Square / Truman had his White House there', the official summer residence of the other named

334

US president in the song, Harry S. Truman). There's also the wildly inaccurate implicit claim that radio stations Luxembourg and Budapest could be picked up from over 3000 miles away in Florida, and the very particular inaccuracy that they are 'pirate' radio stations: they are not. Their mention here, though, is another calling across between songs, given that the names of these stations and others are memorably incanted by poet Paul Durcan in the midst of 'In The Days Before Rock 'n' Roll', a 1990 album track by the real subject of 'Goodbye Jimmy Reed', Van Morrison.[147]

That mention of 'pirate', of course, ties in with the song's subtitle, and though it's not mentioned, there is a Key West radio station named Pirate Radio Key West. And though we know this small island ('island of bones' in Spanish) is one that Dylan has sometimes frequented in real life – including, apparently, when he did have a boat and sailed those Caribbean winds – an extra 'pirate' connection exists between him and Key West's best-known resident musician, Jimmy Buffett. Buffett's so-called 'signature song' is 'Margaritaville', a more simple celebration of the place's sybaritic pleasures than Dylan's 'Key West', but another of his songs is 'A Pirate Looks At Forty': a song Dylan attempted to sing (with Joan Baez) in his brief appearance at Peace Sunday in 1982. Buffett's lyric begins with 'Mother, mother ocean, I have heard you call', soon adding 'Yes I am a pirate, two hundred years too late'. (And if we hear this *after* the Dylan album, we reach the line 'You've seen it all, you've seen it all' – and hear it as if an echo of 'Black Rider'.)[148]

Another 'Key West' verse surely does switch to offering Dylan himself as narrator; its first three lines are these:

> I was born on the wrong side of the railroad tracks
> Like Ginsberg, Corso and Kerouac
> Like Louie and Jimi and Buddy and all the rest.

[147] Van Morrison (& Paul Durcan), 'In The Days Before Rock 'n' Roll', cut February 1990, London; released on *Enlightenment*, Polydor 847 100-2, UK 1990.
[148] Jimmy Buffett, 'A Pirate Looks At Forty', cut 1974, Nashville TN, released as a single 1975. Bob Dylan & Joan Baez, 'A Pirate Looks At Forty' performed Peace Sunday, 6th June 1982, Pasadena CA.

What a contrast to that lovely song from his début album, 'Song To Woody'. In that early work he names 'Cisco and Sonny and Leadbelly too': people who, along with Guthrie, were his heroes in folk music and what was then called folk blues; they were the people he aspired to earn a right to join as an artist. Now, the Dylan of *Rough And Rowdy Ways* is putting himself firmly in other pantheons, declaring his right to be up there with the poets and writers of the Beat Generation (in one line) and with musical greats (in the other). It may be a true and reasonable enough thing to say, though possibly less than seemly that he says it himself.

What the song has established, very early on, is that Dylan's Key West is neither simply a dreamland nor simply a real island, but both at once, just as the 'I' in the song is both Bob Dylan and his old philosopher pirate. (The latter sounds akin to those Victorians who were amateur astronomer/vicars, or physician/explorers.)

After the real-life poets and musicians, we're back in the land of pseudo-Oz, this 'paradise divine', this 'enchanted land' with its named streets, its alluring flora – hibiscus flowers, fishtail palms ('ponds' is a mishearing, a mistranscription), orchid trees, tiny blossoms, bougainvillea and those southern Florida natives, gumbo limbo trees – but no tourists, no branches of McDonald's, and no hurricanes: only 'the healing virtues of the wind' and unceasing summer.

Mallory Square is right at the tip of Key West, famous for its sunsets, and where the cruise ships dock. But it's also where brave indigenous 16th-century traders, truly 'tough sailors', came back and forth from Cuba and landed in dugout canoes; where Jesuit priests arrived during Spanish rule, and built a Catholic church, the fifth in Florida, in the 1850s, calling it St. Mary, Star Of The Sea. The Convent of Mary Immaculate followed – the song's 'convent home' (balancing the 'monasteries' in 'My Own Version Of You') only a mile from Mallory Square. It's been a school since 1886, though not till six years later for black children, and a further year before Cuban girls could go. When the voice sings that 'Wherever I travel ... I'm not that far from the convent home' it suggests that we may have been wrong to assume this old sea-dog is male. She might here be a 'Rambling Female Sailor'.

But there's no Mystery Street, the convent lost its roof in the devastating hurricane of 1919, and the 'tiny blossoms' are 'of a toxic plant'. And some of this flora 'can give you that bleeding heart disease': a nicely double-edged phrase.

South Florida is also soaked in a history of notorious crime. Long after the pirates and shipwreckers came moonshiners and bank robbers, Al Capone and the Mafia, Meyer Lansky's gambling empire; and now the smugglers bring in cocaine. Serious criminals, like old blues musicians, move south in winter. Maybe Mystery Street is another boulevard of crime. 'Key West' is 'under the sun / Under the radar, under the gun'.

It's a mixed picture, then; if Key West is, to swap the narrator's persona again, the Elysian Fields, that final resting place for the souls of the good in Greek mythology and religion, then some of the song's detailing suggests less an objective correlative than the objectionable relatives in paradise. Every Eden has its serpent. Our unreliable narrator(s) would have it differently, though, maintaining that 'Key West is the gateway key / To innocence and purity'.

Naturally the titles of other songs are strewn amid the foliage and streets. In the first verse, its phrase 'he was going down slow' is a very old blues line, and a blues record most notably by Howlin' Wolf; 'Down In the Boondocks' names a record also mentioned, as noted, in 'Murder Most Foul'; 'Beyond The Sea' was an international hit single by Bobby Darin (his follow-up to that Brecht & Weill song 'Mack The Knife', and based on Charles Trenet's 'La Mer'); 'Shifting Sands' is both a complete song (by the West Coast Pop Art Experimental Band) and part of one, 'The Shifting Whispering Sands', recorded many times in the 1950s; 'Try A Little Tenderness' is a so-called standard from 1932, notably revamped by Otis Redding in 1966; 'Pretty Little Miss' is a traditional bluegrass song; and 'Wherever I travel, wherever I roam' comes almost straight out of that jolly song 'The Bare Necessities' ('Wherever I wander, wherever I roam / I couldn't be fonder of my big home'), sings across from the rambling and roaming inside 'Mother Of Muses' – and might remind us by poignant contrast of 'Wherever we travel, we're never apart' from 'Sara' on *Desire*.[149]

In reminiscence he has finished travelling and is back there, 'way down in Key West', but he implies that it's wishful thinking. In telling 'you', us, about this elysium, he never sings that you'll find your lost mind or immortality 'here' – it's always 'you'll find it there'. He's somewhere else now. It's paradise lost. It's always on the horizon line.

And why not just 'on the horizon'? Why the 'horizon *line*'? It's one of Dylan's purposive doublings: Key West is another 'final end'; and when you 'go right to the edge', the world has drawn a line.

You might hope for it on the edge of your vision whether you're straining to see it from the Florida mainland or sailing towards it, the philosopher pirate, waiting to catch sight of it from out at sea. It might be on that horizon coming in from either side, too: the parish boundaries of the real Key West are the Atlantic Ocean on one side and the Gulf of Mexico on the other.

What does it all amount to? What does the song mean? I asked, privately, several Dylan critics that question. Only one could answer, and that answer was: it's a dreamscape, and the crucial test is the voice. If it feels an authentic Dylan performance, believe it. If the voice convinces, that's enough. Feeling rather than logic, vocal performance rather than any persuasive rhetoric.

That makes a certain sense: it does have to offer an authentic artistic vocal performance – but as F.R. Leavis insisted, form is inseparable from content, so that what is sung affects whether the voice can ring true. And voice can cover many a deficiency. Dylan knows he gets away with a lot in this way. Innumerable poems by others are more concentrated, more thoughtful, and express

[149] Bobby Darin, 'Beyond The Sea', 1959, Atco, and, with 'Mack The Knife', on *That's All*, Atco 33-104, NYC, 1959; The West Coast Pop Art Experimental Band, 'Shifting Sands', on *Part One* EP, Warner Brothers, CA 1967; Otis Redding, 'Try A Little Tenderness', cut Memphis TN, Volt 45-141, November 1966; Phil Harris and Bruce Reitherman, 'The Bare Necessities', *The Jungle Book* film soundtrack, Walt Disney Studios, CA, 1967.

themselves more intensely. It's the music and above all, yes, the voice, that can so enrich a song (and its creator).

Which brings us back to the question of what 'Key West' means...

Perhaps more profitably my correspondents could have told me it's the wrong question. And in a way it is. No-one likes those school exam questions along the lines of 'What is Keats telling us about autumn?' – and with 'Key West', perhaps an attentive focus on the detail of the song is enough, granted that the accumulation of detail, in any poem or song, are always truly what it is.

So to pull back from those detailed ingredients in this case, perhaps it suffices to call it a 'dreamscape': to say that what we're left with is a state of being, both momentary and immemorial: flatness, heat, light. 'Key West' burbles on for over nine and a half minutes, and in it he can sing 'Such is life – such is happiness', without ever having said much about either.

So many have declared it the album's greatest track. I don't think so. It offers a long and pleasing beguilement, the old sea-dog pleasantly adrift, enacting that in slow, swishing rhythms. It holds out the pleasure of some of Dylan's enterprising rhymes for the title phrase 'Key West', too: 'Budapest', 'overdressed', 'your last request' (and this last calls back to the start of the song, its 'Say it to me if you got something to confess'). But there's an untidiness that dissatisfies right there at the very end of the track. It's because he finishes by virtually repeating the first bridge section, and it seems off-kilter, a repetition too far.

You don't feel it as a structural fault as it plays (you may feel it has no fault at all, like Michael Glover Smith, who also knows what it's about: 'The subject of the song is the thin line between life and death, and Dylan uses Key West ... as a metaphor for some kind of peaceful afterlife. The lyrics and Dylan's phrasing are perfect'). But that last insistence on 'Key West is the place to be' doesn't quite fit: it's felt as an unease but that unease does derive from a structural problem. If you count verses and bridge sections you see why. (It's easy to dismiss counting verses as gradgrinderish and soulless, but if it helps, as here, to explain a song's leaving you with vague dissatisfaction, then so be it. As Christopher Ricks suggests in his lecture on 'Barbara Allen' and 'Scarlet Town', it's in part by patterns such as verse endings that 'a song builds up expectations', adding: 'counting counts'.)[150]

This song starts out with a clear pattern: after two verses we get a bridge – 'Key West is the place to be' through to 'Key West is on the horizon line' – and after another two verses, another bridge: 'Key West is the place to go' through to 'Key West, Key West is the enchanted land'. It establishes that pattern, but then disrupts it. Now we get not two but three verses before the next bridge – 'Key West is under the sun' through to 'Key West, Key West is the land of light' – and then another three verses, before reaching for that first bridge to serve as its conclusion. Such pattern disruptions can be intentional and deliberate, to serve a purpose; that isn't true here. There's no cunning plan or virtue behind this quiet structural dishevelment; and because the first two bridge sections begin so similarly, and all three end so similarly, it makes reprising only the first seem a random repetition, a dissatisfying awkwardness.

It's often been said about Dylan's records, though admittedly in general by people who don't much like them, that just because a song is long doesn't mean it's a masterpiece. And that's true. There is probably no masterpiece on *Rough And Rowdy Ways*, and 'Key West' isn't one – but it seems to me that the closest we come to a great song, a great track, is the one I have saved to look at last: the modestly shorter, awkwardly titled 'I've Made Up My Mind To Give Myself To You', a declaration that might sound arrogant and patronising, but is neither here. (And it's one syllable shorter than 'It Takes A Lot To Laugh, It Takes A Train To Cry', two shorter than 'Stuck Inside Of Mobile With The Memphis Blues Again' and the same number as 'The Ballad Of Frankie Lee And Judas Priest'...)

It's the moving, mature and multi-layered song that comes closest of any on the album to the high impersonality of great art, while remaining expressively personal, charged with a majestic

---

[150] Michael Glover Smith, 'The Best of 2020: Dylan's "Key West (Philosopher Pirate)"', December 2020, https://whitecitycinema.com/2020/12/01/the-best-of-2020-dylans-key-west-philosopher-pirate/. Christopher Ricks, op.cit.

warmth. It's complex, vulnerable, perhaps a real farewell, and I find it utterly, bravely beautiful.

It opens out for us first with slow, emphatic guitar and bass chords, and a mysterious tension in the tone of the chorus voices humming that lethally catchy part of Offenbach's 'Barcarolle', from the unfinished *Tales of Hoffmann*, his only opera. This mix of stately, deliberate chords with the cautious intimacy of the voices annuls any sense of the 'Barcarolle' as sentimental. (Dylan flirts with the danger of that very sentimentality later in the song: his 'I don't think I could bear to live my life alone' is an answer of sorts to 'Please Don't Go', the previous English-language song that uses the 'Barcarolle' tune, in which the likes of Vince Hill and Donald Peers sing 'If I don't see your sweet face / My life I'll live alone'.)[151]

When Dylan comes in, he doesn't sing along with what he now makes the background tune, but cuts ingeniously across in front of it, the voice almost broken but full of depth. The contrast is thrilling.

He holds so wide a range of feeling across the song, and such sweet, acute specific touches. In the opening line – 'I'm sittin' on my terrace, lost in the stars' – it's the *terrace*, or the *my terrace*, that gives it that strength – and in the choice of 'terrace' there's extra pungency: and not only because it's comically pleasing to picture *Bob Dylan* on his terrace. He could have opted for 'garden' or 'staircase', or been altogether vaguer, but *terrace* enfolds terra, as in terra firma, so that its juxtaposition to 'the stars' is acute.

In the matching line of the couplet – 'listening to the sounds of the sad guitars' – it's that *the* in 'the sad guitars' that saves it from being unimaginatively limp: it's rescued by specificity: that it's particular guitars being heard.

Then comes 'Been thinking it all over and I [immaculate pause] thought it all through'. Dylan's timing enacts that thoughtfulness, while the words are alert to the fine distinction between the two:

[151] Jacques Offenbach, *Tales of Hoffmann*, 1880, incomplete at his death that October at age 61. 'Please Don't Go', credited to Jules Barbier, Michel Carré (for the French-language song made from 'Barcarolle', 'Belle Nuit', 1881), Jackie Rae & Les Reed; single by Vince Hill, covered by Donald Peers, both UK 1968.

thinking something over can be a cyclical, inconclusive process; but to have 'thought it all through' means through to the end, to a decision. And he sings that second half in a quietly energised way, free from irresolution, which makes him sound fleetingly youthful before the more sombre task of commitment declared in the title line and explored throughout the song. Its theme is the push and pull of accepting the idea of commitment, the teetering on the brink of it, the perils and relief to be encountered in the *act* of a wholehearted 'yes'.

The 'you', as so often with Dylan, isn't easy to pin down: there seem to be several in this song, and while there's a very personal, intimate tone throughout, its predominant 'you's are surely death and God.

The second verse, like the fourth, shifts the title line into the simple past tense: 'I made up my mind' instead of 'I've made up'; but as he moves towards it, the voice expresses, with a kind of wonderment, the prolonged pain recalled from having reached this commitment. On the webpage, the lyric is 'I don't think anyone else ever knew'; but the voice sings a far more stretched out second half that dithers between the 'else' and the 'ever', such that one of the two seems duplicated but it's hard to hear which, and it seems to end by being 'I don't think that anyone ever, else, ever knew'.

Then it's up into the bridge section with the more emphatic repetition of 'I'm giving myself to you, I am', a renewed avowal, though admittedly it's just as likely there to give him a rhyme for 'From Salt Lake City to Birmingham' before 'From East LA to San Antone'; and for a moment as you hear the first part of that great geographic American sweep, you might recollect the far briefer, historically correct trip, back on 'White House Blues', when McKinley's body was taken 'from Buffalo to Washington' (D.C.), and perhaps that great but thematically inappropriate Emmylou Harris song 'Boulder To Birmingham'. (The brain doesn't always obey the mind in these matters.)[152]

The third verse echoes another Bob Dylan song ('Shooting Star' from *Oh Mercy*), opening with 'My eye is like a shooting

[152] 'Boulder To Birmingham', Emmylou Harris, *Pieces of the Sky*, Reprise, US, 1975. 'White House Blues' op. cit.

star', and two lines later, when we reach 'No-one ever told me------
-----', the exquisite sustained curve downwards on 'me--------',
as it falls into 'it's just something I knew', enacts vocally the falling
of that star. And in turn that returns us to a phrase right at the
song's beginning: he's 'lost in the stars'. That in itself calls another
song into lower-case service, and with it a renewed recruitment
of the 'Pirate Jenny' composer: *Lost in the Stars* is a 1940s musical
composed by, yes, Kurt Weill.[153]

A counterpoint to 'My eye is like...' comes in the final bridge
section, with 'Well, my heart's like...', each one a simile he
doesn't explain but does elaborate on. This time it's 'like a river
/ A river that sings', and it's paired with the psychologically true
and gracefully expressed 'Just takes me a while to realize things'.
And a double echo whispers to us here from the album's wheel of
self-reference. Take the more literal, formal meaning of 'to realize'
– to make real – in that sentence and you have a restatement
of 'It'll be done when it's done', which he sings on 'My Own
Version Of You', the preceding track; while in the informal sense
of understanding things, 'Just takes me a while to realize things'
also sits in a kind of dialogue with 'No-one ever told me: it's just
something I knew' – both lines as personally human as, from an
aeon ago, 'You're gonna make me give myself a good talkin' to...'

As in so many songs on this album, there's a significance
attached to travel. Not only the implicit travelling from Utah to
Alabama and California to Texas, but *two* contrasting pairs – yet
another *two* doublings – of explicit travel contemplations. In the
song's second bridge (the bridge that he travels on), he addresses
another traveller: 'Take me out traveling, you're a traveling man'
(in musical spirit, that's Ricky Nelson, of course) and in the other
he has already travelled – travelled 'the long road of despair' and
'met no other traveler there'. But this narrator *is* 'going far away
from home with her', and by the last verse he has 'traveled from
the mountains to the sea' (as singing rivers do).[154]

[153] *Lost in the Stars*, 1949, lyrics Maxwell Anderson & music Kurt Weill, based on the
1948 novel *Cry, the Beloved Country* by Alan Paton; the musical was Kurt Weill's last
work for the stage.
[154] 'Travelin' Man', Ricky Nelson, cut April 1961, Imperial Records X5741, US, 1961.

This last 'traveled' became an explicit one only when Dylan reached the studio: in the draft of the lyric published on bobdylan.com the line is 'From the plains and the prairies – from the mountains to the sea', which I'm sorry he deleted. The line that rhymes, either way, is 'I hope that the gods go easy with me', with 'ea-----sy' sung with the longest-held downward curve of any in the song.

Given that he knows the gods are full of vengeance, and keen on torture and death as punishments, it's a forlorn hope, said with a wink perhaps. But he hedges his bet, his Observance again divided, and he turns to God instead. Unlike the vengeful narrator of 'False Prophet' or the sectarian of 'Goodbye Jimmy Reed' who can 'tell a Proddy from a mile away', this one would rather 'preach the gospel, the gospel of love'; and when he follows that line, immediately, with 'A love so real – a love so true / I made up my mind to give myself to you' it has to be God's love he aspires to here.

In turn that gives a weird piquancy to the humour at the end of the song, in which on the face of it the 'you' is mortal, when he sings 'I knew you'd say yes'. If he just might be addressing Him, we're confidently far from 'Tryin' To Get To Heaven' or 'If indeed there ever was a door'. Whoever the addressee, it's a flash of the youthfully comic Dylan who adds 'I'm saying it too' – as if it wasn't his own idea all along.

There's one more hugely endearing line in the song, and which is a further part of Dylan's self-referencing: the candid and realistic 'I'm not what I was – things aren't what they were'. It's a lovely, and in most ways truthful, thing to hear Bob Dylan sing; and it echoes something he said in an interview almost a quarter of a century earlier: 'We try and we try and we try to be who we were … Sooner or later you come to the realisation that we're *not* who we were. So then what do we do?'[155]

The song also holds one more of those curious half-contradictory resemblances within it that we so often find in post-1960s Dylan songs. You might say its lines about travel offer this feature: on the

---

[155] Bob Dylan interview, *Newsweek*, published 6th October 1997; quoted in *Song & Dance Man III: The Art of Bob Dylan* p.548, op.cit.

one hand he wants to be taken travelling by the 'traveling man'; on the other, he's going 'going far away from home with her'. A similar disjointment of sense shows up here too: for while he's going away with *her*, he'll 'lay down beside *you* when everyone's gone' [my emphasis].

We're used to these personal pronouns being jumbled and elusive, but the assured intimacy of 'I'll lay down beside you when everyone's gone', so gorgeously delivered, also works as a reminder of that cumbersome but key line in 'I Contain Multitudes', the one most clearly of an emphatic duality: 'I sleep with life and death in the same bed'. (There's an untitled poem by Ginsberg that puts it like this: 'death / waiting inside life'.)[156]

Dylan's line gives us, here, the over-arching theme of *Rough And Rowdy Ways*. It isn't focussed on death, but on old age, and whether one reaches it, and how that involves much thinking about death. It *is* a portrait of the artist as old man (78 when he recorded it), and all these mentions of death and of its being overdue (including, from the ghost-voice of 'False Prophet', 'I forgot when I died') are ways of saying 'I'm alive' but that, like painting your wagon with Abandon All Hope, the future is uncertain and time is short. Death waiting inside life. Which isn't quite the same thing as a farewell, but feels close. It's an album addressed to all of us, and especially those of us of, as they say, a certain age.

It may prove to be Bob Dylan's non-posthumous last album, his farewell. It sometimes feels like a long goodbye. If so, it's a worthy piece of work. Its rich sound and overall expansive feel make it a real Dylan album, his convivial best since *"Love And Theft"*, a companionable and restorative pleasure.

Rough And Rowdy Ways is a work built from layer upon layer upon layer of reference, allusion and interconnection, with tunnels built under its sprawling city linking fragments of narrative from song to song; and within it, so much is built upon meditative, even wistful recitation, sometimes more spoken than sung, on that quiet bed of ruminative music.

---

[156] Allen Ginsberg, untitled poem in *Family Business: Selected Letters Between a Father and Son*, op.cit.

Among its riches and delights, some of those to relish are the tinier ones. With a lifetime of loving Dylan's work behind and inside me, these include: the playful tease of those fleeting, whispered harmonica notes, unbilled on the album's credits; the similarly quiet aside 'Oh lord!---' said under his breath towards the end of 'Crossing The Rubicon' – the finest, most expressive 'Oh lord!' ever put on record by anyone; the intriguing, never quite pindownable tone of his voice as he lands on 'Virginia', last word of 'Goodbye Jimmy Reed'; and the incomparably comic way he tackles 'Ballinalee' on 'I Contain Multitudes', a name he seems to encounter as most bizarrely exotic, difficult for his mouth to handle. Best of all, hearing 'I've Made Up My Mind', the most exacting critic, if also a fan, must surely forgive him anything for the sound of his pronouncing the single word 'snow' in that second verse.

On vinyl what we have, too, is a double album on which the whole fourth side is one song, just like on *Blonde On Blonde*, so that the album, so beautifully recorded, is unlike any other he's made and yet full of reminders of others, and at the same time, uniquely in his catalogue, a work full of sweet sadness, regret and appreciation for what has been and gone.

'I'm not what I was – things aren't what they were': it isn't a masterpiece, but it's a work of depth, warm resonance, invention and generosity. The sub-text of every song is 'while there's still time', or 'while I still have time'. But Bob Dylan has long been trying to stop time. There may be more to come.

Thanks & Acknowledgments

Grateful thanks to Magdalena Gray and Scott Morton, and especially to Sarah Beattie Gray.

I also thank Alex from Grand Rapids MN, the late Wolfram Altenhövel, the Authors' Licensing & Collecting Society Ltd, the late John Baldwin, Eugen Banauch, Barbara, the late Stanley Bard, David Barker, Derek & Tracy Barker, Ruth Barolsky, M.D. Barr-Hamilton, Dylan Beattie, Jessamyn Beattie, Bryan Beck, David Belbin, Darren & Frances Bell, Andy Benson, Olof Björner and his website www.bjorner.com/bob.htm, Simon Blackley, Eric Borgman, Chris Bradford, Paolo Brillo, Alasdair Brown, Mick Brown, Diana Bryan, Paul & Evelyne Bubernak, Hanns Peter Bushoff, Catherine Butler, Joe Butler, David Cameron (not that one), John Carvill, Ron Chester, Dave & Irene Chesterman, Irene Clarke, James Cody, the late Ray Coleman, Mike Cooke, Neil Corcoran, Wendy Coslett, Rob Couteau, Ian Daley, Anne Margaret Daniel, Jill Daniel, Susanna Daniel, Andrew Darke, Howard Davies, the late Michael Dempsey, Steve Diggle, Nick Dodd, Brian F. Doherty, John Doran, Jean-Yves Dulac, Ian & Jane Duncan, Glen Dundas, Robert Eaglestone, Dave Engel, Michelle Engert, Jack Evans, the late Larry Fabbro, Waldo Floyd III, Nigel Fountain, Raymond Foye, Alan Fraser and www.searchingforagem.com, Larry Furlong, David Gaines, Isabel Galán, Frances Gandy, Karl Gedlicka, Kurt Gegenhuber, Steve Gibbons, the late Dave & Jackie Giff, the late Tony Glover, Mick Gold, Michael Goldberg, Marian Goldsmith, Nina Goss, the late H. Mervyn and Diana Gray, Gabe Gray, John Gregory, the late Sally Grossman, Eileen Gunn, Samantha H, Gregory Hansen, Lucas Hare, Jane Harrison, the late Peter Harrison, Steven Hart, the late Mary Amelia Cummins Harvey, Pamela Lois Harvey, Pernille Hasselsteen, Hugh Haughton and the University of York Department of English & Related Literature, Jim Hickman, Nigel & Rolande Hinton, Jonathan Hodgers, Duncan Hume, Patrick

Humphries, the late Frances Hunter, the late Michele Hush, Antonio J. Iriarte, Deborah Irish, Andrzej Jakubowicz, Debra & Denny Jensen, John Jobling, the late R.T. Jones, Barb Jungr, Roy Kelly, the late Terry Kelly, Michael Kerr, Andrew Kershaw and the other Andy Kershaw, Lewis Klausner, Robert Köhler, the late Dave Laing, Nat Leach, Eric LeBlanc, Spencer Leigh, Ray Leng, Harold Lepidus, Jonathan Lethem, Tristan Leveque, Bob Levinson, William T. Lhamon, Lars Lindh, Sharon Linney Lovelock, Valerie & Ron Lowe, Alex Lubet, Angela McRobbie, Joe McShane, John Maher, Anne-Marie Mai, Cecily Marcus, the late Mike Marqusee, Keith Marsh, Memorial University of Newfoundland Department of Folklore, Keith Miles, Christer Molkom, Robert Morace, Andrew Muir, Geoff Muldaur, Joy Murphy, Petter & Vigdis Myhr, the late Peter Narváez, Susan Neiman, the late Cleophas Newhook, Margaret Newman, Scott Newstok, Diana Nicholas, Michael Organ at the University of Wollongong, Andrea Orlandi, Tom & Carolyn Palaima, David Phillips, Rose Phillips, the late Stephan Pickering, Robert Polito, Michel Pomarede, Tom & Ellen Prewitt, Alasdair Reid, Louis A. Renza, Arie de Reus, Steven Rings, Seth Rogovoy, the late Leona Rolfzen & the late B.J. Rolfzen, Chris Rollason, Jeff Rosen, the Royal Literary Fund, Tony Russell, Naomi Saltzman, Laith Sayigh, Martin Schaad, Burkhard Schleser, Stephen Scobie, Amanda Sebestyen, Gisle Seines, Gavin Selerie, John Sellards, Kerry Shale, the late Robert Shelton, Andrew Shields, Brian Smith, Ellie Smith, Max Smith, Wesley Stace, the late Gloria Stavers, Pat Stead, Harriet Stein, Kevin Steinman, the late C. Keith Stevens, Sue Hurrell Stevens, Julian Stone, Christer Svensson, Linda Thomas, Sherill Tippins, Margaret Toivola, Jeff Towns, Happy Traum, Sue Tyrrell, Lauri Umansky, Sam Umland, Rainer Vesely & Uli, J. Andrew Wainwright, Jon Wainwright, the late David Widgery, the late Bob Willis, David Willis, Arthur Nevill Wilson & Kath Wilson and Stefan Wirz.

Acknowledgments are due to Universal Music Corporation for permission to quote more than is covered by fair usage from the following songs; quotations are taken from Bob Dylan recordings and may in some cases differ slightly from the versions on the official bobdylan.com website: 'Hard Times In New York Town', © 1962, 1965 by Duchess Music Corporation; renewed 1990, 1993 by MCA; 'Mother Of Muses', © 2020 by Special Rider Music; 'Murder Most Foul', © 2020 by Special Rider Music; 'Rambling Gambling Willie', © 1962, 1965 by Duchess Music Corporation; renewed 1990, 1993 by MCA; 'Sad-Eyed Lady Of The Lowlands', © 1966 by Dwarf Music; renewed 1994 by Dwarf Music; 'Seven Curses', © 1963, 1964 by Warner Bros. Inc.; renewed 1991, 1992 by Special Rider Music; 'Song To Woody', © 1962, 1965 by Duchess Music Corporation; renewed 1990, 1993 by MCA; and 'The Times They Are A-Changin'', © 1963, 1964 by Warner Bros. Inc.; renewed 1991, 1992 by Special Rider Music.

Songs quoted briefly and within fair usage are as follows: 'A Hard Rain's A-Gonna Fall; 'Ain't No Man Righteous, No Not One'; 'Angelina'; 'Are You Ready?'; 'Black Rider'; 'Blowin' In The Wind'; 'California'; 'Chimes Of Freedom'; 'Crossing The Rubicon'; 'Death Is Not The End'; 'Dignity'; 'Don't Think Twice, It's All Right'; 'Early Roman Kings'; 'False Prophet'; 'Forever Young'; 'Forgetful Heart'; 'Girl From The North Country'; 'God Knows'; 'Gonna Change My Way Of Thinking'; 'Goodbye Jimmy Reed'; 'I Contain Multitudes'; 'I Shall Be Free'; 'Idiot Wind; 'If Not For You'; 'If You Gotta Go, Go Now'; 'Isis'; 'It Ain't Me, Babe'; 'John Wesley Harding'; 'Jolene'; 'Key West (Philosopher Pirate)'; 'Lenny Bruce'; 'Like A Rolling Stone'; 'Love Minus Zero/No Limit'; 'Most Of The Time'; 'Mr. Tambourine Man'; 'My Own Version Of You'; 'Nettie Moore'; 'Peggy Day'; 'Rita May'; 'Sara'; 'Scarlet Town'; 'She's Your Lover Now'; 'Shelter From The Storm'; 'Simple Twist Of Fate'; 'Solid Rock'; 'Something There Is About You'; 'Soon After Midnight'; 'Stuck Inside Of Mobile With Thee'; 'Subterranean Homesick Blues'; 'Tell Me Momma'; 'Tempest'; 'The Death Of Emmett Till'; 'To Ramona'; 'Tombstone Blues'; 'Tryin' To Get To Heaven'; 'Visions Of Johanna'; 'When I Paint My Masterpiece'; 'When You Gonna Wake Up?'; 'Who Killed Davey Moore?'. Copyright information for each of these is given on https://www. bobdylan.com/songs/.

Michael Gray is a critic & public speaker. He pioneered the serious study of Dylan's work with *Song & Dance Man: The Art of Bob Dylan*, 1972, the first such critical book. Born in 1946, he grew up on Merseyside and studied History & English Literature at York University, where he interviewed British historian A.J.P. Taylor and chatted with visiting American guitarist Jimi Hendrix. His books include the massively updated *Song & Dance Man III* (1999), *The Bob Dylan Encyclopedia* (2006), and *Hand Me My Travelin' Shoes: In Search of Blind Willie McTell* (2007).

He is married to the food-writer Sarah Beattie and has lived in southwest France since 2008. His website is www.michaelgray.net

For more information on this book,
plus Route's full list of books, please visit:

www.route-online.com